Praise for *The Treasure of Montségur*

"In *The Treasure of Montségur,* Sophy Burnham crafts a beautiful, wondrous novel . . . Burnham weaves nimbly between real and surreal, between magic and mundane."

—*Los Angeles Times*

"Sophy Burnham crafts a beautiful, wondrous novel out of the persecutions the Cathars faced for their beliefs. . . . Burnham weaves nimbly between real and surreal, between magic and mundane."

—*Book Review*

"Her characters leave no good tale untold . . . In matters of the soul, Burnham is as sure-footed as those mysterious mountaineers of Montségur."

—*Washington Post BookWorld*

"Burnham . . . paints a vivid picture of the Cathars' struggles. . . . an intriguing and ultimately haunting tale."

—*Washingtonian* magazine

". . . a fierce yet tender heroine . . . the quality of the writing makes what could be an obscure topic . . . enjoyable to read."

—*Library Journal*

"Ms. Burnham recreates her setting with integrity. . . . she paints historical detail over her narrative with spare but sure strokes. *The Treasure of Montségur* is worthwhile for its illumination of the Cathars' plight and for the extraordinary character of Jeanne."

—*The Historical Novels Review*

"Mixes romance with religious history in an evocative prose that should thrill the spiritually intrigued."

—*Kirkus Reviews*

The Treasure
of Montségur

THE

Treasure of Montségur

A Novel

Sophy Burnham

HarperSanFrancisco
A Division of HarperCollinsPublishers

HarperCollins books may be purchased for educational, business, or sales promotional use. For information please write: Special Markets Department, HarperCollins Publishers, Inc., 10 East 53rd Street, NewYork, NY 10022.

HarperCollins Web site: http://www.harpercollins.com

HarperCollins®, 📖 ®, and HarperSanFrancisco™ are trademarks of HarperCollins Publishers, Inc.

FIRST HARPERCOLLINS PAPERBACK EDITION
PUBLISHED IN 2003

Library of Congress Cataloging-in-Publication Data
Burnham, Sophy.
The treasure of Montségur : a novel / Sophy Burnham. — 1st ed.
    p.   cm.
Includes bibliographical references.
ISBN 0–06–000080–5 (paper)
1. Albigenses—Fiction. 2. France—History—Philip II Augustus, 1180–1223—
Fiction. 3. Heresies, Christian—Fiction. 4. Montségur (France)—Fiction.
5. Languedoc (France)—Fiction. I. Title.

PS3552.U73242T74 2002
813'.54—dc21   2001051543

03 04 05 06 07 RRD(H) 10 9 8 7 6 5 4 3 2 1

For my sister, Anne

The mount of Montségur

Preface

The historical events described in this novel are little known to Americans. But recent atrocities and religious wars from Ireland or the Balkans to Somalia and Kashmir (not to mention in the U.S. itself) led me to this period, when Pope Innocent III called for a Christian Crusade against another Christian group.

The largest army ever seen in Europe, perhaps as many as three hundred thousand men, gathered in the Languedoc region, which is now the south of France, to fight the heretics. The targets of their assault were known as Cathars, the Pure Ones, or Albigensians. Among themselves, they were called Good Men or Good Women or Good Christians, the Friends of God all joined in the Church of Love. By the enemy they were called *haeretici perfecti*—perfected heretics.

They worshiped Christ, were pacifists, vegetarians, with strict rules of poverty, work, chastity, charity. They believed that humans were fallen angels, spiritual beings captured by demons in a physical form, and they eschewed all physical matter—pleasures in things of the world, including sex—as wrongful or illusory. They had, of course, various orders of believers. Not everyone was called to take the robe and live as a Good Man, a *perfectus,* or Good Woman, a *perfecta,* or to follow the most serious vows.

We know little of the Cathar faith, and most of it only from the point of view of its enemies. A hundred years after the events depicted here, Jacques Fournier, the fanatical Inquisitor who served as Bishop of Pamiers and later became Pope Benedict XII of Avignon (1334–1342), provided our principal information by tenaciously investigating the inhabitants of the village of Montaillou. His work,

Registries of the Inquisition, furnish us with the detailed inner working of the Inquisition, and some view of the Cathar Friends of God.

But for the most part we can only surmise at that religion. The Cathars were Christian, but their true sins may have lain in translating the Bible into the vernacular, in refusing to tithe to the Catholic Church, and in dismissing the authority of the Pope as well as the sacraments of Baptism and the Eucharist in place of their own spiritual baptisms. Certainly the seeds of their rebellion fed the later Protestant Reformation and fueled the subsequent religious wars that pitted Catholic against Huguenot with such slaughter that many Protestants fled France for Germany, Holland, or the New World.

There is a tendency to romanticize the Cathar Church of Love. Heresy is a relative concept, but even within the parameters of Christianity you can see why the Cathars (as well as the Waldensians over to the east, who were known as "the Poor Men of Lyons") presented a threat to established Catholicism. They believed in the divinity of Christ, but not that he had died and been resurrected—a foundation of Christianity!

Apparently they believed in reincarnation—and felt a desperate need to do something drastic to avoid that dreaded fate. So fierce was their determination that sometimes (though who knows how often) a *perfectus* might starve himself to death, undergoing the *endura* rather than continue to live among the evils of the world.

They had a strong belief in dualism, although precisely how their outlook differed from that of the Roman Catholic church of the thirteenth century is hard to ascertain. Some scholars link the Cathars to a reflowering of Manichaean thought, the ancient form of Christianity to which Saint Augustine had belonged as a young man, before converting. Although stamped out as a heresy, Manichaeanism may have continued underground. Whatever the answers, I imagine that the theology of the Catholic Church and the folk-beliefs of the common people probably differed widely.

To raise his army in 1209, the Pope promised any soldier who fought for forty days a freeze on his debts, the remission of all sins, and the possibility of plunder. Moreover, no one had to travel as far as the Holy Land, as in earlier Crusades, but only down to the rich, lush lands of the Languedoc, owned by the Count of Toulouse. This made it a popular war, and it lasted twenty years, first under the leadership of the French Count Simon de Montfort and then of his son, Amaury. In 1229, Raymond VII, the Count of Toulouse, surrendered an independent Occitanie and became vassal to the king of France.

Soon after, Pope Gregory IX asked the Dominicans to form the Inquisition to stamp out the dissidents while bringing order to the atrocities perpetrated by wild mobs. The harder they worked, however, the harder the Resistance grew—as often happens when an invading conqueror imposes a repressive rule.

Events came to a head on May 13, 1243, when the French laid siege to the fortress of Montségur. It was one of the longest sieges in history, lasting some ten months. Two hundred Good Christians, the cream of the Cathar Church, were trapped on the mountaintop, together with a protecting garrison.

In January of 1244 the Cathars, seeing the end was near, smuggled their treasure of gold and money *(pecuniam infinitam)* off the mountaintop and hid it "underground."

They held out for another six weeks, but on March 1, 1244, the fortress fell. On the night of the surrender, three *perfecti* and one other, who may have been a guide, were lowered down the cliff on ropes and vanished into the woods. Their task: to keep their church alive.

The Cathar treasure has never been found. I'm told that Hitler sent an expedition to the south of France to search for it. Strange tales make more of the mystery, connecting the treasure and the Cathar heresy to the Knights Templar and various occult brotherhoods.

For the record, the last *perfectus,* the semiliterate Guillaume Bélibaste, was burned in 1321 in Villerouge-Termenès, in the Corbières (Aude) district. With that, after nearly three hundred years of effort, the Catholic Church succeeded in stamping out the heresy and establishing the political boundaries of France. The Inquisition then turned its attention to new enemies, finding them in dissidents and Jews.

Even today, if you visit the Languedoc in the south of France, you will find an easygoing people, more "Mediterranean"—more Italian perhaps—than in the rest of France, for they take their heritage direct from early Rome. As late as the Middle Ages their cities were governed, as they had been under the Roman Empire, by elected consuls. The three major religions lived side by side in peace, and women, Arabs, and Jews all had civil rights as well as opportunities for education. The Cathar faith provided, at least by implication, an equality between men and women, while Catholicism remained staunchly antifeminist. We find no women, however, among the Cathar bishops and deacons, since men were more suited for the hardships of that wandering lifestyle, but women *perfectae* could transmit the power of the Holy Spirit by the laying on of hands. They were much concerned with girls' education and often acted as nurses and doctors, especially to their own sex. More of them devoted themselves to the contemplative life than did their male counterparts.

Describing this period offers a challenge. The times were harsh, the speech and attitudes so foreign to our modern comprehension, so violent, cruel, and bloody, that if one of us were somehow sent back in a time machine she would lose her mind. Lives were short and brutal.

People did not wash often; they knew nothing of cleanliness. Their rooms were incredibly hot, with roaring fires kept blazing even in summer, and their many layers of clothing were rarely removed. They stank. They were filled with fear: they distrusted night, the dark, witches, wolves, werewolves, demons, and anything unknown (and this at a time when everything was unknown). They were afraid of one another, and especially mistrustful of anything or anyone who lay beyond their own village. I said that women, Arabs, and Jews were permitted civil rights in the early period. In some jurisdictions they were allowed to hold public office. As time passed, however, these rights were gradually removed. By the full Middle Ages, women were so little valued that their births and deaths went largely unrecorded.

I am told that 73 percent of women died in childbirth, although the figure seems high. Despite the high mortality rate, many people in the Middle Ages lived as long as people today. Both the Lady Esclarmonde and Guilhabert de Castres lived well into their eighties, and died peacefully in their beds. And Esclarmonde was the mother of six children, and grandmother to more.

When the Inquisition began its questioning, some people, including the Lady Esclarmonde, were too important to arrest. Others, such as her son Bernard-Otho de Niort, were arrested, held for ransom, then released. Still others—deemed less important—were tortured and burned at the stake or thrown down wells or stoned or buried alive, as befitted those, it was felt, who denied the one True Church.

The principal characters in this book are fictional. Some, however, lived, and performed the acts recounted here. These include Jean Tisseyre, who walked through town shouting out his innocence, and the randy cleric Gervais Tilbury. In addition, the two bishops of the Church of Love, Guilhabert de Castres and Bertrand Marty, as well as the Lady Esclarmonde, Raymond de Perella, and all those named at Montségur, are based on historical figures. We know the names of those who were burned at Montségur, their station, and even something of their lives.

What happened to the four who escaped is unknown.

Concerning the Bible, I am sorry to say that the prohibition on ordinary people reading the Scriptures themselves lasted for centuries, although today, of course, Roman Catholics are permitted to read in his or her own language the Word of God.

Acknowledgments

I'm often asked what led me to write about this period. Two people independently brought the story of the Cathars to me within a few weeks of each other, and I have come to trust such strange coincidences. The history of this period is known to any French schoolchild, but it came to my attention just at the breakout of the Bosnian war—which saw Christians and Muslims attacking each other with a ferocity so horrifying that I thought we might as well be living in the thirteenth century! Have we learned nothing at all?

A book is generally considered a solitary effort, but it's never written alone. I give special thanks to John Pearson and to Annie and Addison Edwards, who brought the story to me, and especially to Addison, who, living not far from Montségur, helped with my researches in France, leading me to many books and maps; to Georges Passerat at the University of Toulouse, to Jean-Louise Gasc at the Center for Cathars in Villegly, to Lily Devézy in Carcassonne, to David Maso, who acted as my guide in Montségur, to my friend John Hirsch, a medievalist at Georgetown University, to Kim Stevens for research, and to the many books by the Cathar authorities, both in English and in French, especially those of Michel Roquebert, Jean Duvernoy, Zoe Oldenbourg, René Nelli, and Emmanuel Le Roy Ladurie.

Jenna Paulden and MeLissa Bauer helped with information on the birth scene. Professor E. Ann Matter of the Department of Religious Studies at the University of Pennsylvania read the manuscript for accuracy and brought various matters to my attention; and my friend and literary agent, Anne Edelstein, never lost faith in a book that has taken nearly nine years to produce. Her constant good humor and encouragement buoyed my spirits whenever they flagged. A strange thing happens when you write a novel: the characters become as real to you as if they had really lived. I thank Chris Hafner, my brilliant production editor, as well as my editor, Renée Sedliar, whose enthusiasm has rekindled my love for this story, the people, and the courage they demonstrated. Her guidance is shown on every page.

The Treasure
of Montségur

⊞ ONE ⊞

They say I am mad.

Listen, I have seen enough to drive anyone mad, and when the townsfolk see me now, straggling down the street in my ragged gown, sometimes leaning on the rough stone walls of a house or stopping at the fountain to look in the water, when they find me leaning on both hands on a fence to catch my breath before picking up my pack again and hobbling on, then I feel them ease away. The children come out of the byways, calling, "Witch, witch!" They throw stones at me. They are like rats or buzzing flies swarming at some undisclosed signal to my plight; they throw mud and stones at the poor madwoman, with her wild gray hair, which is me. They hoot and point and run in circles round me, touching my torn gray dress and making me forget who I am and what I came out for.

I cover my face with both hands and weep, because I am afraid; because I am a clod of dirt and should have been burnt with the others.

I told them so. "Burn me," I cried. I ran to the two Dominicans, the Preaching Friars in their black robes and stark white hoods, who like our *perfecti* live in poverty. There were two of them begging outside the cathedral doors. I threw myself on my knees, there on the flagstones, and made obeisance as I used to do to the *perfectus* bishop Bertrand Marty, bowing in *adoratio* at his feet. "Burn me," I begged the friars, "I am not worthy," and held out both my hands to show the rope-burns on my wrists. But they pulled away, repulsed. I could see the younger one curl his lip at my smell. "I am not worthy to live," I cried. "In the name of Christ! I have lied. I have sworn oaths. I have drunk, fucked, killed. I am unclean."

They gathered their garments and scurried away from the cathedral, away from me.

Then I sank in the dust, leaning against the heavy wooden doors. Not a large cathedral, this one beside the monastery. Not a large monastery either—only ten or fifteen brothers living there. I scratched my fingers in the dust as our Lord did once when passing judgment on the adulteress, and I thought of all that had happened to bring me to this pass, and all my lovers gone, my friends, a way of life wiped out, and I, the wanderer, lost and trying to do right and trying to serve Christ.

Esclarmonde used to say that misery and self-pity are the lies of the demon. "Take control," she would command in that firm, impatient way she had. I laugh out loud, remembering. "Esclarmonde," I whisper. I can see her crossing the square in her long black habit with a white cord at the waist, and the way she used to cock her head and purse her lips at scrawny me, one reproving eye trying to push some sense into my head. Her *socia,* Ealaine, would be at her side. Es-clar-monde, the light of the world.

"Jeanne, you don't let horses run away with you," she used to caution me. "You rein them in. The same with the wild horses of your mind. Take control of your thoughts. Curb the dismal thoughts, and force forward those of blessings and thanks. They are horses at your own command."

After a time I picked myself up from the cathedral stones and took my cane and let my feet lead me slowly over the cobblestones, out of the town, past the vineyards and into the woods. My feet knowing where to go.

They took me right through the forest into the pastures where cattle grazed, tended by two little boys. There were some geese too, I remember, and one little goosegirl about six years old with hair as black as night. It fell into her eyes like a straggly pony's mane.

I stopped to stare at her for a long time, leaning on my stick.

But she was not mine, that girl, for mine would have been much older, I think, maybe grown by now, though I cannot say for sure, for time has flooded through my brain, days into nights and seasons into seasons, and I don't know how long I've been like this or even what year it is anymore, and maybe my daughter's older than I am now; it's not impossible.

I went on a few steps, carried by the inner spirit that was guiding my feet, and then I sat on a stone by the side of the road and cried. I cried first for my dead daughter, and then for Esclarmonde, whom I miss so much, and Baiona and William, then for all the children of Montségur, and finally for all the children everywhere, including myself, that other child, who was also born in war. She wore a white dress with little pearls sewn down the front. I used to turn it in my hands. I watched it shrink smaller and smaller every year, until it seemed impossible that I'd ever been so tiny, no bigger than a kerchief, it seemed. One day I put it on my own child, and tried to ignore the brown bloodstain that ran all down the front. I should not have done it. Baiona claimed it didn't bring a curse, but I buried my baby soon after. She died of pox, not war. She lay in my arms, that cold little form. That's not a thing a mother can forget. I suppose if she hadn't died, she would have been burnt up too.

Guilhabert de Castres said the first burnings took place two hundred and fifty years ago, in 1002. Three men burnt here, ten there. They hunted witches too—and still are doing it.

They would burn me for apostasy, poor crazy Jeanne. Someday I may be burnt, as my beautiful Baiona was, or William, or my beloved Bertrand Marty, two hundred of them weeping, holding one another as they hobbled down the hill.

No. No! Don't think of that.

How strange is memory. All jumbled up together in my head, just behind my eyes, and some things I see as clearly as if they happened yesterday, and yet I was a child, and other things I forget—closed doors, dark rooms. It's like the castle storeroom, wandering among the trunks and dusty boxes, cobwebs, musty smell, and every now and then a shaft of sunlight illuminates a moment, or a person, or a word. One of the Ancients says you can't step in the same river twice, but I step in the rivers of my memory again and again. And also in some where I never was.

Hoofbeats. I lift my head. *Hide!* I pull to my feet and hurry back from the road, pretending to stoop to do my business behind a bush. I remember when the Inquisitors didn't ride at a gallop, surrounded by their guards. They are magpies, flapping in their black and white garb. I remember when there were no prosecutors poking their noses into every life. I can't remember, though, a time without war—war inside, war outside, war in the heart of that black-haired girl I was, poor ignorant little child, so proud and defiant, and look where it got her.

It seems another life, so long ago, another person, nothing to do with me or with anyone I know. Foolish girl, rebelling against life, against the very ones who tried to teach her happiness. First fighting the marriage. Then just fighting. But maybe that's how God intended it, for each new generation starts from scratch, learning the lessons all over again, and we older ones can't teach or tell the children anything, poor tots; each one starts at scratch, so that hardly any progress is made at all. Her war was always with herself. She didn't even know how rich she was, how happy in her friends.

◈ TWO ◈

She was sewing in the window-seat overlooking the racefields at the castle near Foix, and had the women come in ten minutes earlier, they would have seen the young girl twisted on the stone bench, her head and shoulders outside the open window, looking up at the ivy that covered the exterior stone and down at the course below, the fields, *les champs,* where the champions raced their horses, jousted, fought, and practiced military moves. The war was still on, though the demon Simon de Montfort had been killed the year before when he laid siege to Toulouse. But now the exercises were over, and the horses clip-clopped over the cobbles back to the stables, and the laughter and shouting of the young squires was fading, muffled by the back of the castle, and Jeanne was left to finish the hemstitching in her lap.

She stole another glance out the window, then flopped back onto the window-seat and picked up her needle, sullenly stitching an open fretwork design with almost none of her attention on the needle and most of it on Rogert and the siege that had been laid against Toulouse. People said the women had fought on the walls beside the men, shooting arrows and stones at the French siege engines. They said it was the women who had killed de Montfort with a missile from a stone-gun.

Already the minstrels were singing about that day:

> *A stone flew straight to its mark*
> *And smote Count Simon upon his helm of steel.*

He had just come from his prayers, and rushed into battle, to be killed.

With a sigh Jeanne forced her attention back to her handiwork. She was not good at sewing, like Baiona. Her fingers seemed too big. Her thumbs got in the way, and even now, when she was age thirteen, her stitching sometimes came out careless and coarse. But it was not only her fingers that wouldn't work: it was her dreamy mind. Baiona, on the other hand, only a year older, worked stitches tiny as fairy footprints, and the way she fell into a perfect rhythm and meditation made her sewing a delight to behold, as from her needle—and likewise from her brush and paints—would grow flowers and insects, imaginary and visionary, a whole bestiary of wild creatures climbing and clawing their way up castle walls or across a landscape of trees and fields. From her needle came peasants and nobles so real that Jeanne thought they might jump out of the cloth and walk about, telling of their hopes and dreams.

Baiona had gifted hands. Everyone said so. Jeanne dropped her napkin in despair, onto the pile of its unstitched mates, and let her eyes rove about the room. It was a beautiful, airy space into which the sunlight streamed through arched windows. In it were several carved chairs, high and heavy, and on the wall two tapestries: one showed the meeting of Christ with the woman at the well, when he offered her the water of eternal life; the other (her favorite) depicted the sacrifice of Isaac, and there was Abraham's beige hand lifted as always, his head just turning toward the angel who reached down to stay his knife, and over to the side stood the horn-trapped ram hidden in the greenery. It was lovely.

Usually Jeanne could look at the stories for hours, but today she turned restlessly once more and caught the slender column that divided the window space, scanning the outdoor view of woods and meadow-land. She should have been a boy down on the riding fields. She was not made for napkins and tale-telling tapestries. She would rather the stories were made about herself! She imagined herself as Ovid's Diana, goddess of the hunt, a boy-girl, shooting a bow and running down a stag with her own hounds. She wished she were one of the women defending their city from the French devil Simon de Montfort. No needlework.

She leaned out the window, the soft air on her cheek, and she wanted to cry aloud, to sing and swing her body out to scale the castle walls. She wanted to pitch herself out into that sweet heavy air and . . . fly. Perhaps she would return as a bird in another incarnation, although they said you never go back to lesser forms once the human form has been achieved. But surely, in that case, she had once been a bird, for she remembered flying, and sometimes in the night she dreamed of swooping on the mountain winds, a hawk unhooded, free. She swung back inside and picked up her linen with a sigh.

Just at that moment the Lady Esclarmonde came in, followed by her cousin Giulietta, a young widow. Jeanne rose and bobbed a curtsey, and she felt the blush rising in her cheeks as she thought about what they would have seen had they come upon her a few moments earlier, sprawling out the window.

The Lady Esclarmonde, now sixty-two, had taken the habit thirteen years earlier, at the age of forty-nine. She'd borne six children to her husband and then left him to take the robe and become a Good Woman. They had remained friends, she and her husband—no animosity. She always wore a long black dress, very plain, tied at the waist with the cord that bound her vows to Christ. She carried her spindle from room to room, spinning as she walked. Her eyes moved quietly here and there, mindful of what was happening around her, even as her hands wound the thread and her thoughts spun out her prayers. Each drop of the spindle represented a full round of the Lord's Prayer.

Now she paused in the doorway to finish, because a Good Christian did not pass through a door without saying the Lord's Prayer, did not lift her spoon at dinner without first saying the Lord's Prayer, did not breathe without remembering our Lord.

Giulietta, on the other hand, was a fashionable young woman, still in her twenties, and dressed in rose-colored skirts. Her light step, as she entered the room, was too exuberant for the Good Christian's stately pace. Giulietta lived at the castle and was a believer of sorts, but she had no intention of taking the robe. Her fine eyes darted everywhere. She liked to flirt. If Jeanne had any ambitions, it was to Giulietta she looked, not the Cathars, though Esclarmonde, her adopted mother, had raised her, and though she loved the perfected woman with all her heart.

"It's the path to happiness," Esclarmonde would say quietly, dropping her spindle against the Devil's idle hands.

"To become a Good Woman?"

"Yes, if you choose. A Friend of God."

But Jeanne wanted to dance, to eat, to sing songs, to ride fast horses. She wanted to hunt, wear bright colors—live as a Catholic, actually! She laughed. That was a celebratory church, it seemed.

She made a face, but Esclarmonde smiled into her eyes and straightened her cap with an affectionate tug. "Later," she said with a laugh, "when you've finished with the worldly life. We don't want young girls."

Giulietta took from Jeanne the napkin she was working on.

"See, Esclarmonde," she said, "how fine her work is. You're getting better, Jeanne."

The Lady Esclarmonde examined it approvingly, then said gently, "Stand up, child. Turn around."

"She's getting tall," said Giulietta. Jeanne was annoyed at being spoken of as if she were not present, could not hear. She turned slowly, however, under the inspection. She felt her hands hanging like hams at the ends of her arms. If she were a beauty—if she were Baiona, with slate-gray eyes and gleaming honey-colored hair—she wouldn't mind such an inspection, but being raven-haired and strong, she felt a flush of shame spreading down her chest.

When Jeanne was eleven, Esclarmonde had collared her neck with a prickly wicker neckband, to make her stand up straight and hold her neck in the high and graceful pose of a true lady. Apparently it did some good, for it was removed after six months. The collar did not always help, however, for another orphan girl, Raymonde Narbonne, wore one for three years without success. Her back grew ever more twisted, and one leg developed shorter than the other, until they gave it up.

"Turn again," commanded Esclarmonde.

"What is it?" Jeanne asked, anxiously.

"It's nothing, darling," said Giulietta. She pushed up her soft rose sleeve so that the blue-gray lining shimmered and shot out at Jeanne, "We're admiring you, that's all."

She glanced up. Were they teasing?

"What do you think about marriage, Jeanne? Would you like to be a bride?"

"Now, now," said Esclarmonde. But a smile quivered at the edges of her lips.

What *did* she think about marriage? It depended. For herself or someone else?

"What do you mean?" she answered cautiously.

"Rich black hair," said Giulietta. "Fine eyes. She'll be a beauty."

"Esclarmonde—?" Jeanne turned to the older woman, who dropped her spindle at that moment, the carded wool spinning into one long thread. Jeanne watched it, mesmerized, waiting for the prayer to end.

"It's true," said Esclarmonde finally. "It's time to find a husband for you, Jeanne."

The Lady Esclarmonde never acted in haste. Her movements, like her thoughts, were contained and grave, exuding an aura of peaceful happiness and reserve. No one acted familiarly with the Lady Esclarmonde. But Jeanne wanted to fling herself into the older woman's arms, to tell her, No, she didn't want to marry yet.

Esclarmonde must have seen her face. "Don't you want to marry?"

"I don't want to leave you," Jeanne said passionately. "And anyway, who would marry me? I have no money, no fortune. Don't send me away." She stood bereft, the napkins having fallen at her feet. "Couldn't I marry one of the squires here?" Her face flared red. "I don't want an old man." She could imagine the battle-scarred husband who would be chosen for her, a knight twenty years older than herself. Or more. He might even be forty, like the husband chosen for Blanche de Pepieux. His skin was leather, his mouth set grimly under a grizzled moustache.

"Every girl needs a husband, Jeanne, someone to protect her. As for your dowry, it's true that without any money we can't find you a suitable husband, but you have the pearls on your natal dress, and I will add a suitable sum."

"Ah, you see how generous she is!" cried Giulietta, clapping her hands to make Jeanne pleased. "You should be happy!"

Jeanne felt her anger rise—the silly woman! How had she ever admired her? Her thoughts wheeled like birds, circling—her friends Baiona, Rogert—and then if she were married she'd never fly! Because she knew that the moment she turned from the ceremony, she would be an old woman, a wimple on her head, expected to walk with stately majesty, never again to run. She would grow fat with childbirth, if she didn't die of it first.

"I don't want to go away," she whispered miserably.

"Jeanne, some girls are married much younger than you," protested Giulietta.

But Esclarmonde, with a sharp, appraising glance, spoke quietly: "Don't be afraid. It won't happen tomorrow or next week; but it's not too soon to think of what will happen in your life. I have your well-being in mind, and that includes settling you in responsible hands. This is a good time for such concerns. There's a lull in the fighting."

The war was still going on. Sometimes a messenger would clatter into the courtyard on his lathered horse, throw himself off, and dash into the palace. Then Esclarmonde, brows furrowed and eyes downcast, would join the men to confer in low voices with him, and sometimes she would come to her feet to pace the floor as they spoke. Now and again it was news of a death the messenger brought, and then a hand would reach out to touch another, the touch of consolation. Sometimes the news was of the progress of the war, of battles and losses and secret operations or the movement of troops, for the Lady Esclarmonde, although perfected, kept up to date. Sometimes a peasant woman might leave the palace hurriedly, to disappear across country with memorized dispatches, or a man on horseback would gallop off in haste. But what exactly the news was, the children were never told.

"The men are coming home soon," said Esclarmonde. "They'll be tired of fighting; they'll be thinking of replenishing their fortunes, planting fields—"

"And planting other seeds," said Giulietta with a merry laugh.

"The war has drained us," continued Esclarmonde with a glance at the younger woman that could have felled an ox. "I want to find someone special for my special girl, my angel-orphan."

Jeanne felt her heart go out to Esclarmonde, yet she resisted stubbornly.

"Baiona's a year older than me, and she's not yet betrothed."

Esclarmonde touched Jeanne's cheek with the back of her fingers, so delicately, so gently that the child wanted to kiss her fingertips. "Don't worry, Jeanne," she said reassuringly. "We will do nothing without your consent."

When Esclarmonde had left, Giulietta put her arm around Jeanne's shoulders and drew her back to the window-seat. She whipped out a white linen kerchief and wiped the young girl's eyes. Then she handed Jeanne her sewing and took a napkin for herself.

"So, whisper in my ear. What's wrong? Here, take your sewing, and I'll take a napkin for myself and help you as we talk. Come on now, aren't we friends? Haven't I known you since you first came to the orphanage at Pamiers? You threw yourself at the Lady Esclarmonde and would not loose your grip. Do you remember? Maybe not, you were so small. The two *perfectae* had brought you in from Béziers, where they'd found you— little foundling—in a meadow in the grass."

"The peasant woman found me," Jeanne corrected her. "The mushroom woman."

Giulietta laughed. "So you're talking to me again? Yes, it was the mushroom woman who found you in the meadow just outside the walls of Béziers, the smoke still rising from the burning city and the cries of the dying inside; and you playing all alone in the grass, babbling to yourself in your little white dress with seedpearls sewn on it."

"She took me to the two *perfectae* hiding in the woods," said Jeanne, who loved the story of how she'd been found.

"And they in turn walked for days to bring you to the orphanage that the Lady Esclarmonde had founded at Pamiers. No one could get you to speak. You wouldn't say a word, but you flung yourself at her knees and held tight her skirts, and somehow you drove an arrow into the heart of the Lady Esclarmonde, and she took you with her from the orphanage to raise in her own house, as her own child. Her special angel-child she always called you, come from nowhere, falling from the sky."

Jeanne ducked her head over her sewing. It was true. The Lady Esclarmonde—sister of the Count of Foix, and thus a wealthy woman in her own right—had founded several orphanages, and a hospital too, and she fed the homeless tirelessly; yet for all her prayers and busyness, she'd found time to favor Jeanne.

"Now why so glum? Really, this is a time of celebration, not of despair—and you with your long looks. You'd think we were sending you out into the forest by yourself to live as a hermit instead of telling you it's time to take a man! You'll have your own name and a chateau and children of your own to raise. You'll have a position of your own. What's wrong with that? You'd want to stay a spinster all your life? Or take the robe, perhaps?"

Jeanne wiped her nose with her sleeve.

"No, no, with a kerchief." Giulietta laughed. "By Saint Anne, why do you think we're hemming these things?"

Jeanne, heavy-hearted and submissive, took the linen.

"There's someone you like, isn't there?" asked the wily Giulietta. "Go away, now." She nudged Jeanne, laughing. "I'm not so old I haven't been in your shoes, sitting here overlooking the field where you can watch the boys. Come, give me a smile. That's a girl. Now stab it with your needle, like a good girl, and we'll talk about girlhood and womanhood and love and marriage, and we shall have your napkins done in no time, because I've been where you are. So have we all. *All* women."

Giulietta looked pensive. "You know I was married at fourteen to a noble lord," she confided. "He was thirty at the time." She had thought him as old as the moon back then, but she had borne him four beautiful children before he was killed in battle, and as she stitched, she told how a man of that age might seem wrinkled and worn out to a tender girl, but her husband had shown himself all gentleness and had given her much pleasure too, before he died, for a man that age is experienced in the ways of love. Then she told how, after her husband's death, she had married a second time and again been widowed, and now she had several lovers ("though that's not to speak of to a young girl, except to say that a woman's life is by no means over just because a marriage is arranged"). And what did Jeanne think she would do if she didn't marry? And how would she live? And who would give her children? Because the philosophers have proven that the happiness of all of society rests on good marriages. Moreover, she added, love, despite the cynical songs of troubadours, often coincides with union ("Don't forget it, Jeanne"); and she named three couples—husbands and wives—who were deeply in love, two having fallen in love after marriage.

"Now tell me, is there someone you like?" Giulietta asked. "We'll see if we can't make a marriage to suit everyone's needs."

Thus with whispers and nudges she pulled Jeanne's secret out—that Jeanne had eyes for Rogert of Foix, whose father was a cousin of Esclarmonde.

"I watch him all the time," she confided, "but he doesn't know that I'm alive."

◈ THREE ◈

The sight of the Inquisitors riding past has upset me. I huddle by the river here, hugging my knees and feeling the sickness waver in my stomach.

They say the war was fought against heresy. I say they want our land. You don't see war up north, near Paris. Here they kill everyone—Moors, Jews, Cathar heretics. They say we are demons, and no trace must remain. Burn our bodies, expunge all memory. They exhume dead bodies buried fifty years or more, dry skeletons buried in holy, consecrated ground on cathedral land. They dig up the bones and toss them on the flames, tear down our houses stone by stone. Nothing must remain, they say.

They burnt two hundred and ten people at Moissac, not without resistance. Was I still married then? When were the Dominicans expelled from Toulouse? It's all a muddle in my mind. And yet the first one, the Spaniard Dominic Guzman—he was a good and holy man. Everyone said so. If he were alive today, I wonder if his Preaching Friars would be behaving so. He asked Pope Innocent III to send him as a missionary to convert the Tartars in Russia, and instead the Pope sent him to evangelize the heathen Christian Albigensians here in the south. He'd already taken up our Cathar ways: he walked barefoot in sandals, ate no meat, lived in poverty, like the Cathar priests. He preached the love of Christ just as the Good Christians did in the Church of Love. He took the same vows of kindness and constant prayer, and in fact he converted a handful of men and women to his order—and now look at the Preaching Friars, killing the Good Christians because they refuse to leave the Way.

They call us the Cathars, or "Pure Ones," because we trace our path right back to the original apostles of Christ. We are the sons and daughters of Jesus, following His Way. "I am the Way," He said. "Anyone who wants to enter the Kingdom of God must come by my Way." That's from the Apostle John. We have followed the Way, handed down one on one, mouth to ear, for more than a thousand years, the direct heritage of Jesus Christ our Lord, whose children we are.

The Inquisitors call our priests the "perfected heretics," *haeretici perfecti*. We call them simply the Good Men or Good Women, the Good Christians, the Friends of God. There are Good Christians up north too, in Paris, Orleans, Reims, and around Champagne, worshiping in the Church of Love. But mostly in the south, stretching from Aragon across to Lombardy.

It's strange to think we cannot live in tolerance and peace. First the Pope tried to argue people back to their Catholic faith. He sent out missionaries, but the Catholic Church had become a laughingstock, the province of illiterate or foolish priests, and often drunken ones. Some kept their women right in their houses, concubines and mistresses. It was a scandal. Certainly it scandalized our chaste Friends of God, who taught that we were fallen angels, struggling to return back home. The Friends were opposed to unwed sensuality. Once when I was a young married woman, I came down to the village at Peyrepertuse and saw the priest, Pierre Laclergue, coming out of the house of Na Mengarde, hitching up his hose under his skirts with the satisfied smile of a cat; and I had only to look at Na Mengarde to know how well the priest had done. That's the true sign. If the lover has not yet achieved his prize, his eyes will follow the woman, while she appears indifferent. But once he's gained his goal, it's the woman's eyes that follow him, while the man seems careless and indifferent. So that's how I knew about the priest and Na Mengarde, but it's nothing odd.

You can go to any monastery in the Occitanie and see the wives and girlfriends living in outlying houses, or the whores leaning out their windows right nearby. I know one abbot who keeps his mistress in one house and his wife in another. And I'm not saying anything against them, but they'll burn a heretic for chastity. For shame!

Take the cleric Gervais Tilbury. It was common gossip at the time. One day he and other clerics were walking with the archbishop in the gardens outside town when they spotted a young girl in a nearby vineyard. Gervais nudged his brothers, leering, and made a bet that he could take her, and they all hooted and catcalled at him—even the archbishop!—as if they hadn't each one taken vows to God. And then Tilbury strode through the vineyard, jaunty and polished, to seduce that poor country girl. There—I see how she shies away with downcast eyes—she knew about these priests—and picks up her pace, eyes glued to the dusty road before her. He slips one arm around her waist. She freezes. He bends over her and whispers pretty words ("No," she twists away) about her fine breasts and her lips that should be used for more than words (haven't I heard such whisperings myself) and how he can provide food and drink such as her tongue has never tasted, should she go into the bushes there with him, and there he will show her pleasures known only to the angels in heaven. It would be no sin, he says, since he is a man of God.

But this girl was a believer, a *credens*. She had taken a vow of chastity until she married.

He tried to kiss her anyway, and he thrust his hand under her dress—at which she pushed him so hard that he fell in the dirt. Then she lifted her skirts and ran as fast as she could, back to the safety of her peasant home; and all the while the archbishop and the other priests were howling with laughter and egging on their comrade and calling for payment on their bets.

"It's a scandal!" I shout so loud that a raven flies up off the tree with a raucous croak and flaps away like a loose-shouldered, black-garbed cleric himself. The demon-birds.

Gervais Tilbury accused the girl of being a heretic. Because of her vow of chastity. She was burnt at the stake, alive. Hair on fire. Clothes on fire. Feet hands eyes, *ahyiiie!*

That's the Catholic Church that invaded the Languedoc in 1209. Pope Innocent III called up a Crusade not against pagan Saracens but against good Christian folk who follow Christ Jesus, the Son of God, who could not die on the cross because He was more than human. The Pope called for a Crusade against those who believe in Baptism not by water but by the Holy Spirit, as Christ taught. Who believe in the power of prayer, and rebirths, and our climbing steadily toward the godhead Light. Who believe in the laying on of hands to heal us with the holy Spirit of Christ's Light. And believe in women serving also as the priests of Christ. But I don't think the Pope cared about those things; I think his Crusade was because we wouldn't tithe.

Esclarmonde says that in the end we shall win, in God's own time, that the others will eventually come round to our Way; but I remember when even women—myself among them—were taught to read and write, when the Bible was translated into the common tongue, when the free towns were governed by freely elected consuls—as had been done for eight hundred or a thousand years, ever since the time of the Romans—and when Jews and Arabs were elected to high office too. Now the Jews wear a yellow circle on their breast, released heretics wear a cross on both sides of their breast, lepers wear gray clothing with a red hat, and I have no more bright, gaudy, green or azure gowns.

◈ FOUR ◈

The memories come in flashes, like sunlight shining in a forest grove, while all around lies the blind blackness of lost time. But I'm scared. In the blackness the other memories lunge out at me, but I won't look at them. I'm angry. Control the horses of my thoughts. Hurrying, I stumble to my feet and walk. Te-tum-tum-tum: I hum a tune to keep the fear away. "Be grateful; count your blessings," Esclarmonde used to say, "because God loves us when we sing"; and pretty soon my mood brightens. "You're only as happy as you decide to be," she'd say, and so I sing to the joyous air of Christ.

Look at me, so blessed here. I have a place to live, that only leaks a little. I have clothes and food; I'm never hungry for long. And if I hadn't lost everything, including my mother (indeed, two mothers), and my husbands (two), and country, friends, and all my money and lands—everything material—would I be so rich as I am now? So why am I weeping? I can't stop crying. I could cry for a thousand years.

The others envy me. That's why the little boys throw stones: they're scared of my happiness; it confuses them. And the ladies in the convent pray for me—imagine!—as if they're luckier than I.

A butterfly has landed on that leaf. It's so pretty, with its blue and yellow markings, that I stop to marvel, and it waves its wings as if its little fanning cools the very earth, so sweet a butterfly, cooling my heated memories. And now I'm crying for the beauty. The Friends of God believe this earth, all physical matter, was created by the Evil One, all pain and wickedness masking itself as beauty and delights. (They also think that we ourselves were angels once, except that we've forgotten.) I'm weeping for love of Satan, then, but how can that be when my heart curls around the tender butterfly? Scripture says that God created the world in six days and rested on the seventh. And wouldn't the God of power and love bend over the earth and all the animals—except (slap!), all right, except the black flies. I'll give Beelzebub the flies that buzz on the bleeding carcasses of war, or are they God's way of cleaning up cadavers? Oh, now I'm confused again.

The Good Men want to leave this life of suffering and move into the Light—Christ's Light—but I cling to my life with both white-knuckled hands, terrified of dying, in spite of pain and flies. That's why I'm not perfected yet. Because it seems to me, looking back, that each moment has moved me inexorably to this imperfect moment, as if my life were writ in the Book of God before I even agreed to come be born; and I had no more choice in what's happened than in where the wind decides to blow—not in Rogert, who led me to Montségur, not in loving William, or finding the cave, not in hiding the treasure, not in my weakness—and then I whimper and throw my shawl over my head, because if that were so, then it would mean that God *meant* for me to lose the treasure of Montségur, now gone, now lost. Ah woe, ah me! Unless it was the crafty Devil. Or was the fault mine, made by my free will? How do I tell?

Now I'm walking faster, trying to outrun my thoughts. It begins to rain; the big, scattered drops are like the tears of God, and between the rain and my own tears I think we'll have another Flood.

The age-old question eats at my heart: Was it my will or God's? I have always felt different. With cause, of course—the foundling, found playing among the grasshoppers in the hot green July meadow-grass. How old was I? Two or three at most, in my white silk gown with its tiny pearls sewn down the front—the garb of a noble's daughter, so they said, but smeared all down the front with blood. One red satin slipper on one tiny foot, and no sign of the other, and I not crying in my orphan-state, but singing little baby songs while pulling at the stalks of grass, as if the black smoke of the city weren't still rising in the silent, hot, blue summer sky.

How had the baby gotten there? Some said she was an angel-baby and some a changeling or the Devil's spawn. But Esclarmonde, who called me her angel-child, said I was only an orphan, saved when the city fell.

Twenty thousand people were massacred at Béziers. I've heard the story many times. The slaughter went on for days. Men, women, children, babies. Were the soldiers' arms tired from wielding their knives and heavy swords?

"How will we know the heretics from the Catholics?" one soldier had asked.

"Kill them all," replied Bishop Arnard-Amalric, commander of the Crusade of 1209. "God will recognize His own." (My arm flailing at the raindrops in my rage!)

In the cathedral alone they butchered two thousand screaming people who had fled there for sanctuary. Blood splattered the painted walls and dripped in the dusky shadows to pool around the bodies on the stone floor; while outside, amidst the constant screams and shrieks, blood flowed in the gutters, and the corpses, beheaded, stabbed, mutilated, lay in the alleys and streets and in the rooms of ransacked houses, while the drunken Crusader *routiers,* the mercenaries, roared and raped. Other citizens were whipped out of Béziers, their hands or noses chopped off, or their eyes put out, and they were bumping blindly into trees and stumbling over roots, their bleeding, handless stumps held helplessly out before them, these homeless, mutilated ones. They wandered through the forest until they starved or until the peasants bludgeoned and pitchforked them in mercy. (My arm exhausted from the sweeping and the stabbing.)

And then the fires began—no one knows quite how—and burnt up this rich city, while the French knights fought their own men, swords swinging, in an effort to restore order amidst the roaring, screaming blaze; and when they'd put the fires out, nothing at all was left.

And then the silence.

When it was all over, the French marched away no richer than they came. The silent wind whipped up the empty streets, where the rats gnawed on the silent corpses, toasted by the flames. The only sound was the buzzing of Beelzebub's black bottlenose flies.

A child was found in a field outside the walls, a baby, singing baby songs and playing with green stalks of grass. She was dressed in a white silk dress with pearls sewn down the front. The Lady Esclarmonde took her in as one of her orphans, to raise Cathar. But I remember nothing of either massacre or field, nothing of the mushroom woman who found me or of the two perfected women who walked me to Pamiers. I remember only one moment shot with light. It comes as a glimmer, fragile as if seen through water, of a lady dressed in shining white. She is smiling sweetly down at me. She takes my hand, a Lady in light, sheltering me in shimmering love. We are walking in tall grass together. I'm not afraid, but follow trustingly. The grass is higher than my head.

To this day I don't know if it was a dream or not. . . . I wish I'd see her again. But how did the infant get into the field? And another miracle: the mushroom woman didn't smash the baby's head against a rock and steal her little pearl-strewn dress.

My gnarled old hands. Knuckles knotted. Nails torn. Baiona used to clip my nails and massage my hands with creams; we'd laugh and talk and braid each other's hair, kissing one another, my other heart.

Ah, there's my cozy stable, and the rain is coming hard.

◈ FIVE ◈

nger! Anger! It beats like waves of fire in my spine.

I've hurt my foot.

"Beware of what you pray for," Esclarmonde would say, "because you might get it." Instead, surrender everything to God. "God knows what will bring you happiness," she'd say. "Leave everything to God and to His angels, and do you try only to love like God, to live like Christ." I've never succeeded at that. "Pray, Jeanne, that you can have the heart of Christ."

It's raining. I'd like a mug of hot wine or cider. Something warm and thick running down my throat. I must be close to forty, and yet I want to snuggle down in a featherbed and hide. I want my mother to care for me. Instead, I scrunch down in the straw of my lean-to shed and pull my cloak around me. I could boil some hot water to soothe my throat. That would be good. Especially if I had some honey to put in it, which I don't. Next door I can hear the donkey moving about in his stall, and the bleat of the three black-faced sheep, and there is a fine, thick animal smell.

My shed is roughly three feet wide, with barely space for me to stretch out. Still, it feels good to lie down. Beneath my throbbing foot, hidden under a board, is my treasure. The gift from Poitevin. If I take it out, if I remove the green oilcloth wrapping, I can stroke the silver inlay on the black, hard calf-leather cover. It has silver clasps to hold it shut. My eyes are too weak to read the beautiful inked print, and I could be

burnt for owning it, not in Latin but in the common tongue—all four
Gospels, and each title letter illuminated in gold and red and lapis blue. I
don't dare remove it from its nest, but I rest my ankle over the straw-
strewn board that covers it. Perhaps it will heal my foot.

"Hey, beggar-woman!"

I look up. It's the mistress's servant here, the one who doubles as the
stableboy. He stands in the stableyard, under the dripping eaves, holding a
tray covered with a napkin. The rain is pouring down the thatch into his
collar, and he's wet as a drowned cat. I give a cackle.

"What are you laughing at, old hag?" He pushes into my little lair
that's hardly big enough for me roll over in. "Move over." He shoves me
with one foot.

"What do you want?" I ask, but I move back lest he step on my hurt
foot. I won't get up for the likes of him. He's dressed in his rich black velvet jacket and black hose, pretending to be a squire in the castle perhaps,
instead of the gardener and the stableboy. Oh, he's a dandy, he is. He likes
boys. I have seen him strolling at dusk, or standing on the stone bridge,
looking out for fun. Now he tosses back his fine brown curly hair, which
does not toss easily since it's dripping wet.

"What do you come here for?" I ask.

"Not by choice," he snarls. "Move over, damn you, witch. I'm getting
wet."

"Well, don't come out in the elements," I say, laughing up at him, "and
they won't turn on you."

"Mistress Flavia sends you this," he says with a black look, laying down
his tray. Then with his free hand he crosses himself quickly against my
witchery. I see him make the Devil's fork against the Evil One.

"What is it?" I lift the white linen napkin.

Now tell me that the angels don't take care of me! The mistress of
this place has sent me a pot of hot water and a little jug of wine, and I
can mix the two and stretch the wine out all the afternoon. Blessings
poured on me!

"But why?" I look up at the boy, ready to like him for having brought
me something nice. But he glares down at me, lip curled.

"She's celebrating the return of her little son," he says.

"Her son?"

"Aged five. He's been visiting her sister and their mum, and now that he's come home she says everyone in the household must have wine, and that includes the destitute old beggar-woman in the shed."

"Me?"

Me, destitute?

"I said you were a witch," he whispered, "and should be stoned. Or else a heretic, and burnt."

"Watch your tongue." We glare at each other, but I am first to lower my eyes.

"She's a good woman to think of me. Tell her I shall work for her," I say, "if she gives me wool for spinning and the loan of a spindle. I am no beggar. I can sew and spin. I can mend for her. I'll work for my food and lodging."

He turns away. He won't take back my message, I know. And I'm sorry.

"Tell her thank you." I pour the wine into my bowl and mix it with a little water. He watches sharp-eyed. Then I hand him back the napkin and the jug. I don't want him watching me drink, ruining my taste of warmth. "Tell her I shall pray to our Lord Jesus Christ for her, and her husband, and her son. Tell her that this kindness shall be remembered in heaven above."

"She'll kick you out." He leans down in my face. I cover the wine with one hand. I don't want his spit in it. I don't want him kicking it over with his foot. But he picks up the tray and jug, leaving me the pot of hot water, and he dashes out into the rain, running through the raindrops. Poor boy. Trying to keep his black velvet from getting muddy and wet. It's a sad thing, that he has to wait on me, and suddenly I feel pity for him.

The mistress is a beautiful woman, always neat, her headdress clean. I'm glad I thought to ask for work. Na Jeanne, she calls me formally, as if I were still the chatelaine of my husband's lands. She has a pretty smile. Another woman would have turned me out, my being the reminder of what all else she has to give. The poor are not beloved anywhere.

But I am not poor, as I'd tell her. I am blessed above all women, because I have shelter, and not just anyplace either, but in a stable. I live in this crack between the shed and the stable wall, and who could ask for more? Wasn't our Lord born in a stable and laid out in a manger? I am graced, perhaps, to live the end of my days according to His birth.

So I hum to myself and drink the wine and listen to the rain drip into the courtyard there, splashing on the stones. Once I lived in the palace at Pamiers, and sometimes in the one at Foix; and once I thought a young man's love was the treasure of the world.

⬟ SIX ⬟

Was it God's will or hers that made things happen?

Rogert was well built, with his broad shoulders and his narrow hips. His dark hair fell over lazy black eyes. She watched him under her lashes when he served the wine at dinner, noted the way he rested his weight on one hip. She watched him during military exercises, when the young men were taught the code of arms. And sometimes, as if a teasing universe were testing her, she would come around a corner unaware and there he'd be, leaning olive-skinned against a wall, perhaps, as he chatted with his friends, or carrying armor for his lord, so that even though in her head she wanted freedom from him, her heart would give a sudden leap, her knees go weak. Eyes down, she would hurry past.

Once he was coming off the training field at Foix with a gang of boys, all of them jostling, wrestling one another, trying to throw each other down. Jeanne was standing at the stable gate, and at their approach her feet seemed glued to the ground, unable to move. They came closer. A pulse pounded in her throat. She thought she might actually faint: it was as if he gave off a magical scent, or a bow-wave of heat. She had to support herself with one hand on the wall. The boys took up all the road when they walked, and as they passed, Rogert put one arm around her waist.

"Here's Jeanne," he said. "And how's my little Jeanne?"

She was stunned. For a moment she could do nothing, aware only of his breath on her face and his hand on her waist, and then she twisted away.

"I'm neither yours nor little," she answered. "If you—"

But he'd already passed on with a laugh, leaving her red-faced and for some reason ashamed. She picked up her skirts and ran across the courtyard and through the stone arch, legs pounding down the road that bordered the training field. Running, running, though she didn't know why or where. She wanted to feel her body moving and the breath searing her lungs. She ran all the way to the river and threw herself down on the grass. Then she burst into angry tears, because she'd dropped into a nest of stinging nettles and it seemed the final straw, though whether her tears rose up for twisting away or for wanting his arm around her or for the pain of nettles she could not say. She soaked her legs in the soothing river and thought of him.

That night and for many nights afterward she dreamed about his arm around her waist, his body pressed against hers. She snuggled up to Baiona in the dark—Baiona, friend of her childhood, her other heart. As children they had eaten and played and slept together. If separated for a few hours, they would fly into each other's arms as if they'd been apart for weeks.

"Baiona!"

"Oh, I love you, Jeanne!"

One fair, one dark, they lay in their shared bed and breathed each other's breath from sleepy lips, their legs entangled and arms entwined or thrown casually over the other's back.

"Baiona, are you awake?" Jeanne whispered this night.

"Hmm."

"I have something to tell you."

"What?"

"No, I've changed my mind."

Baiona raised herself on one elbow, peering in the darkness into the white moon of her friend's face. "We don't have secrets," she said solemnly. "Telling me something is like telling it to yourself, and telling you something is like telling another half of myself. We're the same person, you and I."

"I'm ashamed," Jeanne murmured.

"Ashamed of what?"

"Bend down." She could feel Baiona's soft hair tickling her cheek. "I like . . . Rogert," she whispered into her friend's waiting ear.

There was silence. Baiona pulled back.

"Baiona?"

"No. I was thinking about it. How does he feel?" she asked cautiously.

"I don't know, I'm miserable. I can't tell. Do you think he likes me?"

There was a pause before she answered with impatience. "How would I know?"

Then: "I don't like Rogert."

"Oh." For a moment Jeanne was stunned. She wanted to ask her, why—why didn't she like him? But lying there in bed she thought, *What difference would the answer make?* Maybe Baiona was jealous, or afraid she'd lose her best friend. Maybe she didn't know Rogert. There were a hundred reasons why one person liked or disliked another. Maybe Jeanne didn't want to know.

"Giulietta says I must put myself in his way and see how he behaves," said Jeanne. She looked over at Baiona, lying on her back and staring at the dark. "What do you think?"

"I don't think anything," said Baiona. "Do it, I guess."

"What do you mean? How?"

"Take her advice. Perhaps he wants your heart." She turned her back to Jeanne. "I have to sleep."

"Tell me that he likes me," Jeanne urged, innocent as a mourning dove, but Baiona had already gone to sleep. Jeanne ducked deep into the covers, her head bursting with the idea that Rogert might love her, might want her heart. The words were like a *trouvère*'s song: "He wants your heart." In a single moment Jeanne felt that she'd changed from girl to woman, the shift so subtle that it happened in the time it took to turn from her left side, facing Baiona, over to her right. She lay with her back pressed against that of her closest friend and wondered if Baiona knew. One half-turn of her body in the bed, and she had become a woman. One who wanted a man.

But it wasn't so easy by the light of day. Jeanne compared her own stocky body to Baiona's lovely rounded one. Baiona could no more keep boys from her than the apple blossoms can repel the bees. She admitted their attentions—mildly. Nonetheless, she seemed indifferent, preferring to paint or sew.

Jeanne pined. She snapped at the others. She started looking at her image every chance she got in the one precious glass in the women's rooms. She dropped hints about a new dress. She asked Giulietta to help refashion an old cloak and show her how to fix her hair. She didn't say what any of these things were for, but Giulietta knew. She would have known even if Jeanne hadn't shared her secret some weeks earlier. In fact, the entire palace knew, so fast does gossip spread—and perhaps even Rogert himself had been apprised of it. Giulietta teased her, but she also gave advice, and Jeanne listened, thinking that when she had a daughter of her own she would pass such precious information on to her: the wisdom of women.

"Before you enter a room, pause, lift your chin, and say to yourself, 'I am the most beautiful woman here.' And only then go in."

"Yes."

"When you see Rogert, lift up your heart and send him a wave of light, a wave of love."

"How?"

"You'll know how. He'll feel it. He won't know what he feels, but he'll respond."

"What else?" Jeanne prompted.

"Sometimes—but not too often—look right into his eyes."

"Is that all?"

"That's a lot!" said Giulietta, laughing. "And smile. Keep a happy expression on your face. No one wants to be with someone glum."

She wanted to tell Baiona about her love, but whenever she tried, Baiona bent her head over her embroidery and did not respond. Once, with a tense, impatient laugh, she gathered up her sewing: "Jeanne, I don't want to hear about it." She left the room.

Jeanne looked after her, astonished and angry. She decided Baiona was jealous. Baiona preferred no suitor, and no one was planning a marriage for her. Jeanne's love cut a path between the girls.

"This crush," Baiona called it, with a disdainful toss of her head. "It's not real love."

"How do you know?"

"He's not worthy of you, Jeanne. Stay away."

"Why? What's wrong? Why do you hate to talk about him?"

But Baiona would only shrug.

One night at dinner as he poured the wine, Rogert's shoulder pressed Jeanne's arm, leaning in on her. She looked up. His head was so close that his lips almost touched hers. Instantly he pulled away, leaving her with a heart beating so fast that she thought everyone nearby must hear it. She sipped her wine, hands trembling.

That evening, when the singing was over and the storytelling about to begin, Rogert worked himself to her side.

"Anybody want a walk?" he said idly, to no one in particular, and then as if only just noticing her: "Come walk outside?" He didn't use her name.

They slipped away, as happy, she thought, as two puppies, bounding under the starry sky. The bushes in the garden loomed black. The air felt sweet. Rogert put one arm around her and drew her toward the maze. She hesitated, pulled back, not quite a woman yet.

"Come here," he whispered. "I want to show you something."

"What?"

"Curiosity killed the cat."

"Satisfaction brought it back," she said, laughing silently, keeping her voice low lest others hear. "Tell me."

"Do you want to be satisfied, Jeanne?" he asked. "Little Jeanne of Béziers."

"I'm not so little."

Step by cautious step, he led her into the fragrant boxwood maze, secret and dark. The brush stood higher than their heads. Jeanne felt uneasy, but also excited. The sour scent of the boxbushes mingled with the rich scent of Rogert. He kissed her on the lips. She could feel his body swelling against hers, and she leaned in to meet him. He pulled her deeper into the shadows. In the faint starlight she could not make out his expression.

"We shouldn't be here," she murmured.

"Shh. Shh. I want to show you something. Something you will like." With one hand he fumbled with his clothing. With the other he took her hand.

"Here." He slid her hand downward between his legs. She gasped at the touch of his skin. She had not touched a man there before. The skin was smooth and soft. So delicate. Rogert groaned under her fingers, guiding her hand. She held her breath. She didn't know whether she wanted this or not. Fear already sent her running home—to safety indoors—while excitement held her here. And Rogert. He gripped her hand in his, stroking himself up and down as he grew larger under her fingers. Jeanne knew about sex. They were not fools, the children, but she could hardly breathe. The frantic thought came, wondering how *that* could fit inside a girl, inside of her. Now he was nuzzling her neck, and he released her hand, which knew its task now, in order to free his own two hands to roam her flanks, her breasts. She was frightened. He pressed his pelvis against hers. She liked it and at the same time wanted no part of this. Surely it was wrong. What if someone saw? She froze.

"Don't stop," he said. To reinforce the words, his hand returned to guide her own. And now he groaned again, butting her with his head and pulling up her long skirts roughly, his hands sliding along the bare skin of her thigh. She wanted to push him away. She wanted to press up close. Also she wished that he would speak sweet words, to say that he loved her. She wanted him to talk to her, but then she thought how ungrateful she was, when his actions spoke clearly of his love.

"Don't." She pulled away, holding his wrist.

"Don't what?" he whispered, both hands exploring still. He was too strong for her. "Don't leave me like this," he said, and pulled her hand back down to the manliness between his legs.

"Rogert, I—"

"Jeanne, Jeanne," he whispered. "Yes, like that. Like that. Don't you like it?"

But she couldn't answer, for his mouth was on hers, his body lurching against hers. His breath was hot in her mouth, and she felt frightened by the quickening movements, the strangled, gasping sounds. He clutched at her once, twice—and suddenly her hand was wet and something was spurting all over her hand, her dress, the grass.

He held her a moment longer, quivering and almost unsteady on his feet, then pulled away. He wiped himself off with his handkerchief and then looked at her appraisingly, his lazy dark eyes gleaming in the starlight. Then he offered her the handkerchief to clean her hands, but she passed up its dampness and wiped her hands on her dress and on the grass.

Suddenly everything was different, her earlier elation gone. She wanted to burst into tears. She realized that in all that time, they had never sat or lain upon the grass, but only stood on their square four feet. Rogert was adjusting his clothes with the little jerks men make as they tuck themselves in, and she was left there standing in the dark. Abandoned. She felt dirty.

"Rogert?" she whispered, her voice weak.

He laughed quickly, a dark, earthy sound, hugged her in a comradely way, and kissed her. But it was a quick, cool kiss, when what she wanted was simply to be held until her trembling stopped. She felt that something terrible had happened, though she didn't know what, nor how to ask about it. She had seen into the Devil's creation, perhaps, for surely she never felt lonelier in her life—and yet she ought to feel proud. For had he not chosen her, the orphan Jeanne Béziers, for this secret love?— and that made her, she supposed, his lady, though she had never imagined it would be like this.

"Good girl," he said, brushing her breasts with the fingertips of both hands. Numbly, she nodded.

"Go inside," he whispered, "before you're missed." His white teeth flashed in the dim light as he nodded a dismissal.

So she went, obediently, but more confused than ever—for why, if she were his lady, had he sent her away? She felt bereft. She hurried to her room and undressed quickly. The dress was stained with his spill, and she could smell his maleness on her skin.

She washed and crept into bed quickly, and when Baiona came up and slid beneath the covers, she pretended to be asleep.

After that night she didn't mention Rogert to Baiona again. Was it a sin she had committed? She didn't want to ask, didn't want to know. Did God see them in the Garden of Eden? Did the God of Love approve?

▨ SEVEN ▨

his morning I awaken to the bells all ringing gaily from the church. I lie on the straw in my cozy nook, happy and content, and bless the rough wood roof above me with its sweet-smelling thatch—a sturdy roof that keeps out most of the rain. I am lucky. On the other side of the wall I hear the donkey in his stall sound off with his braying like a bellows, enough to wake the Devil (if he should ever sleep), while the little flock of black-faced, narrow-nosed sheep bleat and run into one another in the silly way of sheep.

So I begin my prayers, content.

Yesterday I found half a loaf of bread. Sometimes someone gives me an onion or a handful of olives or some greens. I've gotten thin.

Sometimes I eat only part of the food. *Wait,* says the inner voice. I listen, waiting. Last Sunday the mistress sent me a wooden bowl of porridge and some wool to spin, for to my surprise the stableboy delivered my message. I took the food to an old woman in the upper story of a house.

Here's how it happened: I had eaten half the porridge when the Knowing came. It always comes suddenly, of its own accord, and when and where I never can predict. Sometimes it appears as a light behind my eyes and a swift lift of the heart—because that's how God speaks to me, with joy. My heart leaps up and shouts out, *Yes!* Other times it comes only as a subtle understanding of what I ought to do; and I have learned to obey.

Last Sunday, when the Knowing came, I dug up my treasure, protected in its green oilskin, and hid it in my underskirts, together with the skein of wool, then pushed up to my feet and got my stick—my feet going where they were led, and I on top of them, just tagging along, the bowl of porridge in one hand and my cane in the other, and the Good Book knocking on my knees. Me hobbling as fast as two old legs can go.

I walked down the Street of Tinsmiths. The houses there rise two and three stories high, with their upper stories hanging out over the narrow, dirt street so close that they almost blot out the sky. The ground-floor shops are open to the busy traffic of passing feet, as well as to donkeys and goats and pigs. Inside the open doors the smiths and their boys sit cross-legged, as they have for centuries, beating on big tin sheets with their hammers as they shape kettles, pots, and pans by turning the tin round and round between their bare feet. My ears hurt from the ringing hammers. Banging, trinning, a trillion hammers, pinging to no set time. And above that noise, the tinsmiths were shouting to one another or laughing at some ribald raillery over the din of hawkers selling "Milk! Good milk!" and "Apples! Fruit! Nuts!" From the second floor came the cries of women who leaned out their windows, screaming to their friends in the street below. One woman shook her carpet out the window, creating clouds of dust, and another gave a warning shout before she tipped out her chamber pot. I dodged. Swift, cunning me.

I stepped along as quickly as I could over the rough cobbles, glad to leave the noise behind. Then into the Street of Blacksmiths, with their iron forges bellowing. The men there are huge, strong, hairy creatures, black with cinders and smoke. They grinned at me too, with gaping, red, gap-toothed mouths, and two of them, pausing for a dipperful of water as I passed (the glistening sweat streaming off their bare backs), were making lewd remarks to each other about the fire in their loins and how they could enflame a *femme*. One howled at me to be off and made a gesture. But most of them concentrated on their iron hinges and door locks and armor plates, for I am too old and dirty and poor for men to look at anymore.

I dodged around a horse that blocked my way, his hind hoof resting in a blacksmith's leather lap. The acrid, smoky smell of his cut hooves, together with that sweet, horsey smell of hair and manure, filled my nostrils, pleasing me. I've always liked that odor of hot horse hoof, of sweat and fires.

And so I proceeded through the twisting streets, past chandlers and ink-grinders and various other tradespeople, and out through the city gate to the mud-and-wattle huts that cling to the protective walls. Then I passed those too and moved on into the lower town, where the tanners have their foul-smelling cauldrons bubbling with hides.

I held my rag to my nose, gasping against the stench. The steam rose high into the brown air as the apprentice boys threw their weight against the bellows, building up the fires. Hell itself could not smell so vile or feel so hot as this hellhole of the Street of Tanners.

The muddy road was slippery with the tanners' waste. I stumbled, almost falling in the mess.

A pack of boys came out of the alleys there, throwing stones and dancing round me, trying to knock the wooden bowl out of my hand. Like cockroaches, how do they sense I'm coming?

The boys could not hit the bowl, but I was afraid anyway, as I always am, and held it high above my head or else I cradled it under my arm, and I shouted at them to go away; didn't they see I was only an old crazy woman, curse them all to hell?

I came to the house and stopped. It was just another wooden struc-ture leaning up against its neighbors, with nothing to mark it as the one for me. Except that my feet and eyes stopped there. I paced back and forth, trying to move on—or better, to go back to the stable where I belonged—but my feet would not let me free. I sat down on the wooden steps in front to rest and reason with my feet.

They wouldn't move forward, and they wouldn't go back, so I knew that my heart was beckoning me in, but I was nervous anyway, anxious about what I'd find inside.

Then suddenly the thought—it might be Amiel Aicart inside, or Poitevin, or Hugon—and my stomach lurched.

I limped up the steps to the door, a wooden door rocking on a broken hinge. *Open it,* whispered my heart, and I pushed it gingerly, frightened by the awful creaking of the rusty hinge. I think I could not have entered except for the thought of the Good Men I might find inside, but that thought gave me courage, and I stepped into the dark hall with its smell of dusty abandonment. I sniffed the air. I asked if I was supposed to stay here, make a new home; the answer came back, *No*. That made me glad. It didn't smell good to me, and I listened furtively to the dry sound of empty rooms.

Then I crept slowly up the steps to the second floor, managing the cane and bowl in one hand and holding the railing with the other. It was so dark I could hardly see, and the stairs so steep, almost a ladder indeed, that I had to stop, gasping, my goodness, short of breath. I remembered my Lady Esclarmonde shooing me up the stairway at Montségur that day—and I, a maid, flying up the steps by threes.

I was always running back then; they couldn't stop me. Diana, goddess of the moon. Even later, when I was married and riding on the stag or boar hunts, I rode astride, like a man. I could shoot a bow, train a hawk. Now I can barely pull the stairs.

At the top I heard a whimper. I stopped, frightened, and then I stood trembling, listening, hoping (oh, praise God!) it would be them! So I pushed forward, feeling with one hand along the rotting wooden wall and wishing for a window in this narrow corridor.

I came to another door, sagging like the front door on its hinge. I pushed it open.

"Who's there?" I called.

The stench hit me first. It took all my courage to move into the bedroom against the smell of urine and feces and death. From the light of the narrow window I could make out a tousled form on the filthy bed. Gingerly I approached. No *perfecti* here. Only an old woman, at the point of death.

Involuntarily, I stepped back. I didn't know what to do. Even in the dim light I could see her face was covered with boils and the scabs of half-healed pustules—signs I'd seen before. I knew that pus filled her groin and the nodes under her armpits. She tugged pathetically at the air with little birdlike gestures. Clawing for my hand, writhing on the straw mattress, which was vile with her urine and the release of her bowels. She smelled.

"*Con*—" she croaked. She could hardly speak. "*Conso*—"

Ah, I knew what she wanted to say, and pulled my hand from hers.

"*Consola—*"

-mentum. I knew that word.

I crept back from the pallet and sat on the floor, resting my shoulders against the bare wood of the hut. A cold wind blew through the cracks, chilling my neck and shoulders, and I drew my cloak tighter, praying for guidance, because I am not a *perfecta*. I needed one myself. Hadn't I been looking for Amiel and the others all these months? And what if I caught this woman's plague?

"Oh, Lord, dear beloved Christ—" I prayed.

And then I felt the Presence there. My heart leapt up with joy. My Beloved was back, and you can say it's my imagination, but I know when it comes and when it leaves, and my Friend had just returned. Now I'd know what to do.

But I sat with my back to the wall and rested my head on my knees, praying helplessly not to do what I was being told. One more sin on my soul. Because I don't like that cup; let it pass from my lips. I refuse. But you can't refuse, it seems.

After a time, I pulled heavily to my feet. I cradled the head and shoulders of the poor woman on the bed and wiped her face and hands with my dirty rag, which was all I had, and then I fed her slowly from my cold porridge, which the good mistress had provided for me to give to her. She took a few mouthfuls and seemed to rest easier.

I carried the bowl downstairs and out to the fountain. That's a long way. It took a while to make my way back with the bowl washed out and clean water in it, but I climbed the steps again and even found a scrap of not-too-dirty linen in one of the rooms, which I used to wash her hands and face.

I tried to talk to her.

But mostly what I did was sit with my back to the wall, just waiting. When it grew dark, I fell asleep.

I woke up with a jerk. The room was filled with light, and before me stood a form all made of light, an angel, probably, beckoning with her luminous hand. She smiled at me so lovingly that I felt the warmth go through to every part, and all I could do was to look back, loving her. The white light was so intense, the bliss so ravishing, that I had no power or even need to form my questions into words.

Neither did she answer me in words, but filled my mind with knowledge so that without a care I approached the bed. The beautiful being came too, surrounding us in light. The dying woman was awake, eyes glittering feverishly, though I don't know if she could see the luminous beautiful form that directed me to place my hands upon her head. I could feel the heat pouring off my hands. Not for a moment did I think about the plague, for the bed was no longer a pallet of dirty straw but was shining with its own cool, glowing light. My hands rested on the woman's head, and I could see how the life-force that surrounds the physical body was irregular and shattered, and how dark spots had formed where the disease was worst. Slowly the woman relaxed under my tingling hands. Her eyes closed.

I didn't give the *consolamentum* properly. I've been present at this ceremony and know how it should be done. First the *perfectus* asks if the believer comes willingly and by her own volition to accept this spiritual gift. This is important, for the person asking to take the *consolamentum* must be willing thereafter to observe the customs of *abstinentia,* and from that time forth she may eat no meat or eggs or cheese or any other food derived from the copulation of animals, and she (or he, or course) must promise to live thereafter in chastity and celibacy and to follow all our Cathar rules and to pray the Lord's Prayer at all times ceaselessly. The proper *consolamentum* is performed with the Good Book and legitimate rituals and prayers.

But this woman on the bed was dying, and I felt disoriented by—no, absorbed in—the juice that poured out into her from my shining hands. The intention was pure. But I could not remember the exact order of the ritual. In my garbled state I even forgot about my treasure wrapped in its oilskin at my knee. Instead I made up rites.

I found a little block of wood in the corner, and I blessed that wood, as being a piece of living wood, the same substance on which our Lord had died. Assisted by the light, I said the whole Lord's Prayer over it and sprinkled it with the light of my hands and the stardust of my heart, until it became the Holy Book. Inside that wood was writ all the history of our world and our creation, impregnated in its blocken memory.

"Good Christian," I said, placing the good wood against the Eye of

Wisdom at her brow. "May God and all those present and far away forgive you all offenses you have committed knowingly and unknowingly, and may you be cleansed, absolved, and pure."

Oops. I'd forgotten she was supposed to ask for the forgiveness first, and only then could the absolution be given; and I should have asked her to name the mistakes for which she prayed forgiveness. She is supposed to be conscious and aware, rich in her intent. And the intent is this: to cleanse the thoughts of her heart by the inspiration of Christ's Holy Spirit, that she may fully love and magnify the name of God. But now she was clawing at my hand, and her thick tongue continued to mumble her desire for the *consolamentum*. I got even more flustered then. So I said the Lord's Prayer to her, giving her the prayer that I myself was allowed to take and that I knew, God knows, after all these years, and thought our Lord would not mind a layman giving comfort to a dying woman, with a block of wood in place of Scripture on her brow.

"This is the prayer that Christ Jesus brought into the world," I said, "and taught to the Friends of God. You are never to take a bite of food without first repeating this prayer." And then I repeated the rest of the Cathar directions—about celibacy and purity of soul, about having a *socia*, or fellow-believer, for her lifelong companion and never going anywhere except in pairs, about the vows of poverty and owning no possessions that might interrupt her concentration on the presence of God, for where our thoughts are, there will be our heart. Then I gave her the four directions of the Way. From henceforth, with this ceremony, she would vow

Never to tell a lie.

Never to take the life of any living being—not even a fly or a mosquito, which might have been our mother in another life.

Never to take what isn't freely given—which is to say, never to steal, not so much as an idea or another person's dream.

Never to indulge in wrong sexual practices (as I have done so often, God forgive me, please).

Never to swear an oath or take the name of our Lord God in vain, for is it not said in Saint Matthew, *Swear not at all; neither by heaven, for it is God's throne; nor by the earth, for it is His*

footstool. . . . But let your words only be Yes, yes, and No, no; for any-
thing further comes of evil?

And then I ended the ritual with the pardon: "And we pray God grant
you His forgiveness." After that I stayed with her for some time, my hands
on her head, praying with all the love in my heart for the joy of this
woman and the journey she was about to take beyond the stars. I prayed
that she be liberated from the pain of her body and never need to return
to the suffering of this life, but go into the Light.

Indeed, I could not remove my hands. I loved her beyond comprehension. In that moment I was composed of love. I had no physical body, but
only the sense of being in the Light, and of the Way; and for the first time I
knew what the Lady Esclarmonde had been telling me all those years ago:
how we are formed of spirit, our bodies are filled with the Christhood
Light, the dove. When I opened my eyes, I could see light streaming from
my hands and radiating off my skin, the shining beams of love, and light was
filling the beautiful old dying woman before me on the bed.

She was no longer sick and hideous. I closed my eyes, the better to see
her there.

"Thank you," she whispered. She reached up to touch my hand.

"You are forgiven," I whispered. "Now may you forgive all those who
have offended you knowingly or unknowingly by thought, word, and
deed."

I cannot say how long it lasted—a minute, an hour, a movement of the
sun across a hayfield—but gradually the interior singing stopped, and
slowly my spirit sank back into my body, and the Light withdrew some of
its great power from me, leaving me still flaring with fire but back in my
own trembling body once again. After a time I took my hands from the
woman's head. The room was so dark that I could hardly see.

That's how I gave the *consolamentum*.

At first pearl light, when the shapes in the room emerged gray against the
darkness, I saw that the old woman had died. I was glad for her. Her
mouth had fallen open. Maybe it was a scream or maybe the leftover
shout of joy that flickered at her mouth.

I laid her hands in prayer across her chest. She was significantly smaller without her spirit in her body, but I was still filled with the Light of the Holy Spirit and with joy.

When I stepped from the bed, I found in the pocket at my knee the forbidden Book that I should have used. By then it was too late. I was annoyed with myself—and with that annoyance, I felt the first fading of my inner Light. I wondered if the *consolamentum* had been pure. If intention alone was enough.

I crept from the room before anyone could find me. The early sunlight sparkled on the rain-washed streets, making the stones glitter and flash like jewels. I wanted to laugh. Rain! I'd never heard it, that's how absorbed I'd been in the Light. I hurried along the rough wet cobblestones to the village square, to the fountain. I felt weak. My knees kept giving way. All the way home my Inner Judge, the prosecutor, alternated with my joy, though for a long time I paid him no attention, being still absorbed in Light. Gradually, though, his words began to sink in. Who did I think I was (he scolded) to give that holy rite? To absolve the woman's sins? I was hardly even a Christian, much less a *Good* Christian. Like Esclarmonde. Like Bertrand Marty. Like Guilhabert de Castres. What would *they* have said? Yet here I was, still burning with the Holy Spirit, shining with the Light.

I smiled, remembering my instructions to the dying woman about the abstinences—no greedy eating of meat or eggs—when, after all, she'd never eat again. No lies or false reports. No acts of sexual perversion, passion, and lust that might harm another person. Then I started to laugh aloud into the clear blue air, and the pigeons all rose up in a flurry of white wings, like angels. I turned round and round with them, arms lifted to fly into the sky. I stood on tiptoes twisting with their flight. Then I fell flat in the mud and picked myself up quickly, embarrassed lest anyone had seen me, arms flapping and sleeves waving, crazy Jeanne.

To make up for my exhibition, I sat demurely at the edge of the fountain under a plane tree, its bark as etiolated as a leper's shedding skin, and I pulled out the mistress's wool and started my spinning, singing under my breath and laughing aloud every now and again at the pleasure I'd just had. No one had ever told me how much fun it was to be perfected. My knee didn't ache, and indeed I'd forgotten all my woes. The best-kept secret: getting old. Don't tell the foolish girls.

The sun moved higher overhead, and my Inner Judge began to rail at me again about the sins on my black soul, and soon I wasn't laughing anymore: there were so many sins. I had little enough food, it's true, but whenever I got a piece of meat I ate it greedily. "I'm not perfected," I defended myself, and anyway, Bishop Guilhabert himself relieved the *perfecti* of all dietary principles. He ordered them to stop fasting and to eat meat; they would need their strength, he said, to survive. Moreover, their extended fasts and adherence to a holy diet gave the enemy the noose to hang them with—like the believer who was burnt at the stake because he wouldn't kill a hen.

"Kill that chicken," commanded the Inquisitors, knowing full well that killing is against the Cathar principles. They could as easily have simply asked, "Are you perfected, heretic?" and the Good Christian wouldn't have been able to lie.

But my Inner Judge was adamant and condemned me in louder tones and howls of rage, passing on to other sins. Often I forgot my prayers (which I could have been doing right then, after all, while spinning, instead of cowering with shame). I had sins enough on my soul that I wept when I remembered, for hadn't I lost the treasure of Montségur— who knows where?—and no one around to give me the *consolamentum* now, and what would happen at my death? I could wander endlessly the great black space, looking for my friends, who would by then be gone, absorbed into the Light. And if these weren't sins enough, what about the lechery that took me first to Rogert, then to William (not counting others on the way), or my wicked betrayal of Baiona, my closest friend? Was all that God's doing? No, only mine—only that of sinful, prideful, unperfected me.

I spent the whole day at the fountain, spinning and thinking. As a chill settled on me, I realized it was getting late and that I could feel hunger like a live animal gnawing and chewing inside my belly. It hurt. I crept to my hole beside the stable, lay down, and drew my cloak over me, grateful to have my torn, worn wrap and the warm animal snufflings nearby. I shivered watching the sun go down and the darkness come. For I was afraid again.

The next day my Knowing told me to stay away from the lower town where the old woman had died. It sent my feet far off into another part of town and placed me at a foreign square, telling me to wait. All morning I waited, spinning wool. The women came to the fountain with their earthen jugs on their heads, usually in companionable twos and threes, chatting amiably, but occasionally singly. Casting suspicious glances at the stranger-woman spinning there, and hurriedly drew their water and departed, for a woman without a history is not to be trusted. The littler boys floated leaves on the water, staging boat races in the horse trough, and bigger boys, roughhousing, tried to dunk each other. Every now and again a teamster came by with his horses to drink, man and animals alike. Once it was a man coming from the fields with one strong, white ox. (The beasts drink from the lower pool, not from the basin we humans use.)

In the afternoon a funeral procession passed, led by a devout Dominican, and sure enough the body the men carried on an open litter was the old woman's.

I followed the procession for a spell. Raggedy it was—two brutes carrying the litter, and the girlfriend of one of them, with her hair wild and loose as a prostitute's, chatting him up and jiggling his arm, while the friar walked disdainfully ahead, with his mouth turned down in the grimace of a grouper, obviously not liking his spiritual duties one whit. The Dominicans are proud to preach and convert, not take bodies to the paupers' field. I followed all the way to the *camposanto,* and sure enough the friar buried her with full Catholic rites, though where he was when she was alive I don't know.

I went home to my lean-to by the stable feeling tired and fragile and weeping a little. I was full of memories, for that old woman makes the first time I've given the *consolamentum.*

And I'm not pure.

◈ EIGHT ◈

During Ascension Week she heard about the joust. It was scheduled for a Saturday, and though it was only a mock event, to teach the squires, it would be conducted with full pageantry, with the flags flying and a ceremonial entry parade, because the war was over now. With the French in retreat, it was a time of rejoicing. The women and important visitors would watch from raised stands, and the jousters might have a token from their ladies if they wished. Some were so young, at fourteen or fifteen, that their token might come from an auntie or their mother even, but the older ones took pleasure in proclaiming their loves openly, as did the experienced knights.

Jeanne wanted Rogert to wear her scarf. It was a soft blue, and gossamer-thin—a whisper of silk so sheer that you could see through it. She was proud of Rogert. She thought he'd unseat every opponent easily. With romance burning in her heart, she planned how she would bring him her token on the night before the joust. "If you wish, sir knight," she would say, or something equally fine, and he would drop to one knee and accept it with the courteous, sweet words expected of a lady's swain.

Man proposes, God disposes. And what a maid wants, a man may never give.

At dinner that night Rogert served a different table. Jeanne heard his laughter in another room, and once she saw him dancing with Baiona. Her heart went hot with jealousy. But when the dance ended, he looked her way and gave a secret, quick wave and smile. It was then that she hurried into the garden to wait for him, certain of their tryst, and she walked in the quivering shadows of the starlit boxwood maze until the stars tilted and her tears told her that he wouldn't come.

She made excuses for him. She told herself that the young men, like true knights, had prayers and ablutions to make before the joust, preparations that women could not take part in. But she felt hurt nonetheless, and angry too. And jealous. Thinking of Baiona, she wound the scarf around her fist until the fragile fabric tore, and then she was angry at herself. She pinched the tiny tear between her fingers, trying to heal it. She would sew it up later, or ask Baiona with her fine hand to help, and then remembering her friend, and the teachings of a tender and forgiving soul, she forced herself to go inside and smile at Baiona, her other heart, who had done nothing wrong, but only danced one set with him. She told herself that. Indeed, Baiona may have danced a set with Rogert only to ask about his feelings for Jeanne.

Nonetheless, that night she felt confused as she climbed up into the curtained four-poster bed they shared.

"What a sigh," said Baiona. "What's wrong?"

"Nothing." She wished she knew what to say. She wished she were a man, allowed to ride in combat and joust against the other knights. She wished she were the woman for whom Rogert would perform a thousand deeds. She felt jealous of her best friend, and yet she wanted Baiona's arms around her, the way they used to sleep. She didn't know what she wanted; she wanted reassurance from Rogert.

That night she prayed with all her heart that he be safe, that their relationship be blessed by God.

The next morning she shot out of bed, hopeful once again, as happens when morning dawns, and excited at the festival day. Today she would wear her new embroidered silver dress.

"Come on, Baiona! Up!"

By the time the two girls were clattering downstairs (Jeanne hopping as she pulled on one shoe), the palace was abuzz. Already the experienced, older men were stomping with much shouting through the castle, helping the lads and cursing broken armor; and the grooms were readying the horses and the grounds. Already, this early in the morning, the peasants had come in from the fields and the tradespeople were set-ting up stalls to sell ribbons and sweet tarts, braces of rabbits and meat pies, and all the foods and toys a festival-goer likes to see. A puppet show in one corner, games of bowling and clowns in another. Bright colors and tempting smells. Beggars everywhere. Shouts from the spectators as the early foot and horse races got underway.

Several young men hunkered down on their heels on the grass, listen-ing to last-minute counsel from the knights, or they stood together in small clumps, swinging their swords or else adjusting a buckle or leather strap or weighing various lances in their hands. Jeanne caught sight of Rogert over near the stables, leading out a horse. His back was to her, and she stood a moment willing him to turn around and send her a com-plicitous look. But his entire attention was on his horse and the coming fight.

"Come on," whispered Baiona, pulling Jeanne away. She slipped her arm through Jeanne's as they climbed into the crowded stands. "You look so beautiful," she said softly, and Jeanne felt her heart soaring, a dove wheeling in the empty air. Jeanne wore a silver dress with a bodice embroidered in red and gold. Her wild black hair was held in a silver net. Her eyes sparkled with excitement as she took her seat. She *knew* that she was beautiful today; she felt it.

"You too," she answered generously, squeezing her best friend's hand. She could not imagine why she had been angry with Baiona the night before. "You look good in blue," she whispered. Baiona's dress was a quiet blue, the sleeves slashed with gussets of a deeper tone. She looked more demure than Jeanne—as always, quieter and more reflective. But she too craned her neck to see the action below, smiling and waving to friends.

For Jeanne the scene was insupportably magnificent: the noise of voices raised in exhilaration, the wind-whipped flags, the clatter of armor, and the stamping of the horses' hooves.

Then a trumpet sounded.

"Oh, look!" she cried, as the forerunners of the parade took the field. Soon all the participants would ride out and tip their lances to the duke and duchess. Some would also acknowledge their mentors or their ladies in the stands. Jeanne hoped that Rogert might dip his lance to her and bow, and then she'd have the chance publicly to offer him the scarf that she wore loosely round her neck.

As if reading her mind, Baiona turned to her. "I wonder if anyone will choose *you* as his lady," she said, smiling.

"Oh, I hope so," Jeanne answered fervently. She hid her face in gratitude on her friend's shoulder. "I'm so scared."

Baiona hugged Jeanne to her fiercely. "I love you, Jeanne. Don't you ever forget it."

But Jeanne did not respond. She sat up straight, for now the young warriors were lining up for last instructions, and onto the field rode first the battle-scarred and experienced, older war-knights, who would not fight this afternoon but would watch and criticize their squires and the young men under their tutelage. They were splendid in their gleaming armor on their huge, caparisoned warhorses. The following week a *real* joust would take place, offering both single combat between different pairs of knights and a mêlée in which a hundred knights and horses might fight on the field at once. At that time they would ride for rich prizes of armor and horses and money from the men defeated and ransomed on the field. That joust would outdo this minor one a thousand times in color and gambling and the peril of real hurt: fifty, sixty knights could be wounded, even killed, in the mêlée, and scores of lances would be shattered and horses hurt.

Neither the Friends of God nor the Catholic Church approved of jousts, and both had tried to ban these mock wars. In vain. Too much money lay at stake. Even the Good Christians watched. Jeanne noted two *perfecti* on the sidelines now, their modest black garb standing out among the brilliantly colored crowd. They were waiting to carry off the wounded, bind up injuries, set bones, and lay their healing hands on hurt or dying men. The Church of Love did not like any wars. Jeanne, however, loved a tournament, and for her, no greater battle the following week could equal this little practice joust.

Behind the real knights in their glistening armor, who now circled the field to loud, enthusiastic applause, rode the young men in training— those who would fight this afternoon. They wore leather and chain-mail, in most cases handed down from an older brother or father or borrowed from their sponsoring knight. They carried wooden shields carved from a single block and covered with several layers of hard black leather. Some shields were decorated too: there came one handpainted with the figure of a dragon, and behind him a shield with two lions, and there to the side was a rearing stallion—all insignias of power, courage, speed. But some shields were empty of design, and these looked the more menacing in their black leather starkness. The competitors also carried true wood lances and sharp swords.

These weapons were heavy; it took strength to handle lance and shield and sword. Slowly the aspiring knights circled the field. Each stopped at the dais and bowed to the duke and to his wife, their lady. Three of the youths wore scarves on their arms or wrapped around their necks. Rogert wore none. He rode on the inside pair of two, and as he passed Baiona and Jeanne sitting side by side, he dipped his lance. Jeanne clapped her hands in open delight.

"I wish I'd had a chance to give him my scarf," she exclaimed.

But Baiona looked away.

"Whom do *you* like?" Jeanne asked. Her friend's lack of interest in Rogert did not displease her—Baiona, who could have any man she liked.

"I'll bet on . . . Gilbert de Mirepoix," Baiona answered with a wicked laugh. "He'll fight your Rogert, most likely. We'll see who wins." The two girls made a little bet on the side with their pin-money, while the workmen adjusted the wooden barrier that ran down the center of the field, marking the runway for the horses.

Then, with another trumpet flourish, the joust began. The young men took their numbers, and two by two they thundered down the field toward one another on their armored chargers, their long lances extended. It was magnificent to see: the horsemanship alone brought the crowd to its feet in a roar, for each lance-point bobbed and wavered with the horse's gallop, and yet the men aimed so flawlessly that they could catch their opponent's breastplate, or hit him square on the shield, and with a single twist of the lance unhorse him. If the point of the lance were to find the place at the throat where the helmet joins and overlaps the breastplate, it could kill the jouster right there. Once one combatant was unhorsed, there might also be hand-to-hand sword combat, depending on the joust. However, in this practice meet, with knight-aspirants only, there would be little hand-to-hand work with swords.

One pair after another met on the field, clashed, and ended up with someone unseated; and each winner took on another combatant later in the day, until finally only two men were left—the best of that day's meet. One was Rogert, and the other was Baiona's Gilbert de Mirepoix.

It was late afternoon by now, and the sun lay low, tangling in the branches of the leafy trees and casting a golden glow over everything. Rogert changed horses for the final combat. He chose a large bay with one white stocking. The horse's huge breast and head were covered with armor. Jeanne bounced in her seat, no longer a woman but only a girl, until Giulietta, two seats away in the row of women, teased her openly. But Baiona sat still and proud, lovely in her blue dress, her honey-colored hair gleaming.

"I can't believe your calm," said Jeanne.

"Yes, but I don't care who wins," she pointed out.

The horses paced to the opposite ends of the field, standing sideways to each other across the distance. The two combatants held their lances upright, the stubs resting on their right stirrups. The herald blew his trumpet once, and the horses were nudged into position, facing each other down the field. Both mounts were experienced chargers; they knew what they should do. The herald blew a second time, the signal for readiness, and Rogert and Gilbert lowered their lances, bracing the hilt in the armor-notch. The horses arched their necks and pawed the earth, eager for action. Then came the third blast of the horn, and the two chargers bolted from their positions with a thunder of hooves and a creaking of leather, running toward each other so fast that Jeanne came to her feet, hands covering her mouth. There was a crash of splintering wood on shields, and then the horses had passed each other—and both jousters were still on their mounts.

Again they ranged themselves in place, taking new lances, while the grooms checked the horses' chests and legs for wounds and patted their necks. Again the crowd heard the three blasts of the horn. Again the horses pounded toward each other. This time Rogert unseated Gilbert smoothly, though he lost a stirrup and pitched forward. He caught the pommel of the saddle with one hand, lost his rein, and only barely managed to stay on the giant warhorse. One of the grooms at the far end of the field quickly caught the bridle, and Rogert righted himself, pulled off his helmet, and lifted his lance in victory. Gilbert limped off the field on his own feet—not badly hurt.

Jeanne was squirming in her seat. She could hardly contain herself. "He is so splendid," she said. "He's magnificent!"

Baiona shrugged.

"What's the matter with you?" Jeanne demanded, turning on her angrily. "Why are you so ungenerous? It was perfect."

"He did very well," she answered. "If you like."

"If I like!"

But there was no time to argue. Rogert kicked his horse over to the duke's stand, where his lady placed the wreath gracefully upon the tip of his lance. He had won a purse as well, but that would come later.

Then, for the second time that day—this time to wild applause—Rogert walked his horse around the perimeter of the field. He was alone this time before all eyes, and on the tip of his lance he carried the wreath he had won. His horse jiggled and nervously switched his black tail up and down against his burnished bronze rump.

Jeanne ducked her head and blushed, for offering the wreath to one's sweetheart was the custom. She waited, sitting on her hands.

Rogert nudged his horse to the center, then held him in place. The big bay pawed the earth and tossed his head, tail switching, nervous in the applause. Then Rogert reined the large animal over to the general stands, toward Jeanne.

Giulietta leaned forward to smile at her. "Give him your scarf," she whispered—and suddenly Jeanne realized that, yes, if she hurried she could still remove her scarf and place it on his lance, a fair exchange for the wreath. She hastily unwound it from her neck as she rose.

Except—how could this be?—he tilted the lance before *Baiona,* and so deftly that no one could mistake his intention. Jeanne was stunned.

She fell back on the bench, the blood rising in her face. Baiona, sitting right beside her, froze. She too went red, and she refused to hold out her hand. Still he stood before her, skillfully controlling his fretting horse, the wreath extended on the tip of his lance.

"Take it," called out a chorus of girls. "Take it, Baiona."

Baiona glanced at Jeanne, her face wretched. Then she reached out and lifted off the wreath, while all the ladies applauded the sweet act. She held it limply in one hand. Rogert gave her a dashing smile and backed his horse away.

"Put it on," cried the girls in exasperation, and someone reached over, laughing, and crowned her with the twining green leaves.

Jeanne felt numb. Her mind was still grappling with the scene. Because Rogert, who only two nights earlier had taken her into the bushes to touch his most private, rearing parts, had never—not for a moment—so much as glanced her way, but had gazed with his black-lashed, indolent eyes at the girl he'd crowned. Then he'd turned his horse and galloped off the field.

Everyone thought it very pretty.

"Jeanne."

"Don't speak to me!" She backed away, her rage exploding not at Rogert but at her friend.

"Wait, Jeanne," urged Baiona, willing her to withhold condemnation.

By custom Baiona should wear the victor's wreath all evening, but as soon as she left the stands, she whipped it off and dropped it on the ground. It lay between the two girls now, a symbol of their rift. Jeanne snatched it up and thrust it in her hands.

"Your wreath!" she spat. And ran toward the castle, as far from Baiona, from her shame, as she could get. Ran across the grass. Ran through the graceful archway to turn and press her hot face against the cool gray stones of the wall, scraping her fingers on the stones, hurting her hands. Finally she wandered to the dinner hall, distracted and distraught. She spoke when spoken to, polite phrases here and there, but she would have nothing to do with Baiona.

That night, when the festivities ended, Baiona came into their bedroom. Jeanne sat perched, legs dangling, on the high bed, waiting. They stared at each other. Neither spoke. Baiona tossed the wreath on the floor with a contemptuous flick of her wrist. Jeanne leapt on her, hitting, scratching, kicking, pulling her hair. They fought silently, their blows punctuated only by muted grunts, until Jeanne bit Baiona's ear. At her scream of pain several older women ran in.

"Pull her off!"

"Separate them!"

"Stop!"

"Demon-child!"

A slap to Jeanne's face snapped her head sharply and sent her reeling backward. She looked up, dazed at the realization that it had been Giulietta's hand. This second betrayal ran so deep she hardly heard the other voices, outraged cries.

"How dare you!"

"What do you think you're doing?"

"The Devil's own brood."

Jeanne picked herself up, fighting back tears of confusion, anger, hate, and hurt.

The next day the Lady Esclarmonde came to the room where Jeanne lay on her bed. Doing nothing. Staring dry-eyed at the ceiling. Hair unbrushed. Clothing awry. Esclarmonde paused at the door. Under her arm she clutched her spindle. In her hands she held a roll of soggy blue cloth.

"Get up," she said harshly. Jeanne came slowly to her feet.

"The washerwomen were down by the river this morning and found Baiona's dress, the one she wore at the joust." Esclarmonde tossed it at Jeanne's feet. Jeanne looked away.

"The woman said that she had walked downstream to relieve herself when she saw a bit of blue fabric caught in the water. She had to wade out knee-deep, she said, to reach the garment, and when she pulled on it, it came up from under a rock. Torn. Bleached out. She brought it to me."

Still Jeanne said nothing. Her dark eyes were cold with hurt, her face pinched.

"Jeanne, what do you know of this?"

"Nothing."

"Jeanne, don't lie." Angrily, the older woman pinched her tender inner arm between her strong flat thumb and spinning fingers, bringing tears to Jeanne's eyes.

"You did this, didn't you? Baiona is in tears at what happened to her favorite dress. Jeanne, why did you steal and destroy her dress?"

"Why do you ask me?" Jeanne demanded, her voice coming out too loud. "What do I have to do with Baiona? We're not friends."

"Then you're a fool," said Esclarmonde. "Why are you so jealous? Ugly, spiteful child. No one sensible lets anger interfere with their good sense. Have I taught you nothing? Baiona is your friend. She loves you."

"She loves me," Jeanne repeated icily.

Esclarmonde searched the girl's eyes. "You know nothing about love," she said finally. "I've failed. I don't expect you to love your *enemy* yet, but not to love your *friend?*"

"My friend." The words were a mere whisper.

Esclarmonde regarded her, mouth pinched. "So what are we to do with you? Are you imp-driven, as they say? A Devil-child? Possessed?" She sat in one of the carved wooden chairs with curving arms and legs and stared impassively at Jeanne.

For several minutes she sat in silence, her lips moving in quiet prayer. Suddenly, her decision made, she rose from her seat and addressed Jeanne firmly.

"Come. You're going away."

"What do you mean?" Jeanne felt a rising panic.

"Perhaps it's true, as those who saw your rage last night say, that a demon has possessed you. If so, you'll need the care of someone better trained than I. Bishop Guilhabert de Castres will rid you of it."

Jeanne stared out the window, chin quivering. Was she really a child of the Devil? She didn't want to be. She wanted to be lovable and loved.

"He is the finest of Good Christians. He lives at Montségur. Pack your clothes straightaway. We'll depart in an hour. Before you go, you are to leave your silver dress with all its fine embroidery for Baiona. Put it on the bed, and I'll see that she gets it. You'll need no festival clothing where you're going. Now hurry. We have a long way to go."

"Just like that?" Jeanne was dumbstruck. She and Baiona had had a fight, nothing more.

"Just like that."

"How long will I be gone?"

"As long as it takes you to learn your lesson. Now pack your clothes. We leave before noon."

Jeanne turned on her, furious. "Why send *me* away? Why not Baiona? What have I done wrong?"

But Esclarmonde merely drew herself up to her full height. Her lips, tight pressed, formed disapproving tendrils along the upper lip. She stared Jeanne to silence by her look. When it was clear from Jeanne's despairing look that the outburst was over, Esclarmonde said, "From now on, your silver dress belongs to Baiona. I have nothing more to say."

In less than half an hour Jeanne had packed her belongings. She descended gloomily to the courtyard. There she saw two men gathering provisions in panniers and packing weapons for protection. Esclarmonde and her *socia,* Ealaine, were there as well, counting the supplies. Jeanne looked defiantly about.

"We're going to walk?" she exclaimed.

"Oh, Jeanne." Esclarmonde looked as if she'd been slapped. "I've taught you nothing, nothing." Tears spilled from her aged eyes. The eyes of a turtle, each in a wrinkled shell. "After all these years you'd still ask me to burden an animal with carrying me."

Jeanne felt a stab of remorse. Why did she say such things?

"You can walk like the rest of us, on the feet God gave you," said Ealaine stiffly. "You're strong enough to walk."

"I've brought my spindle." Jeanne held it up in apology, but the two women had turned back to their baskets.

"Jeanne! Wait!" It was Baiona, crossing the courtyard at a run.

"What?" she demanded, unwilling to unbend without an apology.

"Don't look at me like that, Jeanne," she pleaded. "I didn't want all this. I didn't even want the wreath. Talk to me."

"I can't. I *can't* talk to you."

"Don't leave like this." Baiona stepped forward. "I don't want your dress." She swept at the strands of fine hair that the wind whipped round her face. "Oh, Jeanne."

"Leave her be." Esclarmonde intervened, addressing Baiona. "Someday she'll understand what she's done; it has nothing to do with you. Now go back in."

She nodded to the two men. "Are we ready?" At her signal the group set off.

Esclarmonde and Ealaine may have been old, but they set a steady pace, walking side by side before the men and murmuring their prayers.

Jeanne walked behind. After an hour she pulled up beside the two women.

"Esclarmonde?"

"Be quiet," said the older woman firmly. "This is a time for you to rest in silence. And to pray." Such was her displeasure.

Jeanne tried again. "How far is it to Montségur?"

"When we reach Lavelanet, we shall talk. Until then, be still and listen to the guidance of your heart."

Jeanne dropped back a pace, irritated at how Esclarmonde loved to quote the Book of Isaiah: *Be still and know that I am God.* But Esclarmonde often changed the passage to reinforce her constant, boring asseveration that God is found in silence, stillness, and prayer. Her girls heard over and over (it made Jeanne want to shriek) that God is found inside, in their own meditations, and that whatever the true heart told them, *that* is the voice of God.

At the moment Jeanne's true heart told her she'd been betrayed. She felt sorry for herself. She wondered if anger, hurt, and vengeance also formed the speech of God.

❖ NINE ❖

This morning, as I'm gathering my things together getting ready to hobble out and collect my herbs and see where God wants to put me today, the mistress of the house comes out. She wears a white wimple. She is a young woman, still in her prime. I've seen her with her two fine children, a boy and a younger girl, who run and play around her skirts, but today she is alone, looking at the sky. She spies me in my hidey-hole beside the stable and starts toward me, then changes her mind and ducks back into the house.

I have been here now for twice the ringing of the Sunday bells. Perhaps she's going to make me leave. I hurry to push out to the road before she brings bad news, but before I manage more than two steps she's back.

"Good morning, Mistress."

I am startled. I look up and down the street to see whom she is speaking to, but here she is crossing the stableyard toward me, skirts lifted, dainty feet picking through the mud. She laughs good-naturedly at my confusion.

"It's you I'm speaking to, Na Jeanne." Her eyes flicker like insects over my clothes and face. My fingernails are black with dirt. They never used to be dirty. When I was a lady.

She has dark eyes. She has a broad face and a fine plump body and two rounded hills for her breasts, half-hidden under her laces, a pretty, plump dove to make her husband proud of her, but then I see the bowl she's carrying. My mouth begins to water, but I feel a disquiet running through me. I can't put my finger on it. I want to rush away.

Then I see the sneaky servant-boy peering out from the doorway of the house, and I know the source of my anxiety.

I curtsey politely. I am no longer a noblewoman but a poor beggar-beast, a wandering ewe; and I take my proper place, as I was taught. And anyway, who am I to put on airs?

"I've brought you a warm soup," she says. "Eat."

She holds out the wooden bowl and spoon, and a husky smell rises to my nostrils. My stomach twists in delight.

"It's a good bean soup," she says, as I take it in my surprised, awed hands. "A thick broth, made with beef."

I bow in prayer, a silent *Thank you, God,* and take the offered bowl.

"Mistress," I say, "this charity shall be seen by God. Blessings on the provider." The trace of a whine in my voice, as if beggar-born, though on reflection, I've had time to learn. We're all beggars in the end, beggars of God and fate.

She steps inside my little lean-to, out of the stable mud, although short as she is she has to duck her head to avoid the beam. She looks around, hands folded on her stomach. I think that she's *enceinte* again, curling her fingers over the secret babe that's right now hiding in her womb. Her eyes dart about my snug little nook, taking in the clean straw for my bed, the stones that I have gathered for a hearth outside. I get nervous with her staring and put down the wooden bowl and begin to rummage in my sack among my things, wishing she would go away. Suddenly she does not look as pretty to me or as welcoming.

"I am careful with the fire. It's not dangerous." I hear the words tumble from my lips too fast. "I placed the stones outside, as you can see, out in the yard, lest a spark fly out. I watch it carefully. I don't wish to disturb."

"No, no," she answers quickly. "You disturb nothing. Here, though. Sit. Eat."

She picks up the soup that I have not touched and hands the bowl to me a second time. "Eat."

I crouch down and take a spoonful. The soup is good, and I feel my belly twist in appreciation; my hunger is a monster sleeping in its cave, and it's just been wakened with a bone. So I send another wordless prayer to my Lord, to transform the flesh that I'm eating into the natural, living food of God, suitable in His eyes. My Lord could do that, make the unclean pure, as Christ turned water into wine, and I wish He would do so with me, forgive my faults, make me a vessel of pure love. Slowly I sip the soup.

The mistress remains close by. Clearly she has something on her mind.

"It's good." The soup, I mean.

"Where are you from, Na Jeanne?" she asks boldly, smiling down on me. "You're not from here."

"Ah, no," I say. Noncommittal, though I begin to feel the confusion rising in my brain. A loud singing. A singing cloud. The Inquisitors wanted to know that too: Sieur Anselmo and his friend. "Where are you from?" they asked, two Dominicans in their terrifying black and white. Black panthers in disguise. And I, stumbling by, pretending to be mute, not knowing if I wanted them to take and put me to the stake—get it over with—or if I wanted to escape. Edging away from them. "Where are you from?" they had asked, as she did now, this pretty, buxom matron with hot soup. And later the questioning about my Voices and where I've been.

"You say you have seen God," the Inquisitors challenged me. "How do you know it is not your imagination?"

"It is my imagination," I replied.

I saw Sieur Anselmo's face go black.

"Well, which is it?" he thundered. "God or your imagination?"

I was so frightened. I tried to explain: "That's one of the ways God speaks to me," I whispered, wishing I had more courage, wishing I had no fear. I dropped a curtsey and looked over my shoulder for help.

In my imagination, in my sorrow, in my longing, in my fear. And what's oddest of all, I forgot the most important one: in my joy! I wanted to shout. "In my singing! In my happiness comes God." They let me go, I don't know why. They set me free to wander off again.

"If not from here, then where?" Mistress Flavia snaps me back to the present. "You have no family?"

"I had a family once," I answer. "But no, they are dead now, scattered."

"So many have been killed in the wars," she says, urging me to further confidences.

"May their souls rest in peace." I know the responses I'm supposed to make.

"Are you from the Languedoc originally? I can't place your accent. You speak like one of the aristocracy."

A chill goes through me. To be alone, without family, without the protection of friends or place, is dangerous. But to speak like the aristocracy is to be marked. The boy is still watching furtively from the house.

By now I have finished all but a couple of bites of the soup, and I rise stiffly.

"I am no one, Mistress Flavia. I am the lowliest beggar-woman on this earth. I am sorry if I inconvenience you," I continue, rushing on, annoyed by the whine that I cannot leave out of my voice. "I do not mean to be a burden. I shall leave tonight. I have spun your wool, Mistress Flavia. It is here, on this nail."

"No, no," she says hurriedly, but I see she takes the yarn, and she is looking at my work with interest. She shall not find a flaw. "That's not what I meant at all. Only that I'm curious. You know how women are. I see you here, so neat and tidy in your dress, so well spoken. It's easy to see you weren't always like this. You stand upright. You have dignity—the way your fingers smooth your dress. You have a strange, wild beauty, and I wonder who you are, that's all. Also—" she stops. "People see you collecting herbs in the meadows."

"What do you want from me?"

"Only tell me what country you're from."

"Born in Béziers," I say. That's safe enough.

"They say you were at Montségur."

"Who says?"

"A peddler at the fair last week told Na Rixende that he'd seen you there."

"Many people have been at Montségur," I say. "And many have never been there and pretend they have. They've torn it down now, every stone, and scattered the foundations. Nothing remains of Montségur. Hotbed of heretics." I cross myself quickly. After that I put the bowl back in her hands, curtseying my thanks. "Here is your bowl, and thank you, ma'am."

She doesn't take the hint. "They say you have healing powers." Again her eyes flicker round the humble shelter. Her mouth turns up in a little smile, and she takes my arm intimately.

"Na Jeanne," she says, once again giving me a title of courtesy. She lowers her head and whispers, "Tell me who you are. Ever since you came . . . such strange things. Look how our garden grows, the hollyhocks a foot taller than those in the neighbor's yard, and the herbs around our house, everything springing up green and lush. They say you have magic. Look at the donkey. He's so old you can see every bone in his back sticking up like spikes. But the stableboy says that he doesn't limp the way he used to. The donkey could hardly take a step a week ago, and now he's gaining weight. He holds up his head. It's clear that his knees don't hurt as much."

I say nothing. She looks at me. The silence drawing out.

"Yesterday my little boy, the one who's just returned—"

She watches me as she talks, but I'm suddenly intently absorbed in rummaging in my sack.

"Guiscard is five years old," she continues. "Yesterday he fell down while playing with the bigger boys." My heart is pounding. I know what she's going to say. "His head was bleeding. The skin was torn off the palm of his hand, the left hand. He was crying. He says you came up to him in the road."

"I don't know what you're talking about!" I say angrily. "I don't know any children. I have nothing to do with the children. I dislike children."

"The other children ran away. They were afraid of you. He says that you picked him up."

"Lies, lies! I'm an old woman, that's all. Now you'll slander me with lies!"

"He says you pressed your palm on his forehead and the wound stopped bleeding." Her voice a whisper now, her words pushed out intently. "He says you took his bleeding hand in yours and stroked it. Like this." She sets down the bowl and runs the palm of one hand flat across the other.

"I don't know what you're talking about."

"He says he saw the skin repair itself, and when he climbed down from your lap, there was nothing to show that he'd been hurt."

"Never trust children," I say. "Known liars."

"Where are you going?" She grabs my arm.

I start across the muddy yard, she following.

"Na Jeanne," she calls. I stop. She stands, both hands at her sides, looking so forlorn that my heart goes out to her. Perhaps I am mistaken.

"Yes?"

"Please," she whispers. "I want to thank you for what you did for Guiscard. Jeanne, are you a Friend of God?"

"There are no more heretics. Everyone knows that. Now go away. I have my rounds to make." I turn to leave again.

"Will you come to supper tonight?" she asks. "My husband and I would like you to join us tonight."

I stop, stunned. Listening. Trying to gauge the direction of the wind. I shut my eyes to hear better, but I cannot catch the drift. When I open them again she's watching me with her round black eyes. I reach out my spirit, trying to feel her aura.

"It's a true invitation." She senses my hesitation. "Go on your rounds, whatever you do of a day, but this evening, come eat with us. We are good people," she continues. "We remember the old days."

I do not answer. I press on out of the stableyard and into the byway. But she follows me.

"The stableboy saw you the other day." Ah, there he comes again, the traitor. He's the one will turn me in. By now we're standing on the cobbles of the street. "He says you were sitting still as a tree."

"I was probably asleep." I turn angrily.

"He says he touched you on the arm. You didn't move."

"Old woman's sleep."

"No, when an old woman sleeps, her mouth falls open and her head rolls to the side. Or perhaps she lies down on the ground. But you were sitting bolt upright. You had left your body," she says insistently. "And you healed my little boy."

"I don't know what you are talking about," I shout, and I pull from her grip. "Get away from me." I turn my back, groping for my cane. "I need the latrine. Excuse me, please."

She frowns, but she takes the hint and leaves with a quick, irritated toss of the head. She thought I didn't notice her exasperation, but not much escapes me now; and when she's picked her careful way back across the stableyard to the house, I return to my lair, glance about to see it's safe, then quickly lift the board and feel in the straw-packed hole for my treasure. I slip it, still wrapped in its green oilskin, into the inner pocket of my skirts and take up my stick and my little sack with my own wooden bowl and spoon, and I stagger across the yard.

Halfway across I go back for the bowl that the mistress brought me, and I gulp the few remaining beans hungrily. But I leave that bowl behind. I won't be accused of stealing. My heart is anxious, not knowing where I am to go but my feet moving along anyway. I know this feeling. It means that something is about to happen, or that soon I shall meet someone. I know where to go too, when this anxiety comes to me, because any step in a false direction feels wrong, and any step in the right direction fills me with a kind of lightness, though I have no idea where I'm heading or what for. I feel led, as if by the metal finger an Arab merchant once showed me, the magic needle always pointing north. Or led by the magi's star.

I hurry out of the town, past the smiths and the weavers and the scribes, out the gate and on toward the fields, but a little whimper catches in my throat as I remember the other times, when they were after me, and now the fires are burning in my head again.

❈ TEN ❈

I don't slow down until I'm out in the dirt lane, over the hill, and walking as fast as three frightened legs can go over the stony road between the hedgerows. What did she want from me? Yes, I *had* been on one of the journeys. Yes, I *had* healed the little boy. I couldn't help myself, for I can no more stop the flow of that force through my hands than I can stop the sun from shining. It is only love. No harm in love. The touch of love.

But that's no protection now. "Any person is entitled to hunt heretics on another's land, and he can force the owner's bailiffs to help in the hunt as well." I know the decrees by heart.

"If any heretic is found on your land, your property is forfeit, and the heretic's house shall be burnt to the ground."

The French promulgated the laws after the war ended. When would that have been—about 1229 or 1230? It was just after our beloved Count Raymond VII was scourged before the crowd in Paris. Everything's a jumble in my memory. William went to Paris with him, and also Roland-Pierre, my two men riding together in his escort. They both told me of the trip. Count Raymond had surrendered, and afterward the French passed laws to encourage us to spy and turn our neighbors in. Mistress Flavia's servant-boy will hunt me down. And if he catches me, he can probably take over his mistress's land. If he's cunning enough, if he knows the laws—though I think he's just out to make trouble.

A cramp in my leg. I can walk no farther.

Yes, it was 1229, after the war ended, and long after the death of Simon de Montfort. Roland-Pierre and William and three hundred knights rode to Paris with Raymond, Count of Toulouse, cavalcading up to the Languedouil, land of the Francs, where they say "oui" for *yes,* instead of our Languedoc "oc." He signed the Treaty of Meaux with Louis IX, the boy-king of France, and also with the Pope, and the three signatures stood as equals on the document.

Yet afterward they whipped him in the new cathedral they're building in Paris, the one named for Our Lady, Notre Dame. Both William and Roland-Pierre were there.

The twelfth of April, 1229. Raymond was barefoot and dressed only in breeches and a white shirt. They stripped him naked and put a cord around his neck, as if he were a common slave. (Or was he exalted as Jesus Christ our Lord, who was also whipped for us, a living sacrifice?) Count Raymond knelt at the altar, white buttocks bare before the surging crowd, and Cardinal Romanus of Saint Angelo, the Pope's own man—the one whose mistress was the queen-regent, Blanche of Castille herself, mother of the young king Louis—Romanus himself lifted his arm at the altar of Christ and brought down the leather whip. Afterward the cardinal and the other papal clerics took the Holy Eucharist.

Count Raymond left twenty hostages behind in Paris. One of them was his sixteen-year-old daughter, and they say he's not seen her to this day. That's what happened when he signed the Treaty of Meaux. The Catholic Church imposed a fine of ten thousand marks—imagine!—just for defending his lands against their invasion. Ten thousand marks! It would take a hundred years to raise such a sum. That was 1229. When he signed the Treaty of Meaux. When he was publicly flogged at the high altar. I heard about it from Roland-Pierre.

When Count Raymond rode back from Paris in defeat, we gave him a hero's welcome. He rode into Toulouse, the City of Beauty, where the banners were flying at every window and tower and the trumpets scrawled. The mighty warhorses, draped in tapestry run through with red and gold, paraded heavily through the thrilling crowds; the knights, armored in leather and mail, carried lances decorated with bright red and green and white silk flags. All the windowsills were hung with rugs, and

we ladies leaned out to toss roses on the returning count and his cortège.
A shining day! And I so happy that I left my post to run beside the parade,
throwing flowers at my splendid men. I could have flown to the stars,
swept round the universe with joy!

Cardinal Romanus accompanied our count. William said his presence wouldn't matter. We thought we would live in peace now that the
treaty had been signed. We would rebuild, we thought, and life would
go on as before—though perhaps not on the scale we'd known before.
That was too much to ask—to return to that time when the feast of a
nobleman might last three weeks and gifts enough to ransom a king be
handed out: gifts of horses, armor, lands, and cakes of Oriental spices,
wagonloads of salt or bolts of wool or silk. The greater the gifts, the
greater the prestige of the one who bestowed them. Never would we
see those days again, but we comforted ourselves that the peasants were
tilling their fields again, and the first wheat crops would soon fall to the
scythes. The *perfecti* were baptizing *credentes* again, and the Cathar
Church, the Friends of Love, was the stronger for having been driven
underground.

We thought the war was over, when in fact it was only changing form.
The day the decrees came out, William took the palace stairway two steps
at a time, holding the scroll high overhead as he ran into the great hall.

"Listen! Listen to what they now demand!" he exclaimed.

I caught my breath, he was so handsome. His strong square hands, the
way held himself, the turn of his fine head, his generous, open smile
flashing in his copper beard, the vulnerable curl of his hair at the back of
his neck. My patriotic indignation entwined itself with my love for him.
Whatever cause William fought was mine as well—we, the freedom-
fighters. He handed the scroll to a clerk to read to us aloud.

"Quiet! Quiet!"

"Listen!"

We crowded round to hear how our days would pass from now on.

"Any heretic who renounces his false faith must wear two crosses
sewn on his breast, and the crosses are to be in striking contrast to the
color of his clothes. He must change residence. No heretic or reformed
heretic may hold public office." (Well, no one will renounce, that's all!
And laughter follows.)

"Every boy over fourteen and every girl over twelve shall swear loyalty to the Catholic faith, abjure heresy, and promise to hunt out heretics. This oath shall be renewed every two years." (The laughter dying on our lips.)

"All persons, without exception, must attend Mass on Sundays and take Communion thrice a year—at Easter, Christmas, and Pentecost.

"No one suspected of heresy is to practice as a doctor, and no sick person may have a heretic near him when he dies." (That's in case the helper give the *consolamentum* on the sly.)

As I recall the reading of the decrees, my present danger hits full force: the danger of healing that little boy, of staying with the dying woman. And I am on my feet again, up from the stone where I'd paused to rest, and moving on, hobbling on my stick. I'm running from the Inquisition that is already on my heels.

As I run, my mind takes me back to reading the decrees. William stood in the Great Hall, commanding silence with one arm raised, his head bowed, listening to the clerk. I squirmed through the jutting hips and elbows to his side. He reached out and pulled me to him, and I felt a welling up of triumphant joy—in contrast to the horror of the decrees. Around me, the silence deepened as the reality sank in, our dismay at this invitation to denounce our neighbors, betray our closest friends. ("But who would turn his neighbor in?" we asked.)

There was worse to come. "No one may possess a Bible or translate it from Latin or read it in the vernacular."

We looked at one another, stunned. "But who will receive the Word of God?" we asked. If we could possess only a psalter or breviary, and these written in Latin, the scripture would be of no use at all to the ordinary person.

There were many more decrees.

"We shall not give in!" William shouted, leaping onto the table. My heart swelled. I promised myself right then that I would fight beside him all my life. I would die for him. And yes!—we would not give up!

For an hour more we milled around, repeating and discussing the decrees, this tightening of the noose of tyranny. We would refuse—simple as that—to turn our friends in, our cousins, husbands, wives. The hall rocked with our angry disbelief, our voices echoing off the stones of the vast hall.

"Demons is what those Francs are!"

"Now anyone can accuse a neighbor of heresy and take his land for free."

"But look, there aren't enough bailiffs and priests in the land to execute these orders!"

Yet William had his arm around me, hugging me to him, and I could feel my ferocious and exultant excitement: we would fight and love together, he and I.

Two weeks later, the first arrests took place. They took us by surprise.

The *perfectus* Vigoros de Baconia, whose preaching was so passionate that people came from fifty miles around to hear him, was condemned and executed before a lawyer could be called. He was burnt so fast (alive, of course) that we hadn't time to organize a protest.

They arrested the two elder sons of our Lady Esclarmonde, and Bernard-Otho was imprisoned for a year before he could buy his freedom; Esclarmonde herself went underground, poor old woman. She was sixty-nine by then. She retired to her country estate with her youngest son and her beloved orphan girls, the ones like me whom she'd adopted and schooled and tended so lovingly. She engaged in no more politics.

The spying and betrayals spread after those first arrests. And here I am still running, this time from the velvet-liveried stableboy, who's looking for a lover's favor, I suppose.

I stumble on another mile. The sun grows warm at last—amazing in early autumn, when at night I'm goosebumped cold. The last grasshoppers leap out from under my feet, but they are chilly and listless, though you might have thought it summer still with the tall grass and the last dim poppies and wildweed flowers bursting yellow and red at the edges of the road. The land begins to climb, and a river paralleling the road narrows between its banks, running over rocks and tumbling faster in its fearful, white-spumed rush.

We thought we'd been afraid during the twenty years of war, but in those years we could curl up in each other's arms for comfort. We knew who the enemy was. Now the Inquisitors ride through the townships with their bodyguards and men-at-arms; they move in herds of twenty, fully armed.

Advisedly.

Afraid.

Advisedly.

For the Resistance roam the countryside as well. Not long ago, they caught one Dominican Inquisitor and slit his throat and hung him upside down on a tree, his cassock falling over his head to expose his naked brown private parts. "Stupidity!" I whisper now, watching the water spill down its channel, though there was a time I'd thought it fine. "Stupidity." Such actions only spawn more retribution, more moiling hatred, anger, violence, war.

Like the vengeance that William and the band of fighters wreaked at Avignonet when they cut the throats of seven Inquisitors. Afterward, they rode all night back to Montségur, softly in the moonlit shadows, their horses hanging their tired heads, and the men tired too by the time they reached home: their laughter dulled; riding in silence toward the end and some a little worried at the repercussions of their actions, but most of them still glorying in the raid. They arrived at dawn to announce their mission, thinking the murders a great blow against the enemy; and the tired men stomping their boots before the fire and tossing down their swords and bucklers with a clatter of relinquished steel and an air of celebration. Pons Diego guzzled beer in great slurps, laughing, the liquid running down his beard, with righteous pride, his cup running over; and William laughing with the others, his head tossed back, his blue eyes flashing. The *perfecti* were shocked. They shook their heads, fearing that this one foolhardy act would call down on them a siege of Montségur.

I can't walk another step. I sit on a stone in the sun, sheltered from the wind, and look out over the rolling hills and green pastures so good for sheep and goats. *He maketh me to lie down in green pastures. . . . I shall not want.*

Suddenly a great cry rises from my throat, erupting in a wail of anguish and grief. My shoulders shake with the gush of tears. The sunlight is flashing gold and silver off the violent grass, and I am no longer a righteous freedom-fighter but only a fugitive, running for my life.

❖ ELEVEN ❖

Well, that was a good cry.

Buck up, old girl. Things are never so bad as we make them out. I remember Bishop Guilhabert de Castres reproving me at Montségur for worrying. "But it works," I teased him through my tears. "I've worried about a lot of things, and none of them have come to pass."

Bishop de Castres, that good, sweet soul, folded my hands between his own gnarled, work-worn, knobby-knuckled hands. "Remember, child," he said, "all things change. The wheel of good turns round to bad, and bad wheels on to good. But our Lord has made a covenant with us. We may be in pain, but we will never be alone in our suffering. We have a spiritual cavalry at our disposal. Remember, Jeanne, we are always taken care of."

I was only fourteen. I didn't want to say it outright at the time—and certainly not to a bishop—but I wanted nothing to do with any covenant with God, not when our Father would slam His only beloved Son up on a cross and watch Him die, as hard-bitten as Abraham with Isaac. It seemed to me that Christ could have had just as fine a resurrection after a quiet, happy, old-age death in bed (I wanted to say). What was the point of being crucified? Watch out for fathers (I wanted to say). God may have made a pact with humankind, but it didn't include our knowing the terms, exactly. Better to stay out of His holy sight. Don't draw attention to yourself. Of course, I said none of this to my beloved, kindhearted bishop; it would only have made him unhappy.

Oh! A mouse, scampering in the thick grass at the roots of the hedge, just sprouted wings and flew off as a little bird! Goodness. I thought it was a mouse, rustling in the hedge, and instead it was a bird. It was beautiful, the way its wings lifted it into the air, mouse or bird, flying off so free. Suddenly my eyes can almost taste the yellow and red and pink wildflowers, they're so alert with joy; and for a time I feel as if I can hear the grassy growing color green, and then to my surprise I notice that I am not alone on this road.

There's a peasant woman with her basket of eggs coming toward me, and behind her a pair of reapers, scythes over their shoulders, going home perhaps, or moving to another field. The men swing their shoulders as they walk, as if still plying their monotonous harvest trade; their heads bend toward each other. They're father and son, I think, as they approach and pass me seated on my rock. We nod good-day. *Buon giornata. Giorno. Gior.*

When they have passed, I push to my feet and pick up my stick again, trailing after them. If I were a Good Christian, the Our Father would run like music through my steps. I could do it now, as I have done it many times before; praying the sacred words for an hour at a time or more, and watching how the meaning changes with each repetition, watching how happy I become. The meaning of *Our* extends outward to encompass the various green grasses, the hard road, the mice that change to birds on the wing, *Our* Father. And though He sent His Son to die, my arms lift up like a child's for its daddy—for Him. I'm climbing on His lap, enfolded in His arms; and heaven (when I continue minute by minute to say the prayer as my feet eat up the road) is no longer somewhere in the sky, the paradise to which I shall go upon my death, but lounging in the trees, slouching at my moving feet, sifting in the scent of mown hay, inside the very center of my being, the Kingdom of God within, right inside me here, and I am breathing the spaces between the limbs of trees.

Ahead of me the road forks. I lean on my stick, waiting for direction. To the west the sky is lowering, the clouds piling up gray and purple with a coming storm, and suddenly I remember I have no place to lay my head this night.

I push down the rising panic. This is no time for fear: I need clarity. I reach out, listening. Which path? The reapers have stopped on the right-hand road a little ahead, deep in conversation, leaning on the shafts of their scythes. The peasant woman has also taken the right-hand road. I wait at the Y, shifting from foot to foot. There's a little altar here, with a cruci-fied Christ hanging skinny from his bleeding hands and honored by a vase of withered flowers. I've heard that there's a saint in Italy who had stigma-ta—the true nails of Christ—embedded in his palms. When he died, they tried to take the nails out and found them curled so tightly across the backs of his hands that they couldn't pull them out. So they left them in when they laid him in his grave. I myself would have opened his grave, once the body had rotted, and removed the nails from his bones. Out of curiosity alone. To see if they had healing power, or held the key to love.

There: the nudge of Knowing. I turn left, toward the steeper, narrow-er path, and as I climb the mountain I think back on my youth with the Friends of God. In those days we worshiped in ordinary houses. "Your house on Saturday," we would say, and the host would prepare a room with a simple table on which would be a striking pure white linen cloth. And that was all. No image of the bleeding, hanging body of our Lord. No crucifix. No images of God or Mary or the lovely angels—only a table, a white cloth, our prayers, our selves, sitting in the silent privacy of our most secret hearts, as the Master taught: to go into our close—our close-et—and there to listen humbly for the resurrected touch of God.

Some believe that Christ did not die on the cross, but being pure spir-it jumped happily down and walked away. And others add that He met His mother and some of the apostles, and Mary of Magdala, who they say was His wife, and together they all took ship and landed at Marseilles and taught the Cathar faith. Still others affirm that the Good Men and Good Women are descended from the sons of Christ and the Magdalene. I myself don't know what to believe; I wasn't there. But I always liked it when one of the *perfecti* would visit and we would gather for *adoratio* and for spiritual baptism by his light-struck hands.

Of course, we worshiped in the Catholic Church as well. Many of us took the sacraments on Sundays, confessed to priests, and undertook Catholic pilgrimages to Santa Maria Maggiore in Rome, where you could see the actual manger where Christ was born, or to Saint John Lateran, where they display the holy steps He ascended while wearing a crown of

thorns. In later years, the Dominican Inquisitors sometimes sent converted heretics on pilgrimages to Santiago de Campostella across the
Pyrenees or as far away as Jerusalem sometimes, or north to visit the new
cathedrals being built in Chartres or Canterbury or Paris or Reims. It was
one of the penances required of Cathar believers. It had the advantage of
forcing them out of town. And then they'd come home, reconstituted
Catholics, and kneel to the *perfecti* as before.

We worshiped both ways, many of us. Why not? We were all cousins,
brothers, wives, mothers. We'd been raised in the same families, were
tolerant of one another's thoughts. I know a Catholic priest who used to
come to our Cathar services and said he found no heresy.

Unless you count our stifled laughter during prayers when we were
young, green, golden girls, and the flashing of our eyes at the boys across
the room, or how we dropped them in self-conscious modesty. I laugh
aloud remembering—it was so good!

This steeper path has no one on it. I am climbing up a cartroad so little
used that grass grows not only in the mounded center but also in the two
rutted wheel-tracks—though not so high, of course. And I notice how
the air is getting cooler, the sun lower, and there's a hint of orange in the
sky behind me against the dark gray, purple piling clouds; and a tremor of
fear passes through me when I think of spending one more night in the
cold, exposed to bears and wolves, shivering under a tree perhaps, with
no food or fire unless I can collect some wood.

Just then I hear the creaking of wheels. I turn on my two swollen feet
to look behind me. Up the hill comes a slant-floored, two-wheeled cart
drawn by a sturdy Basque pony, a shaggy dun with a thick, white mane that
hangs below its neck and a long, white tail dragging at its muddy heels.
Beside the pony walks a farmer, his face hidden under his soft, slouched
hat. I step off the path to let them pass, for there is hardly room for the
cart on this mountain lane, and I wish I could get a ride with him. My
poor knees.

"Do you wish a lift, Mother?" He pulls the pony to a halt. He is
youngish with a broad face and a flat, short nose. His beard is all pepper
and salt. I wait, listening for direction: friend or French?

"Why, thank you, yes."

"You look tired plowing up this hill," he says, looking me over. I give him a once-over too. Eyes the stormy color of the gray salt sea. On closer inspection, I see he's no spring chicken anymore. He sucks a blade of grass. He is missing one tooth and two fingers of the left hand.

"I'll be glad to rest my feet a while, very kind of you."

I haul myself onto the cart and wedge body and satchel between the baskets. He slaps the pony with brown cracked-leather reins.

"Eh, nice to have a lift," I remark. "Be carried for a bit." I'm amused to hear myself using a country twang—I, who can read Latin and speak the French tongue too, and who learned her high-caste accent from the Lady Esclarmonde herself. "Good-hearted pony," I add.

"Aye," he says amiably, smacking its back affectionately.

We travel up the hill in silence. I appreciate the man's ability to walk without chatter. I take the time to look around me at the twisting road with its views of distant mountains, and to straighten my hair and wonder why my heart is singing uncontrollably—a lark leaping in the air. But then I notice that my hands are as big and coarse as a cook's. Good hands. They lie in my lap like sausages, ten sausages, the nails split and black with dirt, and the skin burnt brown with the sun. The white hands of the nobility are cleansed in milk. I used to wrap my hands in gloves filled with goat-cream batter. Baiona and I would comb each other's hair and paint our eyes and lips; then we would put on our milk-gloves and dance around the room with our hands held high, singing songs and patting at each other's gloves.

What's queer is that I don't feel any older now, so that it's a shock to see in my lap these good, hard-worked hands, the appendages of an old woman, when inside I don't feel more than twenty-two. I mash down my rambunctious hair with both hands, and then I do an odd, flirtatious thing: I take out my hankie and tie it round my head. Why am I so happy? As if a man would look at me!

"How far are you going?" he asks, spitting out the blade of grass he's been sucking on.

"Till I arrive," I answer openly, and break out laughing. Not often do I feel so comfortable with anyone. Then, to my surprise, I hear myself whisper, "To Montségur." Until it's said, I hadn't known my destination.

He gives me a quick sideways glance, and I'm giving a similar marveling one to myself.

"That's in the hands of the French now."

"Hmm."

"Have you seen it recently?"

I say nothing. What does *recently* mean?

"I remember the massacre," he says.

Again I say nothing. I'm sorry I brought the subject up.

"Two hundred heretics burnt," he continues. "The smoke was so thick
the sky went black. And the stench? Faugh!"

He glances over at me, but I'm staring into the distance, thank you
kindly, quite absorbed by the view.

"I don't know what you're talking about." My accent no longer country. I want to cry again; my throat working. Was he there? One of the
French murderers?

He grunts and spits into the grass. "It must be haunted now. I wouldn't
want to go."

I want to change the subject. "You soldiered for the French," I hazard.

"No. Not I. But everyone's heard of Montségur. I work the farm. My
father's and grandfather's before me. My wife died five years ago. We had
two daughters, one boy that died. The girls are gone now, both married. I
live alone up the way. It's not bad," he added. "I've lived here all my life,
just about, except conscripted into the army for one little while when I
was young, and one time on a pilgrimage into Aragon."

"You never remarried?" Get off the subject of war.

"Not yet. At first I couldn't find a woman I liked, and then I couldn't
find one that liked me in return or wanted to live so remote. It's all
right—a bachelor's life."

We lapse into silence for another mile, the only sound being the comfortable creaking of the wheels, the whistle of birds in the brush, the soft
stamp of the pony's hooves on the sweet-smelling, grassy road.

"I live up the hill." He breaks the silence suddenly, gesturing with one
thumb. His words spill over themselves in a dialect so fast that I can hardly grasp them. "Listen carefully. My name is Jerome Ahrade. I have this
pony, three sheep, ten chickens. Quick, what do I have?"

I stare at him, my mouth open in astonishment, then hear the hoof-beats behind us. "The pony, three sheep, ten chickens," I repeat.

"I'm coming back from market. I have two hectares. The house is made of stone and wood. And *your* name?"

He speaks so urgently that I turn in the cart to look behind.

"Jeanne. Jeanne Béziers."

"From Béziers?"

"I was perhaps a babe at the massacre. No one knows."

"You're lucky to be alive. Do you know these?"

I have only time to shake my head, for now they are almost on us, two Dominicans on horseback and two bodyguards in leather and chain-mail. The four horsemen of the Apocalypse. The track is so narrow that they cannot pass, but pull their horses' chests up against the cart, their foam-flecked muzzles and hot breath right at my back.

One of the soldiers slaps his leather whip on the wood of the cart with a curse. "Hyaa! Goddamn you," he shouts. "Move over; get out of the road."

The pony jumps forward at the same moment that Jerome leaps to its head. He leads the pony by the bridle up onto the verge, and the monks and their bodyguards swarm around us.

"Get down," says one of the monks to me.

I hardly dare to look at them. The magpies. Straight and narrow— God save us from the righteous of this world. They tower over us on their dancing horses, and one of the beasts rolls its eyes, exposing the whites, and tosses its head, gnashing at the bit. Flecks of foam shake loose onto my skirt. I stumble off the cart to stand beside Jerome, who puts one arm around my shoulder.

"Who are you?" demands the taller monk.

"No one, Father," says Jerome. "We're returning home from market. Selling butter, eggs. Mushrooms gathered in the woods."

I look behind me. The sun's antlers are caught in the branches of the trees, and the fiery orb is bleeding across the purple sky.

The soldiers lift the tops of the two baskets in the cart. Peer inside. Jerome squeezes my shoulder. I drop a curtsey to the Dominicans, as the peasant women do. I consider crying for a blessing, but I distrust my voice and my peasant accent. Instead, I stand, hands folded before me, and my eyes make lace on the ground. Praying. Listening. I'm afraid. Why does my Knowing leave when people come around?

"We're looking for a woman," says one monk. "A witch or a heretic traveling alone. Crazy, babbling to herself. Gray hair flying loose down her back, without a wimple."

"Not seen her," says Jerome. "There were many people on the main road, down below."

"They said she took the mountain road," says the monk.

"Unless the two peasants were lying," murmurs his companion, and they confer for a moment quietly. Their horses still prance slightly from the exertion. The pony drops his indifferent head to crop the grass with brisk sideways swipes of his strong teeth. The two monks whisper together, looking over at us every now and then.

"Take off your clothes," says the younger monk, looking my way.

"Father!" cries Jerome piteously. "She's my woman, my own wife! What are you thinking of? A good woman, she's borne children, and—"

"Strip her," orders the other monk. He nods at one of the bodyguards to assign the chore.

I give a shriek. "Keep your damned bloody hands off me, you shit-face," I scream in as flat an accent as I can muster, and I fight the soldier off, kicking and biting. They are looking for the *perfecta*'s cord around my neck or waist, and if they look much harder they'll find my treasure too. I scream like a ghoulie, and not only the soldier but now Jerome is trying to hold my hands.

"Woman, stop it!" he cries, then hits me across the mouth.

I stop. He takes my face in his hands. "Hush now, Jeanne," he says, speaking in a slow, loud voice, as if talking to a baby—or for the benefit of the men.

"Sirs, we are poor peasants. We are good Catholics. We go to Mass."

I stand quietly, but my heart is pounding.

"Where do you live?" the soldier shouts at me.

"Up the hill," I say, gesturing imprecisely with my whole arm. Which hill? Where?

"How much land do you have?"

"Two hectares."

"What animals?"

"This pony, three sheep, a few weak, scraggly chickens. Honored sirs, we're not rich." I'm not about to tell the tax-collectors what there is.

"Almaric, go investigate."

The soldier who's still mounted turns his horse and gallops on ahead, up the mountain.

"Go on," says the monk to Jerome. "We'll follow you. If you have a well, you can give us a drink."

The procession begins again, with the little pony trotting along and the horses stepping at an impatient walk behind.

"Meanwhile, the woman gets away?" says the other monk to his partner.

"Don't be impatient," says the first.

"I *am* impatient. I'm impatient for the purity of my Lord Jesus Christ, and to flush out every unsanctified heretic for the glory of His name. So this one gets away while we waste time with peasants?"

"We'll have time."

"Brother, the two scythers misspoke. The woman took the main highway, down below. Why would she come off on the mountain track?"

At this point I remember what I should be doing—that's how stupid I am, forgetting my help in times of peril—and silently I pray to my Lord Jesus Christ, to whom these monks offer reverence as well. But praying is hard, because I'm frightened, coward that I am. My hands shake. I want to vomit.

I pray first simply for the strength to pray. Then I place myself in the light of God and send my Lord Christ to the soldiers and monks to make them go away. Giving thanks that it is done, giving thanks and sending the light of Christ from my heart to theirs as best I can, as Guilhabert de Castres taught me long ago; and this is hard when you are afraid, when what you want to do is run. Or kill. Instead, I need to send the light.

My heart is stone. It is locked in a box and the key thrown away. *A new heart I will give you. And a new spirit I will put within you; and I will take out of your flesh the heart of stone and give you a heart of flesh.* That's from the Book of Ezekiel. Guilhabert made me copy that passage. I take a breath. Begin again. *Take out the heart of stone and give you a heart of flesh.* A heart of flesh is human and afraid. How can I pray? God, help us, please!

Jerome is walking beside the cart with me, and suddenly I understand that he is praying as well. The two of us are praying in a golden wave of light, and then I feel my heart open—click!—and I know the prayer is finished. It has flown to the Source.

"You're right," says the senior monk suddenly. "Turn back. We still have time to catch her on the low road."

"Go get Almaric," the other monk orders, and without a word the second soldier pushes his horse ahead and gallops up the hill after his comrade. We could kill them now, the two Dominicans, unarmed as they are. Jerome and I—it's a passing thought—but I return to my original duty: send out the light of Christ, though it's hard when I'm so afraid.

"Do you wish to be shriven while we wait?" asks the first monk. His expression has softened, his lips turning up into a quivering smile. Suddenly I see that he is only a boy, young enough to be my son, and he seems sweet to me, his shaven neck exposed and his beard hardly more than fuzz.

"Oh, yes!" cries Jerome. "Confess me, Father." He falls to his knees right there in the middle of the grassy mountain road. The pony instantly drops its white-muzzled head again, canny and practical, unpolitical animal, to yank the short-stemmed grass.

The monk slips off his horse and hands the reins to his brother. Jerome and I both kneel before him.

"I have lied, Father," says Jerome. "I have sworn foul words and taken the name of God in vain. In fact, only a few moments ago, as you came up to us, I was cursing my fate and poverty. I missed Mass last Sunday. . . ."

And so he went on, while I made up my own confession. We confess in the Cathar faith, but it is done before the entire congregation, first asking the indulgence of the collected gathering and then in painful detail describing the mistake or sin. Confession is not complete until we've named the flaw in our character that led to the sin, and also the lesson learned from it and how we intend in future to benefit from this lesson and handle such a matter differently. It's not complete until we've asked for forgiveness from all those who have been harmed by our action.

Esclarmonde used to say that if we truly understood the repercussions of our actions, no one would ever do a harmful thing or say a hurtful word. For always what we do turns back on us. It takes a week or a month or year. Or later lifetimes. *Do unto others what you would have them do,* said Christ. *Treat your neighbor as yourself.* The scripture passage omits to explain the reason—that it's a spiritual law: whatever you do or say will swing back onto you. Good actions draw blessings to you, and bad actions bring down trouble on your head, lifetime after lifetime, inexorable justice rewarding our right and wrongful deeds.

Now Jerome is on his feet, with his Hail Marys and Pater Nosters prescribed, and it's my turn, kneeling before the Dominican, right in the dirt of the road, my hands clasped. Suddenly I burst into tears! "Oh, Father, I have done so many wrongs! I have not loved my enemies. I've shouted at my neighbors. But mostly I lose faith. Again and again I give way to doubt. I wonder if my Lord Jesus Christ or the Blessed Mother do indeed watch over me, noticing each feather that falls from a sparrow's wings— and now you are here to counsel and teach me, and it must be by the grace of Christ Himself. I'm so prideful that I rebel against surrendering all things to God, who must know better than the likes of me how things are supposed to be! But why is there such misery? People killing one another? People starving? Righteous and heretics? I get angry with God. 'Why are You permitting disease and pain?' I shout. *That's* how little faith I have, Father.

"I don't even remember all my sins. Greed. I have greed, to be sure, and yes, jealousy. Envy. Hatred. Lots of fear and hatred even of my friends, and only today I lied. My tongue is a terrible liar, and then this day it answered my man back sharply in my mind when he was hurrying me along. I didn't say it out loud in words, but in my mind, which is just as—"

"That's not a sin," the monk corrected. He was impatient with me.

"Yet it's said a woman must obey her husband. It's just that I get so impatient with him," I say, warming to the task. "Two days ago, when he tried to beat me, I lifted my hand to him! And then, Father, I feel compassion for the . . ."—I was about to say the Friends of God when I remembered that sympathy for the heretics is the same as heresy—"for the dumb animals in our yard, that God hasn't given them a soul, and that they die without the glory of heaven before them; and such thoughts are only further sins against the word of Christ! I shouldn't question the way God made the world in only six days, to finish His creation. But I think if

He'd taken more time——. I think how nice it would be to have my little pony in heaven with me, if I'm going there at all, which perhaps I won't, and Father, I want to cry—"

"For heaven's sake!" mutters the older monk. My confession is cut short by the two returning soldiers clattering down the road.

"Compassion is not a sin, my child," says the young boy, my shriving monk. But he is smiling at me kindly. "Jesus Christ was filled with forgiveness for all us sinners. We are told to love all living things—including the pony, I'm sure. But you must obey your husband, and obey the tenets of the Mother Church. And watch out for the evils of the heretics."

"Yes, Father."

He gives me ten Hail Marys for a penance, together with his hurried blessing, and he is already mounting his palfrey, one foot in the stirrup as he signs the cross over me, his mind already on the hunt.

I do not rise from my knees until they've turned the corner and ridden out of sight.

Stiffly, I come to my feet. Fretting. Irritable now that the danger has passed.

"Hurry," says Jerome, as if reading my thoughts. Already he is pressing the little pony forward.

"Wait then, let me get my foot up," I say angrily. Again I feel the urge to burst into tears, and only as I settle in on the cart do I realize how frightened I have been. I can feel a tingling down the middle of my back, running off my fingertips, weakening my thighs.

"A fine lot," I huff. "And you! Whatever were you thinking of to say we're married? Your woman, indeed!"

He shrugs and spits. "It may have saved your life, and that's the thanks I get." He laughs then. "You're the one claimed me as a husband who beat you! I've never beat you in your life."

I'm embarrassed. I'm not going to take up that one.

"Saved my life!" I say. "What about your own?"

"Mine too. Since if they caught me with a heretic, it's as good as the Wall for me as well. It was a woman they were looking for. Did you want to be dragged to prison?"

"Let them try!" I claim courageously, now that danger has passed and the friars are out of sight.

"They'll be back tomorrow, and then you'd better be prepared. And I too," he spat onto the path to send away the Devil. "The neighbors know I'm not a married man."

"What do you mean?"

"Do you think they won't be back? Tomorrow, next week, next year—sometime they'll come snooping up to the farm, to make sure that you and I live there together. Do you wear a cord around your waist?"

It was such a jump of subject that I blush.

"No." Then, with a gush of tears, I want to confess everything. "Yes, I tied one round in memory, but it's not a real cord. I made a little ceremony. I laid out the sacred cord and blessed it and said the prayers, invoking the sainted martyrs of Montségur, and especially the name of my teacher—"

"Who was that?"

"No one," I answer impulsively. "And before that the Lady Esclarmonde." I want to tell. I want to confess to this stranger who might turn me over to the Preaching Friars. And here comes the story pouring out like cream from a jug, spilling over the pony's back.

"I was in the forest. They had all been killed, and the stench still clung in the air, and the smoke was rising thick and black. But I had been saved—or punished, if you will—not going with the others. And so I tied the cord around my own waist and blessed myself in the name of our good Lord.

"You won't believe me, you think I've made it up, but it was so, and she said that this wasn't a sin but a good thing I was doing, in secret in this way. No one was there to give the *consolamentum,* the consolation. For a feast I boiled a handful of groats, and for company I spread some on the forest floor for my friends, the mice and voles."

The tears are running down my cheeks, my burning eyes. Hands wringing. Agitated.

"You think I'm crazy," I continue. "Everyone was gone. And it took hours and hours for them to—two hundred of them—you were there. Did you see it?"

"I wasn't there. I've only heard about it."

"Afterward I tied a twist of wool round my waist, but I am not a perfected heretic."

"Hey, hey," he murmurs, slapping the pony with the reins.

"I want to be a daughter of Christ."

"From the looks of you," he says, "you need food instead." I look away, sniffling. I know when to keep my mouth shut.

"Well," he says after a moment, "I don't know why I didn't let them drag you off. Now it turns out I'm harboring an imaginary true believer. But we're in this together. We're bound to each other by a lie. Can I count on you to keep me safe?"

"I haven't thanked you," I say humbly. "And yes, I'll keep you safe." But I'm thinking the best way to do that will be to go away. I like this man. I like the quiet way he walks beside his pony, one hand on its withers, in silent communication, man and horse. He ignores my tears but gives such a soft and satisfying pat to the pony's neck that my heart twists, as if it's me he's comforting.

Not long after, we turn into the gate of his little stone house, nestled in the dip of the hill. The sheepfold leans up against the house; the pony stable is a shed dug into the hillside. The house has a thatched roof and a door that latches with a stick and a coil of line. We look inside and I see hard dirt floors spread with straw. Two rooms, one big and the other a storeroom. Each with a window.

"I sleep in the main room," says Jerome. "You can have the storeroom." I go in to check it out. It smells of earth and roots. In one corner is a jumble of sacks and broken tools, and from the rafters hang a smoked ham and chains of onions and garlic.

Jerome ducks to enter the room too, then sweeps some sacking off a wooden platform. "I'll bring in some straw," he says, "and there's a hempen cover for your mattress. You'll have your cloak as a blanket."

It's so inviting that I'm pleased to stay the night. Tomorrow I'll move on to Montségur.

✠ TWELVE ✠

Jerome may have been, as his friend Bernard said, the last person on the face of the earth to hear about the treasure of Montségur or the woman the French were looking for. Jerome did not go frequently into town. He had his animals to tend, and crops—a hard job for one working alone. Even going into town on market-day required making special arrangements with the neighbors to feed his animals.

It was the end of the summer, therefore, before he made the trip on which he would encounter Jeanne. He had risen that morning in the pitch dark and lit the tiny oil lamp that hung on a nail by the door: a bead of light. He had quickly pulled on his shirt and rough trousers, dug his feet into clogs, and carried the earthen lamp (cupping it against the thin, chill wind) into the hay-sweet stable, where he'd set it on a rough plank shelf and woken the sleepy pony. The barn smelled deliciously of horse and rich manure, leather and hay. "Gee-up." He had slapped the little horse to its feet and tossed a handful of feed in the manger. The pony licked and lapped the grain as he threw the harness over its back and buckled and knotted the ropes. By the time he had backed the shaggy pony into the cart shafts and tied the cords, the sky was opening with pale, hopeful streaks of gold and Jerome had long since blown out the lamp, watered his pony, and finished loading his produce onto the cart. The birds were twittering and the trees rustling their tiny fingers at him like men at prayer.

He had packed his goods the night before so that he had only to lift the baskets onto the two-wheeled cart: onions and turnips, eggs, wood mushrooms, apples, pears and some grapes, one bale of wool, and two roosters, their legs tied helplessly with twine. The fowl twisted their necks in nervous, clucking concern as they peered from their wooden cage. Jerome hoped to exchange the roosters for nails and perhaps a useful leather hide.

It took half a day to walk to town, so Jerome didn't arrive until midmorning. As he pulled his cart into the central square, it was already bustling with the early crowds of buyers and sellers. It smelled, as cities did, of urine and rotting vegetables and of bodies packed too tightly. The kerchiefed women with their baskets over their arms roamed the stalls. The farmers—men and women both—shouted out their wares. Jerome unhitched the pony and lowered the back of the cart, tilting it aslant to make a display for his goods, all the while greeting old friends, joking, shaking hands. He found Pons Peter, his regular boy, and handed over the care of the stall (as he liked to call his cartload) to the lad, with careful directions about prices and bargaining. Then he moved off on his regular rounds. Jerome was a man of habit: he liked the steady ways.

His first stop was the church. He entered the shadowy dark structure, with its cool stones underfoot. It had small round windows set high up, and one, made of beautiful colored glass, spilled red and blue diamonds to the pavement. Jerome knelt at his favorite side-altar to the Virgin and made his solitary devotions, then lit a candle for the soul of his departed wife. It was quiet in the empty church, and he rested there a moment, his broad hands splayed on his thighs, to regard the lovely wooden statue of the gentle Virgin. He liked the way the folds of her skirt fell, so lifelike, and the tender tilt of her head, as if she not only knew his every thought but quietly approved.

Behind him he heard the slurry of the priest's skirts.

"Jerome?"

"It's I. Yes."

"How are you, my good friend?" Their low voices echoed in the little church, with its high, vaulted roof and thick pillars.

"Been better. No complaint."

"You're looking well."

"You too. What news?"

"Ah, these are troubled times." The old priest shook his head.

"What's happened?"

"More burnings," said the priest with a shake of his head. "Hunting the heretics."

"Well." Jerome sketched with the toe of his shoe on the stone floor. He didn't know what to say. "Well, they're heretics."

"I tell you, Jerome," said the priest, tucking his arm through that of his friend and walking him back toward the sacristy. "I tell you—"

"What?"

He sighed. "What have you heard up there on your farm? Anything about the troubles here? About Alzeu?"

"I? No."

"They burnt Alzeu last week, and confiscated his property for the friars. His widow is impoverished. She's lucky not to have been burnt at the stake herself."

"What for?" cried Jerome, horrified. "What did he do?"

"They say he was a heretic. I don't like it," whispered the priest. "He came to church. You must be careful, Jerome. I'm telling everyone: watch your tongue."

The old man wrung his hands and glanced around as if afraid of being overheard. "I don't think this is what our Lord asked of us, Jerome," he continued. "They're hunting anyone who has ever seen or heard of a heretic. Heretics by association, as it were. If they find a heretic, he's burnt. Or *she*—they're after the women too. Even someone known to us all, some good, decent burgher, whose family has lived and worked in the town for a hundred years and more—Alzeu." He shook his head. "I'm getting old. I'm old, Jerome. I don't have the heart for this. I'm supposed to want to fight for our Lord. But Alzeu. Who would think—?"

"I remember Alzeu," said Jerome.

"He was a good man. I'm not saying I sympathize with the heretics. They're mistaken. But Alzeu—. Be careful, Jerome. That's all I have to say."

"I don't even see anyone, up on my farm."

"Well, you're better off that way," said the priest. Suddenly he burst into tears. "Alzeu. He always came to Mass."

Jerome shuffled his feet uncomfortably. The old church smelled of dust balls and candlewax. Golden motes drifted in a ray of light. He didn't know what to do or say.

After a moment the old man regained control. "Well, you're not here for that," he said. "Do you want prayers for your wife?"

In the darkness the priest couldn't see his friend flush.

Jerome mumbled, "Not this time. I don't have money today."

"Money! Jerome, you don't need money. I will pray for the soul of Agnes without pay. Haven't I known you both long enough to say a prayer?"

"I would appreciate it," said Jerome quietly. "Yes. Thank you."

"Take care of yourself," said the priest, laying a hand on Jerome's shoulder.

"You too."

"Troubled times. Watch your mouth and feet, Jerome."

Jerome stepped out of the shadowed church and blinked against the blaze of sunlight. He hadn't expected such a conversation with the priest, and he was still thinking of the woodcarver, Alzeu, who only last week was arrested and burnt. Jerome did not remember his being heretic. He chewed over the news as he set off on his second task: to find his friend Bernard, with whom he generally spent the night.

Jerome liked market-day. The noise and bustle fell across his shoulders as a kind of shiver of excitement. His senses were assaulted with smells and sights and sounds—the hurry of the crowds, the voices calling out, the horsemen on their mounts, the lords parading with their retinues and women in their fine skirts and handsome headdresses, the young boys playing or flirting with the girls, and the older men sitting at the alehouses or dicing in the shade of the arcade or bowling on the grass at the edge of the square. The toothless aged sat in patches of sunlight, hands folded on their canes. There was always something to look at in the busy town. Not to mention the business of hawking, selling, buying, bartering, carrying, and loading goods. This particular day he noticed large numbers of Preaching Friars too—the black-and-white-robed Dominicans—moving among the crowd: they were everywhere.

Jerome interrupted Bernard at his counting house. The old friend was a short man with a round bald head and popping eyes. "Jerome! You're in town—welcome!" He threw one arm around Jerome's shoulder.

"Greetings," said Jerome. "It's good to see you. Can I stay with you tonight?"

"Of course. Where else would you stay?"

"I'll see you later then!" They clapped each other on the back, two boyhood friends, openly glad to see one another.

"Can you sup with me?" invited Bernard.

"Gladly. Until later, then."

At the end of the afternoon, having sold or traded most of his goods, including the two cocks, Jerome hitched the pony to his almost-empty cart and screeched over the cobblestones to Bernard's establishment—the house of a wealthy merchant. He led the horse under the arch into the courtyard and called for a servant, who ran out to welcome him, take the horse's bridle, and unlock the wooden stablegate. Jerome was as familiar with the household as the servants were with him. By the time he had stabled his horse and pulled the cart to one side out of the way, Bernard had closed up his shop at the front of the house and walked to meet him at the back.

"Bravo, Jerome. We never know when you'll decide to blow into town. Come in, come in. Ready for a drink and supper now?"

It was not until supper was over and they sat at the table with cups of wine that Jerome brought up the disturbing words he'd had with the priest. Bernard stared into the fire, nodding solemnly. "Keep your voice down. It's true; it's true."

"But Alzeu. What had he ever done?" asked Jerome.

"He knew some Good Men."

"Is that all?"

"He had the misfortune," whispered Bernard, rubbing his hands together—rubbing them until Jerome realized that he too, like the old priest, was wringing his hands—"he had the misfortune to be well off. These are dangerous times. Yes, he'd met some of the Good Men. Who knows how often?"

"*Everyone* has met a Good Christian sometime in his life."

"Yes, and we're all afraid, I tell you, Jerome. Did you hear about Jean Tisseyre?"

Jerome shook his head.

"In Toulouse. A workingman. I don't know what set him off. Someone must have made an accusation against him. He lived on the outskirts of town, and one day he got mad and took a stool and started walking through the city. Every few streets he'd step up on his stool and shout to the crowds, 'Citizens! Listen to me, citizens. I'm no heretic! I have a wife. I sleep with her. I swear oaths, I tell lies, and I'm a good Catholic. I eat meat.'"

"What was he thinking of?" Jerome said, laughing.

Bernard could hardly keep his seat; he jumped up and down, whispering and gasping out his story. "As I say, he must have felt himself accused. 'Don't believe their lies,' he yelled. Crowds gathering around him. 'We must join against them. They'll accuse you too—and you, and you, and you—as they have me. These bastards are trying to stamp us down.'"

"What happened then?"

Bernard shrugged. "The bailiffs picked him up. They threw him in prison together with some Pure Ones, and guess what? The *perfecti* converted him. He took the robe as a Good Christian and went off happily to be burnt at the stake."

"So the Dominicans got what they wanted: a heretic."

The two men sat in silence for a time.

"Are *you* safe, Bernard?" asked Jerome.

"Who knows? I was in town when Alzeu was arrested. It was the middle of the night. Two men in masks came beating on his door. One of the servants answered it and was met by the leaping shadows cast by their torches, and the terror of their masks. Scared the Devil out of the man: he can't stop talking of it, even now. Go to the alehouse; you'll hear him—how they pushed past him and up the stairs, lighting themselves up the passageway."

"Friars?" asked Jerome.

"No. Bailiffs, probably, but in the service of the Inquisition. But who knows? They wore masks.

"They dragged the poor man from his bed, still in his nightcap and gown. He had no idea what he'd done. They grabbed him by the shoulders and pushed him ahead of them down the stairs and out the door. His wife was shrieking and following them down the stairs, still in nightgown and cap. They took him to the Wall."

"The Wall." Jerome shuddered. Even the mere name of that dread prison inspired fear. It held every torture machine. Few prisoners ever left the Wall, and never whole. "And then?"

"He confessed . . . whatever he confessed." Bernard's round eyes popped even wider. He ran both hands over his bald head, as if to smooth down nonexistent hair. "Who wouldn't confess? You'd only have to show me the instruments and I'd confess—anything they asked.

"Alzeu was arrested on a Tuesday and burnt the next Saturday—this Saturday last. We all went down to see. The whole town turned out. Actually, we were ordered to go watch as a lesson to us all, but a lot of people went for fun. Jerome, I knew the man. Imagine seeing him in his nightshirt—he was burnt in his nightshirt, they took his very clothes—no reason to waste good shoes and shirt—and he stood on the pyre, hands tied at the stake behind his back, eyes wild, hair flying round his face.

"He searched the crowd with his eyes as if looking for someone, something, turning his head this way, that; and he was so scared you could see the stream of piss running down his leg, turning his gown yellow in the front, but it couldn't put out the fire that leapt up around his feet. When the flames reached him, he let out a howl to curdle milk.

"His wife was there, his widow now, skulking along the edge of the crowd, watching her husband burn, weeping and wringing her hands and not knowing if she would be picked up too, since she had consorted with the man who had consorted with a heretic."

"Don't." Jerome waved one hand and turned away.

"And the stench. Have you ever smelled burnt flesh? There's a sticky black smoke everywhere. The wind picks up the ash and lays it on your skin and you think it's Alzeu climbing onto you.

"It's all about money." Bernard leaned forward to whisper in Jerome's ear. "Of course they've taken his house, his land. He was a free artisan. He'd acquired a little place, some gold. Now they've taken everything. You're safe if you can buy your freedom again. He didn't have enough."

"What's happened to his wife?"

"She's gone back to her family in Navarre. She came from there."

"The thing is—"

"The thing is, no one is safe, Jerome." He leaned in again, voice low-ered. "*Everyone* knows a Good Christian, or has known one in the past, or knows someone who knows one. The Inquisitors can come after any of us. They're closing their net because of the treasure."

"What treasure?"

"What treasure! Why, the treasure of Montségur, man. Where have you been?"

"I don't know about the treasure." Jerome threw out his hands with an amiable smile.

Bernard leaned back in his chair, laughing. "You must be the last man on the face of the earth to hear about the treasure, then. It all hap-pened months ago. Shall I tell you about it? I think the loss of the treas-ure is what's made them so mad. They're like hornets that come out buzzing when you've hit their nest with a stick. They're flying round and round, and none of us is safe: the loss of the treasure first and then three *perfecti*."

He stepped to the door and peeped outside, then closed it quietly again. He checked each shuttered window, then reseated himself at the table, hunching his chair close to Jerome's. Behind him, the dying fire flickered in the low-ceilinged room, casting a reddish glow on the grim faces of the men.

"Speak softly now," said Bernard. "The very night has ears. You know about the siege of Montségur?"

Jerome nodded, but Bernard's voice rolled on. "How the fortress had been a monastery at first, a holy place for the heretics, and when the French laid siege to it, two hundred *perfecti* were living there, both men and women, the cream of the Church of Love, including the Cathar bish-op, and in addition there were two hundred archers, soldiers, mercenar-ies, and knights who had come to defend them. And their women too, of course. But you know about the siege, at least?"

"Go on, though. I like to hear."

"Last, the whole treasury of the Cathars lay up there in Montségur, and they say the real reason for the siege was not to burn the two hun-dred perfected heretics so much as to gain the treasure. I won't say. The siege began a year ago last May, and it lasted all the way through

February. Longer than any place has ever withstood, longer than anyone imagined it could. Here they had a whole army surrounding the foot of the mountain, and four hundred starving defenders trapped up top.

"Finally, in dead winter—this is what we've pieced together—when it was clear that the fortress couldn't hold out much longer, the heretics smuggled their treasure down the mountain and hid it somewhere. The area is riddled with caves. That was in January. The fortress held out another month, then capitulated."

"Wasn't there something about a traitor? I heard talk of that," said Jerome.

"Yes, a Basque who showed the French a pathway to climb up the cliff face. Once the French took the barbican, they were only a few hundred feet from the fortress itself. After that it was all over. The heretics surrendered."

"And burnt."

"Yes. Everyone was wounded or sick or starving. They couldn't have held out. You know the laws of war. If the French had taken the fortress, every man, woman, child, civilian or soldier, would have been slaughtered. But if they surrendered, everyone except the heretics would go free. I'm told that the perfected heretics were the ones who insisted on surrender. They agreed to die rather than have the soldiers hurt. They surrendered at Easter."

"And the treasure?"

"That's the joke. When the French marched in, they found no treasure. Gone. But they didn't discover that until they'd already burnt all the *perfecti* who might have known its whereabouts."

Jerome gave a laugh.

Bernard nodded. "You know, of course, the Pure Ones can never tell a lie. When asked if they're heretics, they have to admit it. So it was easy to corral the *perfecti* and burn them. But here's the thing that's just recently come out: the night before the French entered, apparently three of them escaped." Bernard looked at Jerome expectantly.

"Three of whom?"

"*Perfecti,*" he whispered at Jerome's blank look. "Well, don't you understand? They burnt two hundred perfected heretics. But three of them are missing. That means the heresy can still go on. Those three will baptize others and make new heretics. The Church was not stamped out."

Jerome gave a grunt of appreciation.

"I heard today that they're looking for the guide," said Bernard.

"The Basque guide?"

"Not the one who led the French up the cliff. No, the one who led away the heretics. They say there's a woman involved too, who was either the guide or knows who he is, and now the friars are out in force to find her. Maybe you saw the crowds in town. They want the treasure of course."

"And who is this guide?"

"Ah, that we don't know. They're looking for an old woman; I know no more than that. They've asked everyone to look out for her."

"And that should get a lot of women killed," said Jerome with a bitter laugh. "If I came across her, I'd have her tell me where the treasure is!"

Bernard shuddered. "Don't even joke about it. Not when they're sending artisans and merchants to the Wall." He stirred the ashes, banking the fire for the night. "No, it's bad times now. Inflation. Prices are too high. You can't buy anything. Look at the kind of produce you get in the market now. It's a disgrace, and if they caught me talking like this, I'd be arrested too. So I've not said a word tonight. I see nothing wrong with our good Catholic Church or the Dominicans cleansing us of heretics. I'd be the first to rise up publicly and say so. This war's gone on too long. It's time to get rid of heresy, go on with our lives. The sooner the heretics are disposed of, the better all round. I'm not against the cleansing. But Alzeu—"

"Poor soul," said Jerome, standing to stretch.

"And masked men breaking into our houses."

"And I'd not like to be in the shoes of an old woman now—not unless she has a family to protect her."

"And even family won't protect anyone anymore."

"Troubled times, the good priest said."

"Troubled times," repeated Bernard, handing Jerome a flare. "Good night, now. You know your room. I'll see you in the morning."

It was late afternoon of the next day when Jerome had climbed the mountain track for home, step by slow step, one hand on his pony's mane. When he'd seen the woman by the side of the road, his thoughts, far from Bernard's troubled tales, had been roaming the peaceful, light-struck hills, lambent in the angled sun, and the rise and fall of the pony's withers under his hand, and the work that waited him at home. He'd been watching his feet, the grass, the sky, in the slow, observant way of countrymen; so that when he saw the woman sitting on the bank he thought nothing of it. The words had risen to his mouth unbidden, spoken to the poor old creature as naturally as to a wounded dog.

"Do you wish a lift, Mother?"

It was only when she was seated in the cart that he'd taken note of her worn shoes, her dirty, untamed hair—and he'd turned his face away. A woman should not be seen with her hair unkempt. It was as bad as walking naked. He'd felt a twinge of irritation that she'd let herself go wild. At the same time he'd wanted to place a comforting hand on her, soothe her as he would the pony, with voice and hand, tell her things would be all right. "Whoa, there," he would croon, if she were a horse, and he'd stroke her withers and curry her a bit.

At that moment she had lifted both hands and smoothed her hair, then tied it with her kerchief, and in that practiced gesture, so smooth, efficient, and even elegant, he'd felt a shock. He'd looked up at the woman sitting on the cart, back straight and head high as she gazed across the hills, and for a second the light striking through the trees hit her fine cheekbones. She was lovely. Jerome tore his eyes away and set them firmly on the path in front of him. Who was this woman? A witch? Witches had such power over men. Yet even as he'd stepped along the dappled path beside the creaking cart he'd felt his heart lift and a smile quiver at his lips. The air seemed brighter, the colors stronger; the light flashed silver off the undersides of the wind-tossed leaves. He hadn't noticed before how good he felt.

When he'd dared to flick a look at her again, he'd seen nothing distinctive—just a nice-looking woman sitting in his cart. She had the ability to sit quietly, though, which he liked. In fact, he liked her presence there.

"How far are you going?"

"To Montségur," she had answered. He'd whistled softly and lifted his eyebrows, remembering Bernard's story of the treasure and the friars who were hunting for a woman. They'd talked idly, he and the woman, but his thoughts were sniffing the thickets of this situation, like a hunting dog that works birds in cover: if she were a witch or heretic, he should tip her out of the cart right then—except he wanted her to turn her fine eyes on him once again. No sooner thought than she'd shifted on the cart, tilted her head, and looked down into his eyes.

She was bewitching him, and he was only a simple and defenseless farmer, while she was an aristocrat—anyone could see. He'd stared, mouth open. At that moment he'd heard the hoofbeats cantering behind, and once more words had tumbled unbidden from his mouth.

"Listen carefully. My name is Jerome Ahrade. I have this pony. . . ."

And yet the words didn't surprise him. At the sound of the hooves, Jerome had felt a stubbornness fall over him like a mantle, the sullen rebelliousness of a countryman who will not be pushed aside or forced out of his slow and plodding rut. Why should the Preaching Friars get the treasure? Alzeu—Bernard—the old priest—troubled times. Well, yes; but that was in town, and here Jerome was on his own ground. He could help a defenseless old woman if he wished.

Afterward, the monks had mounted their horses and plunged down the hillside, pell-mell, hurrying after one poor peasant whom they would burn; and Jerome had taken the pony's bridle and walked steadily up the path. The woman—Jeanne—had sat quietly, and he'd been glad of that. The encounter with the friars had unnerved him badly. He needed time to think out what to do.

❖ THIRTEEN ❖

He hollows out a loaf of bread and pours the stew in it, handing me my loaf. Roots and grain with a lentil base.

"Good."

"Hmf," he answers. It is nearly dark. We eat outside, at the door. The first star glows in the globe of night.

"Are there wolves in these mountains?" I ask. Still afraid of wolves, after all these years, though I've never seen a wolf. Gobert's wolfhound, my husband's dog, was as big as a wolf or larger, with his coarse gray shaggy fur and long running legs. Loup-Baiard, he was called. My husband's dog. He protected me that whole first year of my lonely marriage, lost in a foreign chateau. Alone with my beloved Loup-Baiard, who would thrust his rough gray muzzle under my hand and nudge me for attention. Before one summer passed, Loup-Baiard belonged to me, my dog, my wolf-protecting dog. The shift of loyalty annoyed Gobert.

"They come down in the winter sometimes," says Jerome. "When the winter's hard and the snow's deep and they can't find food."

He chews his food slowly. "Stay indoors and you'll be safe."

I laugh. "Once I heard of a friar who tamed a wolf. Do you want to hear? His name was Francis; I hear he's been declared a saint. He lived in Italy. He was so holy that the birds would come eat out of his hands. One time a wolf came right into the town near where he lived—the town of Gubbio—looking for a child or chicken to eat. He'd eaten others—

children, I mean. The townsfolk wanted to kill the wolf, but the saintly man said we are not allowed by God to kill, not even a wolf."

"That's nonsense."

"No, no, this is a true story," I say. "Listen. He said he'd tame the wolf, and the next time the wolf came trotting into town, all the women ran screaming indoors and locked their children behind the wooden window shutters, and the wolf strolled through the village, turning his head this way and that."

"You do that just like a wolf." Jerome smiled his happy, gap-toothed grin.

"The townspeople gathered with pitchforks and spears and knives and nets to kill the wolf, but just then Francis stepped out. He held out his hand, and the wolf rubbed up against him like a cat, and stretched out his forepaws and knelt down in a bow."

"No! Is that true?"

"Then the holy friar took the wolf's head in his hand and told him it was wrong to eat the villagers' children and livestock and that he must stop, and that God would take care of him always. And also the townsfolk. What's wondrous: the wolf understood, and after that the wolf lived or maybe still lives in Gubbio like a dog. The townsfolk fed him as if he were a gentle dog, and never did he kill again."

"You wouldn't find folk doing that round here," says Jerome, after a minute of chewing over the tale. "Taking in a wolf." He shakes his head. "But now I remember, not long ago a man across the mountain found a wolf-pup and brought it home with him. He tamed it. It acted like a dog, and he loved it like a dog."

"Did it turn wild?"

"No. It stayed a dog," he says. "It had white eyes."

Then, because I've been thinking about Loup-Baiard, I tell another famous story in return.

"Once there was a valiant knight who had a fine, big, loyal staghound. Its name was Berenger. This dog was renowned for his gentleness with his lord and for his ferocity in the hunt. He was a king of dogs. Nothing pleased the knight so much as the fact that the dog loved him with unbounded love, and he returned that love in kind. They were inseparable, knight and dog."

"What did he look like?" Jerome asks, loving a good story.

"He was gray, with shaggy, wiry fur," I say, describing Loup-Baiard. "Big head. Strong white teeth. Ears half flopped like this. But let me get on with the tale.

"The knight married, and soon his lady gave birth to a healthy, strong son. The knight was pleased; he loved the boy. When he left his house he put the dog in charge, to guard the baby—that's how loyal that dog was, and how much the knight trusted him.

"One day the knight and his lady went hunting. They left the baby in its cradle in the garden, protected by the dog. And a wolf—!" I shoot out my claws at Jerome, who jumps, then laughs into my laughing eyes.

"A wolf came out of the forest," I continue, pleased with myself, "and you should have seen the fight that followed—fur and fury, growling and groiling—and for a time no one could tell which was stronger, the wolf or the dog, until the one was dead, and the other bleeding bitterly.

"That evening, when the knight returned with his lady, he ran up the steps and through the archway into the garden to see his fine young boy. Imagine his horror! The cradle is overturned, the bedclothes bloody, the baby gone—and up leaps the great dog, Berenger, to greet his master. His jaws are red with blood, and blood drips down his shaggy chest. With a cry the knight pulls out his sword and cuts the big dog's throat."

"Ah!"

"There." (Dropping my sword-arm.) "The huge dog fell at his master's feet, and still he tried to crawl forward to lick his master's hand. The knight pulled back. He would not touch the dog. He leaned on his sword, the tears running down his cheeks, and watched his dog die—the noble Berenger, whom he had loved and who had killed his babe.

"Then suddenly he hears a cooing in the underbrush. He looks, and what does he see?"

"His baby?"

"His baby chewing happily on his toes and gurgling to himself, and next to him the wild, dead, bloody body of a wolf."

"Ah!" groans Jerome again.

"At this moment the knight's good lady appears.

"'What have you done, my lord?' she cries.

"'I have killed my best friend,' answers he. 'I have killed a dog so noble that nothing can replace him. Alas! Ah, *ahimé.*'"

We sit in silence a moment, thinking about the dog named Berenger.

"Well, what do you think?" I ask. "It's a sad tale, isn't it?"

"That's what comes of having a sword to hand. If it had been a peasant, you know, he'd have had to go get a pitchfork from out behind the stable or find a knife to kill the dog, and by the time he'd come back he'd have found the living baby and the dead wolf."

"It's a lesson about acting in too much haste," say I, "in heat."

"On the other hand, I think anyone would have done it," says Jerome thoughtfully. "It's a sad tale, but who wouldn't kill the dog that killed your child? That's the way life is, full of blunders and mistakes. It's a nice story, though."

He thinks a while longer. "Still." His voice shakes with anger. "Who leaves a child with a dog? I fault the knight. What stupidity! Where was the wet-nurse? Or an older child to watch for it? That's what children are for, to help out, and the nobility have plenty of servants. Where were the servants?" His eyes flash.

"It's just a story." I am laughing. He looks over at me, abashed.

"It's a nice story too," he says apologetically. "I liked it. Do you know more?"

"I know a lot of stories. About the lovers Tristan and Iseult. Or Roland the knight of Charlemagne. Or I could tell you about Orpheus, who searched in hell for his wife, Euridice." Why do I want to impress him with my tales? I want him to admire me. I want to have him let me stay. "I'll tell more later," I promise.

Night has fallen, and the stars are blinking down at us. They cover the sky like grains of sand, like golden dust, so cold, so close.

"It's time for bed," says Jerome, but neither of us moves. Then: "Here's a knife," he says, pulling it from a pocket. "Cut off the cord and give it to me."

"What cord?" I feel the rush of blood to my face, the tingling of terror.

"You said you wore a heretic's cord. Give it me."

"It's not real."

"Cut it off."

I turn the knife over in my hand, feeling little waves of shock run through me. It's so long since I've held a knife. I'm moved at its shape in my hand, but how can I cut the cord that binds me to William and Guilhabert and Poitevin and Hugon? To the siege, the cave? I want to flee. I could stab Jerome right now and run. Or slip the knife under my skirts and slice into my own belly and follow the others, and suddenly the tears are coursing down my cheeks and the knife is singing in my ear its high-pitched metal siren-song, the whine of blades, because how could Jerome know what he's asking me to do?—he who never met the lovely, gentle Baiona or saw the way William would tip back on his heels or spread his ungainly large hands, lifting his copper head and laughing down at me. I could cut my own hand off. The knife wants blood. It wants to cut.

"It's all right, old girl. No reason for tears."

I'm standing inside the house now, near the fire, and Jerome has taken back the knife. How did I get here? I don't remember moving. The red eyes of the fire glitter on the hearth.

It's late.

"Come on, now. Let me cut it off."

"Cut what?"

"The cord. You said you're wearing a cord."

"What cord? What are you talking about?" I cry. "Always ready with a lie. Dirty old man, trying to get under my skirts."

"Come on, you've been standing here with the knife in your hand and bawling. It's not safe to wear it. And you know"—he speaks in the gentle, wheedling tone he would use to a wounded animal—"your friends wouldn't want to see you hurt. Or me either. It's dangerous for me too."

I remember now. He's right, of course. I look around me absently. What am I doing in this house? Everything looks strange and unfamiliar, but this farmer is standing foursquare in front of me, steady as a rock, watching with the patience of a countryman.

He holds out the knife again.

"Or untie it if you don't want it cut. Then hand it over to me. I'll keep it safe until you leave."

"Turn your back."

"I won't look."

I take the knife, reach under my skirts, and cut the string that I wear at my waist. After a moment I hand it to him. So easy. It seemed so easy with him nearby.

Sophy Burnham

"It's wool," he observes irrelevantly. "Not even white. Now, no more about the heretics and all your fantasies. Whatever happened to you is done and finished long ago. Come on. Stop shaking now. There, there. It's time for bed."

He eases me into the storeroom and lights me to my bed with the little oil lamp.

"Tomorrow we'll have to figure out what to do about you."

"I'll move on."

"Not without putting me in prison," he murmurs, covering me with my cloak. All his moves are soft and thoughtful. "It was a foolish thing I did, to call you my woman. Just blurted out. It means you'll have to stay a while."

"Well, I'll stay a day or two, no more."

"I'll think out what we tell the neighbors. Sleep well."

He drifts away. I lie there thinking. He doesn't know that tucked in my skirt is something more dangerous than the imitation cord, which was only a fantastical fantasy, a make-believe. Underneath my skirts rests the precious Word of God, and if that were found it would send us both to the stake.

In the beginning was the Word, and the Word was with God, and the Word was God. He was in the beginning with God; all things were made through Him. . . .

That night my dreams are of being chased, and I am running eternally, a stag before the hunter's spears, antlers high, and terrified because I've lost the treasure, and in the dream I'm hunting for it before the others find it first.

◧ FOURTEEN ◧

It took two days to walk to Montségur, and by the end of that first day, she was entranced, despite the disapproval of Esclarmonde. What an adventure! She'd never been so far from home, and she could hardly stop looking at the beauty of the landscape: the wind rippling a field of wheat, the silver olive trees shivering as they waved the undersides of their thin leaves. Were they praying too? Clapping their little hands? There were moments when she'd be trudging along, look up, and see the snowcapped mountains in the distance, and the beauty would take her breath away.

On that long walk, Esclarmonde and Ealaine told her about Guilhabert de Castres, bishop of the Cathar Church. Rumor had it that the bishop was so holy that he did not need to sleep. They said he had lived in a cave for twelve years as a hermit, and in that time had never spoken, though he'd met with God Himself. Later, after he returned from his isolation, it was so hard for him to enter ordinary life that he wept constantly. People were afraid his eyes would fall out from the abundance of his tears. But gradually the weeping stopped, and gradually he took his place at the forefront of the Cathar Church. Esclarmonde said he never ate even now. Food hadn't passed his lips in eight long years.

Once a knight met him on the road. The knight leapt from his horse and made *adoratio,* and when the bishop had walked on, the knight turned to his squire: "I would rather be that man than anyone on earth," he said.

The bishop was a small man with tiny, well-shaped hands and feet, they told her, but he was so powerful that when he walked the crowd parted before him, in respect, as if he emitted an invisible bow-wave: people stepped back. He bowed to left and right, smiling joyous blessings to everyone as he walked. People wanted to throw themselves at his feet. He had an air, said Esclarmonde, of such gentle kindness, such jolly, warm-hearted happiness, that when you met him, you felt he had been waiting all his life to meet and talk to you: how happy your presence made him!

"It's his smile," said Ealaine, "and his shining eyes."

"It's his love," added Esclarmonde.

But what truly set him apart, they agreed, were his visions—what he called his Knowings and Showings. His exquisite intuition could pierce the veil that covers the invisible. Because of this gift he had asked the knight Raymond de Perella to donate Montségur to the Cause and then to rebuild and fortify it: apparently he knew something about Montségur that others didn't know.

"What?" I asked.

"We don't know; he will not say. He knows *something*, though. You'll be surprised when you see the fortress."

But nothing prepared Jeanne for that first view of the mountain sticking straight up from the plain like a thumb. Or the fortress perched stonily on its peak, or, once they had climbed to the height and arrived—breathless at the top of the *pog*—to see that colossal wooden gate built into the surrounding wall. The gate was so large that two smaller portals had been cut into it—one large enough for a loaded haywagon (if such a vehicle could climb the twisting path), a smaller one that was only large enough to let a single person through on foot; and both were set within that formidable, monumental gate: the work of giants, it seemed. A short distance away, the cliff face fell twelve hundred meters straight down to the valley floor.

This was Montségur. The "Safe Mountain," impregnable.

The three women had climbed up the winding path alone, leaving the guards below. They had pulled themselves over up the path, sometimes holding on to the scrawny pines and boxwood trees that grew every-where and that filled their nostrils with the acrid scent of pine—and of boxwood—the same odor (Jeanne thought) as in the castle maze. The woods sent out tangled roots that twisted and writhed across the boulders, thick as snakes and just as ready to whip around her feet. Jeanne had had to watch each footfall as she climbed.

Now, though, they stood before the fortress, catching their breath, chests heaving, and surveying their surroundings.

Every foot of land here at the top of the mountain, under the fortress walls, was terraced or cultivated, every outcropping of rock amidst the numerous wooden or stone huts sprouted herbs or edible vegetation.

"Who lives in those?" Jeanne asked, pointing to the huts, some no more than shallow caves, a partial bricked-up wall built around a jutting rock.

"The *perfecti*," answered Esclarmonde. "The fortress can't hold everyone. Some are hermits, some more companionable."

Jeanne looked about her in dismay. The huts leaned like children against the fortress wall or bulged or burst dangerously out into the sky from their precarious perches on the cliff. And everyone was old—old men, old women—and they were all dressed in their perfect black. She wanted to throw herself at Esclarmonde's feet and beg forgiveness, but the older woman was already stepping through the open gate.

"Come. Let's get you settled with the bishop," said Esclarmonde.

Jeanne cast one last horrified look about her and saw a workman grinning at her openly. He wore a leather jacket and leaned on his crowbar, a blue-eyed man with copper hair, not yet perfected, clearly. Jeanne tossed her head disdainfully and looked away, but as she followed the two women through the fortress gate, she slyly managed to shift and look back over her shoulder. He was still watching her. Her eyes flicked over him coldly—up, down, swiftly—before she entered the castle courtyard.

The following day Esclarmonde and Ealaine bade her farewell and made their way down the steep incline, while Jeanne stood, hands dangling and tears pouring down her cheeks at being abandoned here among the ancient Pure Ones.

"Don't go, don't go." She thought her heart would break, and shatter, and spill down the cliff face after them like so many pebbles, and afterward, when she could not see them anymore, she ran partway down the path and flung herself to the earth, sobbing with deep, gasping cries of loneliness and loss.

To her surprise, as the days passed, Jeanne grew happy. She lived in a cramped stone hut with an old, old lady, Marquésia de Forli, already in her eighties, and she may as well have been a thousand years old in Jeanne's eyes, for over her parchment skin lay a network of wrinkles and grooves as fine as the veins of a leaf and as fragile as her wispy smile; her hands were mottled with liverspots, and her eyelids drooped until Jeanne wondered how she had space between the skin to see. Her *socia* had died. Jeanne prepared her food, ran errands, helped her to the latrine, and walked her where she needed to go.

Here was Jeanne's day, as ordered by Bishop Guilhabert de Castres:

Rise at first light, with the pearl shadows opening up the valleys below. She staggered sleepily to the doorway of her stone hut to greet and praise the day. *Hello! Thank you for coming! What a good day you will be!* And, dutifully: *Lord God, this day is Yours.* She washed her hands in a earthen pot, brushed her teeth with a shaggy twig, dressed, and helped her old lady wash and dress. They went together to the meditation hall, her companion lurching on her cane. There almost everyone except the cooks sat in silence for an hour. Sometimes Jeanne squirmed in boredom. Sometimes she dozed and snapped awake. Or sometimes she slyly played with the shadows that her fingers flashed on the floors or wall. Occasionally, though, she felt great happiness, and as the summer progressed she began to look forward to this time alone with her own thoughts.

Later still, William—now she had a name to put to the man with copper hair—began to attend sporadically as well, and then she found pleasure merely in watching him (when he deigned to come), allowing her eyes to caress the curve of his throat or the spread of his awkward hands on craggy knees. Yes, she came to like this quiet time.

After breakfast, she settled to her studies with one of the perfected women. Jeanne already knew how to read and write both in Latin and her native tongue; she had studied grammar and rhetoric as well. She'd heard that in Paris the scholars also studied dialectic, or the art of logic and reasoning. But that was too advanced for her. Instead, de Castres—Bishop Berto, as she called him—had her copy and memorize long passages from the Good Book. He set her mathematical problems too, and he had her practice composing on the mandolin (at which she showed little talent).

On other mornings she learned to write in different styles—a business letter, a diplomatic letter, a courtly letter, a letter of condolence.

At home with the Lady Esclarmonde in Foix or Pamiers, her afternoons had been spent in the woman's duties of preparing herbs or else in learning embroidery and all the fine points of stitchery, practiced often while someone read aloud from scripture (and then her body would twist and squirm, longing to run outdoors) or French romances (to which she listened raptly); but at Montségur her afternoons were free, for the Lady Marquésia wanted to nap or spend her hours in prayer.

In the evenings Jeanne cooked her charge a gruel for supper, then helped her eat and afterward prepare for sleep. She was a good old lady, and Jeanne grew fond of her. But it was de Castres whom she came to love. Everything that Esclarmonde and Ealaine had said about him was true.

Each night she met with the bishop in the little stone cave that he shared with his *socius*, Bertrand Marty. Sometimes Marty was present, sometimes not. Jeanne would sit at the old man's feet, and he would give the young girl his total attention, leaning forward in his seat and watching her with approving eyes. He was in his forties then, in powerful mid-life, a tiny balding man, and no topic seemed forbidden her (though she didn't always get an answer to questions she raised).

"Is it true that you never eat?" she asked one day.

"I eat all the time," he responded. "I eat the air and the spiritual food of Christ."

"No, but they say no food—no real food—has passed your lips for eight years now."

"Ah, do they? And who might *they* be?" He laughed deep in his throat, his tiny body shaking with amusement.

"The Lady Esclarmonde and her *socia*, Ealaine."

"Well, well, what people will think to gossip about."

Nevertheless, Jeanne never saw him put so much as a berry on his tongue, and yet he was strong and wiry and hard and tough. He could walk for days, she knew, and could outstrip younger men at many physical tasks.

He knew everything. If she caught a butterfly in the field, he could tell its life history. He knew the cures that different plants could bring. He knew his Bible. He could sing and make people laugh.

He knew about boys as well, and the heart of girls, so that one day Jeanne found herself pouring out her shame and rage at Rogert, and her confused feelings about Baiona. He listened, nodding occasionally but saying only, "Yes."

The next day he told her that she was to speak at the weekly public confession, the *aparelhamentum*.

"I will not!" she cried. "I've confessed to you and to Esclarmonde both. I won't do it publicly."

"It's the only way to wipe away the shame," he said.

"Well, that's your way. I don't want to be perfected. I don't have to."

"In that case, for two straight weeks you must spend one quarter-hour every day in prayer for Baiona."

"No!"

"Here is how you do it," he continued, as if she had not spoken. "You draw Baiona's image up before your eyes—"

"I hate her."

"No matter," he said, laughing affectionately. "It has nothing to do with how you feel about her. In your imagination you are to lay at her feet everything you've ever wanted for yourself—goods, clothes, jewels and baubles, anything, your missing mother and father, Rogert and all the other boys, the victory wreath. You give her a happy marriage, love, children, wealth. You give her qualities and virtues too. Bestow upon her beauty, insight, honesty, tolerance, patience, sweetness of nature, courage, love and happiness, an understanding heart. Whatever you would like for yourself, offer it to her.

"Then give Baiona whatever you know she wants. She has artistic talent, you say; so give her lapis and crushed gold for paints, a paintboy to grind the colors for her or prepare her brushes. That's what forgiveness means—to 'give for.'

"'Give what?' you ask. Give everything."

"I can't do that." Jeanne pulled back her long black hair with both hands and plaited it into a stubborn braid. She would not do this thing he asked.

"Yes, you can," he answered gravely. "It's the only way to set yourself free."

"I hate her." She leaned forward passionately.

"Exactly. And if you won't confess it publicly—"

"I'll say that publicly," she said. "I'll stand up and tell everyone what she did. That I hate her."

"No, Jeanne. It's your own failings that you must confess, and if you're not ready for that, then try this other way. I promise you you'll like the result."

The first day Jeanne beat and battered Baiona's image instead of praying for her. She told the bishop what she'd done. She could not do his exercise.

"Ah. You are very angry with her?"

"Yes."

"And with what else?" he prompted.

"With everything. I'm angry at Rogert. At Esclarmonde for leaving me here. At myself. I'm angry at being a girl!" she shouted; and he did not even blink, but nodded, sweetly watching. "I'm angry at this ugly place. And you. I'm really angry at you!"

"And God?" he asked gently. "Are you not also angry at God?"

"Yes. I'm angry at God."

"Good," he said. "That's good."

Instantly her anger was gone.

"What?" She was startled. All he'd said was "good," and all her passion had vanished.

She searched his face. "What did you just do?"

But he only smiled and told her to run along.

It was not easy to forgive Baiona. Her anger and shame did not instantly disappear.

"God doesn't ask it all to be done at once, but only that we be willing," the bishop said. "It's enough to try. If the intention is there, then all the forces of a spiritual universe will help you reach your goal. I'm proud of you. You're doing very well."

Such sweet words. Jeanne felt herself expand under his approval, the ice melting in her heart.

I will sprinkle clean water upon you, she copied in her careful hand. *A new heart I will give you. And a new spirit I will put within you; I will take out of your flesh the heart of stone. . . .*

From that day on, to her surprise, she no longer wanted to hurt Baiona, and within a few days it even pleased her to bestow on Baiona all the things she liked herself; and later still she felt as happy as if she were receiving the blessings and gifts herself, so that she was the one to gain.

"Is that true?" she asked de Castres one night.

"Good for you." He smiled into her eyes. "You've found the art of happiness. Love your neighbor, not because it's a rule or right, but because it's the law of the spiritual universe. It's what Jesus was teaching us. Many people don't understand why they should follow the Way. They think it's in order to become holy in some way, or to get to heaven; when in fact it's only in order to be happy now, at this moment—free of hatred, anger, indecision, fear."

"Free."

"Now you are to pray for yourself," he ordered.

"Myself?"

"Pray to forgive yourself." Which she did until one day to her surprise she voluntarily found herself rising to confess at the public *aparelhamentum*. She spoke not of her lust for Rogert, or precisely what she'd done with him, but of her willfulness, her refusal to listen to her betters, which had led to her jealousy and the hatred she had harbored in her heart and that she now saw prevented happiness; the confession ended with her decision to try in the future to self-correct.

Such were the teachings of the Cathar bishop Guilhabert de Castres, who also told her to wander if she wished, explore the area.

"Anywhere? To the village down the mountain?"

"I think so. Everyone knows that you're under my protection. Just don't get lost."

"You mean I can go alone on the mountain?" In all her life Jeanne had rarely been alone, and certainly not to walk on wooded paths. "Aren't there bears?" she asked uncertainly. "Wild animals?"

He laughed. "I'd be more worried about the wild animals meeting you!" he teased. "Stay close to the fortress until you feel comfortable. Or take someone with you if you wish."

"But who? Wouldn't it be against the rules for one of the *perfecti* to accompany me?"

"Take the English soldier, William. I'll speak to him. Then you won't have to worry about bears and wolves."

It was the bishop who told Jeanne the story of the wolf of Gubbio. The friar in the tale wasn't Cathar, but he was a true lover of Christ nonethe-less—perhaps the finest example of the holy Mother Church. Like the *perfecti,* he too had taken a vow of poverty, wore a rough brown habit and donned sandals on bare feet. And when he held out his hand, cupped with love, the wolf had knelt down in a bow.

Jeanne held her breath, imagining such a thing. "Is that true?"

"Absolutely true. And the townsfolk fed him as if he were a gentle dog."

Jeanne thought for a moment. "I don't think I could do that if I met a wolf," she concluded.

"No," he agreed, laughing. "But you shan't meet a wolf. I guarantee it."

"How can you guarantee it? Do you have power over the wild animals on the mountain too?"

"It's not the season for hungry wolves," he said. "All you have to do is to be careful. Carry a stick. If you see a bear, back away slowly. Be con-tained in your own love, and do not disturb it."

"Will I be able to tame a wolf someday?"

"If you learn what I am teaching you. If you so turn your attention to the love of God that you become the vessel of pure love. For love is God, as God is love. That is what we're all learning to do here, Jeanne: to love. The wolf of Gubbio felt that holy spirit's love. That's the first lesson I'm trying to teach you, Jeanne—how to love—in order that you don't need someone else's power to make you whole."

"Was that what Francis did? Became like God?"

"Yes, he is so loving, has so much love pouring through him, that there is no distinction between the man and God."

With one finger she traced the pattern in a stone. "Are you that way?" she asked boldly. "Like Francis, with no distinction from God?"

He rocked back with a laugh. "Me! Oh, no! I'm only this far on the Way." He held up his thumb and finger, almost touching. "I'm the least of the sons of God. But I know that my business is to give thanks and praise for every moment of this life. It's to love as fully as I can. It's to be happy. It's to practice being kind."

"Even to the French? The Pope? The enemy? Do you pray for them?"

"Yes, I pray for my so-called enemies. I pray that they too may be happy. Now go away and think about these things."

Jeanne wondered what he would do if he knew what she actually thought about—matters far less godly. But at the door he called her back.

"Jeanne."

"Yes?"

His face was in shadow, his voice a disembodied hollow sound. "As you explore, mark every path and shrub and rock and stone. There will come a time—" He stopped abruptly.

"What?"

"No, nothing. Go on now, child." Jeanne blinked. His voice was his own again, and to her surprise she could once more see him seated in his cave. What had happened? She slipped away, trailing her fingers over the rocks and laughing to herself, shaking her head in wonderment at a bishop who could disappear at will. And at what the Lady Esclarmonde would say if she knew how her orphan was passing her days, roaming the open fields, or that she'd fallen in love again, this time with an Englishman fifteen years older than she.

❖ FIFTEEN ❖

Who can tell the tortuous ways of God? Or even if there *is* a God? Occasionally on a cloudless night Jeanne would stand on the highest parapet at Montségur, marveling at the myriad stars that filled the dome of night. *What is it all about?* she wondered, and sometimes, *Who am I? Why am I here?*

That was the summer that they found the cave, the same summer that she was banished from her home after a boy took her into the boxwood maze, itself a kind of cave, the same summer that she fell in love; and later a treasure would be hidden in the cave (but she didn't know this yet) and people would be hunted, killed—and all because of the lust of an olive-skinned boy with lazy, hooded eyes and a girl who in passion drowned her best friend's dress. *Are You there, God? Show Yourself!* she'd think, staring upward at the stars. Was everything already preordained?

Then there was William, blue-eyed and light complected.

As a lad, William had ridden with a party of English knights to Jerusalem and fought the Saracens on the hot, white desert sands. He had seen Paris and Rome on the way to the Holy Land, and on his return he had landed by ship at the water-city of Venice, where he'd watched as dockworkers had lifted his kicking warhorse out of the ship with a sling under its belly, himself a rich man then, he told her, with armor and weapons and money from the war, before he was set on by brigands in the countryside, who stripped him of everything, including his expensive

horse, and left him as destitute as the hermits whom he ended up with
here at Montségur. Helping with the fortifications, he'd learned to speak
Occitan. Jeanne listened to his tales, enthralled.

They scrambled down the slippery hills on paths so steep that at times
they had to hang on to the branches of the trees to keep from falling, and
more than once William grabbed for Jeanne when she fell. They fished
with their hands in the icy, gushing rivers and set small snares for the animals that William cooked and ate (being no believer himself, and scorn-
ing the ascetic vegetarian diet). They clambered over mossy rocks, and
when the thickets grew too tangled to pass, Jeanne took off her shoes and
stockings, belted her skirts, and, laughing, ducked under the hanging
brush, wading up the bubbling streams, the laughing water-paths.

Never had she been so happy, so tomboy free.

"Why don't you come to the morning prayers?" she asked William
one day.

"I don't believe in God."

"Don't believe!" She was taken aback.

"I don't believe in heaven, or in hell either," said William seriously,
"unless it's here on earth. I think heaven rests in our happiness, and hell
lies also in our hearts. I've seen hell on earth. I saw it in the Holy Land
when we were fighting. No, not for me the ascetic ways of the Friends
of God."

"Oh, William, you are wrong. How can you dare? But I will pray for
your eternal soul. I'll pray that you turn to God, because otherwise you
will rot in damnation forever and ever. Of course there's God, for didn't
Christ tell us so? How could you not believe?"

They argued for hours. Jeanne found their discussions frightening, but
also thrilling. Never had she met anyone who cared so little for his soul,
his future life. And yet he was a man of principle.

"I lost my faith in the Holy Land," he explained, "fighting for the one
True Church. I think it's only mumbo-jumbo priesthood now."

"Don't say that, William; don't. You must listen to Guilhabert de
Castres when he preaches. He'll tell you what is true. He's a holy man, an
incarnation of the Christ."

"And so, little Jeanne, you believe?"

"Of *course* I believe. I want to be good. I wish I were good. I'm not good. They say we are spiritual beings living in bodies of decaying physical matter. Well, if I'm a fallen angel, I've brought nothing but disappointment. Still, I'd like to be good. Baiona is good. But, William, you must try to believe. Promise me that you'll believe."

Had it not been for a rainstorm that day, they never would have found the cave. A summer squall sent them running to the shelter of an overhanging crag that jutted from the grassy hill. They were miles from Montségur, in an area of spurs and cliffs. Jeanne crouched against the cold stone, her skin tingling at the warmth of William's arm pressing against her own. Beyond the fine, thin slashing rain the black storm-clouds surged and rolled across a uniform gray sky, but Jeanne trembled, more alive than she had ever felt. She wondered if he touched her on purpose—was he aware of her? Or did the cramped space force him to press against her breast? She didn't dare to move. The rain slashed down, then gradually stopped; the last big, scattered drops sprayed across them, catching the light and glancing off the thrashed and beaten thick wet grass. Above them the cloud-scudding sky opened into patches of blue.

Suddenly William said, "Wait."

"What?"

"Do you feel that wind?" he asked.

"No. Where?"

"Here, from the rocks behind us." He turned slightly and surveyed the slope behind them. "Look, there's a hole, and a wind blowing right out of it." Two tall boulders leaned like sentinels against each other, and between them a crevice opened into the earth. William moved a bit farther down-slope into the long grass and dug at the base of the rocks with his bare hands (blue eyes flashing up at her in his excitement) until he'd increased the crack into a sizable hole.

He stood up slowly, marveling. "It's a cave," he exclaimed. "Look how deep it goes."

Jeanne peered at the mouth of the earth—a slit, a yawn of darkness. "Is it an animal den?" she asked.

He laughed with delight. "No. I'm going in."

Crouching, he twisted sideways and squeezed into the hole. "Come on."

"William!" She protested, but she followed timidly, tugging at her dress when it caught her knees.

The floor pitched steeply downward almost at once. She groped forward after him, step by step into the dark, bent double, almost crawling into this, the maw of the earth.

"Look, it gets bigger and bigger. It's large enough to stand. By Saint Martin! It's huge."

"It's the pit to hell, William. William, let's leave it alone."

But William left nothing alone. "It goes back so far."

Groping, one hand against the rock wall, he disappeared into the dark. "It's getting larger. It's enormous," he reported, his voice sounding distant.

"It's late. Come away, William." *Enter the caves of the rocks and the holes of the ground,* said the prophet Isaiah. *Hide from the terror of the Lord, when he rises to terrify the earth.* She was terrified.

"You're right." His voice echoing in the dark. He appeared then beside her, pushing her toward the sliver of light at the entryway. "We'll come back with torches and ropes. A cave, Jeanne! Think!"

Jeanne thought it less marvelous than he. She followed him slowly home across the wet fields, head down, silent. She was remembering with a confusion of emotions her fear of the cold dark earth, a burial grave, and the warm touch of his shoulder pressed on hers.

William could talk only of his discovery.

A week later they returned with flint and a torch and wiggled through the black slit in the rock. Instantly she was hit by a stale, moist smell, the horror of silent dirt, enclosed.

"I don't like it." The torch cast huge flickering shadows on the walls. "William, let's go back."

"Hold the torch."

Suddenly around them rose a black wave of twittering, squeaking, flapping, small, black forms as thick as flies—but bigger—a curl of demons, peeling chaotically off the walls. She screamed and scrambled back through the entry. Outside, she tumbled full-length to the ground, hands over her head, while the bats swept past her—hundreds, thousands of swirling black forms swooping out into the light, where they whirled and circled, madly cheeping. The sky was black with them. William threw himself on top of her, arms shielding her.

And suddenly they were gone.

His face brushed her cheek. Slowly he came to his knees. "Are you all right?"

"They're demons. From the entryway to hell."

He laughed, pulling her to her knees and stroking her hair. "Dear Jeanne. They're bats. Don't be afraid."

"I am." Clinging to him. "And so should you be too."

"By the Virgin, they scared me as well," he said, and then he kissed her. A spark flew off his lips—she felt it burn into her soul; but the kiss was so swift and shy that he had already pulled away—jumped to his feet—before she understood. She stood up then, looking after him dumbly as he hurried toward the cave.

"William?"

"No. Don't look like that. We're friends, aren't we? Aren't we friends?"

"Friends. Yes."

"I promised the bishop I'd take care of you. Come on, our cave is beckoning."

He thinks I'm a child, she thought. She crept into the cave after him, while he felt for the dropped torch. He rekindled the flame, and again their shadows shot up before and after them, looming against the frightening walls.

"I'm afraid," she whispered.

"Hush. It's just a cave."

Against her will they descended into a kind of groaning stillness. The floor beneath them was smooth, and the walls, where the torch shot light, were colored in various tones of ochre, gray, and green. From a distance came the plink of water falling, its echo clear in that tomblike heaviness— and then they made a turn and saw the paintings on the walls.

"Look!"

The paintings were black and red against the ochre walls, and the colors were burnt into the stone: images of antlered deer and long-horned oxen that fled before stick-figured hunters hurling their spears. In the flickering torchlight the legs of the animals quivered, so that they appeared to race eternally, heads lifted in perpetual flight before the lifted spears.

"Look, a stag. A bull. But what is that animal?"

"Who painted them?"

"Some men or gods." He roamed the chamber curiously.

She shivered. "The torch is burning low."

"Look there. And there."

"Be careful, William."

"Jeanne, we've found a place no one has ever seen—not since the beginning of time, not since these ancient paintings were done. It's *our* cave, Jeanne. We've found a place no one knows about." He could barely contain his excitement.

They climbed back up to the secret entry. "We mustn't tell a soul—our secret," and he thrust once more into the sparkling air, where Jeanne threw herself laughing with relief onto the shining, warm, sweet-scented grass and William grabbed her in his joy: "Look at you, dirt in your hair."

"You should see yourself," she answered, tussling with him, until she stopped. He lay on top of her, his breath hot on her cheek, and this time it was she who leaned forward, upward, to draw him to her with a kiss that this time held and softened, their lips lingering, exploring tenderly, parting tentatively, indecisive, then returning to drink once more, until slowly they untangled. That was their second kiss. He was slower this second time to push away, and seemed almost drunken when he murmured, "No."

He pushed unsteadily to his feet. "No," he repeated. "I can't do this."

So now she had two kisses to dream about, and questions of why he did not desire more—though it was no mystery, Jeanne felt: she was young and undesirable. Hadn't Rogert demonstrated that?

One day William reached out to finger her black hair as it flowed down her back; and on another afternoon—"Wait!"—he pushed a stray curl back under her cap. She trembled under his touch, but he turned away impatiently—and this was what she noticed most, his new impatience with her, his short temper. They never returned to the cave.

William became absorbed with the engineering of the barbican, and that day was the last that they explored together.

Suddenly he had no time for her. Her heart hurt. It was like an animal gnawing at her from inside. It was a rag twisting in her chest. She lost her appetite. She wandered the mountaintop listlessly. Alone.

But Jeanne decided if she had learned anything from Rogert, it was to treasure privacy, her secret honor. She would confide in no one; and no one would see her distress—not William, not her dear old lady, Marquésia de Forli, not even the wise Guilhabert de Castres.

A week after their second trip to the cave (a week after their kiss) the bishop called her to him

"My child." He lifted her chin fondly. "I'm sorry to tell you that your visit is over. You will be leaving in two more days."

"No!"

He smiled. "The Lady Esclarmonde has called you back to her. She's sending a man to take you to Pamiers. Don't look like that, dear soul—well, my goodness, tears. I'm glad you've liked it here so much. I didn't think there was so much here for a young girl like you. There, there, now. You'll come back."

But Jeanne did not explain her rush of tears.

"I truly didn't know you cared so deeply. But do not fret. I think you'll like it back home too. Life has many surprises for us. Perhaps Esclarmonde has one in mind for you." He smiled so sweetly that she pulled herself together.

"Bishop," she asked him shyly, ducking her head, not daring to look at him, "what if a man does not like a maid?" She could feel a blush rising in her throat. And quickly then, because it seemed too close to the bone, she added, "I mean, what if they choose a husband for me who does not find me pleasing? It happens, doesn't it? That a man might not like a particular girl?"

"Look at you blush," he laughed. "How could any man not like you?" He smiled into her eyes. "The passionate, fierce, fiery soul of God."

She did not believe him, but she repeated the words to herself: *passionate, fierce, fiery soul of God*. And the most important part: *How could any man not like you?*

That evening Jeanne brushed her hair and bound it intricately. She put on her single good dress, though it was barely more presentable than her everyday garb. She slapped her cheeks and bit her lips to make them red, and then stared at her image in the hazy steel clasps of a leather-bound Bible.

After supper, she found William. She took him by the hand.

"Come walk with me. I have news."

They climbed the parapet and leaned against a crenellated wall, and the stars shone like lanterns out of the black night, and her heart thudded so fast she could hardly breathe.

"I go home in two days," she said finally.

"So that's why you're all dressed up." Teasing, as usual.

"Did you notice?"

"Of course I noticed. You look very pretty."

"Come to Pamiers." Her imminent departure gave her courage. "Come meet the Lady Esclarmonde." And marry me, she wanted to add, though propriety forbade the words.

He tipped back on his heels, looking down at her. "Jeanne, Jeanne. Don't tempt me. You need a different man."

"I need the man I want," she said fiercely.

He grew grave then. "Maybe I will come to see you in Pamiers."

"Don't treat me like a child. I'm not a child."

"We've had a good time," he said slowly. "But you have to understand: you need a rich husband, and I need a woman of property. I'm too poor . . . too poor for little Jeanne. You need someone who can support you properly."

"You don't like me? You don't think me pretty?" She meant desirable. She didn't know the word.

"I think you're beautiful."

He kissed her then for the third time, and this time he held her, whispering in her ear. What was he saying? His voice was too low to catch his meaning. Except his last words, as he pushed her away, were, "We're just friends."

Alone that night, she wept silently in her lonely bed.

At Pamiers the Lady Esclarmonde welcomed Jeanne home joyfully, exclaiming at how brown she looked.

"You've grown," said Ealaine, her *socia,* who stood beaming to one side.

"I knew the bishop would be good for you," said Esclarmonde. "He says you should continue your studies. That you're a good student. We're all proud of you."

Jeanne had no time to answer, for at that moment Baiona came running across the courtyard. "Jeanne! Jeanne!" She threw her arms around
her friend. "My other heart, soul of my soul, Jeanne." Both girls were
laughing and hanging on each other's necks.

Baiona had grown a full head taller and had fleshed out. "I love you,
Jeanne," she said. "I've missed you so."

"I love you too. Oh, Baiona, I'm so sorry." She stroked Baiona's hair
and hugged her tight, breathing in her sweet scent.

Then other girls spilled out to surround Jeanne and lead her into the
palace, where she heard the latest gossip, including that Rogert had been
banished for his promiscuity to his uncle's estate near Lyon, and she
learned who was pregnant and who was having marital or romantic difficulties, and true to her word Jeanne said not a word about William or the
cave with its strange pictures of fleeing, horned beasts or about the love
that burnt inside her all the time.

A week later, Esclarmonde announced her marriage had been
arranged.

◼ SIXTEEN ◼

J wake up with a start. Where am I? My heart pounding. I dreamed I was sailing in a boat with purple sails and silver lines. Suddenly the wind shifted, blowing to the back, behind the sail, which slammed over, jibing the boat, and we are no longer plowing the green seas but sinking. I am sinking.

At first I don't know where I am, groping blindly in the pitch dark, and then I remember the storeroom. Jerome. The house. I'm trapped. I stumble past his sleeping form, feel my way in the dark to the door and out into the night, where the violent, wavering stars are fading now, and where the demons that attack me will also flee, soon. Soon.

My hair is loose, no headdress. Gray hair streaked with black and flying wild around my face. Sticking out every which way. I smooth it with both hands, and it springs up again like a wild animal. Hair with a will of its own.

Once I had beautiful hair. Raven-black curls pouring down my back, and when I ran, my hair lifted and slapped against my shoulders like a horse's mane. When I ran through the meadows. Long grass up to my knees. Now my knees hurt. Old horse.

"Surrender everything to God," Esclarmonde used to say, "for *He will cover you with His pinions, and under His wings you will find refuge; His faithfulness is a shield and buckler. You will not fear the terror of the night nor the arrow that flies by day, nor the pestilence . . . nor the destruction. . . .*"

I mouth the hopeful words, although the psalm did not keep the others safe. *He will cover you with His pinions.* Was He with me all the time, and I never noticed it? Was I so stubborn that I couldn't let God do His work? For surely I was willful, yes, and determined to have my way.

"Don't send me away." She clung to the Lady Esclarmonde. The full weight of the impending marriage had sunk in, the banishment yet again from this house of peace and piety. She wept uncontrollably.

"There, there, my darling." Esclarmonde stroked her hair.

"I don't want to marry him."

"I know, I know."

"How can you know?"

"But, darling, God will always be with you. And I will too. I'll write to you faithfully. You'll visit often."

"But why? Why do I have to marry?" It came out as a wail.

The Lady Esclarmonde pulled back to look Jeanne full in her face. "Darling, listen. Gobert of Preixan is an accomplished knight, with his own lands. You will be mistress of your own place, mother of your own children. Moreover, he is Catholic. That will also protect you. You are an impetuous, impulsive girl. I want you safe. You won't forget our ways. If you can go under the fold of the Catholic Church, I won't worry about you. Finally, you love to ride and hunt, walk miles outdoors, work a falcon on your wrist—and that way of life can be yours with Gobert."

Esclarmonde smiled mischievously. "I know how you spent your summer at Montségur," she added.

"You do?"

"Exploring the countryside with some wild Englishman."

Jeanne felt the flush creep up her neck.

Esclarmonde laughed. "The bishop told me."

"Was he disappointed in me?" She picked at her fingernail, hesitant to ask; she wanted his approval.

"I think in his eyes you can do no wrong. It was Guilhabert who heard that Gobert was looking for a wife and helped me settle on the dowry.

It's an excellent match. And then, who knows, there may come a time when we need you in the Catholic camp."

But Jeanne was not consoled. Poor little girl. Defiant, angry child. First, she searched out the astrologers and paid them money to tell about her love, but since she knew neither his birthday nor his place of birth, they could not help. One day she heard two castle maids talking of the witch who lived in the lower town, and she grabbed her serving girl, Marie, and twisted the skin at the back of her arm until she squealed and told the name of the witch and where she lived and what she did.

Was she brave or merely stupid? I look back across the years, trying to fit myself into the skin of that rebellious girl. Wanting what she wanted, determined to get her way.

She waited, that younger me, for market-day.

"I need ribbons, Marie," she announced. "I must have ribbons for my wedding linens. Get your things. We're going now. I want to trim the edges with bright ribbons, red or yellow perhaps. Hurry up. If you're not ready, I'll go ahead."

"No, miss." She bobs a curtsey. "I'll be right there. It's not right for a lady affianced to go alone." Though why not, if she could roam the fields of Montségur when not yet even betrothed. Jeanne laughed to herself, remembering; but she was a child no longer, but a woman, wearing a woman's headdress and the betroyal rings, and she paced quietly beside Marie until—

"Oh, Marie, I've lost my glove. I must have dropped it when we stopped in church. Run back and bring it to me. I'll wait here."

Marie ran to do her bidding, and the moment she was out of sight Jeanne slipped away, running through the narrow street, one frightened lovesick girl hurrying toward the witch.

Through the artisans' quarter, where the sculptors carved ivory for the locks of books and boxes that were bought by the nobles and the Catholic Church. These were truly works of art, adorned with a tangle of vines and hounds and stags and hares. But it was not these wares she wanted, but the wizardry of the witch. She slid, her heart in her throat, into that part of town where ladies in such finery as hers stood out, begging to be robbed—or raped and murdered, their bodies tossed (splash!) in the river, never found.

She came to the wooden hovel, door aslant. She pushed it open. Her heart was in her throat.

"Who are you?" spoke a voice from the dark.

She blinked, unable to see in the gloom, and then perceived a shadowed form move out of the shadows of the dark curtains. She heard the curtain beads ring against each other like little bells; the gypsy woman came forward, hips rolling

"Who is this fine stranger who dares to enter my exotic lair?" What a curious way to speak. Jeanne saw only shawls and beads. The woman's earrings were so long they brushed her shoulders and caught in the black disheveled hair that curled around her face and hung disordered down her back. Her throat was covered with gold chains. Her fingers bore a dozen rings.

She took Jeanne's chin in one hand and turned her head to the light.

"What does a lady want in such a place?" she said, and loosed Jeanne's chin and stalked back to her corner, to settle reclining on the piles of cushions on the floor. Jeanne took a shy step forward, her voice a whisper in the darkness.

"I want a potion."

She laughed. "Of course. A love potion, is that right? You are smitten by a man and want to bind him to you?"

"How did you know?" Jeanne sank to a cushion opposite.

"Can you pay for it?"

Jeanne held out one hand. The gypsy took the single pearl Jeanne had scissored from her baby dress. She turned it thoughtfully, held it to her eye, bit it between her teeth, examined it again, and slipped it in her bodice.

"Sit down. Tell me about him."

She spoke about her love for William. She described him, their friendship, her love.

"I want a potion that will bind him to me for all his life."

"Think again. It's a cup of unhappiness you'd drink."

"I want him. I know he loves me. I want him to love me."

"Then come back next week, and I will have one for you."

"Give me back the pearl," Jeanne said. "I will pay you when I have the potion, and no sooner."

"I have it now," the witch answered with a haughty smile, and indeed she had secreted the precious jewel; it had vanished in her breast. Jeanne's heart flip-flopped. The woman must have seen the look.

"Don't worry." She laughed with a flash of white teeth. "Don't worry, little girl. I'll tell you what I'll do. Stay here, and I will come back with your potion. You can drink it now. It will take a little while to make."

"But don't I give it to him too?" Jeanne asked, confused, for in the stories the magic potion must be drunk by both.

"Why?" The curtains tinkled behind her laughter as she sauntered out.

She was gone. Jeanne sat a long time in the dank hut, frightened, playing with her fingers. She wondered what she was doing there and what her people would do if they found she'd come to the witch, alone and unprotected. Twice she started to her feet to leave, and twice sat down again, not knowing whether to go or stay . . . except the gypsy had her pearl. . . .

Jeanne swiveled at the clicking of the curtain beads and the rustle of the witch's skirt.

"Here." Smiling, she tossed back her loose black hair. "Drink this."

"Now?"

"Why wait?"

Jeanne held the cup uncertainly, because she had expected a magic potion such as Tristan took with Iseult, when both together drank the magic draught that Iseult's mother had prepared for her daughter and King Mark. Everyone knew that ancient story. In that tale no one was at fault—not King Mark of Cornwall, who sent his beloved nephew Tristan to Ireland to bring the golden-haired Iseult as his bride; and not Iseult's mother, who prepared a magic love potion for Iseult and who had told her daughter to drink it only when she and King Mark were alone on their wedding night. No one was at fault when the bride kissed her grieving mother farewell and stepped into the royal boat that would carry her to her husband in Cornwall. But out at sea the wind died. The boat lay rocking on a lake of glass. Then the pure knight Tristan, who loved King Mark like a son, called for a glass of wine. The serving girl, all unknowing, found the queen's lovely lapis beaker in the princess's tent, and all unknowing poured the secret wine into two fine cups; and no one was at fault when, looking in each other's eyes, Tristan and Iseult drank the magic draught—and in that moment fell in love. In the story they drank it together, bewitched by gazing in each other's eyes.

The witch was staring at Jeanne, lips curled in pitying disdain. "Don't you want it?"

Jeanne drank. It tasted like wine, perhaps doctored with a bitter herb. She set down the cup. "Is that all?"

"That's enough. Now you are bound to him for all his days," she said, then began to shout. "Now get out of here!" She turned on the young girl. "Go on! Get out!"

Jeanne pushed through the door and fled.

She ran back to the castle, panting, breathless. She was even more frightened in hindsight at what she'd done than when engaged in the daring act; so when she saw Marie she scolded her—and slapped her face as well—for having gotten lost in town. Then she burst into tears. She felt sick to her stomach. What was in the potion—poison? She had downed it without a thought. She refused Baiona's concerned looks, her offers of help.

"Go away," she said plaintively. "I want to be alone."

Then she sat at a table and wrote to William that she'd been affianced, and to come save her from the impending marriage, to come please, carry her away, to be there, help! She sealed the letter with wax and went herself to the stables to find a messenger—a gardener—someone. By luck a tinker had arrived. His pack at his feet. A cup of ale in his hand.

"Will you take this for me to Montségur?"

"If you pay me enough. I'll be moving on in two more days."

"No, sooner," she said. "Leave now."

"I'll leave at my own time. If it's that important, find someone else."

"But you will take it to Montségur?"

"I can go that direction as well as another," he said, laughing.

So it went by the hand of a tinker, urgently, to Montségur—but despite the potion, Jeanne heard nothing back.

At Christmas she stood in the Great Hall whispering her dutiful vows to the gray-haired, elderly knight Gobert, whom she had met only the day before. His face was a geography of folds, furrows, grooves, and drooping eye-pockets. His skin had a faintly bluish cast. He seemed well pleased with his bride, though, and he laughed behind his moustache and tendered her dainty foods from his own plate at the wedding feast.

Still, the ceremony was curiously muted, even pious. Jeanne went through it numb as a puppet on a string, and every now and again she would look up—or across the table at the concerned Baiona—her eyes filling with tears, while the sounds of the gaiety went unheard. Gobert took her to bed that night accompanied as was the custom by the jubilant clang of cymbals and squalling trumpets, by raucous, festive drunkenness and the noisy appreciation of the applauding guests, who walked them to their marriage bed and who, after she'd undressed and been tucked in, still crowded round to yell encouragement and watch. Gobert laughed and ordered them away.

Outside, the snow fell in deep, white, silent drifts as chilly as her downcast eyes, as silent as William, who had not received her letter—did not receive it until the spring: too late. By then she was already five months wed, and pregnant. By the time he arrived in Pamiers and asked after her, she was already living in another palace leagues away, now mistress (at least in name) of her husband's house, though the true ruler was his cool and rigid sister, Irene.

Jeanne was married, and no one in the world knew of her love for William, unless it was the beautiful wolfhound, Loup-Baiard, to whom she whispered all her secrets. No one knew—not Esclarmonde, nor Baiona, nor Gobert, nor her darling old lady, Marquésia de Forli, whom she had served for one full summer and who had noticed nothing; not even the good bishop Guilhabert de Castres, who gave all credit to God that the tomboy maid, his favorite student, Jeanne Béziers, had become so fine and sober a married dame.

❈ SEVENTEEN ❈

I wake up next morning to a cold, white rain that slants in sheets against the little house, rattling the wooden window shutters. It seeps through one hole in the thatch to click on the wet floor. The dirt floor has been mixed with ox blood, I think, and beaten down until it's hard as rock. Outdoors the rain splatters in the stableyard, lifting gobs of mud.

Jerome is nowhere to be seen.

I move out into the muck and find a sheltered place to relieve myself, then come back in, scraping mud off my ancient leather shoes but leaving wet tracks anyway. It is a snug little house, despite its leak, and that can be repaired. My spirits lift. I build up the fire, pulling back the leather smoke-hole flap only a little way, lest the rain find that hole too. The gray-striped mouser comes pattering over on little white paws and mews at me.

"Watching me build the fire, are you?"

She settles neatly to one side, tail curled around her front paws. She licks one paw and cleans behind her ears, and I am filled with sweet sensations that I can't even name. Then I make a pot of porridge, enough for both of us, though I have no idea where he's gone. After that I sweep the house, rummage around and explore the sturdy, rough shelves and what jars and bags of medicines and tools he keeps around. A farmer's house. Not wealthy, but no peasant either. Jerome did well on his two hectares. I am looking for a hidey-hole for my treasure wrapped in its green oilskin. At present it lies under the straw in the storeroom, but I'll need a safer place before the day is out.

I look for flour to bake bread and when I find it, then I find no oven for the baking. I'll have to bake in the fire coals, an unsatisfactory method that scorches the outside crust and sometimes leaves the inside raw.

By the time I'm finished, Jerome comes in, bangs the door behind him against the slashing rain. He drips moisture on the floor.

"Don't come any farther," I call out. "Take off your filthy boots; I've swept the floor."

"Woman, don't nag." But he sits on the bench by the door and obediently removes his wet boots. Comes to the fire, rubbing his chapped hands before the flame. "Raw out there today."

"Here," I say. "Have you eaten?"

"Thanks." He takes the porridge in two red hands, then reaches into his pocket.

"I brought you something."

"Me?"

"I went down to the neighbors," he says. "Bottom of the hill and two miles off. The Domergues. Man and his wife, three children—one married and two helping on the farm. A couple of grandchildren. I told them I'd met you in town yesterday. You're my cousin, come looking for me from over by Montaillou." He cocks an eye at me. "Think you can remember that?"

"Montaillou."

"I figured it's far enough away, up in the mountains. You can cross right over into Aragon."

"I'm not familiar with it. I wish you'd said the plains of Foix instead."

"Well, maybe you came from Foix before that. Anyway, your husband's dead, and your children and most kin."

"What did they die of?"

"You haven't told me yet. I thought the pox." He shrugs and shyly grins, but I'm startled. Had I told him of my lovely Guillamette? No, because he runs on without a thought. I listen sharply, because our very lives depend on my attention. "I said you're my mother's first cousin. My mother's name was Anne."

"Anne."

"Who married my father, Arnaud Ahrade. We've never met before. So the women will want to come visit later and see what you're made of. I told them you were mad with grief, talking a little off, so if your story's confused, it won't be thought odd."

"Did you say why I'd searched you out?" And I feel the tears prick my eyes again, against my will. I grit my teeth. I refuse to cry, though pain is falling drop by drop upon my heart.

"No." His voice softens. "I said I didn't know. I said you were not unpleasant to look at, though, and you looked strong enough to work." He's jollying me. "Here, I brought you a present from Alazaïs Domergue. I said you'd only one headdress, torn and dirty, and we hadn't had time to buy a new one in town."

On my lap he spreads the clean white cloth for a headdress, and my stomach twists. I put down my bowl and smooth the cloth with both hands, hardly daring to look up, so precious does it feel. My headdress. He went out in the rain for me.

"Thank you." The linen is fresh and cool to my touch. I whisper, "Thank you." And then I rise that very instant and dress my wild long hair. Exactly what I'd been wishing for the day before! A wimple, white as Mistress Flavia's. Oh, my most gracious, most beloved God, *Who will cover you with His pinions and His faithfulness is a shield and buckler.*

"Well, I'll stay a day or two." I'm laughing with pleasure. "Your mother's cousin's got some business elsewhere, but she'll stay for a time, and clean the house and cook for you and mend your clothes a bit. Put her cousin to rights. He's got no sense: you'd think he could repair a leaking thatch!" I laugh again, putting on my country airs.

The fact is I like this amiable man. I feel comfortable here, and if the friars leave us alone, I'm happy to give him a hand, in return for shelter. Perhaps in time my hands will stop shaking. I smooth my skirt. It's been a while since I've met company. Real friends. I want to bolt—I'm scared—but at the same time I look forward shyly to the Domergues' visit.

Later, Jerome takes the sheep out to pasture and comes back in to sit by the fire, repairing leather for the afternoon. I sew the rip on my skirt. The rain pours down, a furious, hard, autumn drenching. It's snug and dark in the little house, despite the drip, drip, and after I finish the sewing, I start supper for us, and as it cooks in a pot on the hearth, we tell our stories timidly. He was married, as he'd said before, and his girls have both wed and moved away with their husbands. One girl has two sons. The other keeps miscarrying or losing the babes that are born. That's the woman's lot, ever since Adam and Eve were cast out of Eden, and there's no greater grief.

"You love them beyond anything," I murmur. "You never remember the pain of childbirth, but you never forget the pain of losing them."

There's something about the sound of rain, the safety of the shadows, that draws out confidences. "I've never stopped grieving for my little girl," I tell him. "I named her Guillamette after a great friend, and you were right: she died of pox. I thought I'd die myself from sorrowing." She wasn't for this world, poor little thing, but maybe she's richer than us. The Lord giveth and the Lord taketh away.

"I'm sorry," he says. "And your husband?"

"I married twice. My first was when I'd hardly reached full height."

"What happened? He died?"

"I found him in bed one day with his sister. I came home unexpectedly."

He laughs out loud. I make a face and shrug, and then I burst out laughing too.

"Well, I didn't find it funny at the time. I felt betrayed, and my pride was hurt. I divorced him, though he'd spent my dowry on his wars."

"You had a dowry?" His eyes widen.

"A little one." Suddenly I'm ashamed, for his daughters certainly went penniless to their husbands. I didn't know how rich I'd been.

"Nonetheless." He nods, thinking the matter out. Then after a moment: "That's a sad tale too."

"Yes. But I didn't love him. And it happened long ago. It feels as if it happened to someone else."

True. The raw hurt lies elsewhere, but I'm not going to tell him about William, after whom I named our little girl—William, the husband of my heart.

"Are you all right?—What's wrong?"

"Nothing."

I was four months pregnant when Baiona's letter came. Clutching it, and followed by Loup-Baiard, I ran up to my private chamber in the tower, feeling fortunate that I had so wealthy a knight for a husband that I had a chamber of my own, where I could hug a letter to my heart. My room had a high, well-oiled carved chair and a chest in the same dark wood, a table for my own, and clean rushes on the floor. The table was covered with a tapestry sewn by Baiona's hand.

"I'm getting married," she wrote. "I want you to meet the man I love, and I know you will love each other too. I won't say another word. Come soon. We are still at Pamiers. I want you to stand as witness at my wedding." And then news of the castle there, and of one or two friends, and of the wedding date.

I was happy to leave Gobert and his gloomy sister, with her severe, stern face and sour smell; and as I mounted my horse, she smiled on me—perhaps for the first time with her eyes smiling. She wished me a pleasant journey (patting my thigh in the saddle) and told me to stay as long as ever I liked. And I, poor child, found myself opening to her kindness, starved for affection and grateful to be sent kindly on my way, not knowing yet the reason why. Escorted by two men-at-arms, I rode back to Pamiers, and with each league I grew happier, for I was going home to stand as witness to the wedding of my friend. I laughed with the men and kicked my horse into a gallop, racing with the wind and air.

When I arrived, I leapt into Baiona's arms and we kissed like sisters, laughing in our joy.

"Baiona, you didn't even describe him," I chided teasingly. "Who is this man?"

"You know him."

"Who?"

"It's William!"

I was stunned. "William?"

"Your friend."

"Ah! No."

"What is it, Jeanne? What's wrong?"

"From Montségur?" I asked, certain that I was mistaken.

"Yes. He said that you were friends."

"He told you." My head was reeling.

"Don't turn away. What have I done? Jeanne, don't look like that!"

"He's—"

"He's what?"

"He's mine! I met him first! He lives"—I struck my breast with my fist—"here! He loves me, not you. We're bonded for our lives!" I cried, remembering the potion.

"What are you saying?"

"He's mine, not yours; he's mine!"

Baiona fell back a step, holding herself with one hand on the wall. "I'm marrying the man you—?"

"Yes, love! I love him, yes."

"No," Baiona whispered.

"He only wants you for your money." I spat out the words. "He has to marry a rich woman. He told me so." Would I have said it had Baiona not stolen Rogert earlier? I saw her face go white, her eyes flatten, and a thrill of pleasure shot through me that I'd stung her as she was hurting me.

"Is this some joke?"

"We coupled there," I lied. "He pledged his love to me. He wanted to marry me."

"Why did you never tell me? He said he knew you, that was all; that you'd met at Montségur. Are you making this up? You never said a word about William when you came back—not a word to me, your closest friend." She grabbed my hand, searching my angry face. "But you're married to Gobert."

I said nothing.

"You're carrying your husband's child." She was struggling with the news. "Gobert's."

I smiled wickedly. "Am I? Are you sure it's his?"

"Get out!" she cried. "Get out of my sight! How dare you—"

"My spirit will lie between you on your wedding night," I cursed her. "I will be present in every embrace."

"You lie; you lie!"

It was then that William entered. He found us separated by the height of a tall man and facing each other off. I don't know what Baiona was feeling, but I was torn between despair and outrage, both at this woman standing there, shoulders slumped and tears pouring down her face, and at William, who heedless of what was going on pulled us to him, hugging us one on either side and pumping us like bellows because we didn't properly respond.

"Our trinity of love," he was saying foolishly. "One man and two women, each more beautiful than the next. And all three caring for one another! My love." He turned to kiss his bride.

But she began to laugh hysterically. "Oh, William!" She pushed away, and with a wild look left and right she fled the room. But I stood rooted in my passion, still held in William's arm, and happy to be there, however or why it came about.

"What's happened?" He turned to me in astonishment.

I clung to him, kissing his lips, his face.

"Jeanne. What did you say to her?" He took me by the shoulders and held me away.

"I told her that you belong to me. I told her that we loved each other at Montségur." My arms found their way around his neck.

With one hand he snatched my hands away, and with the other he slapped me across the face.

Still I clung to him. "William!"

But he turned and strode after Baiona, leaving me weeping and lonely and angry and alone.

I was not proud of what I'd done. Later he tracked me down in the common room. He was angrier than I had ever seen him. "Go apologize." He grabbed my arm. Hurting me. "Go tell her it's a lie. Say you've lied."

I searched his face. I'd never noticed before how his blue eyes floated upward under his lids, leaving a white half-moon beneath. It gave him a cold sensuality.

"Go on," he urged.

I went. I did as I was told. She listened from a distance and nodded in the same cool way that the Lady Esclarmonde might have done; and I made no move to approach or touch her. "My child is Gobert's," I added. "No doubt of that."

She accepted my apology with a queenly nod. "Only we will never be friends again," she said. "I do not know you. I do not like you. I do not trust you." There was a pause. "On the other hand, I see no reason to tell Esclarmonde about this. It's never happened."

She was right not to trust me. I went away hurt and angry, and resentful too that the potion was a fraud.

A week later I watched them exchange their vows and rings in the castle garden, under a blossoming apple tree. Baiona's face was pale, but she walked head high with her usual grace, contained and regal, and she was smiling as she accepted the congratulations of the guests. She was very happy. I marveled that I could stand at the ceremony, blessing their union—I'd had to, for the sake of my hurt pride and perhaps for Esclarmonde—but the moment it was over I ran across the grass, running from the sight of the man I loved now married to another. He was kissing his bride, and I was running, running away from them across the grass. I plunged into the walled herb garden and hid, my back to the wall, weeping uncontrollably. My heart twisted in my chest like a writhing animal. It was breaking into two—no, a dozen bleeding fragments, shattering like glass.

The pain was so intense that I bit my own forearm to stifle my cries, to hurt myself, to hate myself, to feel another pain. I bit my own flesh until the toothmarks flared up, imprinted red on my skin.

The day following I mounted my horse with a frozen heart to return to my husband, Gobert, and his icy sister, who would treat me with distant and courteous reserve, and where my baby, soon after deciding that it didn't care to be born, would slip out of my body, leaving a sticky trail of red slime dripping down my thighs.

Five years passed. I had divorced Gobert and moved to a little house in Toulouse (bought with hush-money paid by Gobert to keep secret the reason for our divorce). The war had broken out again full force; and I had joined the Resistance, carrying messages. I was almost twenty, and I'd reached my full height. One night, as I was leaving a meeting to go home, I heard my name called:

"Jeanne."

It was William. My stomach dropped. He too had changed. His body had thickened. The hair at his temples had the faintest sprinkling of gray. He walked with the heavy tread of authority, and he held himself taller, if possible, and with more confidence. I'd heard nothing of him for five years. Now, it seemed, he'd joined the court of Raymond VII, Count of Toulouse.

"Jeanne, I'm so glad to see you. Look at you," he said, laughing and turning me round. "You've grown. You're beautiful."

At first I was embarrassed, shamefaced with memory.

But he was smiling broadly. "Aren't you glad to see me?"

I didn't know what to say. "How is Baiona?" I asked stiffly.

He laughed and swept me in his arms for a big kiss. "She's well enough. She lives in Foix. Come now, I'll walk you home."

He tucked my arm under his and escorted me through the dark stone streets to my little house, talking all the time. I did not invite him in.

In the next weeks, I seemed to meet him everywhere. At first I thought he'd lost his boyish ebullience, but every now and again it flashed forth in a sly wink of those startling blue-sky eyes, or he would rock back on his heels in silent laughter at some joke. When did I realize William was flirting with me—the way he stood full face, legs apart and hands on his narrow hips, or else leaning back on his heels, smiling straight into my eyes? Displaying himself for me. He would hold my eyes in long luxurious looks. It took me several days to understand—I mean, to remember—that he had stood like that even at Montségur. He'd been flirting with me even then.

"Don't you understand, little silly?" he said one day.

"Understand what?"

"There's no one like you. Don't you want me still?"

"What are you saying?"

"I've never forgotten you. Or your wonderful declaration of love. I couldn't take advantage of it then. Do you love me still? Why don't you love me now? There's nothing now to interfere with you and me."

I was shocked. "What do you mean? You're married." I paced the reception room nervously, and yet I was helpless to send him away. I'd wished so often for this moment.

"My marriage to Baiona has nothing to do with my feelings for you."

His hands reached out to touch my breasts. I could not move.

"Don't you like me just a little?"

He was kissing me now. "Oh, Jeanne, I've missed you so."

I was helpless with longing and hopeless with self-hatred. I tried to push him away. "Why didn't you want me at Montségur?"

He stepped back, paced two steps, turned, and faced me. He clapped his hands briskly, as if wiping out that memory.

"Because I wanted a woman of property. I couldn't afford to get you pregnant. But now we're both older. There's nothing to stop us. Unless—" he faltered. "Unless you don't like me. I'm only a landless *faidit*. I have nothing to offer; I'm not worth your time."

Now began a game of hide-and-seek, or hunt-and-chase. We were thrown together by the Cause. But in addition he pursued me subtly, finding ways for us to serve on a mission together. He'd come up behind and wrap one arm about me, then brush my breasts with the back of his hand, teasing to make the nipples stand high. I was a bird caught in a trap. If he found me alone in a passageway, he'd lift my hair and kiss the back of my neck, and when I turned he'd catch me in his arms, seeking my mouth hungrily. Eventually my mouth searched his as well.

He called me his darling love. He said that his wife didn't understand him, that she was a miser, controlling the purse-strings. She didn't appreciate his need for one of the big Lombard or Spanish warhorses, for example, and in fact refused to accommodate him. His horse was old and small and not strong enough to win prizes in the jousting lists; he needed a charger that, by winning for him, would allow him to buy a castle, lands. He needed it for war besides. How could he run down a French knight and hold him for ransom when his own horse was so slow? Yet Baiona kept tight watch on their money, he said, doling it out to him in bits and coins. All the time, we were laughing together, playing, or plotting missions. He was complex. He would fall into brief black moods— the black dog at his throat—and another day come whistling to my house as sunny as a day in June.

Soon we were all but living together. On many mornings during the next ten months I handed him his armor and watched him dress and walked him to his horse. One day we went together to the horse fairs, and I bought him a destrier. It was my pleasure to buy him a new strong horse, though it took nearly every penny I had. He accepted it because of his true love for me, he said, and I believed it. I wanted him well mounted. I wanted him safe. How many times did he murmur his love? He said that when Baiona died, he'd marry me.

Did I suffer guilt? Yes, but he dispelled that too. He explained that he lived with Baiona as a sister. How could what we did be wrong? And anyway (I told myself), I wasn't responsible: I'd drunk the magic drink.

My arms around his neck, and his hands pulling at the laces at my breasts, mine fumbling with his breeches, and we are falling onto the bed with William already inside of me, push and thrust, our lips engaged— while I, near fainting, gasping, hold him deep inside me, swallowing hungrily this man I love. It's all entwined, our love, the Cause, betrayal, love, and war.

"He doesn't sound so fine a man to me."

I shoot Jerome a look. "He was wonderful." How did all that happen to spill out? I wasn't going to confess. The story pouring out like water over a dam, my pent-up longing to talk of William, and the past.

Jerome snorts, unimpressed. "Wonderful how? I've known men like that, dreamers, drifting from woman to woman. No patience for hard work. He couldn't even support himself, according to you."

"He had hard luck."

"What's the difference between his marrying for money and your Gobert's using up your dowry? This William spent his wife's money on big horses for the wars and jousts. A gambler, right? He was unfaithful to his wife and unfaithful to his mistress—you."

"You never met him."

"What did he have then?"

I hesitate. Who can say what captivates a woman's heart? "He was the most fascinating, most entertaining, handsomest man I've ever met. He inspired us. He laid down his life for our *parage,* our Occitan way of life. He didn't have to. He came from a foreign country. He was warm and funny and daring." But my voice shakes. I'm remembering other times.

Jerome lets out a foul-mouthed curse. "Charm doesn't last," he says, concentrating on his leather. He looks up at me. "He was unfaithful. I don't like lies. I tell you, if I found the woman for me and knew her to be true, as true as gold, I wouldn't let her go for lack of money. Or give her up to someone else, neither. And if she married me, I wouldn't cheat on her." He stares at me so fiercely that I blush and drop my eyes.

We're silent then for a long time.

I was remembering those times when I carried messages for the Cause—word of raids or plans of them, reports of movements of French troops, or news of papal Inquisitors. My tasks were simple. I'd pass word to the baker four streets over, who might pass the message on in relays to a shepherd to carry on. I sat in on underground meetings. Sometimes I rode with a message to the fighters at Saissac or Mirepoix or Peyrepertuse or Roquefixade.

I kept a safe house where a Good Man or Woman could find shelter for a night or a week, or where a small group could meet to hear him or her preach. Sometimes I gave a roving knight hospitality for a night.

One night I heard a banging on my door. In my nightshift, terrified, I plunged down the steep stairs to the door.

"Who is it?" I called out, my voice low.

"Hurry! Open up."

I recognized the voice and swung the door open to reveal William on the threshold. He was half-carrying a limp and bleeding man.

"Quick."

"He's badly wounded."

We carried him upstairs.

"Keep him safe," said William. "They're looking for him. I have to go. Tell no one he's here."

"What's happened?"

"A raid. We've killed one of the Dominicans." He kissed me quickly and was gone into the night, filthy and mud-splattered, the blood of his comrade drying on his shirt.

I bathed the visitor, washed the hole in his gut, but anyone could see he would not live the night, not with his stomach seeping out the hole and dirt and wood embedded in the wound.

He died without revealing his name or any information. I had no way to pass the word to William. My problem was to get the body out of the house, without the neighbors' prying eyes. I burnt his clothing and sewed him into a sacking, as if a bag of vegetables. My houseboy helped. We lugged the sack outside and tossed it in broad daylight on a wagon. We drove him out of town into the fields, where we tossed him in a ditch, poor man, unsacked, for the buzzards and maggots. We couldn't dig a grave. Better to make it look as if he'd been set upon by brigands, robbed and left there dead.

The saints know there were enough of them.

I sent the boy across the mountains into Aragon. No use his being caught for what I did, or turning me in either. With money in his pocket he was happy to be gone.

And always there would be William riding in at night to bed down at my Toulouse house if he was in the neighborhood, or to ask my help. I'd have laid down my life for him.

"What about the second time?" asks Jerome.

I jump, startled out of my reverie. "What second time?"

"You said you married twice."

"Ah, the second time. Roland-Pierre. He was a good, generous man. I was fond of him, but not the way I yearned for William. Still, we stayed married almost nine years, and then he died."

"That's the way of it," says Jerome.

But I'm thinking of the lighthearted Roland-Pierre, who went off to fight with the Count of Toulouse and came back from the wars a melancholy man. Afterward, he could not shake his nervous sadness. I tried to lift his spirits with games and guests, and hunts for stag or boar. But his despair lay so heavily on him that you could see it like a dark mantle covering him, black as death. Nothing I did could cheer him up.

The doctors strapped him into a special chair with leather thongs and poured bitter purges down his throat, so vile that he vomited across the room; they slathered him with plasters and poultices as smelly as a stable-yard. I held his hand, my darling friend, weeping at his sorrow and his plight. He could not shake that *accidie,* which the monks call sin.

"He didn't die." I cannot stop myself, my voice too loud. "He killed himself."

"Killed himself!" says Jerome, looking up in horror from his work. "A suicide!"

My hands shake. I put down the spoon.

"So then the Devil has claimed his soul." Jerome's voice is hoarse.

"No! I had him buried decently in hallowed Catholic ground, with a good carved stone for his marker. I wouldn't have him left outside the Church. It was an accident."

And yet I've always wondered and worried for him: they say that a suicide can never find his way into the Light and drifts forever in the gloom, not here, not there; I could not bear to think of it. The Friends of God say that he'll come back to earth once more but in an even worse life, and that's also too horrible to bear.

Jerome is watching me under his brows, considering. "Well, you did right to bury him in consecrated ground."

"Yes." I had to pay plenty for his burial in sanctified Church grounds, though, for he was a good and pious Catholic. The priests demanded most of his estate for the favor of a Christian burial, but I did not grudge him that, poor, gentle soul, not for his eternal life. He hurt, poor lamb. All he wanted was to relieve the pain. I was hurt and angry he would leave me. I felt abandoned. But I'd never condemn him to eternal punishment. He loved me and also my little Guillamette. We had happy times. If I could love him when he killed himself, why wouldn't God the more?

When I first met him, he was one of the Resistance knights, young and merry. I had been warned to expect his proposal.

"What will you do now?" he'd asked that night, sitting before the fire in my little house. He nursed his mug of hot spiced wine.

"When?" I pretended not to know what he was referring to.

"Now that you're pregnant. William told me—do you mind? He says the father died." (At which I sucked in my breath.)

"No," I said quietly, staring into the flames. "He didn't die, but he cannot marry me. I'll have the child. It won't be the first bastard born into this world."

"Why not marry?" he asked, taking my hand.

"And with whom would that be?" I laughed lightly, but my heart twisted cruelly in my breast. I'd already made my decision. It remained only to proceed. He smiled an open charming grin.

"Why not me? We'd do well together, you and I."

Why not? He was younger than I, and not bad-looking. If he was willing tra-la to overlook my condition, why not take the man who wanted me and would give my child a name?

Jerome is squinting at me, askance, waiting for me to continue. I duck my head. "It was long ago. I've had good times too. My life's not all been bad. I'm not complaining. Roland-Pierre was a good husband and a good father to my little girl, who surely is in heaven herself. I have loved and been loved, and what more can any of us ask?"

I smile at him and toss my head. "And what of you?"

And so we pass the evening, the two of us indoors, exchanging our stories, with the smell of stew brewing in the pot and the smoke warm on the hearth, and the cozy sound of rain clattering against the roof.

Then, to keep from thinking about William or Roland-Pierre, I tell him the fable of King Midas and the golden touch, and the Bible story of Susanna and the three men who tried to seduce her. Jerome likes stories, so I tell about Abraham and how the angel saved him from killing his son Isaac, and then I tell the story of how Jacob stole his brother's inheritance, and finally some of the romantic tales of Tristan and the Princess Iseult.

Jerome is impressed. He doesn't know the Bible stories so well as I (not having ever had a Good Book to read, and not being able to read if he'd ever found himself in possession of one). Naturally, he doesn't know the romantic ballads either. But he tells me about the robbers and the barnyard animals. Soon we're laughing at each other's tales.

One I tell him is the vision that Robert, the *jongleur,* had when we were under siege in Montségur, and we laugh so hard I think I'll pee— flying castles and boats that swim underwater, haywagons that roll themselves along without an ox or horse! Such fantasies. Only of course I don't mention Montségur. I just say a man I knew had visions of the Future, and I leave out all the rest.

It was early in the siege, when our spirits still rode high. We gathered after supper in the dungeon, men and women both, to entertain ourselves.

One night Robert came forward, our self-proclaimed entertainer— juggler and jester, troubadour, clown, musician. He struck three chords on his lute to quiet us, but silence took some time to fall over us, with everyone talking and ignoring him. He stood in his absurd parti-colored hose, one leg thrust forward and the toes of his stockings curling up in the air like two scorpion tails. He knew he looked funny. His beard was jagged and thin, and he had a little round belly above thin, shambly legs, and a more ridiculous figure in his diamond-patterned hose you could not find.

Some of us hushed the others and shouted that we would have a song, if they'd shut up. Others taunted him, already laughing and ready for his asshole wit. He struck his instrument a flurry of chords, like rabbits running for cover—and stopped.

We waited expectantly.

"Last night I had a vision," he said in a low, flat voice. We laughed. We thought he was making fun of the Good Men's meditations.

"Listen!" he shouted. (Strum-strum-strum.) Then he did a backward somersault while holding his instrument, and we applauded gaily. (Strum-strum-strum.)

"Last night I had a vision of a Future-time. Now be quiet, and I'll tell the future for you." A murmur ran through the hall, and we all settled down, for who alive doesn't want to know the future, whether a young girl wanting to marry or a man questing for a prize? What we wanted to know was when the Count of Toulouse would send his reinforcements and defeat the French forces that encircled us.

But to our surprise, he said, "Last night an angel came to me." The room grew still. We did not laugh. His face lifted, radiant with the memory. "He was surrounded by light and dressed in brilliant white, and from his head came spears of light. I was awed and filled with joy.

"'Come,' he said, 'and I will show you the Future-time.'

"I hesitated. 'Are you demon or angel?' I asked. 'I follow only those who follow Jesus Christ, our Lord.'

"'Then you may come with me,' said this beautiful creature. 'For I too worship the Light of the World.'"

Robert paused, and his face took on a glorious, distant aspect, as if he were peering into inner realms. Then he looked down at his instrument, remembering. "You will tell me I am lying." He glanced up joyously. "But this was given me, just as I'm describing to you. The angel held out his hand to me, and when I took it, I was pulled upward, spiraling out of my body to I-know-not-where, and there I saw the marvels I shall describe. I know only this: it was not another world, but this very land we live on now, and years ahead."

"Tell it!" we called impatiently. Now his strumming changed to plaintive melodies, the kind that tug mysteriously at the heart, and from that plangent melancholy he moved gradually to gayer, quicker tunes, until his voice broke in full and strong.

"I saw a time of such prosperity" (strum-strum-strum) "as you cannot conceive," he said. "Both men and women were dressed in gaudy foreign clothes of soft fabrics and rich colors. Never has human eye seen such tissue, thin as Oriental silk and yet so warm that people wore neither overgarments nor thick underclothes.

"They were standing in great crowds on a black path in the high-ceilinged hallway of a palace—and then I saw that the floor was moving, and they moved with it, and no one had to walk, because in those days the roads will do the walking for them!" (Strum-strum-strum.)

We burst out laughing, hooting and calling, delighted by the thought of moving roads. He pretended huffiness, but he was pleased withal.

"But I saw more!" he shouted; and when we had stopped hooting him and had quieted down again, he held up one hand for absolute silence, and again he strummed his lute.

"I saw castles that soared through the air with a sound like a hundred waterfalls, a sound like the thunder of an army's hooves, a sound like an earthslide. And I saw the faces of people at the windows looking out. They could fly from here to the Holy Land between dawn and noon. They ate their dinners in these flying houses, and—I swear—with everyone at ease. They read books as they flew through the air!"

Some of us laughed even harder. But we were fascinated. "Where will they go, these flying castles?" called out one woman.

"Anywhere you desire, little heart. You make a wish and you are whisked into the air and set down leagues away. A time will come when these things happen, for I have seen them, as in a dream."

"I dreamt I married a queen," croaked an old man, "but it doesn't mean it's come to pass!"

"Don't give up!" chimed a voice from the back. "You're not dead yet."

But Robert paused, his head cocked to one side. His eyes trailed thoughtfully to the farthest left-hand corner of the room, lost in sweet memory.

"This was not a dream," he said quietly, so quietly indeed that he caught our attention. "There is a difference between a knowing and a wish, between a vision and a dream. This was given to me, like seeing through a crack in the curtains of time."

He looked down wistfully, a little smile playing on his lips, and he plucked on his pretty instrument a watery river of soft chords, gentle and nostalgic.

Suddenly he bellowed. "I saw more!" (Strum-strum-strum.) "In addition to the moving floor and the flying castles, these people have carts as high as haywagons that race each other on their roads, carrying people inside."

"And so do we have carts!" shouted one man.

"Are these roads moving too?" asked another.

"But I tell you," answered Robert, "these are drawn by neither ox nor horse. They push themselves along with noisy growls, howls, screams, and roaring breath. I tell you, in this Future no one walks."

We loved it! How we laughed. It made a happy evening, and for days the children and even hardened soldiers, weary with the fighting, would stand and pretend the ground was moving them along, or that they were climbing into a flying tower that would soar over the walls and over the enemy troops in the valley below. The flying castles would pour boiling pitch onto the Crusaders, and buckets of fire, and then fly on to set us down in the Holy Land of Christ.

"What else?" someone called.

"I saw boats shaped like the fishes of the seas. They had no sails." (Strum-strum-strum.) "They did not travel on top of the water, pushed by the good Lord's wind—"

"They flew through the air!" shouted a young wit.

"No!" He silenced the heckler with a look. "They dove under the waves and swam like cormorants *under* the water, diving and coming up for air."

We didn't like this as well as the moving roads and the flying houses.

For myself, it made me uncomfortable to think of swimming underwater in that way.

"Why?" someone called. "What was the point?"

"I don't know," he answered honestly. "I understood the roads and the air-houses. But going underwater—perhaps it was to escape an enemy. Perhaps to catch a fish. I'm merely telling you what I saw."

"How did they see underwater?" someone asked.

"Blindly," came the answer from across the hall. "The saltwater in their eyes."

After that, every few nights Robert told us of new visions that he had. Or else that he made up. Once he said these people could talk to one another across great distances, their voices carried from Paris to Rome. They only had to think, it seemed, and messages would fly like castles through the air, only fast as thought—not lumbering like stones. He told us of many strange things—how rich will be this world, and without the classical distinctions between men and women, peasant, soldier, servant or lord.

We argued that: "How would you tell your place? How would you know to whom to bow?"

The dress alone, the night he talked more of that, kept us occupied for hours.

Another night he said there'll be no more disease: no lepers, no plague or pox or children dying of the cough; and I remember afterward the little hunchback cripple Esclarmonde de Perella, daughter of our commander, who had already taken the robe, poor crippled girl—how she crept to the *jongleur*'s stippled side. She put one trusting hand on his patched leg and looked up in his face. "And do they have hunchbacks and dwarves in this Future?" she asked.

Robert looked sadly down at her on her wooden crutch. "I don't know," he said.

His visions did not come on call whenever he wanted one but captured him unexpectedly. Was he lying?

One day I approached him in the yard. "Master Robert."

He was leaning against the wall, watching nothing, which was what we did much of the time during the boredom of the siege. He pulled himself up straight and touched his cap to me courteously. "Na Jeanne."

"I have a question." I searched his eyes. "Are they true, these tales you are telling? Are you making them up?"

He regarded me solemnly. "Jeanne, I'm telling you only what I've seen. I don't know if they are true or my imagination. But I believe I am being shown a Future-time, for I haven't wit enough to think of something like that. Even so, it doesn't concern us—does it?—for we shall never live to see it."

"No." I sighed, pleating my skirt unhappily between my fingers. "No, but I like to think it real. They must be so happy in that future age."

One night he spoke weeping about the weapons and wars, for now the visions had turned dark.

"They have stone-guns so powerful that when a missile hits, it explodes in a wall of flame. There is fire everywhere, and the roar of their weapons is like the noise of the flying castles. The earth trembles. Thousands are killed in the thunder of one blow—women, children, soldiers, babes."

"Women and children?" we cried in horror. "The citizens and peasants too?"

"Everyone and everything is killed. The landscape is desolate and bare. Craters of mud."

"But who will till the land?"

"That's not right!" cried one fierce soldier. "War is a profession. It has strict rules. It's not directed at civilians."

"We farmers may not know that," Jerome interrupts me. "The knights ride across our plowed fields; the soldiers steal and burn our crops. May God help anyone who lives in an army's path."

He's right, of course. Didn't Montfort burn the crops wherever he went? And weren't towns destroyed and didn't famine wrack the land?

I shake my head at the memory. "I know."

Indeed, that night at Montségur we argued about this harsher kind of war, with some people crying out that what's the point of winning if everything's destroyed? I remember how that night I crawled to bed filled with the terror of Robert's Future-time. It made me grateful to live in my own time, even under siege, rather than in those years when the stone-guns will belch out walls of living flame and thousands will be burnt alive by one stone alone. For that one night, I felt safe under the rain of the French Crusaders' rocks, because they could not clear the walls or explode in fireballs.

But then came Robert's final vision—and our patience snapped. That last evening he was pleased with himself. He strutted proudly up and down. The notes of his music chased one another in a merry hunt and drew colors in the air, dissolving and reappearing, until he smashed them to a stop with a slap to the side of the instrument.

"Listen to me," he announced, as pleased and proud as a lord. "In that time there will be no more darkness, for people will create light by a wave of their hand. Like gods they will turn night into day! In that time, both day and night will be the same, for there is light all the night long."

It was too much for us. The crowd turned on Robert. He had to flee for his very life. They stripped his clothes off his back, punching, biting, kicking, for God alone can create light. Everyone knows this. Light was the first creation of God on the First Day, when he commanded, "Let there be light," and there was light, and God separated the light from the darkness and called the light Day and the darkness he called Night—and what would these poor people do with their very souls at stake, defying the rules of God?

Then bitter fights broke out, with even our *perfecti* (who up till then had listened as delighted as the rest) joining in. Some pointed out that we have fire now, which gives off light and heat and is ignited by striking flint on flint. But others said that fire was God's gift. Still others disbelieved the prophecy altogether, while some broke out in angry protestations, asking when servants would sleep if denied the balm of night, or peasants halt their labor in the fields? How would we know when war could stop without sweet-tempered, starry night, or the wounded be carried off the field and tended to? And what of the stars and moon? Would they grow pale and die without their nightly exercise?

Robert limped for weeks. After that he had no more visions, or if he did, he would no longer tell us them.

"Do people in that time still die?" asks Jerome, going back to digging at his leather with an awl. His question is as innocent as little Esclarmonde's: cat-curious.

"Yes," I answer. "Robert said they grow old and die, just as we do now. But some live to three- and fourscore years and more, because the babies rarely die."

"So it's crowded!"

We had thought that too.

"Is it as crowded as at Montségur?" someone had called out, and a ripple had run through the termite-hive of that room as we'd considered that Future-time to come, when no one would die until extreme old age (except by the fire of the stone-guns). A nightmare, you would think.

But they'll have creams to soften their skin; and now, I glance in the flickering firelight at Jerome, head bent over his work, and think how I would like to have a cream for my raw, wind-burnt face and hands, which once were soft as the tapestry silk with which we sewed. Everyone will have water to bathe in, without cutting wood for the fires to heat it in, or traveling miles to the hot springs.

Oh, there is nothing you can think of they won't have in that Future-time!

"I don't believe a word," says Jerome, stroking the gray cat, which has leapt up and curled right on the leather in his lap.

"No, nor I," I reply. "Though I suppose if you have roads that move you without effort and castles that fly through the air, if you have no disease, and all the creams and clothings of that Golden Age, then perhaps you wouldn't mind living so long. Especially if your friends lived too. But it would be hard," I finish, "if they all died while you could still creep about."

He looks at me sharply, alerted by the catch in my throat.

I lie, eyes open, on my storeroom bed. The room smells of sweat and leather, of strings of onions and garlic, and most prominently of earth (for the walls were dug out of the hillside, or rather formed by digging into the hill). The mattress is thin and my cloak serves as a blanket, but it's not for discomfort that I stay awake. I keep hearing Jerome's words: "He doesn't sound so fine a man to me."

How do you tell one man about another? The pictures rise like bubbles behind my eyes, like jewels: William's blue eyes flashing with excitement as we planned a daring raid, his face washed by moonlight and only inches above my own when we made love, and then his mouth at my ear as he moves gently inside me: *Jeanne Jeanne Jeanne Jeanne Jeanne*. He whispers my name again and again as we make our baby girl, and my body is rising to meet his, my arms around his back, my fingers in his thick hair, our legs entwined, and my back is arching under his hands, our lips so sweetly meeting, William taking little sips of me—of lips and neck and arms—tasting my skin with his tongue, sucking on my breasts and providing pleasure so exquisite that no one could believe it wrong, not even God himself, who presented Eve to Adam in the Garden and whose Son blessed at Cana the wedding ceremony that would result in these delights. I am coming—oh, ecstasy!—and come again, and once again, while he, still in control, moves softly above me, in and out. His face is pale in the moonlight, eyes open, watching me. I lick my lips and close my eyes, falling into his embrace, his scent. He pulls out so far that only the tip is teasing the lips to the entry of my secret cave, tantalizing, circling the precious entry; and "No!" I cry and plunge him back inside, and soon he begins to thrust, faster and firmer, while a throaty growl fills my ear. I rise to meet his passion, crying "Yes!" and I can feel him splash against my deepest part and William's cry and afterward a series of short, spasmodic jerks as he squeezes himself dry.

William drops his weight on me, heavy in my arms. I stroke the hard, flat muscles of his back, still resonating, upswept, in transport. We are one mind, one heart, one body. He is slipping out of me. Juices oozing down my thigh. He has fallen asleep on top of me.

Gradually I slide out from under him. Still sleeping, he rolls onto his back, and I creep in close and rest my cheek on his heart. I can hear the strong, even drumbeat of his soul. His face is as tender and vulnerable as a teenager's. White moonlight fills the corners of the room, casting a pallor over William's face and his bare chest.

"You are filled with light," he told me once. "I feel as if I'm drinking up light when I lie with you."

William sleeps and I smile, because I know he's just given me his baby, and I sit up on one elbow, admiring him while I can, because soon he will have to depart, and I can't bear to waste one moment lost in sleep. I have so little precious time to watch his face, to trace the line of his jaw, to memorize his lips.

But then I drift asleep, and in sleep our souls twine together with our sweet deep breathing, in union, and all night long we lie together, man and wife.

"He doesn't sound so fine a man to me," Jerome had said. But when William entered the room, I came alive; and when he left, the sun died out.

He could be brutal, even cruel; I knew that. Once, after making love, we went to the castle of the Count of Toulouse where William turned his back. He never spoke to me; he acted as if we'd never met, instead of having just risen from our wild bed.

That was nothing, though, compared to his reaction to the babe. I thought he'd be thrilled at the news. Instead, he'd frowned. "Are you sure?" He snapped his fingers nervously.

"But aren't you pleased?" I asked. "I'm so happy. I'm carrying your child. Perhaps a son."

He held me absently. "I have things on my mind," he explained when I pressed him. He added that he'd been called to Foix and from there on to Mirepoix. He would be leaving in the morning—and yes, he'd see Baiona on the trip. But he'd be back in a week or two, and meanwhile I was to take good care of myself.

I pushed my anxieties away. I felt sure he would marry me, now that I was carrying his son. He would divorce Baiona.

He did not return for several weeks. When he did, he said, "I think it's time you married again."

I was taken aback. Searching his face, then recovering: "Oh, you mean marry you."

"Of course not me," he laughed lightly, as if I'd made a joke. "I'm already married, dear. But we have to find a home for you and my unborn son. I've spoken to Roland-Pierre. I saw him recently in Mirepoix and suggested that if he asked for your hand you would give it to him. And he could have a pretty wife—not rich, but not poor either. He likes you well. If you marry quickly, the babe will appear his own."

I didn't like it. I argued. I wept.

"Darling, I want you taken care of. Do this for me. I need to know that you'll be all right, you and my child. You know I would do anything for you. But my hands are tied. All I can do is make provision. I've spent time with Roland-Pierre. I like him. He doesn't know whose child it is. I told him only that I knew you from the Cause and that I wished you well. He's a good man. He'll make you a good husband."

"What will you do?"

He patted my rump. "I'll think of you while I make love to other women. I'll pretend they're you." He laughed and chucked me under the chin.

"How can you say such things!" I didn't know whether to be flattered, angry, hurt, and was all three simultaneously, and in varying degrees and sequences. "How can you say that?"

"Now don't look so downcast, little goose. Give us a kiss. It's not the end. We'll love each other all our lives. If we met when we were eighty, don't you think we'd leap into each other's arms? This is simply a practical solution. I'm not going anywhere, and after you're married, I'll send word to you. We'll find ways to meet." And then his hands were moving over me, and I thrust him away, shouting at him angrily, until he pinned me in both arms, laughing and kissing me. I broke down into tears then, and wept while he held me, crooning love words in my ear.

I lie awake now, all these years later, remembering as if all this had happened yesterday. It's a sad story.

I lived nine years with Roland-Pierre, and slept beside him most of that time; and yet it's William's face I remember hovering over mine, his arms, his voice.

I loved Roland-Pierre in a mild and kindly way, and he made a good husband and a good father to my Guillamette, and he loved her too, as smiling proud and awed as ever a father felt when he held the new baby in his arms. As she grew, he delighted in her pretty ways, and he grieved her loss with his own hot tears, though knowing that she was not of his own seed.

After my marriage to Roland-Pierre, I stayed away from any place where William and I might chance to meet. I gave up my work for the Resistance, became an honest married woman and mother to my girl. As for William, I hated him, but I knew if he were to walk in the door and beckon, I would go.

▨ EIGHTEEN ▨

Another day: it's time to hide my book.

Jerome has taken the sheep to a high pasture and will be gone all day. I look first all over the house, but it has only the two small rooms, no attic space, no hidey-holes. I step out of doors, patting the treasure at my knee, and as I breathe in the sweet soft balmy air, the clear hay-scented air that always follows a storm, standing, looking out, I realize how much I've changed.

I don't want Jerome harmed. The thought jolts me. It's the first time in many months that I've thought of someone besides myself. Stranger yet, I'm thinking of the future instead of dwelling on the past. I don't want Jerome imprisoned because of me or a foolish cord that I no longer wear, or because of the sacred Word, the discovery of which would mean torture and death. Yet I never gave a thought to Mistress Flavia when I stayed there. She could have been killed too, she and her husband and little boy. I feel ashamed. Had they only known what danger they were in!

I stare at the black flagstone threshold, then out at the view. Overhead the clouds are scudding across a milk-curdled sky like running sheep or like the flash of sea-spume on the crest of waves, and the muddy yard looks homey and familiar with its trodden hoofprints and with the poles of the shabby cart tilted aslant against the shed.

I cross to the gate, half off its rusting hinge, and begin to climb up the grassy footpath. My eyes are searching for a hole, a cave, a loose stone. I walk a while before I see what I'm looking for: a beech tree clinging to the side of the hill. Its roots are partially exposed, and they snake into the earth and out again, forming small cavities and gripping deep. Best of all, the tree is off the beaten path.

It takes only a moment to scoop a hole in the dirt between the roots and push my small book, protected by its green oilcloth, deep under the tangle of knotted roots. I close up the hole with dirt and stones and scrape the wet grass forward to hide the exposed earth. When I step back, I can't see much. Tomorrow I'll plant a little bush right there, to hide it further. Meanwhile I return to the path and then see my skirts have bent down the shining, dew-glittering grasses. Anyone can see someone had business at the tree.

To cover my tracks, I reenter the little trail and stoop down to do my business. Yes: a strong brown stool, lest anyone wonder why someone passed this way. By noon the grass will have sprung up again to hide the forbidden Word of God, held in the grasp of the kindly tree.

When I get back to the house, Jerome is there. My heart skips. I suppose my face lights up. But he is staring at my hands, covered with earth, my sloppy shoes and muddy skirts. Inadvertently, I hide my hands behind my back.

"You're back early." I'm as guilty as a schoolgirl caught.

"Where have you been?" he asks.

"Nowhere. Up the hill. I wanted to take a walk."

"Take a walk?"

"I wanted to see the farmyard from above, that's all."

He stares at me quietly. I can see him chewing over my lies, and he knows I'm lying. I feel the blush rise to my throat and spread over my face.

"Oh, now I can't go out to do my own business? You have some objection? I walked out to look about, if you must know. Now I've come back for the water buckets. I thought to do the wash. Do you mind?"

In Future-time they put the linens and bedclothes into barrels and whisper magic words and the barrels do the work. No wonder the women don't grow old.

"And what are you doing home at this hour? As if there isn't work to do?" My voice goes soft. "You're not sick, are you? You've not been hurt?" I take a step forward and stop myself.

He shakes his head no. "I forgot the grip I need to repair the rake. I came back for it."

"Well, since you're here," I nod toward the waterskins. "Help me lift the buckets on the pony. I can't stand here all day. There's work to be done."

Jerome runs his thumb thoughtfully up and down across his nose, wiping away his thought, and lifts the empty water-sacks on the pony's back.

"Can you fill them? They'll be heavy when they're full."

"I'm strong."

"I'll see you later then." He stands, arms crossed, watching me trudge off, leading the pony by its halter-rope. At least the book is safe. Jerome will not be hurt.

Jerome stood a moment, running his tongue thoughtfully around his teeth, considering this conversation, the way she'd ducked her head and wouldn't meet his eyes. What did he really know about her? He was half-certain that she had lived with the heretics and wholly certain that she was not in her right mind, the way she slipped in and out of her tall-tale fantasies. Perhaps she'd never been at Montségur, knew nothing of a buried treasure. Yet he'd stake a pig that she'd been there, perhaps as a baker's wife or a soldier's paramour. For all he knew, the experience had scrambled her brains so that she imagined herself a member of the nobility, and thence unwound her wild fantastical love-story with a knight. Jerome did not believe half of her ravings, but they were entertaining tales, and then too, he could not shake from his head the idea planted by Bernard on market-day of the Cathar treasure. What if, by chance, Jeanne really had been at Montségur? What if she knew something of the treasure? He kicked a stone across the yard and watched it *plink* against another, skip, and come to rest. Dead as a stone. Bernard had said the Inquisitors were searching for a woman.

From his gate, Jerome stared out at the wood and out toward his back-breaking field. He eked out a hard existence on his farm. What he could not do with even a few pieces of silver or of gold! A peasant never saw the like of that; he dealt in pennies if in coin at all. Imagine treasure! He could buy seed, hire a man to work the farm with him, repair the gate, even buy an ox, for an ox was stronger by far than a donkey or pony. He'd plant a vineyard, and add apple and cherry trees in the orchard, pears and quince, and then thinking of Jeanne going for water, he dreamed that he'd build a spring-fed washpool for her. He would line it with good stones to hold the clean water; he would add a rock at one end for her to beat the clothes on. Perhaps the farm could even be enlarged enough to support one of his daughters and her family; or maybe he'd buy that piece of bottomland down in the valley owned by Raymond Domergue.

He found the grip he'd come back for and trailed out to the field again, fondling his dreams and turning over in his mind the handsome woman who had come so suddenly into his life, like a miracle, come unexpectedly to help him with the farmwork and remove his loneliness. He remembered the way her face had changed to concern for him, just now, when she thought he might be hurt. Yet he knew he had to be careful. She was a little mad. Moreover, she had been badly hurt. She was frightened. A wrong word, an unguarded gesture, and she'd be off. He knew this as surely as he knew how to soothe a shy horse or ease it past a danger point; how to rub its muscles and talk it down with patience and quiet stillness. She was a wild woman, and perhaps even a witch, for surely she was bewitching him with her stories and her laughter. For example, her tales of future life. Imagine common people reading books. He snorted impatiently. Imagine the number of copyists you'd need for everyone to have a book.

He bent over his work, shifting and twisting the blades of the rake back into shape. Then he sharpened his scythe once more and set to work. When he stopped again, the sweat pouring down his back and neck, he still had not decided what to do.

There was the business of the Lady Esclarmonde, sister of the Count of Foix. The only thing Jerome knew about this noblewoman was a tavern tale he'd heard of how Saint Dominic's companion, Brother Stephen, had put her in her place when she'd tried to join a discussion on spiritual matters.

"Go tend your distaff, madam; it is no business of yours to discuss matters such as these."

Some of the men in the tavern had snickered at the monk's cleverness, and others had laughed at the disdain this woman must have felt for the foreigner's boorish remark. She was educated, the mistress of her own lands, and not accustomed to being dismissed.

On the other hand, Jerome remembered also how years ago four hundred *perfecti,* both men and women, were burnt at Lavaur, when the Crusaders took the town. Four hundred in one swoop! They were protected by the chatelaine of Lavaur, Guiraude, daughter of the renowned *perfecta* Blanche de Laurac (and even Jerome had heard of this woman, famous for her charity and prayers). And yet when the fortress was taken, the Crusaders, against all the principles of war and chivalry, dragged Guiraude out of the town gates, threw her in a well, then stoned her until she was buried. Her position was not enough to save her from the mob. What would happen to a solitary peasant woman?

The wars raged on, sometimes with one side acting, then another. At Cordes an angry crowd threw three Dominican Inquisitors into a well. But the following year at Moissac, the Inquisitors burnt two hundred and ten persons at the stake. At one point the Inquisitors were expelled from Toulouse, but on their return to power a hundred eighty-three *perfecti* were burnt alive at Marne.

And here was Jeanne.

One moment he thought to send her packing. He'd tell her tonight that in the morning she'd have to leave. He'd be generous: he'd give her a waterskin and bread and onions, maybe some raw pulse.

The next moment he decided he would take her to church on Sunday; he would watch to see how she sat through the service, and whether she knew the Catholic ways or not. Witches did not like church, and neither did heretics, he guessed, although if truth be told (removing his cap and rubbing his sweating brow with one forearm), he had no experience with either one. He'd never met a witch, but he'd heard of them riding on their broomsticks by night, and weren't they ugly creatures, bent and ancient, with chins that thrust forward in toothless mouths as if to touch their long hooked noses? Well, Jeanne did not resemble that. Moreover, he himself was a good Catholic, a believer in Christ our Lord, and no witch or heretic could harm him so long as he attended Mass and said his sacred prayers—as he did, God knows, every night.

No, she was a good woman, he conceded, to think of drawing water for the wash. And not unpleasing to look at. And what if by chance she really *could* lead him to gold coin? So his mind circled the problem. Who was she?

On impulse, he set down his tools and turned to climb the hillside above the house where Jeanne had gone. It didn't take long to reach the beech tree. Jerome stood, pensively rubbing his nose. The tracks were clear: here she had stopped and moved off the beaten path, cut through the thick grass to the left. Yet the mix of ash and beech trees hid the view that she'd claimed to be seeking, and no one would climb this high anyway, he thought, just to look at the land. You could see across his field from the barnyard gate.

He stared at the grass, partially beaten down but rising as the stalks dried in the sun. She had stepped right up to the tree; that much was clear. Faugh! He bent to part the grass and examine the wet stool, then rose, his eyes tracing the great exposed roots of the beech tree. He looked back at the surrounding brush, the white trees standing silent as sentinels, the footpath winding on up the mountain.

But why had she walked all this way? Above his head the beech leaves shivered gently. He could almost feel the heat of the trees, as if they knew and breathed their secrets to the air. The beech was whitish-gray, with thin, smooth bark. Its thick roots twisted like snakes, gripping into the rocky ground so hard that Jerome wondered if the dirt and earth provided purchase for the tree or if those huge roots, those giant's fingers, were holding up the elemental rock.

He gave one more look about before he turned and made his way back down to the field. His curiosity was still not satisfied: she'd come that far for some reason, and she hadn't told him why. Now what was he to do? He remembered Alzeu. If she was a heretic, his keeping her was dangerous.

I lift the waterbags from the pony. They are heavy, and they will be heavier yet when full. The pony drops his shaggy head to crop the cress and long wet grass beside the giggling stream, and a sudden whiff of mint fills the air. I stop a moment, staring at the light-struck, rippling water, thinking about my conversations with Jerome. For the first time I see myself as a selfish, grasping child. I had not loved William. I had wanted him, and I did everything I could to possess and hold him. Had I ever asked what I could do for him?

❖ NINETEEN ❖

Sunday. We prepare for church, Jerome and I. He has insisted. My heart is battering my chest as if it wants to get out, and my hands shake, but I brush my clothes, wipe my shoes, tie an apron over my gray woolen gown. Nothing I can do to look much better. Jerome puts on the clean shirt I washed, and over this a sleeveless coat. His boots lace up his hose. He looks nice. But though I manage a weak smile, I want to run. How can I go into the church that killed my friends? Pretend to worship? And what am I to do in church? Stand up and confess to everyone, or scream out my anger at God, the cross, the priest who will read the lessons and give a sermon while I squirm? I can hardly breathe, and yet Jerome has taken my arm harshly and is pulling me along, and though my feet are wooden, so that I stumble awkwardly, I cannot find the strength to resist.

"Do you go every week?" I ask, hoping for distraction.

"No, but when I can, and every holy day. To give my thanks and prayers. I'm a good Catholic."

We walk the few miles to the stone chapel, and all the while his grip is firm on my arm. The little church nestles in a fold of the hills, on the outskirts of a few scattered houses that like to call themselves a village. The bells are ringing gaily in the thin air as we approach.

"Ah, Domergue!" Jerome calls out, throwing up his hand in greeting. They stand in a knot at the church door, a clutch of men and women and two children, curious as cats to meet the woman Jerome's found. I hang back shyly.

"This is Jeanne Béziers," Jerome says, introducing me, and they give their names in return.

First Raymond Domergue, solid and square, ruddy-faced. When he smiles, his eyes disappear into the folds and pockets of his face.

"My wife, Alazaïs," he says formally. She's short, tough, a peasant farmer's wife, worn by weather and work, who looks me up and down openly and unabashed.

"Delighted to meet you. He needs help on that big farm."

Domergue is introducing his son, Martin, and then another Raymond, his son-in-law (both strapping men) and Raymond's wife, Bernadette, who is eight months *enceinte* from the look of her protruding belly, or maybe about to foal at any time; and there are several children including a young girl, Fays, barely more than a child, and a toddling granddaughter, Raymonde. All of them, adults and children alike, are examining me from head to toe, and I'm maybe not coming off too well by comparison with Jerome's late wife.

"I thank you for the headdress," I say timidly to Alazaïs. "It was generous of you."

"A loan. Jerome says you'll give it back." She's staring at it on my head.

"Yes. Yes. You'll have it back." I'm blushing—how?

"Next time I'm in town," Jerome interrupts, "I'll buy you material for a new one, Alazaïs. I'll make a special trip this week. But listen, after church why don't you come by the house?" His eyes are sparkling with pleasure, his lips curled up in that merry smile I like.

I open my mouth to protest.

"Why yes," said Alazaïs. "We will."

I haven't time to say a word because Domergue is hurrying us inside, amidst the bonging of the bells and press of the other parishioners.

"It's time for the service."

The bells are pealing, and I am being led to slaughter.

"Why did you ask them over?" I whisper nervously.

"Shoosh now. Come along." Jerome's hand locks firmly on my elbow again. The blood rushing to my face, I hesitate to cross the doorway, enter the tiger's lair, for the thought flashes through me: What if the priest recognizes me for a heretic, a lapsed bad one at that, and a worse Catholic? I am praying for strength and faith, for God lives in this house of prayer, and I remember how Guilhabert de Castres used to tell us to worship in any house of God, of whatever persuasion, for God is always around us, everywhere, and worship is always just. "It is right and meet to give Him praise and thanks, a good and joyful thing, wherever we are."

We used to worship in the Catholic church (and I remember how once William and his best friend, Peter, rode their horses into the big cathedral in Toulouse, clomping up the aisles amidst the sellers of wax candles and wooden figures of the saints, William laughing as his giant horse let loose a pile of manure on the stones. Then he dismounted to say his prayers. Afterward both men were chastised angrily by the Good Christians for desecrating another's holy place). Once Guilhabert attended a Moorish worship, though the Moors were not killing his people, of course, or wiping out all memory of the Friends of God. I drag inside after Jerome.

It is a country church, of low vaults and quiet, peaceful stones: you can almost hear them breathe, and a thousand years of prayers have sunk into its soft, round, comforting curves. At the altar hangs a painted cross with Christ bleeding, his head hanging to his shoulder. My heart gives a tug of pity for the man who suffered on the cross (unless, as the Cathars say, he did not die, since spirit cannot die—but even so, he suffered for us here).

The priest mouths his Latin. He has a curious dialect that I find hard to follow. The congregation consists of five families, not much more. I kneel and rise, intoning the comforting responses weakly while I look about. Even in an Arab mosque, said Guilhabert, God can be found, for there is no place God is not; and God is not to be sought inside any structure built by human hands, but only in the stillness of a pure, cleansed heart. I think how impure is my heart, criticizing the young priest, and no wonder I don't see God. Maybe he can't read the Latin, or maybe he never wanted to be a celibate and had no other way to eat. Look at him, bony and awkward, not much older than twenty.

The sermon is on sin, and how it is pardoned only by Christ through His appointed priests of the Catholic Church, which is the Bride of Christ, His most beloved.

When we leave the church, Jerome introduces me to the priest. I mumble greetings timidly. I feel Jerome's hand on my wrist and I hardly speak, for any false move now will only hurt Jerome. But the priest too is cordial.

"Welcome to our church," he says, smiling and a little forlorn. "I hope to see you often, then."

I mumble yes or no or sounds unknown.

"And remember confession," he adds kindly. "I'm here all Sundays and Wednesdays and all holy days."

The Domergues walk home with us. They will stay to dinner, so my mind is on what we have on the storeroom shelves and whether the place is tidy. The conversation around me is mostly about the passage of time and when the last market-day was, everyone counting how long I've been with Jerome. And then the men—Martin, Domergue, Raymond, and Jerome—go off on crops and rain. With each step farther from the church, I feel myself relax: the service is over, and I am still alive, and now I don't need to go again until Christmas at least. My spirits perk up. It wasn't so bad, after all, and wouldn't Bishop de Castres have been proud of me! Alazaïs takes my arm. "It will be nice to have a woman neighbor close." The smile I turn on her is genuine.

We sit on the benches by the jolly fire, the men along one side, the women and the knee-baby, Raymonde, on the other; the older girl, Fays, sits at our feet. Alazaïs lifts her skirts to warm her ankles and knees, and soon we're laughing together, she and I, as she waves her skirts to draw the warmth to the tender parts higher up. And then the men—the two without hose—catching our drift, lift their own long, belted shirts to bring the heat right up to their bare balls.

The Domergues' daughter, Bernadette, is laughing at them and hits her husband playfully to pull down his shirt, stop that, what does he think he is doing in front of the young ones. Fays glances up in surprise because she wasn't paying attention and wants to know why we're laughing, what she's missed.

Looking at Bernadette, I feel in my own body how the baby catches right up at her ribcage so that she can hardly breathe. The sensation kicks me in the throat. It's her third child, though, an easy labor being expected. She has Raymonde, named after the grandfather; and she has a boy,

Gaillard, who isn't with us this afternoon. Nor was he at church this morning. Alazaïs and Domergue have another daughter, Sybille, married now and living over near Narbonne.

I offer bread and honey, wine, apples, and walnuts to crack before the fire, and we are all jocund this night. God loves us when we sing and laugh, says Esclarmonde, since He laughs through us, and He likes to laugh and love.

I don't tell the Domergues this, lest they ask who was Esclarmonde, but I'm caught up in their high spirits and laughing too, and all the while I peek under my lashes at this man who lets me stay in his house. He has a bald spot the size of a penny on the back of his brown head, though his cap covers it usually. He has a merry smile, and even at rest the left-hand corner of his mouth tilts upward elfishly. He wipes his laughing mouth with the back of his left hand, and the raw scar flashes red in the firelight where he mashed his fingers in a millstone when he was young. I like his looks.

But my attention is drawn back to the pregnant Bernadette. She is telling me of her son, Gaillard. He is sickly. I feel my hands tingle as she talks. The gentleness falls over me.

"I'd like to see him," I murmur. "I know some herbs."

"We had the surgeon come." Her voice is strident, rising with emotion. "He bled him, but it did no good. We paid him well too. What they think to charge! Do you know what he costs now? Don't get sick, I say, because whether the surgeon makes you well or no, you can't afford it."

"Foolish to have the surgeon," says Domergue, the child's grandfather, and when he narrows his eyes they disappear entirely in his cheeks. "I've killed or nursed as many donkeys back to health as he has men. I told you it would be a waste of money."

"I'd like to see the lad," I murmur again.

"Come tomorrow," says the grandmother, Alazaïs. "He'll be home. Don't be afraid you'll miss him. He doesn't move. He can't catch his breath anymore."

His mother looks away.

"White as his shroud," says Domergue, cracking another walnut. "He'll not be long with us." His voice is as rough as a raven's caw. He's already prepared. He'll waste no time in grief. Too many Domergues gone; too many still to go. *Crack,* go the walnut tongs. Protect yourself from pain and just don't think.

"Tomorrow I'll come down," I say, for I like Alazaïs and her family, and it's nice to be in company. "Maybe I can help."

And so I go next day to meet the poor, white, sickly child. He is feverish, as they said. I lift him onto my lap. My hands rest on his chest, where I can hear the bubbling in his lungs. They pause on the back of his neck, on his spine, the joints of his hips and legs.

"I hurt," he whimpers.

"Hush now, darling," I murmur in his ear. "You'll be fine."

"My legs hurt," he says, and then, "Your hands are so hot. They feel like fire."

"You like this? Sitting in my lap?"

"It feels good," he says, relaxing into me. Soon he falls asleep. And my hands are tingling, burning, as they touch his heart, his throat.

"What do you think is wrong?" asks Bernadette, easing her great belly as she sits. The knee-baby, Raymonde, one thumb in her mouth, holds to her skirt, peeking at me with round, suspicious eyes. "We had him bled," she repeats helplessly.

"I'll fix him some tea," says I, already trying to remember where I saw that yellow plant I like to brew. And my hands, like living animals, brush back his hot hair from his sweating brow and cling to his neck and chest. "Let him sleep for now. I'll come by this evening with the tea."

But I do not move for a long time. My hands won't let me leave off touching him.

❖ TWENTY ❖

Night. Jerome is sharpening his scythe, honing it on a stone, and all I can hear in the room is the long, stripping screech of blade on stone as he strokes the iron, wets the stone, strokes the iron, wets the stone.

"Stop it." I come to my feet.

He looks up in dumb surprise.

"What?"

"That. That noise. I can't bear it."

He gives a grunt and continues as if I haven't said a word. Squeal of blade on stone, as if I haven't heard the blades, the stones, and sometimes the stroke is a crunch of bones and screams and screams. "I mean it. Stop."

He looks at me a long and puzzled time, rubs his mouth thoughtfully, and then puts down the tools. "All right. Time for bed anyway."

That night I wake up screaming at the sound of the squealing blade.

"Woman, what's the matter?"

Something is grappling for my hands, holding me down, as I flail my arms. "Jeanne. Wake up." His face is buried in my neck; my mouth is covered, muffling my scream, until I break out of the terror of my dream and suck in a startled breath.

"What is it?" asks Jerome. "Come on, old girl."

He turns my face to him and wipes my cheeks with the end of his nightshirt. "There, there, now. You're all right. Just a dream you had, a nightmare, right?"

I nod.

"See? Everything's all right." He is rocking me in his arms. I am a child being rocked in his strong arms, and my arms creep around his neck to hide my face in the pungent scent of his sleepy shoulder. I nuzzle the soft beard at his throat.

"What is it?" he repeats. But how do I describe the thunder of the hooves? The bloody sword?

I yelp and push away.

"Where are you going?" He calls, following me. "Don't go outside. It's night. Use the chamberpot." And then, "Damn!" as he stubs his toe on the rake, which falls with a clatter.

Outside, the cold stars wink down. I throw back my head, breathing in the cold black pain and loneliness. I'd like to howl my rage at the unfeeling stars, but behind me I feel Jerome watching.

Suddenly it's decided: I leave tomorrow; at first light I'll be off. I whimper. Like a dog. I'm being followed. They will find me. I'm afraid.

Jerome's hand touches my elbow. "Come on, old girl." His voice is the murmur of a river, bubbling over stones. "Time for bed, come on home." He lifts me in his arms, and I'm clinging to him as he carries me inside, lays me on his bed. My arms creep round him again. I know he'll keep me safe.

In the morning I awaken slowly, his arm heavy across my waist. The light is just creeping into the room, enough to make out his dim features, relaxed in sleep, his mouth ajar, his stubbly chin just at the level of my eyes. He is breathing sweetly. He looks innocent as a little boy, and my stomach twists. I want to do something good for him. I lie under his arm, careful not to move or wake him up and taking in his distinctive male scent, the heavy smell of sleep. Happiness floods me. I want to do for him, but what can I do but rise, start a fire, cook a meal? Then I remember that last night I promised myself I'd leave, and now I don't want to go. Will one day matter? I want to go see the Domergue boy today, who seems to be on the mend, imagine, for his breathing has quieted now and his fever has gone; and after that I'll leave.

I edge closer to Jerome, and in his sleep he shifts and pulls me to him. "Treasure," he mumbles, and my body softens; I lie smiling in his embrace.

I shell beans into the tin pot, and they ring against the metal like the silver echo of the horse's hooves. The sunlight is warm here on the stone threshold. Jerome has gone to market; it's not so major an undertaking, with me here to tend to the place, and he promised Alazaïs a new headdress. I'm back from the Domergues, alone here on the farm, and singing to myself as I bask in the blessed, healing silence. The wind whispers in the swaying branches of bare trees, and an occasional stray bird whistles in the autumn light. The chickens scratch and chuckle in the grass.

All morning I've been trying to claw up an image from the mud of memory. Why do I remember one white hoof?

Then it comes back: the ring of the horseshoes on the stones of the courtyard. The jostling horses. Men's loud voices and one man's deep laugh as another shouted to get out of the way.

The horses' hooves are as big as dinner plates, and above them hang the huge bellies of the horses, towering over me, a little child, and on top of those the metal-plated, terrifying knights.

"Out of the way, little maid," Count Raymond bellowed as his black horse reared back, one white hoof looming above me. I scurried to one side. The horse came back to earth with a clatter of hooves on stones, then like the other horses pranced and jiggled in excitement. And then on Count Raymond's cry, "*Avaunt!*" they charged out of the courtyard with a deafening noise through the arched stone gate. My hands to my ears. They have no faces, no eyes behind their metal masks.

The hot bodies of the horses were running past me, and the thunder of hooves was like water falling down a cliff.

Then they were gone.

Silence.

Only then did I realize Count Raymond might have hurt me.

I was in the way.

I put the beans down on the floor. Suddenly nervous. A confusion cloaking me: Am I in the way? Does Jerome want me here? How long have I been here? Thoughts scurrying again, squirrels scrabbling in my head: I'm in danger; he's in danger. They'll take him. He'll be coming back soon, and I have to leave before he returns. Where's my mantle? I need to root out my precious book. But I must put the beans to soak. He'll need his dinner. Leave . . . stay . . . leave . . .

I pour water on the beans to soak, and pick up a trowel to dig up my Good Book, and then I hang it back on its peg. Jerome is a good man. I want to leave and I want to stay, and I'm paralyzed, not knowing what to do; for I don't hear my voices anymore, or else so faintly I can't distinguish them from my own thoughts.

Winter is coming on, and near Christmas Jerome will need help slaughtering the pig (it's owned half with the Domergues). He went to market for salt. And maybe he will buy some fine white powdered peat salt from the Low Countries, as we used to have at Esclarmonde's, or perhaps he will find salt from Bourgneuf Bay in Brittany, which is almost as good, and then he will need help in grinding it and with the butchering, and with packing the meat in salt. I count on my fingers: for twenty pounds of fresh meat, we need two pounds of salt, and that will cost eight-tenths a pence. I don't know how much he took with him. If the meat is to be any good, we'll also need peppercorns and cloves, cinnamon, nutmeg, mace, raisins of Corinth, almonds for the almond milk, and flour of rice. . . . Ah, the meals we used to have! I could make Jerome a blamanger, one day when we kill a chicken. I would take a little of the inferior meat and shred it, then blend it with whole rice that has been boiled in almond milk, seasoning the whole with sugar, sautéed almonds, and anise seeds.

If we had sugar.

Or almonds.

Or anise seeds.

I begin to scour the pots with sand, and count the peppercorns preparatory to his coming home, and after a time I realize I've been saying "we" in my mind, to myself, so apparently it's not yet time to leave. To my surprise I find myself singing once again, as I lay the fire, singing a song of happiness. And then I remember that that is one of the ways God speaks to us: in harmony and peace, and I am peaceful here. *I will lift up mine eyes unto the hills. From whence cometh my help?* How is it that I have forgotten my Lord God in these last weeks? I've forgotten that all things are possible for God, even forgiving me for what I've done; and suddenly I burst into tears at such grace. Forgiveness, yes. For perhaps I did nothing so very wrong, leaving them—William, Baiona, and the others; perhaps it was God's will, and He has brought me here for reasons I will never understand.

If I had my Book and if my eyes could read the tiny words, I could spell out the love of God; or merely hold the treasure in my hands and meditate on Christ, who came to bring us life, vitality, and joy, and bring it most abundantly. Well, here I am lifting up mine eyes, and the hills are beautiful right here. I am in the hands of my Beloved, who leadeth me beside still waters, so that I do not need to leave this farm or worry about the valley of the shadow of death—and neither will Jerome—though (laughing) if I don't gather kindling we'll be in want of fire soon enough; I throw on my shawl then and go outside to gather wood. Because I'm going to stay with Jerome; the decision's made.

I am bent under the load when I hear the creak of the wooden cart. I do not stop. I want to drag out the sweet, exquisite agony before I turn and see his face. I keep on, but my mouth is smiling, and then I cannot stand it any longer and I throw down the load and turn, my face alight. He is walking by the cart, and my eyes are rewarded for their long wait, because he lifts his hat to me gaily.

When he comes even with me, I heave the faggots in the cart and walk along beside him.

"Good day?" I ask.

"Not bad." He is whistling under his breath. It must have been a happy day.

He winds the reins around his bad left hand and puts his other round my shoulder, and so we walk up to the house together, and somehow a decision has been made, and I shall stay till spring.

That night we eat black maslin bread. I hollow out a shallow hole and pour into each a spoonful of the stockpot stew. We each have a hunk of sheep cheese, and are happy as two turtledoves. He tells me the market news and shows me what he's bought: salt, a block of sugar, almonds, and mixed spices for the winter. I'm so delighted that I clap my hands. He's also bought the promised new headdress for Alazaïs—and another one for me, so that I have an extra for a feast day too.

Tomorrow, he tells me, he will go hunting up the mountain for rabbits, grouse, or other small game.

"No, don't. What if you're caught? Only the nobles have the right to hunt."

"I've snared small game before. I'm experienced."

"We don't need it," I plead. "We have a half a pig."

"Don't worry. I'll be all right."

But now I have another fear—that something will happen to Jerome. I used to hawk on horseback with the nobility, and hunt deer and elk with the hounds, and whip the peasants off the land; they'd be hanged if the bailiffs caught them poaching.

"Apparently you used to live another life," he says.

"It's true." Then I tell him of my memory of the white-hoofed horse.

"A good-luck memory," he claims.

I laugh. "What in the world would make one memory good luck and not another?"

"Don't you know the old rhyme?" he asks. Then he chants it for me, all sing-song:

> One white sock, buy him;
> Two white socks, try him;
> Three white socks, nobody knows;
> Four white socks, feed him to the crows.

I cover my ears in mock agony at his rendition.

"That's how you buy a horse," he explains. "But you saw *one* white hoof, so it's luck. I think the horse is me; you should buy it."

Laughing, I shake my head at him. We're laughing. It is dark in the cabin now, with only the feeble red glow of the smoky fire. Jerome is stroking the cat that purrs in his lap.

"Tell me about the siege of Montségur." He's caught me off-guard.

"There's nothing to tell." My voice is hard.

He says nothing, but tilts the cat off his lap and reaches for my hand. "Come over here. I know you were there."

"Why do you want to know?"

"Tell me."

"It was boring, dirty, crowded. We were hungry." I don't even try to deny it.

"I want to know what happened to you. I want to know how you got there. And how you left. I want to know everything."

The cat settles by the fire and licks her paw, purring, and cleans behind her dainty ears, and it seems so dark I shake my head, because the darkness lurks behind my eyes, and even the red firecoals do not dispel it. My lips are moving: *My help cometh from the Lord, which made heaven and earth. He will not suffer thy foot to be moved: he that keepeth Israel shall neither slumber nor sleep.*

"Jeanne?"

I won't answer.

"Jeanne. The siege."

"It's disease, dysentery, dirt, that's all. Lice and fleas and cold. Did I mention hunger? We were hungry all the time." Suddenly tears spurt from my eyes and I strike out. "No, no, no!"

He grabs my flailing hands. "Hush, hush. Whoosh, shh, sh, sh." And in another moment I am caught against his chest and he is stroking my hair with his quiet hand. "Shhoosh, shh," he says, and he is kissing my brow. "Shhoosh, there," until I calm down.

"It's good sometimes to talk," he says.

I lean against him, one hand stroking the soft, worn leather of his jerkin.

"There were four hundred people trapped on the mountaintop," he begins for me. "Two hundred were *perfecti*."

"Yes."

"And the other two hundred were——?"

"Soldiers—either volunteers or mercenaries, who had signed on to support the Good Christians. Their women, camp followers."

"And you were one of these?"

I start to pull away; it's dangerous to talk of Montségur.

He strokes my cheek and then he takes my hands between his and blows on them with his breath and then holds them to his lips and kisses them, and that gesture is so gentle that suddenly the words are pouring from my mouth, a flood. I cannot stop: I've been so lonely. I've been so alone. Yet all I've ever wanted is to be loved.

❦ TWENTY-ONE ❦

It began on May 13.

For seven months, until Christmas, we withstood the siege well, all of us crammed into one small fortress. We maintained a discipline: the knights and their ladies and servants had their quarters, and the common soldiers had lesser ones; and everyone had tasks: the bakers, the cooks, the barbers, the steward, the two astrologers, each working so that food could be properly rationed and prepared and a schedule maintained for feeding everyone and keeping order.

There was a space near the fires for those who were sick or aged, and another area was blocked off for the wounded. The women kept to their own quarters, with their servants—all but the soldiers' paramours, and the prostitutes that follow any army. The Friends of God kept separate, many in the huts that leaned against the outer walls, but we were all crowded and dirty, and after a time tempers grew short and sometimes snapped.

At first it was easy, during the spring and summer months, when we still expected reinforcements; Count Raymond would not leave us there, we knew, but autumn came and the nights grew chill; and then the freezing rains began, and later the winter, the worst winter in memory, the stones slippery with ice. It was horrible to be outdoors in the courtyard (full of tents and wooden shacks), and sometimes the sleet turned to snow, with the wind whipping in our faces, in our eyes.

The French encircled the foot of the mountain, six to ten thousand of them, but we were safe on top: the enemy could not climb the sheer cliffs, while the one well-trodden pathway is so twisting and narrow that we could easily defend it. Any force attempting that climb would have been picked off one by one before they could have grouped to attack. We owned the mountain, and at first, in the early months, we laughed at the siege. I was one of those who roamed the mountain, or slipped through the enemy lines to carry messages. We could still walk down the mountain then, and we knew some of the sentries posted as guards. They came from our area, sympathizers, even though in the pay of the French; and I'll say that friendship and kinship go a long way, further than coins.

I carried messages in my head from the besieged soldiers to outlying resistance groups, and sometimes, just as a prank, I dressed as an old woman and hobbled through the enemy camp to hear what news I could pick up, or else I organized the young girls to saunter through the French lines and bring us back reports. Sometimes I walked to market to buy supplies—eggs, chickens, root vegetables. It takes a lot to feed four hundred men. But my service wasn't special. I was only one of many couriers who organized the paths by which the wagons would proceed or sweet-talked a sentry to let us pass. I was strong and tough. By night whole groups of us helped carry basketloads up the steep face of the *pog,* walking in excited silence lest we be discovered. Our spirits were still high.

All autumn the men could still go hunting, for though the French had chased away the game with their noise and hounds, our men were able to snare rabbits in their lures and down an occasional deer. But as the days passed, the game grew scarce. By full winter we were starving, eating roots and grains as if we were perfected ones ourselves.

The boredom was the worst. Confinement led to fights amongst ourselves: a game of dice or chess would suddenly erupt in shouts and fisticuffs, and even swordplay, and then the others would rush to break it up, because we couldn't afford to fight ourselves. Or else two women would start screaming at each other, competing for a man, or two men would come to blows over a woman or an insult to a wife. After a time we fought discouragement too, for our Count had not come, despite all our messages. He sent word that a great army was being raised to lift the

siege and that we should wait till Michaelmas, and then till Advent, and
then till after Christmas.

I had been there since the beginning, since May, and William had
joined us only a few weeks later, in June. All during my marriage, I'd
stayed apart from William faithfully, but after Roland-Pierre died, we had
come bumpily together again, William and I, because I was drawn back to
the work. For months at a time we wouldn't see each other, and then for
weeks we'd be thrown together again by work or geography, and our love
affair would burst back into flames, always dying down again when we
parted.

Now it happened that we were both in Montségur that summer, once
more defending our noble *parage* and the Pure Ones whom we loved. I
was fiercely glad. He was mine at last, to sleep with openly. I belonged to
him, and he to me; there was no secret to our relationship. After all, we
were trapped up there, isolated from the outside world, and Baiona was
far away. This made my time at Montségur pleasant all that spring and
summer, when we were under siege and sure we'd win in the end.

One day late in August, when we could still easily cross the lines, I
saw a party filing up the hill carrying provisions. A crowd gathered as
usual at the gate, and some walked partway down the mountain to meet
the new arrivals, so dull was life. I too had gone outside to welcome the
travelers, when to my dismay I recognized one figure amongst those
struggling up the path. My heart lurched. How did I know her instantly?
Her head was down and her body covered with a heavy woolen mantle
that would be needed come winter. She carried a pack on her back. She
plodded slowly upward. Perhaps she gave an upward glance as she paused
to catch her breath and gauge the distance still to climb. Perhaps she lifted her hand to shield her eyes or smooth her headdress. I don't know
how people recognize each other, when a face cannot be seen. But we do.
It's as if each person sends out a signal or is surrounded by an invisible
coloration that cries out, "It is I." I knew her immediately, from that
simple glimpse between the pines.

I faded back, peering between the heads of others in the crowd. I
watched William trot halfway down the hillside to greet his wife with a
kiss and take her pack. I crept along the fortress wall, slipped behind the
joyous crowd and back into the fort and across the spacious courtyard to

the far door on the opposite wall. I plunged outside again, and partway down the western hillside, scrambling down the incline until I was alone. I sat down on a rock.

I didn't want her there, the wife. William and I formed a couple there at Montségur, bonded by war and love and memories, and by our baby who'd died, and by that magic drink the witch had made for me. I had not seen Baiona in twenty years.

When I finally went inside again, I found that William had moved my things to another room. The gesture lit a cold fire in my gut, but I said nothing, did nothing.

For two days I managed to avoid her, slipping through the crowded rooms. Baiona no more wanted to meet me than I did her, but there we were, hundreds of people crawling like termites over one another, brushing shoulders, touching hands. We each had space only as wide as our shoulders for sleeping and possessions, and some slept several to a bed, toe to head, and these private areas were so carefully mapped out, according to rank, that though we might have to slide over one another to reach our own bed, no one stole another's possessions: honor bound.

Separated by the length of a room sometimes were Baiona and I, and yet our eyes never met, though I marked her every movement, as aware as a cat is of a cricket on the floor: alert to her every twitch. Did I feel guilty? Yes. And jealous too. It pleased me to see that she had aged. Her skin was lined now, her hair gray. Her eyes were puffy and sunken into dark pockets. Yet from the moment William saw her coming up the path that day, he changed. He no longer brushed up against me in a doorway teasingly, but kept pious company with the men. He waited on his wife, the considerate husband, bringing her a shawl or her embroidery, settling her on a pillow to make sure she was comfortable. He avoided me, or, if that wasn't possible, gave me no more than a smile or a nod in promise of things to come.

Old lovers know each other's ways. I knew to stay apart. I hoped for his return to me, though, and one day I felt an arm encircle my waist from behind. I turned to him with a flashing smile—it vanished on seeing Baiona.

"Jeanne."

My quick recovery: "Baiona! When did you get—?"

"Don't." Her finger almost touched my lips. "Don't do that. Come. I need to talk to you."

Perhaps so, but did I need to talk to her? Reluctantly I followed her outdoors and then out through the back gate. We wound our way to a pile of rocks and each chose one to sit on, side by side, but not too close. It was an overcast gray day with a soft wind ruffling the mountainside. The smell of a summer lightning storm, and in the distance the growl of thunder stalking us.

It was not chilly, but I wrapped my shawl tight, my hands inside, arms crossed on my chest, crossed against her. She leaned forward, peering nearsightedly into my face.

"How are you, Jeanne? How have you been?"

"All right."

We circled each other like two dogs, stiff-legged, sniffing, wary, tails stiff and hackles bristling, not quite growling, but nervous and testing each other.

"And you?" I asked finally.

"I'm older. You look just the same, though——so trim."

"Your hair's gone gray," I said ruthlessly.

"Yes. And yours not so much. Silver streaked. You look . . ." She searched my face. "Beautiful."

Again she took me by surprise. "It's not easy seeing you," I confessed.

"No. Nor for me. But I have to talk to you. I thought about just pretending that we never see each other as we pass, but actually I miss you. And I'm curious."

Missed me? *Me?*

"I've heard reports of you over the years. I heard about your husband's death, and that of your little girl. I'm sorry. I lost four children too, unborn or stillborn, so I know. . . . And then every so often I hear about some daring adventure you've had. You're famous. At least William thinks you are."

I said nothing. Lost four children. He'd never said a word.

"He thinks the world of you," she went on rapidly, the words tumbling out too quickly. "He brings me news, how he's seen you here or there, always working for the Cause."

I watched her hands twisting in her lap. Her gray eyes roamed the heaving, stormy clouds and ranged across the green plain stretched out below and dotted with its white and brown tents and the grazing horses and people like tiny ants. The greens of field and forest changed hue under the darkening sky.

"Don't think it's been easy for me," she rattled on, running her words together. "I'm not complaining; I'm just telling you. You know that Esclarmonde didn't want me to marry William, and many times I've wondered what would have happened if I'd listened to her. Or if we hadn't had the wars. Always struggling for money—that's been hard. And then the children—my being unable to bear children and that's been a weight on my heart. When William wanted them so much." (I freeze: William wanted them?) "And then his women, so many women, and always coming to me for money for his next plan or for a new charger or another wild plan to make a fortune—"

She'd said "many women." But I'd known that, hadn't I? Why did it come as a surprise?

She must have seen my face. "He loves women. Women love him. We used to quarrel over that. Sometimes he'd be seeing two women at the same time. Sometimes three. I've learned he'll never be faithful to me. I've accepted that. And his excuses: 'I couldn't help myself,' he'd explain. 'I felt this mysterious something, it's unreasonable. I didn't want to be attracted.' And then he'd swear he loved only me. He'd hold my skirts as he knelt before me, his head in my lap, clinging to me, and say that he was wicked, no good, nothing, that he didn't deserve a wife like me, that I should kill him right there, run a sword through him; that it wasn't worth being involved with him." Her voice was rising hysterically. "He had these sudden dark black moods. But you know that. You were one of his women, weren't you?" She laughed, a single bark. "Yes, I see it in your eyes.

"'I've deceived you,' he told me once, 'but I've never betrayed you.'

"And then he'd come galloping back to me with some new scheme for making money. He's a dreamer, always hatching some harebrained plot, but they rarely come to ought."

"Baiona," I said, but couldn't manage more.

She looked up then with eyes so anguished I could not tear mine away. "I wanted you to know. I know you love him, have always loved him, you were one of many women, though maybe more special, I don't know; and

I thought you ought to know it's not been good for me; and maybe——"
She stopped.

"Why did you come?" I asked stiffly.

"To show my support. Because finally it was time for me to take a stand,
to fight. I don't mean fight you, or the other women; I mean fight for the
Way, our way of life, *parage*. For William's cause, which ought to be mine——
ought to have been mine all the time, except I'm such a coward." She hardly
paused for breath: twenty years of pent-up emotion pouring out.

"You fight, Jeanne. I hear about you working for the Cause, while I'm
too scared to even ride a horse."

"You didn't come to be with William?"

"Of course to be with William. And with you. I've been so envious of
you, living as you pleased, doing what you wanted, independent,
unafraid, while I've stayed at home——not even my own home; we're
always staying in one knight's castle or another's——not even a chateau of
my own——always living at someone's expense; and just once I wanted to
take a stand with you all. Oh, Jeanne——"

She glanced up at me, the quickest flicker of her eyes, and I realized
she was afraid of me. My thoughts were in turmoil.

"It's brave of you to climb up here." I was posing, too proud to display
my distress, and grasping at the first thought that tumbled from the turmoil. "It's brave. We may lose."

"I want us to be friends again," she said. "I miss my sister. Will you forgive me?"

Forgive her! "Forgive you for what?" I struggled to collect myself,
responding numbly to this flood of information——I, the adulterer, who'd
betrayed my former friend.

"For marrying William when he should have married you."

I gasped.

"You were right," she went on quickly. "You two belonged together.
Forgive me for having been so jealous that I couldn't come to you before.
I want our friendship back. It will take time, I know, I'm not romantic,
but we have time now, nothing but time, as we wait here, wait out the
siege, and you can have William, I don't care," she continued breathlessly,
her words running together without pause. "My love for him is all worn
out. I just want peace. Tranquillity."

"You'd give me William?" As if he were hers to give.

"He's a free agent," Baiona said. "I can't control him. Our marriage is a shell."

I hardly knew what to say, and then I heard the words fall from my lips, unbidden. They surprised me, and yet they resonated with an interior and unexpected truth.

"Then we'll be friends," I said decisively. "I've missed you too." We rose from our respective rocks, twins in our movements, both hesitant, awkward with each other and with ourselves, looking in each other's eyes—gauging, cautious—before attempting our first embrace; but as we held each other, my former childhood love flared up: her scent in my nostrils, her soft breasts pressing against mine, and now we were old women. Tears pricked my eyes. I'd missed our friendship. I'd missed Baiona.

"It won't be easy."

"No, but we can do it."

"It will take time." We reassured each other.

"It's a strange situation, isn't it? A triangle, you, me, William, all three loving one another. Because," Baiona continued seriously, "of course you can love two people at the same time. Justice and fairness are all about laws. But Love doesn't know any laws. William loves both of us, and I suppose that we love him."

"Or he loves many women. Forgive me, Baiona, you, who are so good. I wish that I were good too, that I had your goodness in me. It's I who ask forgiveness of you."

"I don't want any more dishonesty, Jeanne. I don't want—" She paused, searching for the right words. "You must tell me, Jeanne," she continued urgently, "if you want me to go away."

I searched her face. "You're asking my permission to stay?"

"Yes."

What did I want? A skein of confusion. "Yes," I heard myself answer. "Then stay."

As for William, he was delighted by our truce. He moved between us like a stallion among his mares, superior in our admiration. At first he remained on his best behavior, attending to Baiona's needs, but gradually he relaxed. He'd grin at me across the crowd or brush against me in a doorway; his hand would slide down my flank or slap my rump affectionately before he went on to confer with the officers or with Baiona, who (head bent over her embroidery) must have seen the interaction anyway. Later still, as the siege locked in, he'd throw an arm around each of us, kissing us sequentially, left and right, her cheek, mine; so that we settled into a curious *marriage à trois,* except that Baiona and I grew daily thick as thieves. In the end we were all too tired for adultery. Overcrowded. Starved. In the end it was William who in jealousy tried to separate us; and so the seasons passed.

I go on at length about this relationship, because for months nothing happened with the siege. The French could not attack, and we could not run away.

The days grew cooler, and the nights longer, and the stars sharper. September passed into October, and then came the early snows of November. Still the siege continued. We were surprised. The French should have gone home by then, back to their winter castles to take care of their own estates. We fretted restlessly. We waited for Toulouse to send his army to save us. Instead, he sent messages of hope. He was negotiating with the Pope in order to lift his excommunication, he said. He was concerned with his immortal soul. He said he'd raise an army soon.

We waited for relief.

Winter fell in earnest then. It snowed and snowed. We huddled together against the cold.

Christmas approached. One night we awoke to the sound of a horn and shouts for help. *Succor!* We leaped up, all of us, in confusion. The soldiers pushed through the milling crowd, strapping on their swords and grabbing at pikes and staves, as they ran for the barbican. This tower stood just east of the fortress and separated from it by a hundred yards. It protected the promontory, and from it came cries and screams, the clash of swords.

It turned out that by moonlight in the dead of night, by some ungodly chance, a band of French led by a traitor Basque had scaled the sheer cliff face, hand over hand. Who would have thought they could do it, clambering up those horrible precipices? And surely it would have been impossible by day, when they would have been able to see the terrifying drop below them. They took the barbican by surprise. Only a token force guarded it—three or four men at most, and they were probably asleep, though none lived to tell.

The path to the barbican ran along the cliff. At one point it is so narrow that two men cannot stand side by side. That meant one French soldier could hold the path. One of our men slipped on the ice and fell over the cliff. To his death. Inside the fort, we stood by helplessly. We could hear the fighting and our soldiers calling for help . . . and then nothing. Silence. And then the scurry and shouts of further fighting, this time closer, ferocious steel on steel, while the Good Christians lifted their voices in prayer.

The French beat our men back into the fortress. We could not believe it: we'd lost the barbican! It shook us to the core. Some of our soldiers were left wounded or dead outside the walls, to be mutilated or finished off or cast over the cliff—who knows? Others only barely made it back inside the gates. William was one of those wounded in that encounter. He limped along on a crutch, each step a stabbing pain.

That was at Christmastime, when we were celebrating the birth of our Lord. And for the first time the menacing grin leered at us: short of a miracle, we were doomed. What if God wanted us to lose? What if losing were the will of God? *Deus vult.* At dawn the *perfecti* walked among the wounded, laying healing hands on the injured and dying or praying over them.

After that assault we were trapped inside the fort. Where before we had been able to roam the entire mountaintop and even sleep outside the walls, we were now confined to the interior or to the far western slope, and even this was dangerous. Earlier we had been able to descend the steep hillside to spy by starlight on the French encampment or slip through the lines to carry a message to our friends; now we were crowded together inside. The French mounted stone-guns at the barbican and bombarded us night and day.

"I heard there was a treasure." Jerome's voice is disembodied in the darkness of the hut. The oil lamp gives off a bead of light the size of a thumbnail; the dying fire glows red on the hearth, casting shadows across Jerome's face. "I heard the treasure was removed."

"Yes, that's true."

It was mid-winter then, and supplies getting low, and the ice thick. Not quite starvation yet, but all of us cold and shivering, hungry, sick. We were too cold then to flirt or even to care who loved whom anymore. Our situation was grave.

In January, Bishop Bertrand Marty called me to him. I had first known Bertrand when he was the *socius,* or companion, of Guilhabert de Castres. Now, thirty years later, at the siege of 1244, he was extremely old.

I entered his room and made *adoratio,* touching my forehead to the floor. "May God make a Good Christian of me and bring me to a good end," I mumbled.

"May God make a Good Christian of you and bring you to a good end," he answered mechanically. Then: "I need your help."

"Anything."

"Jeanne, William tells me that years ago you and he discovered a cave in this region."

"We did, and so hidden that no one could find it who did not know where it was."

"That's what William said, although he could not give directions for how to get there."

"It's hard to describe. This area is pocked with caves, but that one is bigger than most, and safe."

"Tonight the *perfectus* Matheus and Peter Bonnet are taking our treasure out."

"Out of Montségur?" I was stunned.

He nodded.

"It's that bad, then." I let the information sink in. "No reinforcements? What of Count Raymond's promise?"

"Hush. The question is, How far is the cave? Can they find it?"

"It's no farther than Sabartès. They can go and return in one night. Unless they can't pass through the lines."

"Could they find it without a guide?" he asked.

"Not easily. It would be foolish. And waste time."

"Who knows about it?"

"The cave? Only William and I."

"And William is wounded, and you cannot go."

"Why not?" My temper flared. "Haven't I roamed the mountain all these months? Haven't I spied for you and brought in basketloads of goods?"

"I'm only thinking that you are a woman, and this is the entire fortune of our church."

I said nothing, but I'm sure that my face revealed my hurt.

After a moment he nodded. "You will guide them, then."

Again I said nothing—this time from fear. What had I gotten myself into?

"I have arranged," he continued, "that two sympathizers will be posted tonight as sentries on the last road open to us."

"Can you trust them?"

"They're from Mirepoix," he answered simply. "They're our best hope. The astrologers say our effort will be successful if done tonight, so we haven't much time. Be ready when I call."

"What did the treasure consist of?" asks Jerome from the darkness of the hut, and now the fire is so low that I cannot see his face. "How was it packed?"

"In sacks: great quantities of gold and silver bullion, and sacks of money, as well as sacred books and manuscripts, some of great antiquity, and deeds of property, and silver objects, including one priceless relic, the Holy Grail."

"What's that?" Jerome asks.

"The cup from which Christ drank at the Last Supper."

A gasp from Jerome. Then a whistle. "Did you ever see it?"

"Yes. It was a tall, heavy silver chalice with ornate handles curling out like ears on either side, and scenes from the Bible chased and carved into its base. One scene portrayed the creation of Adam, and another the expulsion from the Garden, and yet another the crucifixion, with three women grieving for our Lord. But I think this cup must have come from modern times, despite what the Good Christians said, for I think that Jesus would have drunk from an earthen vessel or from an ox horn like ordinary people, or a pewter cup, and not a silver goblet chased and graven with biblical scenes including His very crucifixion. Nonetheless, it was a holy object, and it was wrapped in purple silk."

"Go on," Jerome urges, clearly intrigued. "What happened then?" He tosses more moss and kindling on the fire. A single tongue licks up, blue and yellow, then another, a spark, and the fire tastes the wood, licks and eats at the dry, dead branch.

Night fell. Five of us gathered at the western gates: the two Good Men and I; Bishop Marty, who was there to send us off; and Baiona. A fine sleet was falling. We talked in whispers, wary of the French even before we left the fortress. Baiona, wrapped in a shawl, hugged her arms. "Be careful." She kissed me on the cheek. The Good Men prayed, standing in the cold. I shivered and pulled up the hood of my woolen cloak, and then Bishop Marty blessed us and kissed my companions on the lips, the kiss of peace for the Good Men.

"Go with God," he said to each one in turn. He touched my elbow in the fashion that a man gives the peace to a woman, and we turned each one and set out, walking in each other's footsteps single-file. I led them to my cave, and there we left the treasure.

It took longer than I had thought to carry the heavy sacks to the cave, and all next day we stayed in hiding. The following night, under cover of darkness, Peter and I slipped back through the enemy lines, staying as far away as possible from tents and horses. We moved carefully into neutral territory between the enemy lines and the relative safety of the mountain woods, moonlit shadows fading into shadows, and climbed the steep mountain. We arrived exhausted. Our companion, Matheus, had set out for Toulouse to beg Count Raymond one more time for reinforcements. The fortress was in sore need; we couldn't hold out much longer.

Afterward I was tired and depressed. It had been a hard journey, and I didn't find it easy to be back, tormented by the thunder of the stone-guns and the constant thud of stones against our walls; and though almost no one knew what we had done—the secret kept from the garrison—I knew we would not have hid the treasure if our leaders did not expect the worst. For days I did not want to talk.

That happened in January, after we'd lost the eastern barbican.

It is human nature that when you think you cannot go another day, something happens to make you lose what you had; and then you look back on what had earlier seemed intolerable, and, in light of your now-worsened fate, you wish for that bad time—which in retrospect looks to have been a paradise. That's what happened in February. The stone-guns thudded against the walls, shaking them, and we remembered summer and autumn as an idyll, though at the time we'd thought them near intolerable.

We waited. We did nothing. Waited for Matheus to return with reinforcements. Some days we sat in the pale, weak warmth of the winter sun; the icicles dripped. The enemy stones battered and bashed against our walls. We didn't have any mangonels with which to send stones back.

Some days it turned too cold to sit outdoors. We walked, heads down against the bitter wind. We moved like automatons, lost in melancholy. Paralyzed with fear and grief.

We picked lice off each other, grooming one another, and sometimes to keep our spirits up we told each other stories. William especially. He would describe the fresh reinforcements who at that very moment (he would say) were riding toward us on horseback into the mountains—an army of ten or twenty thousand men. They would bring supplies as well. Fresh meat. Oranges. They would encircle the French. There might be forty thousand men in all! No telling how many Count Raymond of Toulouse would arm! In addition he predicted that the mercenary captain Corbario would come up from Aragon, drawn by the thought of plunder when the French dispersed and fled. In the siege of Jerusalem, the angel of the Lord had killed a hundred thousand Assyrians. Who knows what spiritual help might not come to us?

But William's stories didn't change our lives. One man suffered a stroke. His right side was paralyzed, his mouth twisted, and his tongue became a loose lump in his throat. His wife fed him with a spoon and watched as the gruel dribbled out of his lips. He died of starvation, though food was there.

Many of the *perfecti* gave away their food. They would slip a spoonful of porridge or half their bread to a soldier or a sick person. But everyone was discouraged. In one *aparelhamentum*—the weekly confession—Bishop Marty admitted he felt personally guilty at having put so many civilians in danger to protect the Good Christians.

And then Matheus returned. We heard a shout and ran to meet him as he climbed up the dangerous shoot behind the fort. Two crossbowmen clambered up behind him. We stared at them in disbelief. No army of ten thousand! Only two simple bowmen, loyal followers of the Cathar faith who had volunteered to accompany Matheus back; to climb the secret mountain path and join us there, besieged—and they must have known they'd die with us. Suddenly we knew with certainty: we'd die at Montségur. The Count had sent courteous word with Matheus asking us to hold out until Easter: he was still negotiating with the Pope. Clearly we couldn't last that long.

Matheus was not, however, without hope: he told us that the Aragonese mercenary Corbario—the man whom William had spoken of—might come to our aid even without the Count, and his archers could put out the eye of a gnat at a hundred yards. Two local knights, supporters of the Cause, had offered him fifty *livres* if he would bring twenty-five of his men to Montségur. But later we heard that Corbario couldn't break through the French lines. After that we lost heart. The siege went on, with everyone shivering with cold and afflicted by doubt that the walls would hold against the barrage. It seemed endless. We all had bad dreams, and one person or another would wake up screaming almost every night, waking the room with her dreams.

One day toward the end I came on Baiona weeping over the embroidery in her lap. All day long she sewed, and for as long at night as the fire let her see; her fingers embroidered fruits and flowers on many of our dresses. She gave away her work. One woman carried an embroidered tree twisting up one sleeve, its leaves spreading over her shoulder and down her back. Another had the image of her husband worked in black and gold across her breast.

That day in February I came on her in the women's chamber. She was sewing with such concentration that strands of brown hair fell from her cap across her face, unnoticed. Her shoulders were shaking. I sat beside her, put one arm around her shoulder.

"What is it?" I asked.

She shook her head silently. I thought perhaps she'd had a fight with William. God knows everyone's nerves were on edge. But she held up her hands. They were swollen with cold and blistered, langouste red. I covered them with mine, thinking her joints too stiff to sew. Then I saw that she was not adding stitches but rather picking at the thread already sewn.

"What are you doing?"

"Nothing." She pulled away the cloth, but I snatched it to me and spread it out across my knees, and then I saw she was removing the designs.

"Why, Baiona?"

"I have no more thread." Her voice was a cry of distress.

I left her there, tearing at her work. And when she had enough thread free again, I spied her working a different design in the half-used cloth.

Arpaïs, who was one of the daughters of the commander, Raymond de Perella, took a piece of her own underlinen and pulled out threads for Baiona, until the garment was completely destroyed; but her friend had thread again with which to work. I wished I'd thought of it. Every few days Baiona would tear out the work she'd done and begin a new design.

At the end of February we surrendered.

❖ TWENTY-TWO ❖

After that I would talk no more. Jerome undressed me and put me to bed as if I were a child, kissing me gently, and he stroked me until my flesh awoke to his touch and I turned toward his sweet and urgent presence. Afterward I lay awake a long time, listening to this kind man's heavy breathing, and wondering what would happen now and whether I should go to the young priest and confess, as he'd enjoined in his sermon. (No, a bad idea, for it would mean my very life, and Jerome's too.)

Then I remembered that grace comes only through God and through praying for forgiveness to Christ Jesus, whose love is given not by our earning it but by His Being and through our sincere repentance (if only I knew of what to repent). And then I found myself praying with all my heart—praying not only for having spent my life in hatred and jealousy, in anger and in ungrateful fear of not having enough or of not being enough, when all was ordained, but also praying for forgiveness for having lost the treasure, and for I don't know what else—all of it—as I lay in the dark beside this gentle man; and slowly forgiveness came in the form of blessed sleep.

Jerome woke up, instantly alert. It was the middle of the night. Jeanne lay beside him trustingly, her head close, her soft breath on his arm. She was a heretic, or at least she had consorted with them—confirmed, admitted;

and worse (or was it better?), she knew where the treasure lay buried in its cave, guarded by the spears of ancient hunters under the eyes of the fleeing stags. A terrible fear accosted him, a chill fear. He'd brought her here out of dogged stubbornness, an intractable refusal to be pushed around, and he could be killed for harboring her. He slipped out of bed to his knees, praying for help—God's help. What was he to do?

There was a reason the heretics were surrounded at Montségur. She hadn't told of that, but it was common knowledge. He wondered if she'd been involved in that raid too, perhaps run messages back and forth. Not long before the siege, two emissaries of the Pope had embarked on a new inquisitorial tour. One was William Arnald, the first and most hated Inquisitor of the province. He was accompanied by a pair of Dominicans, a Franciscan, several other Inquisitors, and four domestic servants—a party of eleven in all. It was known that on Ascension Eve, the group would stay at Avignonet, as guests of the Count of Toulouse. The day of their arrival fifteen knights and forty-two men-at-arms from Montségur, in addition to others from the surrounding neighborhood, had ridden hard for sixty miles to gather secretly near Avignonet. They walked their horses quietly, speaking in whispers with only the sound of hoofbeats, of saddles creaking or the clink of armor attesting to their path. They halted by the leper-house just outside Avignonet, where a messenger from the Count's bailiff came to meet them, bearing a dozen axes.

At nightfall twelve of the vigilantes moved to the house where Arnald and the other six Inquisitors were sleeping. They battered down the bedroom door. They fell on the Inquisitors, and, without allowing them time to say their prayers, they butchered the men with axes, maces, daggers, and swords. *Va be, esta be!* they shouted, as they competed in battering the skulls and dead bodies, each giving a coup as blood-sign of having participated in the deaths, and each taking glory from the massacre.

After the killing the savage raiding party divided the spoils and valuables: some books, a candlestick, a box of ginger, a handful of coins, some clothes and bedding. They left the bloody corpses in the house at Avignonet and clattered noisily away, without even trying to keep their deed a secret, until they separated that night, dispersing into the countryside, a large group returning to Montségur.

By the next morning, Ascension Day, news had spread like fire through the region, with crowds gathering in every village to acclaim the fighters. The story was soon well known, told and retold with elaborations in every town and tavern. Some thought the raid was carried out with the blessing of Toulouse, whose guests the Inquisitors were—the way these nobles thought! Others believed that the raiders were outlaws, operating without orders in a frenzy of pent-up frustration. The Count's war of liberation had begun.

The effect was immediate. The French in fury called for vengeance. They mounted the Crusade against Montségur, where hundreds of the *perfecti* lived. Death for death, a hundredfold. Again the populace were divided in their judgments, some feeling the murders justified, others that they were a foul and cowardly deed. Jerome waffled between the two sides. He didn't approve of the hunting of heretics, but the Catholic Church was right: you couldn't have holy friars and monks murdered and massacred in their sleep.

And what of Jeanne? Tears choked him.

After a time, he crept back into bed beside the woman, but still he couldn't sleep. If truth be told, he did not like to give her up, not because of the treasure, which she might know nothing of anymore, months having passed—and who knew where it was by now (or even if she were lying or repeating stories she had heard, just common-knowledge tales), but also because (taking in a breath, expanding his chest, stretching his legs straight out like a satisfied cat)—the fact was . . . he felt just fine.

Was his soul in peril? He didn't know. He considered himself a good Catholic, and no question he'd turn her in when the time came, if necessary. But he had no taste for this harsh duty. He'd go see Bernard in town. Bernard would know what to do. He'd go this week, he thought, and feel the question out, without telling Bernard anything about the woman who had come out of nowhere almost, as a gift to him, who kept a house so clean that she'd taken the harvested threshings and spread the straw thickly over the dirt floor, right up to the hold-thresh door-stone—straw as thick as his hand—and her cooking was tasty and waiting ready when he came in from the fields, the fire always hot. She was a strong woman, not too proud to work beside him in the fields or haul in wood and water. How had he managed by himself? She attended church—and everyone knew that no Devil's whelp would enter or pray in a House of God. At Christmas he'd see she took the Eucharist, and surely that would prove her faith. She was the gift of goodness. He stretched his leg over hers; good company, fine stories, and also good in bed. Why shouldn't he like her? When he saw Bernard, he would find out what penance had been laid on the civilians at Montségur, for possibly she'd paid hers off (if indeed she'd been there at all), and if she had, then she was free to stay.

Yet still he couldn't stop thinking about her story. Wasn't it as fantastical as any fable, and ruined moreover with useless bits about her friend and one man who had obsessed her all her life—which thought sent an irritable ripple through him, so that inadvertently he pulled his leg back, the one that had covered her, and she came with it. He pulled her toward him roughly, turning her on her back, a little growl rising his throat. She woke sleepily, smiling into his face, and her arms reached round his back as he slipped into her again, thrusting angrily at her, at all the murderers and heretics, back and forth, pole and thrust, and wondering also, but too vaguely for the thought to rise to full consciousness, if entering a heretic made a heretic of him.

The next morning I rise with a light heart, singing, as if my Lord Christ himself had placed His hand upon my brow: forgiven. I am forgiven! I remember Jerome taking both my hands in his and kissing them in a gesture as sweet and noble as that of any aristocrat. And I remember how gently he undressed me last night and brought me back into my body with his touch. Our ribald night together. I laugh aloud.

So I am singing as I open the door to the new day, and the colors of the grass and yellow fields are bright as the Garden when first seen by Eve—which is how it is, I've found, after intercourse. "Good morning, Day." All things bright and beautiful.

"Someone's coming this morning," I say to Jerome at breakfast.

"How do you know?"

"That I can't say," I answer. "But it's a woman, and something's wrong."

"Well, you either know or not. I'm off to the field with the sheep." And he's smiling into my eyes too, and I know that he sees the colors brighter too. Then he scowls. "I'm going into town tomorrow," he says. "I have business there."

I watch him grab his staff and move away, sprightly, a spring in his limping step, shoulders rocking easily as he sings out to the sheep.

Sure enough, another half-hour and the young Domergue girl, Fays, runs into the yard, pushing away the goat that trots up to butt her in a friendly way.

"Get out, you beast!" High color in her cheeks. She'll be a fine woman soon.

"Push him away," I say. "Go on, get out!" To the goat, that is.

"Jeanne, Bernadette is in labor," she calls out. "She wants you."

"Me? Where's the midwife?"

"She's attending another birth. She can't come. My mother says she's asked everyone she knows, including the far-off midwife in town. There's no one else to help."

"I'll be right there." But I'm scared. What do I know of childbirth? Nothing, other than having given birth to one child and lost two others in miscarriages. I've never delivered a babe.

Bank the fire, collect my few things. My hands are on fire again, throbbing with light and heat. "Is it all right?" I ask as we walk downhill to the Domergue farm. "How long has she been in labor?"

"Since yesterday. All day yesterday and last night. She's groaning a lot," says Fays.

"Groaning's all right," I say. "But that's a long time to push. Is the baby coming out?"

"I only know my mother sent for you. She said to hurry."

At the Domergue house, the men and children have been sent out to the fields. Bernadette is in the birthing chair, hanging on to the cords. But she is exhausted, limp.

"Push," says her mother, almost screaming. "You know how to do it. What's the matter with you, child?" Then, with an anguished look at me, "There's something wrong."

I put my ear to Bernadette's belly and stroke her flanks. "You're tired." Just then comes a contraction, and she digs her nails so hard into my palm that I gasp at the same time that she emits a bellow like a lowing cow, her voice as deep and throaty as a man's.

"It's been like this for hours," snaps Alazaïs. "It's her third baby. She ought to drop it like a bean."

The contractions are weak, irregular, and every now and again I think the poor girl is leaving us, she's so tired. Her skin is dry, hot, red and shiny with sweat. She wants something to drink, but Alazaïs says no, that water will drown the baby. The mother cannot drink until after the babe is born, she says. The room is incredibly hot, with the fire blazing on the hearth.

I knead Bernadette's belly, helping her to push. The baby is turned wrong way, and where is the midwife but tending to another woman, and everything is noise and distress, moans, bleeding in the dark little hut; and we women turn on one another, shrieking angrily, because we're all afraid. I'm scared and helpless, and something's very wrong.

It's a nightmare of moans and bellowing as Bernadette pushes; of blood, feces, urine; of us women jostling one another in filth and angry outbursts and frightened tears—and in the corner the terrified rising and falling of little Fays, repeating her prayers. It's only right to pray, for don't so many women die in childbirth, and don't so many babies die?

The light from the window shifts across the bed, fading, so that the shadows deepen in the little room, pale dove to gray to charcoal black, as the sweat pours down our arms. As the hours pass, a strange thing happens: I begin to see Bernadette as Guillamette, my little girl, who would have been her age, I think, had she lived past five, and maybe lying-in with a baby of her own; so that this woman under my hands, Bernadette, hanging on the birth ropes, this woman so tired she can no longer push and barely hold the straps, her head sunk on one shoulder, eyes closed—or rolling up into her lids—this woman struggling to give birth is my own daughter, and my fear for her increases.

"Come, Guillamette," I urge her.

"What did you call her?"

"My darling, my little one. Rub her stomach with sweet herbs."

Then, with a wash of relief, I see the baby's head. Another contraction, too weak and ineffectual, and I see that it's not the head but the buttocks, and there is poop everywhere, a black, viscous tar.

"A boy!" Its feet are up by its little shoulders, apparently. I put my fingers right up inside Bernadette, tugging on the baby's butt in an effort to pull it out, but it takes all my strength, and now I'm swept again by certainty: a baby is supposed to slip out easily. It should come out fast, not require all my strength. I look up at Alazaïs helplessly.

"What do we do?"

Just then Bernadette falls forward off the chair, landing on her hands and knees, her head in her mother's lap. She is gasping, but in this position I can see the baby easily.

"Hold her there," I say.

Bernadette's shrieks are yellow ribbons before my eyes, filling up my head, but the baby is half out of the mother now. I manage to get the feet loose so the legs are out, but the baby is caught at the navel. The cord is so tight that it's pulling at the infant's tiny tummy; in a moment it will tear away, and suddenly a great calm descends like a mantle over me, and I know exactly what to do. With my fingers I follow the cord up inside of Bernadette; she is screaming with pain, screaming with my fist up inside her, and the moist juices and blood are pouring out, and sweat in my eyes—and "Pray!" I shout helplessly. "Pray to Christ and to the Virgin to help us now. Just pray!"

Off to one side rise the mumbling voices, drowned out by Bernadette; yet I work in a teardrop of silence, listening to the voice that has taken over. I think my hands are not my own, as my fingers feel for the cord, trying to unhook it from around the baby's head. I can't get it loose.

"We have to cut the cord," I say. "A knife—get me a knife and flax."

My fingers, still inside, grope above the baby's head, feeling for the umbilical cord. There! I hooked it on my forefinger. I pull it down and out where I can see it, and quickly tie a string around the cord and pull tight, not knowing how my hands can be so practiced, marveling at my skill; a second tie, and I'm groping for the knife that Alazaïs holds out to me, as Bernadette leans howling, moaning, and weeping in her mother's lap.

Slicing a cord is hard. I'm sawing at it and then the knife cuts through. The baby can come out. I'm turning the poor slippery thing, trying to ease the shoulders out. Bernadette is groaning, too tired to push, so the baby is dangling, its head still caught but no longer strangling on its cord.

"Push!" I slap the girl's behind. There is no time!

"Stop that!" cries her mother, quite rightly. But this is no time for gentleness.

I twist the head, lifting, while Bernadette once again gives one of her deep, lowing, anguished bellows as she tries to drop the babe. Then comes a torrent of blood, and the baby's dark head plops out, with Bernadette flopping like a fish, palpitating, sobbing with pain and fatigue. She is torn and bleeding. She rolls on her side to the floor, her head still in her mother's lap.

The baby's face is black, and the marks of the bruising cord are imprinted on its throat. I thrust the baby onto the mother's stomach, where Alazaïs catches, steadies him.

"He won't breathe. He can't breathe!" She bangs him on his back to bring the breath, but no cry comes, and Alazaïs is swinging from her daughter to the babe and back again.

"He's dead," she cries, "and *she's* dead."

"Not yet," I say fiercely. I snatch up the baby and wipe its face with the hem of my dress, turning the tiny thing in my hands as I wipe away the slime. Its limbs are limp. It slips a little in my grasp, almost drops, but I grab it by one arm—and then we hear the tiny suck of breath and a feeble cry. Praise God!

"Ah, there!"

"Alive!" I cry.

"Give me him."

I pass him to the grandmam, Alazaïs, who swaddles him right well, murmuring, clucking, "His face is all bruised!" while I turn back to Bernadette, who's lying on the floor, too tired to expel the bag. She's still bleeding. There is another gush of blood. I grab her belly with both hands, holding on to a fold of flesh. Slowly the placenta seeps out, the bloody bag expelled. I am ecstatic: everything's all right.

"Catch it," cries her mother, still holding the now-swaddled babe. "We'll cook it for her. It's good for keeping up a mother's strength."

"Come on, darling, don't give up now," I say to Bernadette, pulling down her shift. But her heart isn't working properly, the heartbeat irregular and weak.

"She's dying," I whisper to Alazaïs. "Put the baby in her arms to suck." Sometimes that gives a mother courage to go on. But Bernadette's eyes fall back inside her head and her breathing is too shallow. Alazaïs has to hold the baby to the nipple. It makes small sucking sounds, snuggling, searching, unable to take the breast.

"It's black," I whisper, as Alazaïs had done. "Its face is black. What does that mean?"

"It means it had a hard time coming out," says the grandmam starchly. "I've seen it before. The poor babe couldn't breathe. If he lives, the color will go away in a week or so."

My hands are on fire now. I cannot keep them from descending on the poor girl's head. I close my eyes, fainting from the light.

"We need a priest," weeps Alazaïs, "to confess her quickly."

My hands are stuck on Bernadette's head. On her heart. On her poor battered belly, and at the bleeding tears between her legs.

"What are you doing?"

I feel her drinking in the Light. I rock back, eyes closed, entranced, and let the fire flow into her. I can see it best with my closed eyes: the Light is flowing down from the crown of her head and into her body wherever my hands rest—into her shoulders, around her heart, into her head. It expands out, filling her whole body, seeping, sifting through her soft insides, and down her arms and off the palms of her hands, and down into her poor hurt belly and pouring into her torn vagina, pouring in golden clouds. I see it flooding off the soles of her feet. She is filled with light, enveloped by light. She lies still, moaning softly in her throat.

The light curls off her feet, coiling back and up to my hands, until she is cocooned in light. She is composed of light.

I don't know how long my hands rest on her.

When I come out of the trance and look around me, Bernadette has fallen asleep. I remove my burning hands, feeling dizzy and not a little sheepish.

Alazaïs is looking at me sharply. "What is it? Are you a Good Christian?"

I shake my head.

"We have to wake her," says Alazaïs. "She has to pee and get rid of the waste of birth."

"And then to bed," I say, "and let her rest. She needs some soup when she wakes up. Something soothing."

Full night has fallen by now. The birth has taken all the day. I am exhausted. Bernadette is moaning in her sleep, and feverish, but every now and again she wakes to nuzzle the baby sleeping in her arms.

We stir up the fire in the kitchen. Boil up a lentil soup, and soon the men trail sheepishly in with silly grins, carrying the sleeping children in their arms or over their shoulders like sacks of meal, and they are stamping embarrassed, helpless feet. They have heard the cries, the curse of Eve that resulted from wanting knowledge in the Garden. *In pain shall you bring forth children.*

Bernadette's husband approaches the bed. He rubs his palms together shyly, taking it all in.

"Are you all right?" he whispers, but she cannot hear, her mouth slightly open as she sleeps, her pillow wet with tears and sweat.

We clean up the birthing chair and set pots of water to boil, to wash the filthy rags. We eat lentil soup with onions and carrots, but there is a quiet, restrained air in the little house. Raymond stirs the fire, breaks into laughter—and then we're suddenly laughing, all of us, and slapping each other on the back, happy that the birth is done. We have a baby born, a mother still alive. Everyone is laughing and talking loudly, then shushing one another to choking whispers so as not to wake the sleepers, and Alazaïs is elaborating on what happened, so that with each telling it becomes more fanciful.

"It wasn't like that!" I protest, laughing. "Not at all!"

Jerome arrives. From outside, standing on the dunghill, he lifts one corner of the roof. "Is it safe to come in?"

"Jerome is here!" cries one of the children.

"Come in," shouts Domergue.

"What are you doing, spying on us?" cries Alazaïs, laughing, and then he enters, carrying the blowing wind that makes the fire flare up red and orange like the flame of my heart, and it's so beautiful! I wonder if God loves those colors best.

When Jerome seats himself beside me, I put one hand on his thigh in shy greeting. He slyly covers it.

Bernadette has awakened. "Your wife has delivered the babe."

I look up in surprise at what she's called me, then lean into Jerome.

Bernadette's husband, Raymond, stamps proudly around the dark, cozy room, as if he had something to do with all of this, and wipes his moustache, while his brother, Martin, grins and pokes him proudly on the arm.

"A boy!" He is very proud. "We'll get the birth registered at the church." Strutting. If it were a girl, no one would bother with a birth record.

Jerome gets up to look at the baby, fast asleep on its mother's breast. I see him start: its skin so dark and bluish-black, but he collects himself.

"A fine, good child," he says approvingly.

"But you should have seen your wife," says Alazaïs. It is the second time that word is said that night, and neither Jerome nor I denies it. He puts his arm around me proudly.

"Good woman, isn't she?"

"And handsome too," says Domergue. "I don't know how you've done it, but you've got yourself a good woman. You've never looked better these many years than now that she's come to take care of you."

Jerome just smiles a silly grin.

"I too," I murmur quietly. "He's done a lot for me."

Domergue pulls out a bottle of wine from the rafters. "This is a time for celebration," he says, and swaying on his big farmer's feet, ruddy-faced and weathered in the firelight, he pours us each a tiny drink. "To the babe! What shall we name him?"

"We shall name him Jean," whispers Bernadette, "in honor of his mid-wife, Jeanne."

We have a party, sitting at the Domergue hearth. The young boy, Gaillard, climbs as usual in my lap. He likes to lie on my lap, sucking his thumb.

"Jeanne did it," says Alazaïs. She takes my hand and holds it to her cheek. "What is this power in you?"

"Not mine," I say. "It's God's. Praise God."

"Look at her," says Domergue. "She's shining. You're shining, Jeanne, with God."

I feel it too. I see the light quivering off the palms of my hands—and not only off me, but off everyone. Everyone is flaring with light, light filling up the little house, light pouring off the face and hands of each member of this holy family. Everyone is flaring with light, and my Jerome is too.

I duck my head, they are so beautiful. "If you only knew. You're all shining with God's light."

It's late when we walk home. The stars flicker down at us from a black dome. Jerome rests his arm across my shoulder, and my heart is full, for this day another soul has been born into the world, and I helped. At the door he says gruffly, "You shouldn't do that."

"What?"

"Show off your healing."

I say nothing.

"Are you perfected, then?" he asks.

I take his hand and hold it to my cheek. "If I were, I could not sleep with you."

"I don't hold with that," says he. "That's a custom. It may be that you haven't taken the habit, but I think God made you one."

This night it is I who lead him to bed, and we do pleasurable things to each other in many different ways. I only know that with all the pain I've encountered in my life, my Lord—or the Blessed Virgin—has given me a new life. Never have I been so happy as now, living with Jerome, living as a peasant here.

We waken early. Still dark. Lying in bed with my new love, I begin the rest of the story of Montségur, whispering lest anyone might hear.

◈ TWENTY-THREE ◈

We made one pitiful last stand to take back the barbican, a sortie on the night of March 1: a failure. We were beaten back, the French coming almost inside our doors, and our men fighting but weakened by ten months of enforced idleness and disease, our teeth loose in our mouths, and our spirits discouraged too. How could we expect to win?

That same day, March 1, we surrendered, and the next day, March 2, the truce and terms were worked out. During an initial cease-fire our commander, Raymond de Perella, accompanied by forty knights and men-at-arms, dressed in their best (borrowed clothes and scratched and makeshift armor), descended the steep path to the French camp to negotiate the terms. The rest of us—women, civilians, soldiers, and Good Christians—waited above.

In the afternoon the men returned, climbing the steep path single-file, de Perella walking some ways back from the lead.

The young boy, Michel, had been climbing in my lap. When the cry went up that the men were back, I stood up with the others crowded at the gate and slung him up onto my hip, searching the faces as the men peeled off on the flat, muddy yard. William had not gone with the others, but remained above with the rest of us: walking on a crutch. I set down Michel with a pat on the rear and said, "Go find your nurse." Then I joined the mob around the returning troops.

"Is it all right?" I heard a woman behind me ask. And the soldier's gruff response: "Not bad."

Raymond de Perella, tall and gray-haired with his long horse face, entered the fortress and ascended the steps to the keep, above the crowd. Beside him stood his son-in-law and second-in-command, Pierre-Roger de Mirepoix, stocky and scowling. Their wives, Corba and Philippa, mother and daughter, held hands one step below, looking up at their men (two husbands, one son), searching for a sign about the terms.

Two or three hundred people shoving in the courtyard.

De Perella lifted his hand. Slowly we fell quiet. A cough sounded loud, without the stone-guns thundering in our ears.

"We have finished," he said. He gave one wrenching sob and then was helpless to prevent the tears that gushed from his eyes. He was not the only person weeping. He slashed at the tears with his fist. As if his words broke through a wall of sorrow, a wail arose, for suddenly the meaning of surrender swept over us: the *perfecti* would burn, yes, and the rest of us might languish in prison for life or else be mutilated, and if we ourselves were miraculously saved, we'd see ones we loved burnt or hurt; and such a cry went up as must have rent the heart of heaven.

A moment later de Perella regained control. Raising both arms high, he brought quiet to the crowd, except in one corner, from which rose a woman's muffled sobs. Mirepoix called out, "Quiet! Silence!"

"The terms," de Perella said, "are generous. We could not wish for more. First, everyone is permitted to remain in the fortress for fifteen days, through the celebrations of Easter. During this period the French will not enter our walls. I have pledged that no one will attack them, and no one will try to escape. I ask that of you. Montségur is ours for fifteen days, to make our farewells and to celebrate the Lord's passion." (A murmuring, the buzz of a hive of bees.)

"During this period," he continued, "we shall be treated with courtesy and honor."

He looked around our small community. We held on to one another, embracing waists and shoulders white faces turned up in rapt attention.

"To ensure our good intentions, and our word," he said, "I have offered hostages from our noble families. They are my own young son,

Jordan; Raymond Marty, brother of the bishop; Arnald-Roger de Mirepoix, brother of my second-in-command. . . ."

And so he named the hostages, one by one, who would that afternoon walk down the slope to live for a fortnight in the enemy camp. Each had significant ties to the fortress, to an important family, and to the Cathar Cause. They would be released when the French took possession of the hill.

"In one fortnight," he continued, "on March 14, the French shall enter Montségur. They shall destroy it, stone by stone, even to the foundations, which shall also be dug out and removed."

And then he came to us: "When the French take over, any civilian who is not a Good Christian may leave Montségur with full pardon for all crimes, and this includes the freedom-fighters whom the French call out-laws and who murdered the Inquisitors at Avignonet." (A gasp of surprise that these men would not be put to death.) "All soldiers and military per-sonnel may freely leave, together with their baggage and belongings and women."

Robert was standing next to me. "Amazing," he said. "They're taking no revenge."

"Shh"—this from several people.

"Later," he continued, "the soldiers may be required to appear before the Inquisition and make confession of their errors. I have been assured, however, that anyone who confesses his errors will receive only a light penance, in the form of prayers or a pilgrimage. No physical harm shall come to anyone."

Now a great sigh went up, audible, and the voices rose until our relief was hushed again with shouts of "Quiet! Listen! Silence!"

"All those who do not re—recant—" He stumbled, the words catch-ing in his throat, and he passed one hand across his cobwebbed eyes. "Those who do not recant," he finished sturdily, "shall be burnt alive at the stake."

We fell quiet. The room grew heavy with silence. Our stunned minds groped with the information, and then another uproar: we had two weeks. I watched as Corba, who that afternoon would deliver her son, Jordan, as hostage, and therefore who might never see him again, took him from her crippled daughter, Esclarmonde, gathering him in against her knees. The little Esclarmonde had already taken the robe. She would walk to her death too. The bishop, aged old man, sat in his chair weeping openly for us, his sheep, whom he had not been able to keep, as our Lord directed. (*Feed my sheep,* the Christ had asked of us, and *Feed my lambs.*) We looked around in horror, all of us knowing that the Good Christians, the Pure Ones, men and women both, had each one taken vows. They could not recant.

De Perella spoke again. "Noble lords, my brave soldiers, ladies, gentlemen, we have suffered together under intolerable conditions, and if there is any justice under heaven's eye, your names shall ring forever down through the corridors of time, burnt into memory as martyrs, as the true, pure soldiers of Christ. For forty years we have fought this invasion, and for ten months have undergone a siege as hard as that of Ilium. Never has any city defended itself longer or better than Montségur, though it was built as a holy place, a hermitage, dominating nothing, and never intended for war.

"We thank you, every one. And those who have fallen in battle and who cannot be properly buried—we thank you as well. I pledge you now that any man or woman here who ever needs help has only to come to the domains of Raymond de Perella and remind him that we fought together at Montségur. I will do my best for you."

His son-in-law, Pierre-Roger de Mirepoix, stepped forward then. His voice was likewise thick with emotion.

"I too, at this sacred moment, thank all the men and women who have fought for our freedom. I thank those heroes who climbed up to help us. I too pledge that if ever I am able to help any who fought beside me at Montségur, man or woman, and I fail in that duty and delight—may heaven strike me dead!"

And then it was over.

We milled about. We worked our way through the crowd to reach our special friends. We clustered in small family groups, some talking, some simply holding on to one another silently.

The soldiers were free to leave. Where would they go? How live? The rest of us were free, if we confessed our errors, recanted the Church of Love. And the two hundred *perfecti,* contemplatives, those pure ascetics?

Some had lived as hermits for many years. I clung to my friend Arpaïs. I could not stop my tears. The *perfecti* were the best and gentlest, most loving, wisest, and most forgiving people this world has ever known. It was unjust that they should die: it should be us sinners, soldiers, slayers of God's word.

Later that evening Baiona found me in the common room. She pulled me urgently aside. Her eyes were dry and bright. "Jeanne, I'm going to take the *consolamentum.*"

"Baiona!"

"Yes," she said, smothering me with kisses. "And you will too. Jeanne—my dear, dear friend. William's taking it as well. We'll all of us be together. Forever."

"Us?"

"Come with us, Jeanne."

My mind reeled. I stared at her. I didn't want to die. But she stepped forward to take my arm again. Her eyes glittered.

"We've always been together, a trio, loving one another. We form a trinity." She laughed wildly. "Remember William saying that? And it's true. Come with us."

"What are you saying?"

"Oh, Jeanne, you love William. And he loves you. And I love you and William, and you love us both. When we take the *consolamentum,* that's what's important, and then we'll be together on the other side. Say yes. Say you love me. Say you'll come with William and me."

"Let me think," I said, taken aback. "I'll think about it."

She threw her arms around me. "Oh, my darling Jeanne. We've been best friends since we were little girls. In a way we're both married . . ."—she gave a high-pitched, strangled laugh—"to the same man and to each other. It's only right."

"Let me think," I repeated numbly.

My mind was whirling, for here were the Pure Ones, the Cathars, believing in the worthlessness and baseness of the world, who had spent their lives in abstinence from marriage, wine, eggs, milk, meat, from godless gossip and idle thoughts, hating their bodies—"the grave that you carry around with you," as Guilhabert had once described it—these perfected mystics who believed that only the soul, like a spark from an invisible world, is truly good, and that it is seduced by the demonic powers who created the illusory joys of the world—and these wanted to hurl themselves into the flames that would release them from the chaos and send them to the Light. I had lived all my life with the Good Christians, and yet I was a heretic among heretics; for I cringed from this passionate optimism. I wanted to live.

I found William on the ramparts.

"Baiona says you're taking the robe, that you'll both be burnt."

"Yes," he said. Then he threw his arm around my shoulder and said, "Ah, Jeanne, don't look like that."

"But why?"

"Look at me, Jeanne. I'm tired. I have wounds all over my body. My back hurts. I'll never be able to lift a sword again. My leg will never rightly heal. What am I? An old, beaten penniless *faidit*. Landless. Childless. My wife is taking the vows. She wants me to come with her. And you know what? I can't imagine living without her, Jeanne. It's that simple. I want to be with her."

I stared at him, aghast. All this time I'd held to the dream that if Baiona ever died, William would come to me.

"Silly, isn't it? But what is left for me? I'm an old, worn-out knight. Baiona says you'll come too. Will you? Shall we fight together one more time?"

"I don't know." I didn't know anything. He reached out and pulled me to him for a kiss, but I twisted away, confused.

"Come with us," he urged. "I love you, Jeanne. We can be together always."

I could hardly breathe. I unclasped my hands and found that my nails had driven red half-moons into each palm.

"All right. Why not? If you both are doing it, then I will too. But I tell you, if I don't pass over, if I am reincarnated and return to this earth, I swear that I will fight for my country, I, Jeanne, and I will drive the foreigners out of my land, wait and see. Everyone will know the name of Jeanne. I'll drive them out, you'll see. The next time I will not submit to foreign domination. I won't surrender." Tears of passion running down my face.

"But if you take the *consolamentum* with us," he said, "we none of us will come again. In death we're transmuted to pure spirit, I'm told, and then we travel on beyond the stars. We won't come back.

"Do you remember," he continued, kissing my hair. "Do you remember asking me once if I believed in God? You were just a child and I not much of a man."

"I remember."

"Remember that I said I didn't believe, and you said you'd pray for me. Well, I believe now, Jeanne. Baiona has taught me. Now I'm concerned for my soul. I want God. This has been an important time, here at Montségur, the three of us together—and me with leisure and finally with the wit and will to examine my soul and sins. Because I've sinned. But this way, I can make my reparations."

"While I instead—I love this earth, this life. Look how beautiful it is."

He nodded. "Well, dying will only take a few minutes, and then we'll be in another place that I'm told is pretty too.

"Chin up," he added with a lighthearted punch to my jaw. "We're warriors, you and I. We'll fight in other places yet."

It was all too much, too fast, and here was William acting as if we were youngsters again, kissing me and loving Baiona and choosing to die. And why not, after all, when we'd gone down in defeat? Why shouldn't I join them?

I went to my room and lay on my mat with my face to the wall. I threw a blanket over my head and cried to my forlorn soul. I didn't want to die. But neither did I want to live anymore. What had William been doing with me all these years, just playing? Frightened, confused, I felt betrayed once more by William or by Baiona, or by the French, or everyone. Or maybe not *betrayed,* for didn't they want me to go with them?—except I didn't want to die. Yet I could not imagine being alive without William, without either of them, near at hand. I didn't know what to do. Nothing made sense anymore.

Little Michel came and jumped on me. "Boo! Why are you hiding, Jeanne?" He pulled the covers off my face.

"I don't know," I whispered, hugging him hard. He squirmed away and began to tickle me.

"The siege is over. Let's play, Jeanne."

I smiled and let him lead me out by his innocent little hand. But I had no heart to play.

In the days that followed, a kind of calm descended on the fort. We sat at the doorways to the hermits' huts, looking out over the valleys that flowed out to the horizon. We talked quietly. We prayed. We watched the changing season. (Another irony: with our surrender, spring came rushing in.)

The snow melted under a warm south wind. The sun burned. Flowers sprouted, overnight it seemed, clinging to the rocks, and the trees were greening in the yellow light, while down in the valley the almond trees bloomed pink and white, and the forsythia shot out of the snow ferocious and yellow in the sunlight. You could hear the snowmelt trickling down the rocks in rivulets, singing of spring; and the sun shone hot enough to make us shed our heavy clothes.

The French sent food.

Wine. Ale.

For the first time in months, we ate. We felt warm.

I watched spring come, my heart aching under the beneficent sun. The birds twittered and chattered in the treetops and flitted past our huts, a straw in their beaks as they built their optimistic nests. The years would go on and on, and the birds would remain unconcerned with what Christ said or which church they ought to worship in. But we humans—we would burn up, leaving souls as pure as Christ Himself, pure spirits, no longer captives of the wicked and material world.

Others did not share my despair. The lady Corba, wife of de Perella and long a *credens,* decided that she would take the robe on the last night, in order to stay with her husband and family as long as possible. A few days before the ceremony, she gave her rings to her daughter, Philippa, then reached up and removed the glittering baubles in her ears, the gift of her husband. These too she placed in Philippa's hand, closing her daughter's fingers around the jewels.

"I came with nothing," she said, tilting her daughter's chin, smiling into her eyes. "I go with nothing to meet my Lord Jesus Christ. I'll have only this dress to cover my nakedness, not even underclothes."

"Oh, Mother!" Philippa cried.

"But I leave behind my most precious jewel: you, my darling. And my grandson, your little boy."

Again, "Oh, Mother!"

"Hush. I'll be watching from the other side."

"Mother! Mother!" Philippa threw herself into Corba's arms, weeping. "I lose you and my baby sister too. Oh, Esclarmonde."

Then she turned to the little girl. "Oh, Esclarmonde. I love you so."

"Don't be unhappy," said the little cripple Esclarmonde, her face opening in a radiant smile. Esclarmonde had taken the vows some years before. "We're going to a much, much better place. Don't be sorry for us. If anything, envy our good fortune, for soon, so soon, we shall stand before our Lord. We shall look into His most beautiful face, and into that of our Lady, and we shall be no more than sparks of the divine, absorbed into the divine. It will be wonderful, Philippa—like Robert's Future-time, with no discord and no hatred. Just wait: you'll see."

I vacillated, struggling with myself—to take the vows and walk to my death with my friends and have eternal life, or cravenly to recant, a civilian, worshiping this pretty earth.

"But you didn't die," whispers Jerome. We have been talking in the dark of our warm bed. "You didn't take the *consolamentum.*"

"No."

"Why not?"

"I was asked not to."

My pause extends so long that he nudges me. "Are you awake? Who asked you?"

"Bishop Bertrand Marty, the bishop of Toulouse."

"Why?"

"He knew I was afraid."

"No, that's not why," says Jerome with sudden insight. "He wanted something."

Everyone was in a state of heightened emotion those last days, of sudden bursts of tears, or tempers lost and snappish like two dogs that, circling each other, suddenly attack for no reason and for no reason stop, to stalk apart stiff-legged, maintaining dignity.

One evening I sat with Baiona on the western rocks. High above us, a hawk wheeled in flight, and I remembered the hawk that heralded my first summer in this place: but how to fly up with that hawk and soar to freedom through the air?

Baiona's next words took my breath away.

"I'm looking forward to the sixteenth, aren't you? Soon it will be over."

"Don't say that."

"I'm scared." She leaned against me. "I won't deny it. I'm afraid of the pain. I think about it, walking barefoot, and do you know what I'm most afraid of? It's so stupid. I'm afraid of the sticks pricking my bare feet. I should be afraid of the fire. You know how sensitive the soles of my feet are. I can't bear to have anyone touch the soles of my feet, and I'll have to walk barefoot down the mountain to the meadow and climb up the pyre on the faggots, and it will hurt my feet."

"Wear shoes," I said in a harsh voice.

"They're building a huge pyre—have you seen it? Surrounded by a palisade so we can't escape. They will burn us all at once. To save time. They will herd us into the palisade, and we will climb up onto the sticks and straw and faggots. They'll probably use pitch to make the fire burn, because there are so many of us, and then they'll light it."

"Stop it," I said.

"Corba is taking the *consolamentum* on the last possible moment, so she can spend as long as possible with her husband." Her voice was hysterical. "And so will I, and then in the morning we'll walk down to be burnt. I don't think the fires will hurt for long, do you, Jeanne? The flames will be very hot. There will be a few minutes of pain, of course, as we catch fire, our clothes catch fire, and our hair, but we'll be suffocated by the smoke, then we'll be in the arms of God—"

"Stop it."

"You will see—it will be glorious."

"Glorious!"

"And we shall walk into His kingdom in the Light—"

"Oh, Baiona, it's the teaching that's important, not what happens afterward! It's loving one another right here, right now. The Kingdom of God is within, remember? It's about following Christ's teachings and learning to forgive, and going on with courage even in the dark times. About loving right here—not in paradise, but here on this earth. Look at the hawk. How beautiful it is."

"Well, I shall take the *consolamentum* like Corba on the last day, and then I'll live for a few moments in chastity and celibacy. If you do it with me, you can be my *socia*. Please, Jeanne. We shall be together for all time, you and I and William. Don't you want to be with God?"

"Yes, I do."

But my heart was torn out of my body. I think I went crazy, for I started to laugh nervously as Baiona covered me with kisses, and I was returning her kisses, as we did as children, pawing each other, laughing, crying.

"You will see. It will be fine. A few minutes of pain, and then we're free."

Arpaïs came to me with a soft mantle of white wool, embroidered by her hand. "This is for you, Jeanne. I want you to have it, from me."

I turned it in my hands. "But I'm going to take the habit too," I said. "You must give it to someone else."

"Ah, I didn't know. I'm sorr—" She stopped herself. "No, I'm happy for you, Jeanne. And for me. We'll be on the journey together then."

Thus I agreed reluctantly to take the sacred vows that would make me a Good Woman. I would make a sad ascetic, I thought, but then I didn't have to be one for very long. One night and part of the next short day. I figured I could manage one day.

Before we were burnt.

All the Friends of God were making gifts. The *perfecta* Raymonde de Cuq gave a wagonload of wheat to one of the sergeants-at-arms and his wife. The old Marquésia de Lantar, mother of the lady Corba, gave all her belongings to her granddaughter, Philippa. Others gave the soldiers a purse, a felt hat, a pair of shoes, a lock of hair, a spoon or stone, whatever these ascetics possessed, as a memento of their love. Bishop Marty gave a present to Pierre-Roger of oil, salt, pepper, wax, and a piece of green cloth. And a group of *perfecti* presented Pierre-Roger with corn and fifty jerkins for his men.

I too gave away my things, though mine wouldn't be treasured as either valuable or saintly relics.

And so the days passed quickly. Later in the week I took the *convenensa* with five others. This was a preliminary step—the initiation to become a *credens,* or believer—in which is granted the right to repeat the sacred Lord's Prayer. It is a simple ceremony, led by two Good Men.

Three times we bowed before them, each time requesting their blessing, and each time hearing their response: "I shall pray for you."

Then Bishop Marty gave a little homily on the spiritual Kingdom, the precious pearl that is worth more than all other belongings. Turning to each of us in turn, he recited the Lord's Prayer, and one by one each of us repeated it, following his voice. Then it came my turn:

"We entrust this holy prayer into your keeping, Jeanne," he said. "Receive it, then, from God and us, the whole church. May you have strength to say it all the days of your life, night and day, without ceasing, alone or in company. May you never eat or drink without first saying it. May you never enter or leave a room without first saying it. And if you fail of this, you must do penance."

"I do accept the gift," I said, "from God and you." Then I performed three more genuflections before asking, "May I be blessed?"

All the *perfecti* together then said a double—the Lord's Prayer repeated twice through. They made obeisance, and I too made *adoratio* with the others, both before Bishop Marty and before his *socius*. The Lady Esclarmonde would have been pleased, I thought, that her wild orphan was finally taking vows.

So we prepared our souls for March 14, when the French would take possession, and for the pyre on which we would be burnt.

I was watching the sunset spread orange and flaming pink across the sky when Bonnet approached.

"The Bishop asks to see you," he said. He led me back to Bishop Marty's hut and left.

I ducked under the low wooden lintel and stepped into his flimsy hut. The bishop, wrapped in a large woolen shawl, was seated against the wall. I prostrated myself. He blessed me with two fingers, then gestured me to sit on a cushion before him on the floor.

"Tonight," he said, "is our last night free in Montségur. Tomorrow the French take command." He leaned forward to look at me intently. "I have a favor to ask of you."

"Anything."

"I know that you have asked to take the robe tonight and die as a Good Christian. But I need you alive. We have arranged to hide three *perfecti*. They'll leave the fortress later in the night."

"But by the terms of the surrender——"

"Yes," he interrupted passionately, "but if we abide by that agreement, all our Good Men will die. Then who will be left to give the *consolamentum,* Jeanne? Who will be left to guide souls to their peace? Raymond de Perella made that promise for us, but sometimes it's no sin to evade or tell a lie to save another's life." He must have seen my look. "Oh, not the lives of these three men," he added quickly. "I mean the other souls, who need the light of Christ."

"Oh."

"Three men. They are Poitevin, Hugon, and his companion, Amiel Aicart. Tonight, after everyone has taken the *consolamentum* and prepared to die, after everyone has retired for the night, these three will be hidden in the castle keep, and tomorrow night, after the French have finished separating out those who die and those who live, when all is still again, Pierre-Roger will lower them on ropes down the west cliff-face. I want you to go with them. Take them to your cave, collect our treasure, and carry it to Lombardy, where the Way still lives. Later, perhaps, when times are easier, they'll be able to return to the Occitanie, and three Good Christians will be alive to carry on Christ's work."

He held up one hand. "Wait. Don't answer yet. This is important. Think carefully before you decide. I'm asking you to give up——or postpone, rather——your final vows. Will you do that? Will you lead the men to your cave, then go with them to Lombardy?"

"To keep the treasure safe."

"Ah, Jeanne." He shook his head and smiled in gentle reproof. "*They* are the treasure. Don't you understand? The three Good Men. They are the only treasure that we have. Because only the perfected can give the *consolamentum,* the spiritual baptism that permits a person to find the passageway to Light."

Still I hesitated. "I don't know."

"Yes, you do. This has been ordained from the beginning of time."

"What do you mean?"

"We've known for years that you came to perform a special service. Look at you: found in a meadow, belonging to no one. Dropping from the skies in the midst of war. You spent that summer at Montségur, learning every creek and corner of this countryside, each bush and briar. I used to argue with Guilhabert, I'm ashamed to say. I disapproved of his letting you wander all over with the Englishman."

"You knew?"

"One day when we were talking, he told me, 'She'll need this information later, and we'll need her. It's her training.'

"'For getting pregnant,' I answered tartly, but I was wrong, for you have spied for us, Jeanne, and smuggled in caravans of food, brought us weapons and reported on the movement of the troops. You helped us hide our treasure. Now I'm asking you to guide three men to your cave and help them shake the dust of Toulouse from their sandals. After that, you're free to do whatever you wish."

Still I said nothing.

"Say yes. I need a guide who knows the cave. Moreover, as a woman you provide extra protection. They'll be attired in ordinary clothes. In the company of a woman, no one will suspect them of being Friends of God. Moreover, they can't tell a lie, but you can—as long as you haven't taken the robe."

He looked heavenward then, his wispy hair a halo, face drawn. Soon he too would be burnt.

Then he faced me again. "Last—the final reason I ask this of you: you don't want to die."

"Yes, but I'm pledged to take the *consolamentum,*" I said, "and die with my friends."

"When you're safe in Lombardy, you'll have numerous Good Christians to give it to you. I'm only asking for a delay."

What irony! Only hours earlier I had wanted to live, and now that I was asked to forgo death, I chewed my nails nervously. "Let me think," I said. "I don't know what to do."

"Yes, you do," he said gently. "I've known you many years, Jeanne. You are passionate and impulsive, and not even age has dimmed your quickness of mind—which was put there, I think, by God. You imagine that you'll be failing your friends if you do this, when in fact you'll be helping everyone.

"Now let me give you some consolations to take with you. This scripture passage will be yours. Hold it to your heart. Repeat it with me.

"*The Lord is my shepherd, I shall not want.*" To my surprise, he recited the entire Twenty-third Psalm. "*He maketh me to lie down in green pastures. He restoreth my soul. . . . Yea, though I walk through the valley of the shadow of death I shall fear no evil. . . .*"

When he finished, he looked deep into my eyes. His own eyes, watery with age, had faded to pale gray. "These words are for you, Jeanne. Remember that wherever you are, there too is God. Remember also the words of our Lord Jesus Christ, how He spoke of the lilies of the field, and how they are fully clad by God."

"He meant clad in beauty," I said.

"No, he meant it literally. Listen to me. You need do *nothing,* Jeanne, *nothing* but surrender every moment unto God. You will be clothed, fed, cared for. These aren't idle words. When you give your life totally to God, all the power of Providence shall take care of you. You no longer belong to yourself, but only to God, the Force of Love, and the great I AM will take care of you. You are already a believer, already in service. You are His donkey, His dog. Remember, just to listen to His voice. He will make himself known to you. Go away alone. Listen. Do not speak of it; but always—promise me—*always* obey. Even when it makes no sense, obey it. Do you understand?"

I nodded.

"How do I know the will of God from my own desire?" I asked.

"There are four ways," he said. "First, the will of God is inexorable. It won't be swayed. Nothing that we do can prevent its working out.

"Second, the will of God is constant, steady, strong."

"So if I want something for a long time," I said and smiled bitterly, thinking of my longing for William, "it means it is the will of God?"

"Shut your eyes," he said.

I did so. The silence drew out. Suddenly my little daughter, Guillamette, a two-year-old, was skipping down a road beside me. She dashed to a flower, then to a ditch, dodging first before me, then behind, dancing and twirling, her attention easily diverted by cloud and clod, while I, her mother, walked stately down the center of the road, watching lest she hurt herself; I saw that in just this way is fickle human will—a baby's, by comparison to the steadiness of God.

"Yes." I opened my eyes. "I understand."

"Third, you will know the will of God by its effects in your body. You will feel a tingling or physical sensation, a powerful charge that goes beyond your normal desire.

"And fourth is this: the will of God, difficult as it is to follow— you'll know it by its Joy! It brings you Joy." He leaned forward, smiling as Guilhabert used to smile at me, glowing with his inner wealth. "The joy God gives is more than mere happiness, which comes and goes."

"Yes." I nodded dumbly. Then, aware of my own resentments and impurity, I burst out, "I am not worthy. I am filled with hate. I'm angry. I'm afraid. I'll never be a pure Good Christian."

"Ah, you'll be the best," he said, "because you are aware of it. Don't you think we all have anger and fear? All of us do. It's our lifelong practice."

"The Friends of God do too?"

"Of course." He laughed. "That's what we're doing all the time: watching our weaknesses. The trick is not to be rid of emotions, but to observe them in ourselves quietly, without judgment, to be aware of them so that they don't take us hostage, forcing wrong actions or false words. Do you remember the Gospel of John, where Christ says to be on guard, as alert as the man who is waiting for a thief he knows is coming to rob him that night? That's how sharply we need to stand watch over our evil ways."

"And you? Do *you* hold resentments, get jealous? Do you feel doubt? Are you ever afraid?"

"Of course," he said, smiling sadly. "I watch the dark emotions all the time. If we observe them carefully, and if we allow and love them, they'll go and play elsewhere. But as long as you're alive, Jeanne, you'll have fear, anger, grief, sorrow, jealousy. But they don't need to rule you; you'll feel them, but you won't have to act them out.

"One last word," he said. "Wherever you find love, there you will always find the angels of God. A mother, two lovers, a farmer in his fields, the food you eat, the silver-spilling water—these are nothing but the expressions of God. Whenever you hold up the cup of compassion to another person, Jeanne, whenever you help another or give her something to drink, you are holding out the Holy Grail. Do you understand?

The Grail is your compassion.

"Now let me bless you again," he said, smiling. "You're in charge of our treasure, Jeanne, and with the help of God you'll keep our treasure safe."

"All right," I said. "I'll go tell Baiona and William."

"No! No one must know. You go in hiding with the others now. That way no one needs to lie if any questions are asked."

"I can't even say good-bye? I said I'd take the *consolamentum* with them tonight. They'll think I'm a coward. They'll think I ran away." My hands were fluttering. Tears pricked my eyes. "They'll be burnt in only two days, on the sixteenth."

"Hush now. Come with me."

We went into hiding that night. I lay weeping, trembling in the dark while outside my friends took the robe without me. I tried to send them mental messages that I had not run away or abandoned them, that I was with them as they took their vows. Eventually I fell into a troubled sleep. All next day, lying in that dark hole as the boots of the French Crusaders moved back and forth above our heads, I imagined what was happening in the fortress: how the French were setting up a table in the courtyard, according to the terms of the surrender, and how all the people in the fort were approaching, one by one, to give the scribes their names and stations in life as perfected heretics who would be burnt, or as soldiers or civilians who could be released.

But the four of us lay hidden, barely breathing, waiting for nightfall when secretly we would be lowered off the mountain and sent away.

"Then you're safe!" cries Jerome excitedly, sitting up in bed.

"Safe?"

"Your name isn't on any list. There's no one to say you were ever at Montségur." He pulls me to him. "You're *safe,*" he repeats.

"But I was there."

"Not if no one knows. Not if you never tell. Everyone who knew you was burnt, and your name appears on no one's lists." He catches me in his delight, kissing and snuggling and cuffing me affectionately. "My Jeanne. Go on. What happened next?"

"Aren't you sleepy?"

"Yes, but I want to hear."

◈ TWENTY-FOUR ◈

They lowered us down the cliff face on ropes. We swung in the chill dark, dangling over the precipice, and I prayed as my shoulder smashed against the stones. "Oh, God, help me." I was swinging in the black air on the end of a rope, struggling for my footing and terrified, and the cliffside bruised my arms and hips. And then I was down and slipping unsteadily on the steep pitch of wet leaf-strewn earth, all smelling of rot and mold, finding my footing and clambering to the safety of a level space.

We gathered at the foot of the cliff, murmuring to one another in concern. There was Amiel Aicart, the youngest and most graceful of the *perfecti,* with his pale blond beard and brown eyes; his happy *socius,* Hugon; and the older, speckle-bearded Poitevin, who came unaccompanied.

"Are you all right?" we whispered to one another. I hugged myself under my woolen mantle. Hugon shook each rope to signal Bishop Marty, and we turned, giving thanks, all four of us, and began to slip and scramble down the black hill over the snow-soaked leaves.

I felt Amiel's hand on my shoulder. "Are you all right, Jeanne?"

"Yes."

He put his face close to mine, peering at me intently in the darkness of the wood. "Don't cry," he whispered. "We are doing God's work now. You are chosen, Jeanne. Be glad."

"Pray for me." I smiled bravely back at him. "That I may have a good death." But what I wanted to say was, a good life; for death lay all around us, and I felt it lurking in the four elements of earth, air, water, and fire: lying in wait to trip my feet; or whispering its presence on the wind and pulling at me to fall from the rope; gurgling, should we trip in crossing the churning river; and waiting also as fire, should we be captured that night. Death was a black dog running beside me, close underfoot, and I was afraid of it.

We descended through scrub-brush into the warmth of the valley, where the vegetation changed to long grass and briars. No one spoke. A light rain began to fall, and I wondered whether, if it rained hard enough, the French would postpone the burning, or perhaps if it rained long and hard for days on end, they would reconsider, believing that the hand of God was giving them a sign. So I prayed for an outright deluge, but the sprinkling stopped after a bit. We walked with heads bowed in grim silence. Once I heard Hugon murmur gravely to Amiel, but what he said I didn't hear.

The moon came out, a golden globe riding the bowl of night. The wind lifted, and the moon tore through clouds and stars as if they too were infected with our haste, hurrying through the hours as we were hurrying down below. We moved across the meadows in long single-file, and into the shelter of the woods, the men striding out in their leather jerkins and breeches, I in the lead, though hindered by the muddy skirts that wrapped around my ankles with each step.

A stranger, seeing us by day, might have thought us simply travelers who had lost the road, except no honest travelers would be so foolish as to walk by night. The Good Men were thin, but they looked no worse than artisans in their rough leather, and no one could see the sacred cord tied around their waists, hidden beneath their shirts. They wore strong leather shoes, and their hands were work-hardened, chapped from the elements; their bearded cheeks were ruddy from wind. I could have been the wife of one of them.

By dawn we had circled the mountain and were heading south; we'd had to go out of our way to avoid the enemy troops.

"We'll stop here," I said softly, for by now it was second nature to speak in whispers, murmurs, among ourselves. Hidden in a grove of trees at the edge of grassland, we ate chunks of rich dark bread and drank from the nearby stream. The first pearl light was tinting the sky. We began to make out the looming shapes of trees around us, and in the distance the snow-tipped mountains gleaming white. In a few more moments—how quickly the sun came up!—we could discern white sheep speckling the high meadows before us, dim in that first gray light but brightening with every moment. We strained to see a shepherd among them but could see no human shape or movement.

In the warmth of the valley, it was hard to believe that only a few hours earlier we had slogged through spots of wet spring snow on the slippery mountain. Now the ground gave underfoot, soft and spongy with the smells of spring.

We were far from Montségur by then and would soon be at the caves near Bouan, at the Souloumbriè Pass.

Suddenly a great anxiety fell over me, a desperate uneasiness. I have seen a dog or horse behave like this, unable to move forward. The dog will cast up and down whining and running back and forth as if unable to cross an invisible river at his feet. The horse will stamp his hooves and balk, spin on one hoof and rear, ears flattened, refusing to obey the rider's whip or spur. He bolts backward, shies, clashes his bit, refusing to go past a particular gate or post.

The three men stood up, wiping their mouths with their hands and their hands on their thighs, ready to proceed. But my face turned north, fixed, as the dipper is fixed on the polar star, circling that stable point. Every fiber in my body strained back toward Montségur.

"I must go back," I said.

"What?"

"Why?"

"What is it, Jeanne?"

"I don't know," I said. "Oh, sirs," I cried in anguish, "please, let me go. I told Bertrand Marty that I would guide you to the cave and help carry the treasure into Lombardy. And I shall. I promise."

I threw myself at generous Hugon's feet and turned, bowing in the dirt to Amiel Aicart as well. "Something awful is happening. I must go back."

"To Montségur?" asked the graceful Amiel, perplexed.

"Listen." I scrambled to my feet. "I can tell you how to find the cave. You go and wait for me there. I can go back to Montségur and return to you by nightfall. We can leave for Lombardy at first light tomorrow morning."

"There's nothing you can do there, child," said Poitevin, stroking his speckled beard. "It's dangerous. You could be taken."

Amiel touched my elbow gently in his concern. "Jeanne," he murmured. "They are burning our friends. It is not a thing to see."

But I stood before them helplessly and wept.

"Now let us stop a moment and think," said Poitevin. "Let me see what I can divine."

He sank onto a rock, eyes closed, and in a few minutes his body began to sway gently, like the stalk of a flower balanced in the air. Everyone settled down, sitting or standing to pray or meditate, wasting no time, until Poitevin returned to us.

After a while Hugon and Amiel wandered off together up the stream, deep in conversation. I went downstream to relieve myself and then walked to the top of a small rise that gave a better view of the nearby land. In the distance I could see the hazy hump of Montségur, bluish-gray against the clouds. When I returned to the little group, the three men were hunkered on their heels, heads together in discussion. Poitevin rose at my approach.

"If you go," said Poitevin, "you won't be back."

"I will!" I cried passionately. "I promise! I'll be back before the moon sets. What difference does one day make? We'll take the treasure into Lombardy as planned. I'll pack double-weight to make up for slowing you down one day. Look, you can go into a trance and see what's happening miles away, but I cannot. I want to say good-bye," I said.

There was silence.

"Bishop Marty said I must listen to my inner voice—that it's the voice of God."

"We're afraid we may not meet again," explained Amiel. "We're afraid that something will happen to you, and that we'll be separated."

"Do you wish the *consolamentum* before you go?" asked Poitevin, but he spoke to the blue sky, and his hat bobbed with the jerk of his movement. "Do you want us to give you the consolation?"

I shook my head. "Not yet. Bishop Marty said to wait until we reach Lombardy. I may need to tell a lie or take an oath to help you three."

I was thinking of them and not of my fear of fire.

"Very well," said Hugon. "Tell us where the cave is. We'll wait for you until tomorrow morning. But if you're not back by morn, we must go on without you, lest the French discover our escape. We'll wait only until sunrise tomorrow."

"I'll be there earlier—by nightfall," I said with relief. "I can go and return in one day. Wait for me!"

With a stick I scraped a bare spot on the earth and drew directions to the cave.

"The entrance is found through a crevice in the rock," I explained. "Go up this path heading east. The cliffs rise on your left, and when the trail opens out into the meadows and you think you've gone too far, you will see a weathered pine tree. Its trunk twists almost in a circle. That's your landmark. Watch carefully toward your left, and you will see two giant boulders standing guard, close as soldiers side by side. The sentinels. Approach at an angle, and you will see a crevice between the stones; it's small and down low, hidden at the base of the two rocks. That is the entrance."

Then I gave directions to the treasure hidden inside.

"Wait for me inside the cave," I repeated urgently. "You'll be safe there. You can sleep and we'll be ready to travel in the morning."

"And you? You won't need sleep?" Poitevin smiled bitterly.

I ducked my head. "I have to go."

"Be careful, Jeanne. Take no risks."

"Here," said Hugon. "You'll need food. It's best if we divide our provisions now. Take your part."

The men divided our bread. I tucked my share in my pocket for later.

Then I bowed three times to each in turn and kissed their hands and set my face back the way we'd come, toward Montségur. All I could think was that I must hurry.

I had gone only a hundred yards when I heard my name called and, turning, saw good-humored Hugon running after me.

"Jeanne!" He came up panting, his teeth gleaming in a happy smile.

"What is it?"

"Jeanne, Poitevin says that he's afraid for you. In case we don't meet again, he wants—"

"I promise!"

"He wants to give you this."

He held out a little packet wrapped in green oilcloth. "This is for you."

"What is it?" I asked.

"Open it."

Carefully I folded back the cloth. Inside lay—I looked up in surprise. "A book."

It was bound in ancient calf, as hard as wood, and held together with silver clasps. I opened the lock and saw that the pages, thick and rich, were beautiful in their black lettering and gilt or red or lapis illuminations.

"Bishop Marty gave it to Poitevin last night," said Hugon, beaming down on it, on me. "And he asked me now to give it to you. It will protect you, he says."

"For me?"

I turned the Holy Book in my hands, disbelieving, awed.

"It's all four of the Gospels, Jeanne, and a few of the psalms. It belonged to Guilhabert de Castres. Guard it, Jeanne. It's written in our common Occitan, so that the simplest man may read it, and it's forbidden, therefore, by the Catholic Church. Never let anyone see you with it."

"Perhaps you'd better keep it for me," I said hesitantly. "Until I come back tonight."

"No, you'd best take it now," he said, smiling gravely. "I have another gift for you."

"Another?"

"This one is from Amiel. He says to tell you that the *consolamentum* will be given you. You will not die without it. That's his promise."

I laughed ruefully, for the promise seemed unnecessary. "When I get back," I said. "When we reach Lombardy."

He did not respond to my assertion, but touched my elbow. "Now kneel down to receive my gift," he said.

I knelt before him, clasping the holy scripture, and he placed both hands on my head. I felt a runnel of light score through me, the same light that I had felt as a child with Esclarmonde and later with Guilhabert de Castres—the Cathar Light. I must have made a sound, for Hugon laughed softly.

"Isn't that nice?" he asked. "I give you the Peace."

I rose in awe. He smiled, nodded once, touched my elbow lightly, turned, and walked resolutely away, and as he joined the others they fell in step beside him, all three without a backward look.

For a moment I almost ran back to them. Then I twisted in my tracks, lifted my skirts, and ran down the path as fast as I could go, running back toward Montségur. I felt elated, my spirits high and the Good Book in my hand, not knowing which was the more precious gift, the Holy Word in my possession or the blessing of light I'd just received. But I had no time for reflection.

I was tired by the time I climbed into the cold and snowy foothills; and when I came near I saw that streamers of fog sifted around the foot of Montségur, shrouding the trees.

I worked my way into the heavy woods to the east, across the river from the *pog,* and staying high in the trees, I trudged through the wet until I could see the meadow at the foot of Montségur. My shoes were filled with snow, my feet and hands frozen, and my teeth chattering, for I was higher now than in the warm valley, and the forest held the cold.

I hid in a thicket and chewed on a piece of the bread. By now the fog had burnt off the mountaintop, so that the fortress parapets gleamed in the sun.

Below me, at the foot of the mountain, I watched the French soldiers moving in the white mist about the pyre. They had brought in wagonloads of straw and kindling, covered by huge logs, and the logs slathered then with pitch. In days past, we had seen them building it from the fortress. The pyre was surrounded by a palisade of outward-pointing sharpened stakes. One gate led into this death-corral. Up in the fortress the Friends of God were waiting. Meanwhile, nothing happened. Time dragged. I'd had no sleep since the night before, and I was exhausted. My eyes closed.

I jerked awake at the sound of voices. There, trailing down the steep path from the fortress, came the *perfecti,* some with their hands tied behind their backs, but others unbound. I was too far away to make out faces. I edged down the slope, holding on to trees, inching forward to get a better view (though why I wanted to see my friends in such a state I cannot say). My stomach twisted and my knees went weak. The fog had lifted under the noon sunshine. Above my head the trees swayed dizzily.

"Oh, God, Lord Christ, save them," I prayed fervently, and I held Poitevin's scripture to my heart and kissed it with utter devotion, for had not our Lord Himself promised that our prayers are answered always, if we but have faith?

"Let them live!" I prayed. "Thank you that they live!"

They wound down the mountain path, men and women, in a long line, like ants from an anthill, two hundred of them and more, most of them in their long black robes but some in ordinary garb. They gathered on the wet grass before the palisade. They shifted and moved among themselves, saying their last good-byes, and I thought I could make out some of the women:

Marquésia de Lantar, mother-in-law to Raymond de Perella

Braïda de Montserver, mother-in-law to Arnaud-Roger of Mirepoix

Ermendarge d'Ussat

Guiraude de Caraman

Ramonde de Cuq

India de Fanjeaux

Saissa du Congost

And then the men: there was Arnaud des Cassès with his brother

Raymond Isarn, Guillaume d'Issus, and Jean de Lagarde

Raymond Agulher, who was bishop of Razès

Jean de Combel

Bernard Guilhem

For a moment I caught a glimpse of Corba with little Esclarmonde—mother helping daughter on her crutch—but then lost sight of them. I spotted Raymond de Belis, an archer who had arrived at the beginning of the siege, and there was Arnaud de Bensa, one of those who had massacred the Inquisitors at Avignonet. Oh, and there was Sergeant Pons Narbona, who had taken the *consolamentum* at the last minute, together with his wife, Arsende.

Then, with an involuntary cry, I saw William stumbling on his crutch and holding Baiona by one hand, the two of them not bound. I longed to shout out at them, to tell them of my love, but the next moment I lost them in the surge of people, so many on the open plain.

A bird twittered nearby, and perhaps because it sharpened my ear, I caught the sound of singing. Singing—imagine! At such a moment, singing! Their voices carried in snatches on the wind. They were singing praises to the Lord, and no sooner had I comprehended this fact than in horror I saw they were being herded into the palisade. Those whose hands were free, not tied behind their backs, helped the others up the logs, and once having climbed onto the pyre they held each other in their arms.

"God, You who promise that all prayers are answered: *Save* them!" I cried. I wanted to scream, for the soldiers had lit their torches. The flames leapt up, and then the men were circling the palisade and touching their torches to the straw and pitch-spread faggots. I shouted, "No!" for the smoke was rising black against their feet. Yet still I could not believe that they could be killed. Again I screamed out "No!" and rose to my feet, shouting and waving in anguish to the angels of God. But the red flames licked at the logs, and the martyrs, my friends, were still singing psalms to God, still holding one another, as the tongues of fire leapt skyward, were still praying . . . until the singing turned to screams.

A black cloud hung over the plain and moved out toward the woods, smoke stench screams enveloping me. I ran. I ran from the touch of the black smoke, the fingers of my burning friends. Screams filled my ears.

Or were they mine?

The sound of my own breathing as I ran. And then a stab of pain in my lungs, and another in my side so sharp that I stopped running and, gasping for breath, held to the rough, scabrous trunk of a pine, held hard with both scarred hands, then stumbled on, my feet moving by themselves, over the soggy pine needles, through snowy hollows and across the gushing snowmelt rivulets. Walking, walking, walking. Where was my Lord now? I went mad.

I came round a fallen tree, tripped, and fell at the feet of the surprised young guard. His sword flashed.

"Wotcha doing here?"

With a roar I attacked. I could have killed him in my rage. I saw his face crumbling in fear as he stepped back. But I threw the stone onto the ground and fled, crying to myself—yes, and to that dark smudge that still poured across the heavens, silting up the sky.

How long did I run?

After a time I sat down on a log, exhausted and hungry. It was growing dark. To my surprise I found a scrap of bread in my pocket, and I began to chew slowly, mechanically, tasting nothing, dry ashes in my mouth; and then to my astonishment my hand pulled out a book. I turned it, marveling, in my hands. Where had it come from? I had no memory of a precious book. These things are valuable, copied letter by deliberate letter over years and years. Chewing, I chewed and puzzled over the mystery. I looked around me blindly and recognized nothing. Light failing.

Where was I? I held the Good Book, thinking, *When I open it, wherever my eye lights, that is a message for me.*

It opened to the passage *Behold the fowls of the air: for they sow not, neither do they reap, nor gather into barns; yet your heavenly Father feeds them. Are you not better than they?*

I sat there a long time, surrounded by the gathering dusk.

Slowly my thoughts retraced their path, returned over their lost musings, remembering the black smoke befouling the sun, how I had climbed up the hill, moving from the shadow toward the sunlight, how I'd held the branch of the pine and seen my friends burning on the pyre. Then I remembered walking. Then Hugon and Poitevin! Amiel!

With a start I came to my feet. Night had fallen. I was supposed to be over the Souloumbriè Pass by now, heading for the cave!

In panic I twisted round, first in one direction, then the next, wondering where I was, for I had run a long distance. I'd lost my way. The sky was overcast. No stars. No signs by which to tell north from south. I stumbled on, hoping to find a landmark. The branches whipped my face.

"Lead me," I prayed. "Take me back to the *perfecti*. I have to find them tonight. We leave in the morning. I *must* find the Good Men."

It was full morning by the time I reached the cave. The sun was high in the dome of heaven. Sunlight streamed onto the high, greenish-yellow grass. I was dizzy with fatigue. I knew now why they'd told me not to leave.

At the guard-stones I called out, "Hugon! Amiel! Poitevin!"

No answer.

I ducked into the crevice, then groped along the rocky wall. "Amiel!" I called. "Hugon!" My own voice echoed back in response, and the bats stirred and chirruped in their sleep. One flew out past me, to my horror, and others moved in waves on the ceiling like a single furry body, one black, demonic creature.

When I reached the cache, I felt around with my blind hands and found the bags still there. I lifted their weight and could tell that they were full. I left them and stumbled back out into the light, searching the landscape for the men.

Nothing moved. "Hugon!" I trumpeted. "Poitevin!"

My voice carried on the wind.

Finally I sat on the warm grass, my back to a guardian stone, to wait. The grip of fatigue was so strong that I soon lay down, curled on my side, utterly worn out. Despair had me in its clutches too: I had lost the Good Men. Nor did I know where to search for them. I had walked for a night, a day, and then another night, and now I had no strength left. Exhausted, I fell asleep.

When I awoke, the sun was bleeding low behind the mountain, and long green shadows swept across the meadows. A light wind soughed and stirred the branches of a nearby pine, rippling the grass. I was thirsty, hungry, dirty, lost. I was anxious too. Where were my *perfecti*, my charges? My feet were swollen and bruised. I could hardly step on them; but my physical pain was nothing compared to that of my soul: for I had lost the treasure of Montségur. I had lost the three Good Christians. Where were they? And how would they find their way to Lombardy? My prayers now were for the Church of Love, for the Good Men, for myself, who had failed at every turn: failed to die with my friends, failed to save the Cathar treasure, failed to take the Light. I was left with a cave of money, that was all.

For all that second night and another full day I stayed in sight of the cave, waiting for my darlings to arrive. It was hunger that finally drove me away. When I could no longer ignore the urgent pangs, I went into the cave, opened a bag, and borrowed a handful of small coins, for I had no money, no sustenance. Then I hid the bags even deeper in the cave and began my walk.

❂ TWENTY-FIVE ❂

"And the gold and silver, the bullion and books, the Holy Grail?"

"I left everything there. All but a few coins, and I'll give them back someday. Somehow."

There was silence for a time. Jeanne felt a change in Jerome. He'd pulled away, withdrawn into his private thoughts, and though her head still rested on his shoulder, she didn't know what more to say.

"I'm getting up," Jerome said suddenly.

"It's not yet dawn."

"Stay in bed." It was an order.

"And you?"

"I want to be alone."

When he came in later for breakfast, Jeanne looked up expectantly. She moved from the fire toward him, but involuntarily he shrank back.

"What is it?" he asked stiffly.

"I don't know. Hold me," said Jeanne, with a tentative smile. But he had no resources to assist her.

"No." He shifted past her, eyes lowered, to fill his bowl with porridge. He waved his spoon at her and hunkered on the bench outside the door, uncompromising, swallowing his porridge in stony silence. He ate solemnly, turning over the things he'd heard the night before, and as he did he observed the beauty of the little farm. A white tinge of early frost clung to the ground, covering the choppy, hardened mud and hoofprints. When

Jeanne came outside, wiping her hands on her apron, he frowned and looked away, though not before he saw her mouth twitch, lips pressed together, stung.

"I'm going to visit Bernadette," she said. "I'll be there most of the day. She's still not well, and Alazaïs with too much on her hands to care for one thing more."

He grunted.

She sat down beside him on the bench. "Do you want anything before I go?"

"What happened to the Holy Book?" He shot her an accusing look.

"The book."

"The one they gave you." A Bible was worth untold sums, if it could ever be sold. Jerome had never held a book in his hands, not in all his life, and suddenly he was shot with jealousy of this woman who said she'd been given a book, knew how to read. "The book you say you had."

She flushed. "I don't have it on me anymore." Her voice hard.

"Lost it? Like the treasure?" Why was he going on like this? He felt angry with the woman. "Was it all a lie?"

"If that's what you think."

He saw the hurt on her face. It made him want to strike her, because what was he to do with the knowledge she'd given him last night?

"Are you saying it's *not* a lie? Woman, look me in the eye. Can you swear that everything you said last night was true?"

But her eyes skittered round the yard, the way they used to do when he'd first met her, rolling from side to fearful side; and he realized how much she'd changed in the last weeks, how calm she'd grown in the safety of his careful nurturing; if he did not watch out, she would revert to her former crazy ways. He had to get a hold of himself, lest he make a wrong move.

"What's it to you?" she asked. "It's not important. You wanted my story. Believe it if you want, or not. It's nothing to me what you think."

"Were you involved in the murders at Avignonet?" He could not stop his tongue from pushing on. "Did you carry messages to plan that act?"

She stared at him; for a long moment she held his eyes. "No. I had nothing to do with that. Now I have to go. I have better things to do than stand here arguing with you, defending myself. Bernadette Domergue is sick.

"I'm not going to stand here arguing," she repeated angrily.

As the days passed, everything seemed to shift from bad to worse. One day Jerome tripped and painfully twisted his knee. Now he walked with a limp. And still he had not walked to town to meet Bernard. Each day he put it off, always finding one more chore to keep him on the farm.

One morning he took the pony and the cart up the mountain to cut wood for the winter, his mind still uneasy. The sound of the ax rang out in the chill air, and after a time, as he built up heat, he took off his jacket. He stood a moment, mopping his brow and letting the cool sink in, and then attacked the tree again as if it were the enemy and he were fighting for his life: *crack! crack!* fell the ax, Jerome's body so balanced that the entire force of his turning weight and all his shoulder muscles lay behind each blow.

The tree swayed, staggered, toppled slowly to the ground. Wiry and strong, he straddled the trunk, preparing to trim the branches. It was a good tree, and when it had seasoned it would burn well. He stopped, the ax swinging in a fine arc: "burn well," burning, everything was burning. His mind was on fire, his belly. It was ironic that Jeanne could build up the fire in the house, cook on the fire, odd that she was unafraid of fire after what had happened to her. He had asked her about that one day. "It wasn't the fault of the fire," she'd answered with a shrug. Awkward. Practical. But he could not remove from his memory the images she'd drawn, the dangers she had undergone. He had pushed her to tell her story. She had done so. He hadn't realized everything would change.

Jerome was a simple farmer. What did he know of politics? Or ethics, right and wrong? Or the wars of the religious? Whom could he ask for advice? The priest? He gave a bitter laugh, then shuddered, glancing quickly over his shoulder at the forest that surrounded him, as if someone might be watching. For no one must know—not Bernard, not the neighbors. The truth was, his days were brighter and his nights warmer for Jeanne's presence. He liked to come home in the evening and find her singing softly as she worked—though there hadn't been much singing the last few days—the house cozy with warm smells. He liked the way her face lit up at sight of him, the way she nagged affectionately and pushed him around, the way she made him laugh.

She had taken over the care of the house and farmyard, and when he went to the fields she always had a loaf of bread for him, or soup or boiled eggs, and when he returned at night he was sure to find a good lentil stew, sometimes even with a little meat in it. The house was clean, his torn clothing neatly patched. He wondered if Bernard would understand how a man lives for years, preparing his own sparse (often cold) meals and going to bed hungry and lonely in the dark, worrying that the farm is declining, the work too much for him, and how he feels when a woman comes and everything lights up.

On the other hand, he couldn't bear the sight of her lately. He felt a chill now even as he took her dish of soup. Guilt.

Were there good witches as well as bad? Certainly Jeanne had cast a spell on him. Hadn't he saved her from the Inquisition on their very first meeting, bewitched by her beauty; and even now, when he knew how dangerous she was, what kept him from turning her in? He wouldn't use the word *love;* love was for knights and barons and romance tales, not for the likes of him. But if she were to leave? His stomach twisted at the idea.

Well, take another matter: her healing properties. She said it was "the energy of love" that she conveyed; and the sickly Domergue boy, Gaillard, was getting well, no doubt in that, the way he walked more easily. Moreover, she had delivered the daughter-in-law's baby.

Jerome's thoughts turned to the Domergues, because right now, while he worked with his ax, Jeanne was taking Bernadette another of her healing teas. The girl was dying, never having recovered from the birth. Blood poured from her. She lay in bed, tossing and moaning with pain, one moment moist with fever sweats, the next with her tongue swollen and her dry skin hot as fire. She thrashed with hallucinations as the fever climbed. She thought her mother was a stranger; she said she was swimming down a warm river (she who didn't know how to swim), or else a rat was chasing her. Jeanne reported these things.

They wrapped her in wet cloths, Jeanne said, to bring her fever down. They put her in a tub of cool water until her skin stopped burning, and then she began to shake with chills. Her abdomen was a rock, yet so tender to the touch she cried aloud in pain. She was too weak to take sustenance. A thin gruel dribbled out the corner of her mouth onto the dirty pillow whenever anyone tried to give her food. She had no milk; her breasts were hard as rocks, as hard as her belly, and the baby had been given to a woman far off in town who had a baby of her own still at her breast, a wet-nurse, and Bernadette was dying, so that the mood in that little house was different from the celebratory atmosphere immediately after the baby was born. Now all was dark and grim at the Domergues— one more concern for Jerome, who already had more on his mind than any man should have to suffer.

Jeanne spent much time down there these days. Alazaïs was in tears, she'd told him. They'd even called the doctor in, little as they could afford that murderer. He'd bled the girl and growled at childbirth in general and left his own black concoctions that made her vomit when forced down her throat and that threw her body into paroxysms. The doctor said he was calling her soul back into her body, calling her into life. Then the priest had come and shriven her, calling her to death. Jeanne had report-ed these things too.

But what was most disturbing: Jerome remembered how the baby's face was black. He had leaned down to see the newborn lying in its mother's arms, and just as he'd bent forward, the baby had yawned and opened its eyes. He'd seen that the whites of its eyes were black as Satan's eyes must be. The infant had looked straight up at him with its mud-brown stain. Jerome had crossed himself. Alazaïs insisted it meant nothing, that her own son, Raymond, had been born with bruises on his face and bloodshot eyes, that the baby's skin and eyes would clear. Nonetheless, at first the wet-nurse wouldn't touch the boy either. In the end she could not well refuse: the baby had been christened proper-ly, after all; Jeanne had persuaded the woman to give it suck.

Jerome swung the ax again and again, now splitting the logs he'd cut. Every muscle in his body hurt, but not so much as his insides. Are witches Christian? he wondered. Have heretics an immortal soul? If you christen a demon's baby, and if it turns a proper color white, is it still a Devil-child?

His own behavior with Jeanne had changed these last few days. He'd grown aloof at the same time that she—having told her story—had become more affectionate. Her eyes followed him, appealingly, begging for a pat, a bone. He could not give it. He was in torment.

On the other hand, there was the treasure, tempting him. What if the story were true?

The day before, he'd caught her wrist. "Jeanne. Listen, I've been thinking."

"Always a bad idea." She'd flashed her wide white smile.

But he hadn't laughed. "You say you've been looking for your perfected heretics."

She'd nodded uneasily.

"I'm thinking we could both go look for them. We could take the pony and go to the cave where you were supposed to meet. The treasure is still there."

"That was long ago. Maybe they never found the cave. Maybe they were captured. Maybe they went on to Lombardy without the Cathar funds."

"Well, what if—"

"No!" she'd said sharply. "No, I won't hear any more. I'm sorry I told you anything." Her hands twisting and twining nervously; her mouth twitching.

"No matter," he'd said. "It was just a thought." Then he'd turned on her fiercely. "But don't you whisper a word of what you've told me, hear? Not to anyone."

"No."

"Not to *anyone*. Or you'll get us both burnt up. Do you understand?"

She'd nodded, large, fine eyes looking at him trustingly, and his stomach had lurched. She was like a child. He wanted to shield and protect her. And yet he also wanted to push her away. He wished he'd never seen her.

Yet why shouldn't they go together and bring back riches beyond description? He'd like to touch the cup of Christ. He would give the Grail to the merciful holy Mother Church, and the gold as well, and maybe buy Jeanne's pardon—if pardon needed to be bought. But no sooner did this optimism flood over him than his mind flipped to the opposite pole. Who would watch the farm while they went off? How could he suddenly appear in town with coin? He'd be questioned by the Inquisitors—and his thoughts, buzzing like black flies in his brain, stinging, brought no answers to his questions.

His ax rang out, again and again, chopping at the logs. He pushed the terror away, told himself to pay attention to the tree, that's all. All the thinking he could do would get him nowhere. He didn't even understand the heresy. The Cathars believed that Christ did not die on the cross but had sailed with His apostles and Mary of Magdala and Mary, His mother, to Marseilles. The Cathars believed that their teachings were descended from Christ Himself, but so did the Mother Church, except that Catholics believed that Christ had died on the cross and then come back to life. The Catholics baptized with water and the Cathars with their hands, the holy spirit; but what was the difference, since Christ himself had been baptized by John with water, and He had healed with His spiritual hands?

The Cathars believed the world was made by the Devil, and there were moments when Jerome could believe the same—when Bernadette was dying in agony, when famine wracked the land, when soldiers pillaged and plundered and plagues broke out, when babies were born crippled, maimed, or not quite right in the head, and when women came into your life, tempting you to sin because they were so useful and so beautiful that they turned your head, their logic twisting good ideas until you didn't know what to think, or how. Jerome knew, however, that the Bible said God (not the Devil) had created the world in six days, and so that must be true.

He threw down his ax. He would walk to town right now, he decided—pass the night with Bernard, tell some of this story, find out what he should do. He didn't even stop at the cottage to explain his absence to Jeanne.

When Jerome returned next day, he was surprised that Jeanne didn't come to meet him halfway down the path as usual, or stand at the gate watching for him. He caught a glimpse of her moving in the doorway of the little house, but before he could lift his hand in greeting or open his mouth, she took off up the hill. He was irritated. Why had she fled?

He went inside and poked the smoky fire. The house seemed desolate and dry without her laughing there beside him. After a bit he went outside and called and called her. She did not answer. Damn the woman, where could she have gone, and why?

At sunset she appeared in the doorway, a shadow against the shadows. No greeting.

"There you are," he said. "Why'd you run off?" He knew enough to be the first to attack.

"Where were you?"

"I walked to town."

"Oh, and you didn't think to tell me? Just go off and leave the animals. Don't ask if I want to come along. It wasn't even market-day."

"I had business," he flared up, tired from the walk. Why was she so unreasonable? He didn't have to tell her everything, did he? He clamped his mouth shut on Bernard's advice and turned away.

"And did your business have to do with me?" she asked.

"It did."

He met her eyes then, challenging her. She dropped hers first.

"Here," he said grudgingly. "I brought you a ribbon." He pulled from his pocket a length of soft rose satin. "I'm trying to keep you safe," he added.

She turned it in her hands, twisting the lovely color round her fingers. When she looked up, he saw her eyes were filled with tears.

"Bernadette has died," she said. "The funeral's tomorrow."

❈ TWENTY-SIX ❈

I wept when she died. Alazaïs and I had spent days at her side, bathing the poor girl and washing linens that got dirty as fast as I could boil them. The Domergue hut is small and darker than Jerome's. It holds more people too, so that Bernadette lay on a palette in the main room, surrounded by the family—her husband and her brother, Martin, her three children, and then Fays, Domergue, Alazaïs, me. She died in pain and crying for her mother and her little ones.

The priest came and gave her the last sacraments, which made the Domergues glad: at least her soul, they said, would fly to heaven. They'd see her there again. I no longer know what happens to souls or believe in anything. Whatever sacrament is given may be more for the living than for the dead, for I have seen both Cathar and Catholic sacraments and they do not differ except in metaphor—taking on your tongue (in the one instance) the mystical body and blood of our Lord Jesus Christ, or (in the other) taking into your body the spiritual light and blessing of our Lord. At any rate, Bernadette took the transubstantiated bread, the body of Christ, and died in a state of grace, which meant she could be buried in the churchyard rather than having to lie outside the gate.

"Mother." That was her plaintive word, whispered so softly I could barely hear her.

Alazaïs was holding her hand, crying, "I'm here. I'm right here."

But Bernadette could not see her.

"Where are you, Mother? Hold me."

"I'm here."

"Where are my babies? I want to see them. Mother!"

Her father, Domergue, held one of her hands and Alazaïs the other, and her husband squeezed between the two of them, trying to say good-bye to the mother of his brood. The little knee-high girl, Raymonde, climbed onto the bed-cover, but the boy, Gaillard, sat far off in a corner, his eyes closed and his head on his knees. I stood against a wall and wept for the girl I'd grown so fond of, wept for this family and for all the lone-liness and partings of this fragile life, for my own despair and hurt, for the lost *perfecti* and for those burnt, for myself and for all the things that I don't understand.

Afterward, they thanked me curtly for my work. I clung to Alazaïs, but eventually I left and climbed the hillside to our farm, to find the cold house empty, the fire dead, and the cat skittering shyly away, knocking a dish off the table in her haste. Jerome was still away, having gone off with-out warning or explanation, who knew where. And I was hurt and annoyed and frightened to find myself alone.

When finally he made his way up the hill the following day, I was so angry at him that I ran up the hill to sit and collect myself.

"Bernadette has died," I told him when we'd finished quarreling.

He grunted, and looked into the far distance, avoiding my eyes. I didn't know what was eating at him, but that night I fixed cold bread and cheese for supper and took myself to bed, too tired to care. He said he'd gone to visit his friend Bernard, but he didn't deign to tell me why.

We stand at Bernadette's gravesite with the Domergues and the rest of our small community. The priest sprinkles her body with holy water and off she goes, wrapped in the shroud that she had sewed herself, dropped down into the black hole, while her family stand awkwardly about. The children cling to their grandmother's skirts. Her brothers shovel in the dirt. Jerome is giving them a hand. I am no longer crying, my heart hard: I'm scared and at the same time glad—scared because it will happen to me one day, to all of us, and glad that it's Bernadette and not me being buried in the earth. Yet I know that her soul is not down there: it's passed into the realms of Light. I know that. Nonetheless, a shudder of fear ripples through me and I hug my shawl around my shoulders. I watch the muscles in Jerome's back as he shovels in the dirt, and my eyes take pleasure in stroking his sturdy form, the sensitive curve at the nape of his neck, his splayed hands, his expressive eyes, the wind-whipped leather of his face. Imagine, enjoying a man's body at such a sad moment. Surely, if anyone asked if I were a heretic, I'd have to say no; because a good heretic would never find true pleasure in such lust, much less in other pleasures of this world. But then, neither would a good Catholic; would anyone admit to lusting or to loving as I do?

Something is wrong. Jerome does not look at me. Yet since telling him my story, my eyes follow him like a dog's. I'm aware of every turn of his head; I quiver when he stands up or sits down. I want to run errands for him, bring him gifts, make him talk to me. Only at night, in bed, does he acknowledge me. Then he turns to me in passion and wordlessly takes his rough pleasure, and rolls off; but occasionally he is gentle, as before. I don't know what's happened. For just when I think he does not care for me anymore, he does something special, like last night when he embraced me, breathing in my scent and holding me so tightly to him (was he crying?) that I couldn't have escaped even had I wanted to.

"You are my treasure," he murmured in my ear. His mouth reaching for mine.

By day he goes into brief, sullen silences, walking around me, head down, as if he does not want to see me. We spend each Sunday in church, now, and this is surprising, for did he not confess, when I first arrived, that he attended only sparingly? He had no time, he said; he didn't like the sermonizing. Now he even walks over sometimes on a weekday night and kneels on the cold stones in prayer, as I found by following. I spied him there. Why is he praying? What is he praying about?

"Is something wrong?" I asked timidly.

"Nothing." The answer curt.

"Why do you pray in church so much?" I asked another time.

He answered with a grunt.

It can't be the Domergue baby: his long-lashed eyes have turned a proper black with pure, clean whites, like any Christian babe. He is as pretty and sweet a smiling cherub as anyone could want. Poor Bernadette.

Another day Jerome approached as I fed the chickens in the yard. "What's your opinion of marriage?" he shot at me out of the blue. "A proper marriage, blessed by a priest of the holy Catholic Church?"

"Is that a proposal? Are you asking me?"

"You'd have to be baptized." His voice hard. "You'd have to be a good member of the Church. No heresy."

So that's what was bothering him. "Yes."

"Well? What's your answer, woman?" Again the cloud of anger on his brow. "Or do you want to live in sinful lust and concubinage?"

"I said yes," I answered testily. "I will. Isn't that enough?" That night we hardly spoke to each other, because we'd agreed to marry and it frightened both of us. But the next day and in the days following, we start to move around each other less tentatively, each day coming a little closer, every now and again our eyes meeting and dropping shyly; and then we begin to smile at each other again. This will be my third marriage, a comedown in status and a go-up in happiness. I laugh again, as I used to. I start to lift my voice and sing as I go about my work. At night we lie together, whispering. Making plans.

Our first task is to talk with the priest, and we do this on Sunday after church. He seems pleased with us, rubbing his hands together and smiling and bobbing his head as if he'd come up with the idea all by himself. He says he'll read the banns the following week, and as we walk home together, Jerome and I, down the glade, with the bare trees quivering under a gray winter sky, I feel a weight has lifted from Jerome. Just a few words from the priest, and he's his old self, cheerful and easy with the land, his animals, and me.

The following week we stand together in the church, shy fingers intertwined, and listen to our names read out. The others are looking at us curiously. Jerome holds my elbow possessively as we leave the church, and my head is proud and high. Three Sundays in a row the priest will read aloud our intention to marry, as he is doing now, and on the fourth we'll stand before him to offer our wedding vows. Would we each (in turn, by name) agree to honor and respect each other, and live together and help one another in sickness or health? *I will:* that's the answer I shall make. Meanwhile, we take instruction from the priest in our marital duties.

Back at home after church I whisper the words of commitment to myself: "I will."

"Do you promise . . . ?" he shall ask, and I shall respond, "I do," or "I will." I let the syllables roll off my tongue, my lips pursed in a kiss, "I oo; I oo-ill." I laugh to myself, because the pledge is sealed with a secret kiss blown from heart to heart.

Our marital duties, according to the priest at our first instruction, are severe: we are never to make love except for procreation of children, and then only with the man on top. This puzzles me, for I am too old to have children, unless our Lord should bless me like Sarah with an old-age babe; and as for the one church-blessed position, I don't tell the priest all I know or have already done, and neither does Jerome, although I can see the teaching hits him hard, for Jerome is more serious than I, and if these things we've done are sins, then we have already lost our souls.

On the following Sunday, for the second time, the priest reads out the banns. We stand proudly with the others in the cold stone church, and I look about me at the familiar old building with its four thick pillars (two on each side of the center aisle), its low roof, and its altar. It has two windows, one on each side wall, and both of them with glass. My feet are cold on the cold stones, because it's snowing outside, but my heart is warm with the prospect of my marriage to Jerome. And then from behind me comes a hoarse voice:

"It can't be done."

I turn in surprise. It was Domergue who spoke. The priest looks up, equally surprised.

"Aren't they cousins?" Domergue thrusts the question forward like a piece of meat on a knife. "Jerome told us she was his mother's cousin. And doesn't the Church forbid a marriage to the fourth degree?"

Jerome grips my hand. I sway. The church has erupted into a buzz of conversation, everyone craning to peer at Jerome and me. A lie, one little lie, prevents our marriage. Do we confess to the lie? But who would believe us if we change the story now? Jerome has gone white. His eyes roll helplessly around the church, catch on Domergue, who stares back grudgingly, then turns his face with a shrug. The shrug of the stubborn peasant.

"Is it true?" asks the priest.

Jerome shakes his head, confused.

"You cannot be married until you investigate the relationship," the priest decrees, but he falters helplessly. "The church does not allow marriage between two people bound by blood. Do you understand the degrees?" he asks, stepping toward us down into the aisle. "You cannot marry your own sister or brother, or your aunt or uncle, or your niece or nephew. You cannot marry your aunt's or uncle's child. I mean your own first cousin. These are forbidden relationships.

"You cannot marry the child of your first cousin. You cannot marry the child of your niece or nephew. You cannot marry your mother's cousin's child—your second cousin. That's marriage to the third degree.

"Is this clear? These are forbidden by the Church. You cannot marry the brother of your husband or the sister of your wife. That too is incest. Am I clear?"

Still, neither of us speak. None of it is clear, and a great buzzing has arisen in my ears. I can't keep track of his cousins, aunts, brothers.

"It used to be forbidden to the seventh degree," he pursued us relentlessly, "but our Holy Church is merciful. Marriage is now forbidden only to the fourth degree. So confess, are you two related?"

But what was the fourth degree?

"I . . . we . . . I don't know," says Jerome, looking wildly around.

"We will speak of this later," says the young priest, "privately." And he swings back to the safety of the altar, relieved to continue the comfortable Latin liturgy, while we stand smitten in our places, and now I see how the others edge away from us, uncertain how to behave. After the service, we stagger from the church, bewildered, only to see Domergue talking to the priest, together with Alazaïs. We slink back inside to huddle together and wait.

"What are we to do?" I whisper.

"How do I know?" he snaps.

But when the priest returns and launches into his next lecture, I think from his garblement that he understands no more than I, and the only thing that's clear is that somehow all this relates to children, though the relationships are so confusing I just want the priest to stop.

In the end Jerome confesses all: how we had met on the mountain path (but without reference to the Inquisitors who had come riding up behind), how Jerome had invited me home, and not wanting to create a scandal had told the neighbors a lie, and yes, he ought to have admitted it in confession but had not thought it important, and how filled he now is with remorse, and how he wants to do what's right both by me and by the Church. But we are not related, no.

I say nothing. I hang my grieving, hopeful head.

The young priest nods and listens and fidgets, twisting the tassels of his shawl around his fingers. He doesn't know what to do. Finally he says that when next he goes to town he'll take the matter to his superiors, and he gives us penance and the injunction to chastity while we live together. This he repeats: we may no longer share a common bed, on peril of our immortal souls.

In a few weeks, he says, he'll report back whether we may marry or not. He rises to dismiss us with the decisiveness of someone young and inexperienced who's trying to act beyond his years. But what has shaken me is a new idea, that we're too old for marriage anyway, since procreation is no longer possible.

We walk back home in silence. I feel chastened, chastised, punished for daring to be happy with this man. He stalks one pace ahead, not looking at me. His back is hard and his neck stiff in that stubborn tilt I've come to know.

What are we to do? The snow falls softly, softly, white on his crumpled hat, white on my cloak, white on our footprints, white on the grass and brush—the sky white, the earth white, the foggy air we breathe all white with the purity of snow.

❖ TWENTY-SEVEN ❖

We live now in chastity, as if perfected friends, while the priest waits on his superiors, who take their good time, I might add, to hand us their decision. I tried one night to draw Jerome to bed with me, as we used to do, but he sprang away. He both wants and doesn't want me.

"I cannot jeopardize my soul," he said firmly. Which hurt, because don't I have an immortal soul as well? I wonder what our Lord Christ would have said about our wish to marry. I am shaken by these events, and sometimes I climb up the hillside to walk past the beech tree that holds in the safety of its tangled roots my Holy Book, my treasure. But I do not dare to remove the book: my eyes are too weak to read those lovely pages anyway, the letters blur; and moreover, I don't want footprints guiding people to my only possession. (No, I've not told Jerome everything.)

I pause only a moment, talking from a distance to the tree (because I don't want some footprints to show deeper than the others in the snow, indicating that I stopped), and then I climb on in the snow, and all the while I'm puzzling in my mind the course of events. I'm no longer mad: of this I'm sure. When I was mad, the voices chattered in my head and people sometimes grew large or small, but now I hear no voices and I feel myself solidly on this earth. But I still understand nothing. Why did the Good Christians have to be burnt? Bertrand Marty told me at our farewell that with that pyre all our prayers were answered—the Cathars prayers, because they did not want to live any longer trapped in their bodies on this Devil's globe; and the Catholic ones, because they wanted to have just one True Church. So both prayers came about, God giving us the desires of our hearts.

I want to understand. I want to know what the Good Christians saw that made them throw themselves into the flames; I want to know the Light of God, which they talked so much about and which I don't think I've seen, unless it be the light that came sometimes with de Castres and Esclarmonde or the prickling in my hands when someone is sick nearby. Practical as a pine tree, I know nothing of these spiritual matters.

My thoughts turn to Jerome. The torment fell on him after he heard my story. Several times he has asked me about the treasure.

"Could you find the treasure again?" he asked once. Another time: "If someone wanted it, would you take him there?"

I bolted from the questioning. It's not my place to steal the money of the Church of Love, but Jerome will ask again, I'm sure. What then? Should we go?

The weeks pass, and still no word from the priest.

Jerome asks again about the treasure, and this time I say yes, I'll take him there; and the veil of darkness lifts from Jerome: he laughs with me again, and sometimes he gives me a kiss on the lips. Sometimes he lets his fingers trail down my arm or rests his hand on my lap, familiar as the tabby cat. We'll be married in the spring, he says, he's sure of it; and meantime we can mind our manners in our separate beds, slog our way to church, and keep our souls from hell. Some weeks we cannot make it to the church, but that's no sin, so long as we attend at Christmas, Easter, and Pentecost.

Winter has fallen full force. The snow sometimes packs right up against the door. We have covered the windows with thick hides in addition to the wooden shutters; it's cozy and dark with the fire going, and sometimes we add the bead of a light from the oil lamp and Miss Tabby curls daintily under the table, and the house smells of woodsmoke and oil, garlic, leather, wet wool, and strong body scents, as we talk.

Only once at church have we met the Domergues since Domergue *père* spoke out and stopped our marriage. To my surprise, Alazaïs turned aside before I could greet her. I started after her, but Jerome caught my arm. "No," he said. He's angry with Domergue.

If I didn't know better, I'd say Alazaïs is holding a grudge, but perhaps she simply didn't see us in the dark church, wrapped as we were like round mushrooms in skins so thick that only our noses showed. Besides, what grudge could she bear, when I've helped with her babies, brought herbs? Jerome bought her a new headdress too, but that was months ago. Or is she embarrassed at Domergue's having spoken out? It doesn't matter. At present the snow makes all roads impassable, and in the spring we'll talk. I smile at myself, thinking perhaps I'm not yet finished with being mad: here I am making up stories about my friend Alazaïs. But I would have liked to speak to her; I miss her.

She scurried away right after the service, as if she'd left a pot on the stove. Domergue striding at her side, and none of the rest of the family with them.

Later, when the lanes are better, I'll go visit.

❖ TWENTY-EIGHT ❖

Spring comes early this year. By the end of February you could go outdoors with just an undershirt and dress, no coat, but wearing wooden clogs against the mud; now the snow is melting in the pastures. On the sunny southern slopes green stems are poking up, forsythia and almond trees in bud, and mild breezes are caressing us. It's so lovely I stand sometimes just to breathe and look.

Then one day Jerome comes in with news. "They're burning a heretic on market-day next week." He throws down his armload of wood. "I heard it from the shepherd, Belleperche. Next market-day."

"I can't get this smoke-hole open," I shout, fighting the leather cover. I'm suffocating. I slap at the thick air with the end of my apron. In some new houses they have clean chimneys that carry the smoke—but also the heat—away, but not in old farmhouses off the beaten track. I yank the rope with all my might, but the hide sticks tight. "Get free!"

Jerome takes the line from my hand. "Stand back."

"It's stuck."

"I'll do it." And gracefully, efficiently (as with everything he does), he jerks twice. The half-cleaned hide slithers silkily off the smoke-hole as if it had heard its master's voice, and the gray smoke from my cookfire begins to uncoil from the ceiling rafters, to twist and sift and wind itself like a living thing out of the hole, drifting up into the sky.

"You shouldn't build up the fire until you open the smoke-hole," says Jerome. He stacks his wood, then moves to the bucket to dip a drink of water before settling himself on his bench again and picking up a leather rein and tools. All this while I concentrate on my cooking. I am boiling cabbages and apples, onion, garlic, turnips, herbs and roots, to make a vegetable stew. I have celery and carrots, some pulse. In the stew I shall put walnuts and seasonings, including my few precious grains of Oriental cumin and nutmeg, which go well with apples. To go with it, I'll make some fried bread in the long-handled iron pan.

"What do you think?" he says after a moment.

"What do I think about what?"

"Market-day. Do you want to go?"

"Go!" I stand up, hands on my hips, and turn to face him. "Go see a poor man burnt?"

"It might be a woman," says Jerome. Watching me. His eyes glow in the firelight.

"Poor woman, then! It's all the worse!"

"I'm only asking because it's market-day. I thought you'd like to go. We have eggs to sell, and wood, and sausages." He drops his leather in his lap, eyes boring into me.

"Then *you* go. I've seen enough. Who hasn't? They burn them all the time, and not all of them heretics by any means," I continue in a rush of passion. "They burn anyone who ever knew a heretic, anyone who ate in the same house with a Good Christian—even if sitting at a different table, if you can imagine; that's how afraid they are! They burn anyone who has ever bowed to a Friend of God, anyone who's accepted a piece of bread from one, blessed with the very Pater Noster that we say each Sunday in church. They've killed one million of us so far, an entire population, anyone who shows some Christian charity."

I stop, breathless, shocked by the shock on Jerome's face. He stares at me, mouth agape.

"They'll burn us too, when I tell them what I know," I add, throwing up my hands.

We look at each other in horror. Something has been said that can't be unsaid. A door has been opened that cannot now be closed. It was this that we have been walking around these months.

"What do you know? Why would you tell?"

"I have work to do," I grumble, turning back to my fire. "As if we haven't all seen heretics."

"I suppose," he says humbly. "Yes."

"Well, suppose," I answer sharply. "You can't live in this day and age and not have come in contact with the Friends of God. They weren't bad people, not bad enough to burn. They're only heretics in the eyes of the Catholic Church, *haeretici perfecti,* indeed."

I mutter at the cookfire. Slam the pots and pans.

They are burnt one by one, like this poor man (or woman), or else in twos or tens or in whole companies: four hundred at Lavaur, four hundred and forty at Minerve, one hundred eighty-three at Marne up north, two hundred ten more at Moissac. Not long ago they threw three women in a well to drown, but that was a mistake, poisoning a good well. At Minerve they burnt them on a bonfire surrounded by a palisade of sharpened stakes. Afterward they pushed the ashes and bones off the cliff and into the river below, to the surprise of those downstream, as bits of blackened corpses filtered to their drinking water or filled their fishing holes or washed up on their laundry-beating rocks—corpses eaten by the fish that are eaten by the men.

"Can you imagine being downstream?" I laugh out loud, but it's a bitter, caustic sound.

"What?" asks Jerome, unaware where I've traveled in my thoughts.

Furious with myself, I slash at the tears with the back of my hand and lift my head to the smoke-hole, cursing the smoke that's made me cry. Jerome glances at me quietly and returns his attention to his leather. The cat jumps lightly to the tabletop, sniffing to inspect his work.

But I'm thinking of the black-robed ones who even at this minute are shoveling up the bodies of the dead and scattering the bones to the dogs— great-grandmothers buried fifty years in consecrated ground, dug pitilessly out of their eternal sleep so the Inquisitors can line up the skeletons to hear their posthumous trials. Then they burn the bones. No bodies left to rise at the last trump. On Resurrection Day. Well, it doesn't harm the Good Christians who've already gone into the Light. But I want to be buried in the good sweet earth when I die, just in case, and at a church, in hallowed ground, and not dug up. Just in case. Because I don't know what happens to us, if there's really a resurrection for the likes of me. But I know I don't think they should dig up bodies dead for fifty years.

"Bernard told me once," says Jerome, "that some years ago there was a perfected man. It was the same year that they made the Spanish friar, Dominic, a saint. They'd held a big burning at Moissac. Perhaps you remember it. Afterward, the consuls and the people rose up and arrested the Inquisitors. Remember? They protested to the Pope. Even the other Catholic orders disapproved. I remember hearing that one Cathar heretic took refuge in a monastery and the monks disguised him as one of their own and refused to turn him over to the Inquisitors."

"You're saying there's hope," I answer after a moment. "And perhaps there is, if we could all band together. Well, we tried for forty years. They're too strong for us." Then I give another laugh: it's all too much for me. "Maybe, when we wake up on Judgment Day, we'll discover all of us together, friars and preachers and ordinary people, Cathars and Catholics, all standing at the feet of Christ. Or maybe we'll all come back, reincarnated as the Friends of God assert," I continue brightly. "Maybe we'll return in the *jongleur*'s Future-time, when everyone is happy, and houses fly and people have heat without having to chop the wood or build the fire up, and in that age no one will kill another person or massacre whole populations. There won't be the need, because there won't be prejudice and hatred anymore. They won't go to war for ten years over a faithless woman, as they did at Troy. They won't butcher twenty thousand citizens in Béziers—men, women, babies, running screaming from the sword and club—or kill two thousand innocents who've taken sanctuary in a church. There won't be atrocities in that Future-time, when everyone will have enough. I wish I lived in that time. Yes, I do."

"Hmf." Jerome glances up at me. "They'll probably have developed new and better ways to kill by then. They'll still have massacres."

"No, it will be better. People will be rich, and everyone will have enough to share. Everyone will be educated."

"It's the knights and nobles that wage war now," says logical Jerome, "and they have enough to eat. It's not the likes of us that go to war. But the lords are all family, married to one another, and they *like* to fight. It's in their blood. They're the richest of us all, with their lands and castles and tithes and taxes. It's not the peasants who are busy waging war."

"So?"

"So the nobles could have peace if they wished. They have enough to eat. Fighting is part of human nature. They'll kill in that Future-time as well."

I stir the stew, mumbling to myself, as Jerome works his tooled design on the workhorse rein.

"What are you saying?" I ask finally.

"Nothing you want to hear."

After a time, he stands and stretches to ease his back. "I thought I'd go," he says.

"I don't know," I respond after a moment. "Maybe . . . I don't know. Who is it?"

"I don't even know if it's a man or a woman, perfected or not. Just a heretic is all I heard."

I drop the spoon at my sudden thought: What if it's one of my three? My stomach twists, and suddenly my mind is squirreling round its trees, over the branches, up and down the trunks, searching for a way to meet the heretic alone and ask for a blessing. Or for information about what happened to Hugon, Amiel, and Poitevin, the last and holy treasures of Montségur.

"Where is he?"

"In the Wall."

I shudder. The heretics lie deep in the stone prison, far underground.

We eat in silence, each lost in personal thoughts.

"Aren't you afraid?" I ask.

He looks at me hard. "Yes," he says. "I am." And looks away. Then back in my eyes, direct, but his brow is furrowed with concentration, speaking slowly: "That's why I take you to church every week, why I want us married in the church, why you should come stand with me in the crowd and watch him burnt."

It takes the breath out of me.

I'm a coward, I think, because I don't want to see another person burn. A pause. My mind whirling. Then, wiping my hands on my apron, I say, "Well, I'll go to market with you Saturday. We'll watch it together." I'll go to see if this is one of mine, found and lost again.

But by the next day, it's too late.

❈ TWENTY-NINE ❈

hey rode up the hill at a gallop. They thundered into the farmyard, all hooves and spurs and chain-mail, scattering the chickens, which fled squawking to all sides, and making the goat lunge, bleating, on his rope—as I wanted to do as well. The two armed escorts in their chain-mail jumped from their horses and took the reins of the two friars in their black and white robes. The Preaching Friars, the Inquisitors.

My mind flew to the Bible Gospels, hidden amongst its secret roots. I wanted to run, wings waving like the chickens. Instead, I stood frozen in the yard, hands hid under my apron, while they pulled up their frothing horses; and so queer is my mind that I found myself marveling at these friars astride their mounts like chevaliers, when they could walk.

"Are you the woman they call Jeanne Béziers?"

I nodded numbly. Jerome was running in from the near field, still holding his wooden hoe, limping as fast as possible on his game leg. At the gate, he slowed. Moving on reluctantly. Wiping his hands on his shirt.

"Can I help?" he asked staunchly.

Help! I wanted to cry aloud. Help the Inquisitors, was he crazy? Or perhaps he already had—I didn't know whom he'd been talking to in town.

"How long have you had this woman living here?" one friar asked him.

"How long, Jeanne?" he asked, managing to sound all innocent and unsuspecting. "Six months? 'Twas autumn."

"What is your name?" asked the second friar.

"Jerome," he answered. "Son of Arnaud."

"You come too." And before you could say Jerome Ahrade, the soldiers have us both in leather cuffs and collars, a rope hanging from our necks, like two donkeys.

"What about my animals?" cried Jerome. "I can't leave my animals."

"A neighbor will take care of them, whichever one you name. We'll stop and tell them on the way to town." He smiled, his glittering little piggy eyes disappearing in a fleshy, well-fed friar's face.

Jerome turned wildly in place, pulling on the halter at his neck, for suddenly he understood: anyone he named as a friend would be arrested too. The Preaching Friars need no charges to make an arrest.

"What's this about?" Jerome demanded. "What am I accused of? Who's fed you lies?"

"Come along." The soldier pulled on us.

"There are legal proceedings. I'm a good citizen. I'm a Catholic. I live here with my woman. We're not heretics. Look, I have Christ in my house on the cross. Go look. Over the door. I go to church. I take Communion. Ask the priest. You need a charge, a trial."

"Come on. If you're not lying, you won't be away for long."

"Jeanne?!" He cast another desperate look at me, then turned back to the soldiers. "Let me lock the door," he said.

They laughed, but they let him draw the rope through the hole and tie the latch. Anyone with a sharp knife can still get inside, of course. The animals were simply left in the farmyard, with our hopes that we'd be back by night to feed and care for them.

We were pulled behind the horses, jerked out of our farmyard, and the rusty gate swung squealing closed behind us. The goat bleated and the chickens squawked in outrage, flapping up in the air, but they'll settle into a soft contented buk-buk once the horses have left. I didn't have time to relieve myself, and now, with my bladder full and my fear high, I find myself spilling down my legs as we are hurried along too fast.

"I need to piss," I cry. "Stop!" And when they walk on, I add, "We're not criminals. Christ have pity on you, you haven't even questioned us."

One of the friars must have heard, because he stops his mule and motions me to squat right there in the road. Which I do, pulling my skirts around me modestly and loosing a hot stream of nervous urine in the path. It runs downhill to the horse, and I watch it pool around an indifferent hind hoof, but to me the angry piss is flowing on the man himself.

Jerome likewise takes the opportunity to relieve himself on the verge. And then we are hurried on again, down the rocky hillside road toward town. A thousand thoughts clatter through my mind—about Jerome and the animals, and how Saturday will be the *auto-da-fé,* the act of the faith, as they call it, in which a heretic will be burnt, man, woman, friend or stranger, who maybe named me before he was condemned to death. Named the crazy hobo-woman in an attempt to save his life. Mistress Flavia, perhaps, turned in by the stableboy? She knew my name. One of the women I met at market in the last six months? The Domergues? The egg woman whom I beat at bargaining a month ago?

Named me for what?

"What are we accused of?" I call. They do not answer, but trudge along, lost in their prayers and praise to God.

Jerome, walking beside me, looks lost.

"I'm so sorry," I murmur. "You're here because of me. I should have run away. Jerome, forgive me. It's my fault." And at the same time the violent thought assaults me: Was it Jerome who turned me in?

"Why?" he says stubbornly. "There's a mistake, that's all; and when we explain, they'll let us go. We'll be home again tonight. Tomorrow at the latest. You're my wife. No one knows anything more."

"Not married." I correct him.

"Maybe that's it. They want us to be married in the church."

I glance at him in surprise. Does he believe his own stories now? More likely we'll both be burnt on market-day with the other heretic; but even as I'm thinking this, I think, *I'm already married to this man.*

"I have married you," I say, and kiss him with my eyes. We walk along in silence then, terrified of the friars and their guards.

What's strange: down here in the valley springtime is bursting out in glorious pinks and whites, yellows and greens—green leaves, grass, bush, brush, the earth abloom with joy, and the scent of white apple blossoms and pear and quince warming in the air; while we are led to town like animals, with leather ropes around our necks and the leadlines trailing over the bay rump of the horse afore.

We come into town like criminals. Our hands are pinned behind our backs, our necks in leather collars. A hush falls over the afternoon crowd as we approach the market-square. People gather together in pools, shift away to give us room, move back under the protective arches of the shadowed gallery that runs around the plaza, providing shelter from sun and rain. Wherever we pass, a stillness falls, followed by a nervous buzz.

Some people suddenly find important business at the outdoor stalls or in the doorways of interior stores, and some just stand and stare, turning full-body to watch our progress. Three young boys dash excitedly down the gallery, calling to one another and twisting in and out of the well-clad burghers. One boy throws a rock our way and shouts, "Heretics!" before sprinting straight across the marketplace, dodging around the fruit and vegetable stalls. Followed by his two companions, he plunges down the street by the cathedral, to come out farther down the plaza and throw another stone.

Jerome and I, in shame, struggle behind the two black-frocked Inquisitors and their chain-mailed guards. Jerome is worried too about the animals. I know him well. His forehead is puckered with thought beneath his old felt hat. I'm concerned for him, because I have seen the Inquisitors. They give no quarter, no merciful shades of gray or blue. And I am worried for myself too, but more for Jerome, who has publicly called me his wife. He's not a young man anymore, and they've been pulling him along without regard for his game leg. He licks his lips, dry as hay, reminding me how parched my own throat is.

But what if it's Jerome who turned me in? If it was, it won't save him. They'll burn him too. Didn't he think of that?

We stop at the Wall. The black gate.

My fear is so great that I let go my bowels, and then my shame is greater still. A moan escapes my lips.

Jerome looks over at me. "Are you all right?" he whispers.

I am praying my Lord's Prayer, and trying to remember Baiona and Corba and Arpaïs all walking hand in hand into the fire, high of heart, singing and certain of their faith; while I . . . I glance over at Jerome in desperation.

I am praying, though, and pleading with God for my life. Then I think about the farm animals. Who will keep a fox or dog from killing the chickens, or one of the neighbors from thieving, taking anything they please out of our yard, our house, picking through my cooking pots or the seedlings on the windowsill? I could imagine old Annie doing that, who lives down in the dell and never nods a greeting to anyone. Or the Inquisitors themselves; I don't put it past the friars to send the monks from their monastery back up to lead away our livestock.

"Move!" One of the soldiers pushes me across the courtyard toward another gate.

"Jerome!" I look back over my shoulder.

He is white. Even his beard looks spiky and pale, and we are now so far apart from each other that we cannot even say good-bye. The soldier thrusts me ahead of him down the steps.

"Jerome!" I call out. Oh, I want to say so much: "Don't lose heart. You're a good Catholic; they'll let you go." I want to shout, "I love you. Yes!" Words never spoken. I want to say, "Trust God." But doubt catches in my throat and then it's too late, for I am pushed down the narrow stone corridor so hard that I fall to my knees. The soldier jerks me up and hurries me on, down the women's corridor, with its darkness and the stench of urine and feces, blood and human sweat, and the muffled calls of two women from behind the wooden doors. The sound of dripping water too. I am terrified. The soldier stops at a narrow wooden door and jangles the lock with his keys. The door creaks open. He pushes me into the cell, slamming the door with a bang.

It is black. No window. I cannot breathe. It is so dark it wouldn't matter if my eyes were open or closed, for I couldn't see either way, and my hands are still shackled behind my back. I am trembling with fear. I stand utterly still, shaking, not daring to move.

I can see . . . nothing. Darkness. I can hear . . . nothing; and then, what's worse, the heavy sound of silence, a high whine in my ears, and the voices of memory and reproof running wild inside me, like rampant children loose in the castle without a nurse. How long did I stand like that?

"O Lady," I prayed. "O Lord Christ, O my angels, I need You now. Most desperately. Help me, I belong to You," I prayed, though I could not manage devotion and gratitude at that moment, but only fearful, angry, hopeless cries for help. "Lord Jesus Christ, have mercy; do not forsake me," I pleaded. "I have not served You as I should, but I need You. Please forgive me my trespasses as I forgive—"

And then I stop, for of course I don't forgive my persecutors as our Master asks. How, therefore, can I be forgiven? I have failed the *perfecti*. I failed Baiona and failed the hopes of my true mother, Esclarmonde, the one who reared me and tried to teach me the Way, failed her with my sins and with William and now with Jerome, and failed Jerome. And now I am failing the teachings of our Lord. "And there is no health in me, but You, dear God, are most gracious. Look with mercy on Your daughter. . . ."

I know what I have to do: pray for the Inquisitors. But my heart is cold with hate. I sink to the stone floor praying for the willingness to pray for them. "Lord, help me." I want to burn them. I want to blind them with hot tongs. Strangle them barehanded, my hands locked on their throats, nails in the wattles of their soft skin. I imagine the white necks that rise beneath those threatening robes. I want to mutilate them for their righteousness, tear off their balls, and force them down their throats—rip their ancestors from their graves and scatter the bones.

I am panting. Suddenly I realize I have become not more forgiving but less! I am as bad as Inquisitors, consumed by righteousness and hate. Isn't that what Esclarmonde used to teach me? That the only one I'm hurting is myself.

"Help me, Lord God, for I hate them with most passionate fury, and only You can remove my anger and help me to forgive them, as You demand. Open my heart, O Lord!"

The Friends of God would repeat only the Lord's Prayer, the prayer that was given to Jesus' disciples by His own mouth. *Our Father, who art in heaven* . . . My lips repeat the words now, but my heart is whispering another prayer: "Save Jerome, please God; save my husband, Jerome." And the farm and animals. And me, Lord God! I'm so afraid. Sometimes I remember to put the prayer into the present tense: "Thank You, God, for saving me. And Jerome. And the animals."

I make a bargain: my life for his, although I know God does not bargain, and would not recognize the trade.

I pray as well for light, because I hate the darkness; I'm afraid of the dark. "Make them move me to a cell with light."

And, "Give me light!"

Wild, terrified, and passionate pleas.

◈ THIRTY ◈

I sit on the cold stone with my knees curled to my chest, shivering in the darkness. I have no idea how long I have been here. I am cold. Exhausted. Quivering. I have stopped praying, but now the memories roar unbidden to my mind.

Courage is not the absence of fear, but going on despite it. I'd happily place myself in any moment of the past, even wandering alone on the mountain after the massacre of Montségur, any moment rather than this one here in the blind dark, my hands tied painfully behind my back. My shoulders ache. It suddenly comes to me how much of my life I've spent bewailing my fate; and it occurs to me that if it was wrong to do so in years past, when I had my youth and freedom, surely it must still be wrong, locked in my prison cell. The Lady Esclarmonde used to say that happiness is a state of mind, a habit to be cultivated.

I set myself again to prayer, struggling for gratitude against the cold. *He giveth power to the faint,* says Isaiah: *They shall mount up with wings as eagles; they shall run, and not be weary, walk and not faint.*

It takes a long time, but eventually the soothing words begin to spin their hypnotic effect. *Our Father, who art in heaven*—in the heaven of my heart; and slowly I feel myself relax, feel the fear seep out, feel the loving Presence softly running to my heart. My head on my knees, I'm rocking, eyes shut, blind against the dark. *Our Father, who art in heaven, hallowed be*

Thy name—and as I finally (after what seems hours) reach these lines for the hundredth time, I am aware that I've grown calm.

Thy Kingdom come . . .

The light . . . ?

Thy will be done. The room is filled with Light. It is a being of light. I stare at her with awe and joy. "Come," she speaks in my mind, by thoughts moving from her mind to mine. She holds out her lovely hand and I am ravished. "Come with me." My Father, my Mother, the Kingdom in my heart. She is white, so blinding white, yet it does not hurt my eyes. My lady of the meadow.

Give us this day our daily bread—and this is the rapturous bread I wanted, I am awash with Light. I feel my very bones might crack with joy. I swoon into the Light, so filled with love that at that very moment I am only Love. I hold no rancor for Inquisitors, Domergues, for William, Jerome, Baiona, stableboys, or any other frightened traitors. This is what Christ was teaching, when he said to love your enemies, when he said, *Feed my Sheep.* I am overflowing, my cup running over. My soul is lifted up, the eagle that flies high, so high, into a sky of love. . . . The Light is pouring through me, enraptured by the Light.

She has gone. I'm in darkness again. Yet my soul is throbbing, full, and I am no longer afraid.

The guard comes in with water in a pitcher. I squint against the torch. It throws great shadows round the cell, but I blink against the torchlight, seeing my surroundings for the first time. The walls are damp, though I had known that by the feel and smell. A little dirty straw covers the stone floor.

The guard pushes me aside. "Get over there," he says, and "Here!"—pulling at the thongs that bind my hands. They fall. My hands are free. I want to speak, but my tongue stumbles on the words. I feel dizzy. I see in one corner a drain in the floor, and think, fuzzily, *Good: that is the privy, if I can grope to it again.* He tosses a piece of bread into my lap. The jug of water is on the floor.

The slam of the wooden door, and I am in the dark again, rubbing my wrists, easing my shoulder joints. Hesitantly, I grope for the pitcher and it clatters against the stones. I reach for it with shaking hands, trying in the dark to find it again before the water runs out. There. My palsied hands around it. I right it. Too late. Most of the water spilled. My teeth chatter against the jug as I drink the rest. Moist water.

The dry bread hurts my teeth. I feel sick. I doze, wishing to see that light again, but now my thoughts twist and turn along dark avenues, shadows of my former friends.

I have diarrhea. I scramble to the drain, and think I missed, though it is too dark to see. I feel nauseous, and at one point vomit at the same time that I befoul my legs and skirts.

Soon I cannot stand or sit up straight. I lie on the straw, sleeping, feverish and dull.

I am traveling into Light. I am captured once again by Light. I have left my body down in the prison cell, and what is strange is to see it crumpled there on the floor. Why did I care so much for it? The Light, the Love, pours over me, inside and outside of me, like the waves of the ocean rolling over me, like the petals of a flower, and I am the bee that drops dazed into the center of the sensuous blossom, made faint by dizzying scents and by the whiteness of the flowering light.

I am in a white rose, or else I am the rose. It climbs to the farthest reaches of the universe, and out of the rose (like small flames flaring upward in a fire) comes the even whiter light of yet another rose: out of which comes music—angels, pouring out a praise to God. Their voices blend in a choir so magnificent it makes my senses reel. It does not stop but builds from rose to rose, the inner whiteness growing ever whiter in the music of the praise. My tongue is filled with sweetness beyond nectar; it is the taste of this pure Light, and my soul is borne still higher, until I think I shall be extinguished by the Light. There is nothing but steep love, the love that moves the sun and stars, and creates springtime, autumn, winter too. This love is a lake of fire, and from its dancing flames (rising, falling back) comes every living thing, sparks drenching every living thing.

In my dream I cry out with a silent wordless shout of jubilance, for my heart is pierced with a love so sharp it hurts. I have had this dream before, but cannot remember when, for now I am flying upward into

Light, and on the other side of the meadow I see Baiona running toward me, and behind her comes William. William! I cry. Baiona! They know me. They are calling my name. I race toward their joy. As I approach the stream that divides me from them, I see my Esclarmonde, and she too is waving. All about are other spirits clad in many colors. Far in the background is my beloved Guilhabert de Castres and beside him his young *socius*, Bertrand Marty. They're both so young!

The next moment I am whirling back. I'm not allowed across the stream. Suddenly I am slammed back into my pain, my body, and hear the cries that are as weak as tiny fairy moans and that are coming to my surprise from my own throat. I want to go back there.

I lie on the hard stones, but my mind is still back in that meadow of Light, when I knew . . . everything, and everything was perfect—all birth, death, joy, pain, evil, good, all of it intended and perfect. Every moment of my life has been moving toward this perfect point. I know things. On that meadow I understood there is no evil. No Satan, devils, demons. Only Love. And what seems bad appears so only as the result of ignorance. What seems good carries no more weight than the bad, for in the eyes of God there is only *Yes! I AM!* How can this be? I remember knowing, as the Light swelled up around me, that evil is made by us, by our acting without the aid of love.

Slowly words return, coherent thoughts. But most of what I know cannot be said in words. I am humbled, for *this* was the treasure of the Friends of God. I'd thought the Cathar treasure lay in gold and jewels, in ivory boxes carved and clasped with silver locks. Or in the chalice of the Holy Grail. Or in the Good Book. Or (later, after my talk with Bishop Marty) in the *perfecti.* When all the time it lay hidden in my heart, waiting for me to turn the key, to discover who and what I am, what we all are— made of love.

The pearl beyond price.

I lie on the stones, blinking against the darkness, which is no longer threatening but seems to cover me now in an embrace as safe as the dark and fluid womb, as warm as my nurse's arms. I drift on a sea of love, remembering the rose-white visions, the music of the spheres.

The lake of love. I can swim in it, for what I understand, coming out of reverie yet still in that sublime sweet state of timelessness (the music fading in my ears, my mouth rich with honeyed light)—what I remember is this: that living things are all composed of Light, the Light of love; our souls are soaked in love; and the soul is not found in any single part of the body but permeates it utterly, as water permeates a sponge, so that there is nothing in us not composed of love and nothing real but soul. The French crusaders too were formed of love, the Preaching Friars, *perfecti*, peasants, Pope.

Perhaps I am delirious. Perhaps it was a dream.

I had prayed for light, and light was given me—not as I had imagined in the poverty of my imagination, for all I'd wanted was a window, and instead I was given light greater than anything I could have conceived. (I am so thirsty. I reach for the empty water jug and take a few drops on my lips. My tongue is thick and sore.)

Suddenly I know that I've always been protected. Every moment of my life—how can I say it?—has been, not of no importance, exactly, but more lighthearted than I'd understood. Each evil that I named has led to good, or taught a lesson, or changed the ground of its being to disclose in its dark silk lining the beneficence of God. Even the violence is an aspect of the loving hand of God.

(And so is water: water, please.)

The guards find me raving when next they come. I'm so sick they send a surgeon to examine me. And now they have moved me to a larger cell. It has a window. Thanks be to God, for this pleases me, and didn't I pray for a window earlier? I stare at my blue hopeful patch of sky. They brought me soup. I hold the bowl in trembling hands. I lift the spoon. Must eat.

Days pass. Where is Jerome?

They came for me today. The door opened with a squeal, the soldiers grabbed me under the armpits and hauled me outside. Hands bound again behind my back. I can hardly stand. Blink against the torches. I am dragged up steps and down long corridors until, shaking, all I want is to stop, to rest. But on we go, higher. I ask, "Where are we going?" But my thin voice is no more than a scent on the air, an idea inside my head.

Into a large chamber. A fire in the chimney. High carved mantelpiece. A black-and-white is standing, his back to the room, to me, staring into the flames. I am dizzy and it takes a moment to sort out the shifting shapes: the room holds a long table, at which stands another friar, and seated are two scribes, with quills and papers ready, and they too are wobbly, and sometimes make themselves into three or four and then go back to two. There are various guards and soldiers, some leather books, but these may be shadows only, I don't know.

The man at the fireplace turns to face the room, and slips his hands inside his sleeves. He has a mournful, angry, haunted face.

"Jeanne Béziers," says the guard in a loud voice. Announcing me.

"Sit."

"Stand."

Contradictory directions. I am weaving on my feet, aware in this sumptuous room of the filth on my skin and clothes, my hair loose and uncombed, wild around my head. I smell of cold stones and worse.

They begin the questioning: Name. Age. Where are you from?

My tongue is swollen. It stumbles over words: "Praise be to Jesus Christ," I whisper.

"Are you a heretic? Have you ever known a heretic? What's your association with Béziers? Did you know the Lady Esclarmonde of Foix and Pamiers, known *perfecta?* Were you acquainted with any of her sons?"

"Praise be to our Lord Jesus Christ," I whisper again.

"Answer the questions!"

"Answer on pain of death."

I say nothing, for at that moment I see behind him in the vision of my eyes the face of my Lord Christ and with him is Our Lady, both looking at me so compassionately that my knees buckle. It is she—it is the luminous Lady who, smiling, took my hand in the meadow at Béziers, when I was but a child, and here she is again all draped in light. My Lord Christ moves toward me, into me. The monk gives a nod. The soldiers grab me, strip me to the waist: my breasts exposed. They beat me with their leather whips, but oh, my Lady! Each blow brings only exquisite joy. I am transported, for I am filled with Christ and yet I gaze into the glowing eyes of Christ. It's one more treasure of Montségur.

"Do you confess your heresy?"

"She does not cry aloud."

"Beat harder. Use your arms."

"O Christ!" I exclaim.

"Take her back to the cell," says the monk at the fire. He turns away. He has a heavy heart, unhappy man. Does he not see our Lord shining in the room?

"May Christ have mercy on you," I bless him, "and all the angels of heaven be with you, in the name of the Father—"

An impatient wave of his hand. "Next time the torture."

Then we are staggering back down the corridors, down steps, down, down, along corridors, into the darkness again, to my prison cell. The wooden door slams.

My Lord Christ has left. My Lady has left. My back is on fire. Now I scream in pain.

❈ THIRTY-ONE ❈

I think of Baiona and William happy together in the next world. In my little cell, I pray for them both to forgive me, and I pray also to forgive, for otherwise how can my own misdeeds be overlooked? Forgive us our offenses as we forgive those who offend us. Forgive me, Baiona, I pray. Forgive me, Esclarmonde, for my defiance, for not loving. Forgive me, Jerome.

Sometimes I pray for the animals, and it occurs to me that, being here in prison, I am unable to slaughter another pig next fall. So God has worked His will so elegantly, thus saving me from yet another sin.

Sometimes, though, the pain is such that I cannot pray. Doubt and fear assault me. Shakily, hardly able to stand, I force myself to pace my stone cell, to and fro, ridden with anxiety and trying to think of . . . what? My mind whirls frantically, unable to harbor anything but doubt. And who turned us in? The Domergues? Raymond? I can't believe it. The priest? The stableboy? Jerome himself?

Where now is the Light? But after the life I've lived, I deserve my punishments. I take off my underskirts, which are soaked with filth. The smell is intolerable. I tremble at the solitude, mad with loneliness and guilt.

Then I pull my thoughts under control again: God does not punish, I tell myself, but only my inner conscience. "Try to know exactly what you're feeling," Esclarmonde used to say. (I'm feeling angry, hurt, afraid;

thirsty, hungry, wet.) Sitting in that gloomy cell, the silence broken only by the occasional scurrying of a rat in the straw, or by my breathing or by my fingers scratching my own molting skin, by the muffled shouts or even screams from the other side of the door, I scrape beneath the surface of my thoughts to name my feelings as Esclarmonde had taught: not placing my ruthless anger and hatred onto the Inquisitors, who are only doing their job as they see it, but examining my heart, myself, who can no longer see the Light (that too coming only as a grace, however, unable to be willed).

My feelings shift from fear to loneliness to sorrow, to guilt (which is another form of fear), then anger (which also comes from fear), jealousy (fear), revenge, shame, pity, remorse; until it becomes clear as I sit in the prison cell that none of these emotions is true. Each of them acts as a shield for fear. I am afraid I'll die in prison, never see Jerome again, for no one leaves the Wall. I'm afraid of being tortured. I'm afraid of being burnt.

My back is on fire where I was whipped.

Sometimes I lose control. I scream. The echoes bounce off the walls. Sometimes I pace my cell—three steps forward, three back—like a leopard in his cage. Sometimes I feel utterly alone. Then I force myself again (how quickly I forget!) to pray, and again I struggle to my knees, hands clasped, and once—but only for a moment—I am enfolded in the Light.

Again they take me for questioning. Always the same two friars. Each time they ask the same questions over and over.

"Your name," they ask, although they know it well. "Where are you from?" At first they ask simple questions. They know nothing about me: my name never appeared on the lists at Montségur.

"Name the heretics you know."

"Have you ever praised the heretics for their saintliness?"

"Do you know anyone who has ever been in the presence of the perfected heretics?"

I answer nothing. "The blessings of Jesus Christ our Lord," I repeat, or else I say the Hail Mary or the Pater Noster, trembling lest they put me to torture, but no other words fall from my mouth. They ask about Jerome. They ask about Montségur. They ask and ask.

"Were you at Montségur during the siege? What do you know of the Cathar treasure?" (Yes, I know it all: it's found in prayer!) "What do you know of the *perfecti* who escaped? How many were there? What are their names? Where is the treasure? Who knows where it is hid?"

I answer with my prayers, only prayers.

The soldiers lash me to the rack. I faint. They waken me to try again, but at the first pain I am gone—hovering above my body and watching with detached disinterest as they discuss the body on the rack: "Take her down. We don't want to kill her."

Then back to my cell, where I'm left alone again.

One day it dawns on me that I've already received the *consolamentum,* for I have no more anger at these men. My heart overflows with gratitude; it floods my guards, my dingy straw, my food, my life, my dead friends, my enemies, my own pure soul. Surely I am mad. I fall to my knees in humility. I have found the treasure. This is what everyone is looking for: the treasure is our own immortal soul. I am the treasure. I have found the treasure of Montségur. Crazy Jeanne.

◼ THIRTY-TWO ◼

For the second time: they take me to the torture chamber. This is no beautiful room with its finely carved mantle and writing tables; it is small, cramped, dark, and in one corner the fires smoke and in another the black metal torture machines lie in wait grinning at me, and the smell is of fear and hot coals, and as soon as I see the machines I loose a trickle of pee. My weight sags onto the arms of the guards. I am sick with fear.

"Do you confess that you are a heretic?"

They have not even strapped me yet to the plank. I try to answer——*Yes, yes, I confess to everything, to anything*——anything you want. But when I open my mouth I vomit. The men leap back cursing, and then throw me on the rack. I've made them angry. I'm trying to answer——*Yes, don't hurt me, I confess. I am a heretic.* But the words are stuck. *O God, help me, I'm afraid.*

Today they came and released me. As suddenly as they arrested me, the guards have unbolted my prison door.

"You're free," they said.

No explanation.

"And Jerome?" It comes out as a croak, so long has it been since I spoke. But they don't answer. I am led through miles of corridors, up and down staircases and along dark passages; I'm lost in a maze of corridors, and then I'm at a gate. As it swings open, I blink against the startling light.

"Go," says one of the two men. He shuts the gate behind me, remaining within. The other man pushes me toward an even larger gate. Squinting, disoriented in the painful light, I stumble across the courtyard and through the doorway out into a street. I can't believe I'm free. The gate clangs shut behind me.

I can hardly walk. I have no food or water or shelter. Where am I to go?

People around me staring. I move slowly, with unbalanced gait, away from town, out into the country, along the dusty road. I look down at myself and have to laugh at Crazy Jeanne. Dirty and unkempt once more. The dispossessed. *Exilio.* But I'm alive!

As I climb the hillside, my heart expands, grows, widens in wonder at the beauty of the waving grass! At the blue of summer sky and the sweet warm wind that comes to kiss my cheek! It's full summer. I cannot get enough of it. Walking toward the snowcapped mountains. Going home.

I stop at the river and lean down to drink, then wash the filth from my face and arms and feet. The sun is hot, no one near.

I strip off my soiled dress and slip right into the river. The shock of cold water. I pull my dress into the water and try to wash that too, then put it on the grass to dry in the sun. There's not a lot that can be done.

I duck under the surface and pull the water through my hair.

Crazy Jeanne.

Later, drying in the sunlight, I try to think out where to go. Caution is required. I need food, shelter. But already I know where I am going and what I'll do when I get there. Everything is very clear. I am stick-thin, ribs showing. Still sick. My knees are weak. I shake as I pull my dry dress back on.

It is late afternoon when I reach the Domergues. The yellow dog dashes into the yard, barking. Alazaïs sees me first. She rushes outside to greet me, followed by the wet-nurse—and here's the knee-baby grown so big now, sucking her thumb.

"Jeanne! It's Jeanne!" Alazaïs calls. "Dear God! Look at you!"

"Don't you look a sight!" agrees the wet-nurse.

The dog barks and cavorts in the yard, twisting on his tail. Fays is at the door, carrying the baby, Jean.

They bring me inside, laughing, scolding. The men are in the fields.

"How are you?"

"Are you all right?"

"How did you get out?"

Everyone is talking at once.

"Who is she, Mama?" whispers the knee-high, hiding in her mother's skirts; and I laugh aloud. Who am I, after all?

Alazaïs blows up the fire, sets a kettle on. "You need to wash," she says. "You look awful."

"I need food."

She puts a hunk of bread in my hand.

I am so happy that I can only turn from one to another, smiling, laughing foolishly. They give me ale and a leftover oatcake, and then a sweet apple to break my fast. I feel my strength returning. As I eat, they pass on news. Bernadette's husband, Raymond, has married the wet-nurse, who would have imagined? and the baby had colic but is doing well. The married daughter who lives away had another child, her fifth.

"What happened?" I ask finally. "Do any of you know? They came today and let me out. For no reason and with no more questioning. They simply put me outside and said that I was free."

"We told them you were crazy," says Alazaïs. She throws back her head, laughing, her fine teeth glowing. "We said you were a half-wit." She taps her head. "Too happy, we said. But a good wife to Jerome." Laughing, she throws her arms around me. "Now don't go making liars of us all."

The smiling wet-nurse (I've already forgotten her name again) plops down on a bench, opens her blouse, and pulls out one beautiful, white moon of a milking breast to feed the boy. He slurps milk greedily. I can't stop looking. I can't get enough of life!

"Crazy, eh?" I smile to myself. "Well, you didn't lie." Then in curiosity: "Who turned us in? I thought it might be you."

"We think it was the priest's investigations, when he sent to ask about you. Did they think you were a heretic?"

I'm not ready to talk about all that yet.

"But you're home now, never fret," says Fays, the perceptive woman-child. "Just be glad it's over. It will never happen again."

"Jerome is home," says Alazaïs. "You'll find him at the farm. Waiting for you, I expect, though we didn't none of us know when you'd get out.

Or even if you would. If they would release you or burn you. But they've let you go, you're cleared."

We laugh and laugh. Alazaïs is crouched down, blowing on the coals.

"Gaillard is a shepherd." She offers up the news as if on a banquet plate. "With Belleperche. He's gone as far across the mountains as into Aragon. He's grown that strong. We won't see him from one year to the next," she continues, still down on her knees at the flames. "One moment a little boy, and the next he's gone."

"And Domergue?"

"He's getting older. But he put in the crops again. Thank God for two strong sons to help."

I wash again in the stableyard with two buckets of warm water, heated on the fire. Alazaïs grabs up my clothes.

"I want to get on home," I protest.

"You'll find him waiting for you," she says. "But no point going like that, looking like a hag. I'll loan you my other dress and a cloth for your head."

"What dress?"

"My blue one."

"Your good one? Your Sunday dress?"

"You can return it tomorrow, when you've washed your gown properly. Be careful of it, that's all. I'll need it for this Sunday."

"Is he all right?" I hardly dare to ask.

"He was in prison only for one week. Not months like you." She sits me in the sun between her knees, now dressed in her clean shift. She brushes and dries my hair. Grooming for lice. Snapping them between her fingernails. How fine it feels, her strong fingers stroking my scalp, my temples, as Baiona used to do. I hold her knees and lean back sweetly on her chest, while she tells the local gossip, and her hands caress my head, massage my scalp, filling me with serenity. So-and-so has hurt himself and the younger boy, Martin, wants to marry a town girl, but Alazaïs doesn't like the girl's family. Annie, the woman in the dell, has died. And of course she tells me about Jerome, imprisoned and immediately released.

"How?" I ask. "Why did they let him go?"

"We bought his liberty."

"Bought it?"

"We mortgaged our farm for him," she says. "It took three hundred *livres,* but he's free."

"Three hundred! That's the income of the lord!" I am shocked. Then I reconsider: "What made you think of that? How clever!" I pat her knees in applause and try to turn around to see her lovely, wrinkled face.

"Don't move. Even the Inquisitors need money," she says cynically. "The problem is, now he has to pay it off. So don't think all is well: he's signed over his farm to us, in pledge. It's just a business deal. And we'll be the richer for it in the end, I expect. A good deed with a good outcome. He'll be in debt till his death, and then the farm is ours."

I say nothing.

"Jerome's the one who got you freed. He petitioned the papal legate in Toulouse. He said if you'd been at Montségur, then you had been exonerated once and could not be arrested for the same crime."

"And did they find my name in the records?"

"Well, actually, they did not. There was a problem with the records. But we testified that you were" (circling her temple with one finger) "you know, 'off.' He said if you were not there, then you could not legally be arrested. They agreed a mistake had been made. More money passing hands, I presume. I don't know how he expects to pay it all."

Dusk is falling. I can contain myself no more. I leap to my feet.

"I'm going now," I say with a laugh. "You understand."

She laughs too, embracing me. "I'll walk you to the stablegate."

"Say hello to Domergue. We'll come see you soon."

"Dear Jeanne. It's good to have you back."

I climb the last two miles. Giving thanks to God, who worked it out, and to my Lord Jesus Christ, who is walking beside me, climbing humbly at my side. I feel the golden, friendly presence. He is smiling, delighted with me. And someone else is up ahead, in white.

I think tomorrow we shall pack up, Jerome and I. We shall take the treasure from the cave and pay off our debts, or else we'll travel into Lombardy and give it to the Friends of God. Or perhaps we'll just stay on the farm, marry, and pay off our mortgage to the Domergues, year by slow year, in order not to arouse suspicion. Perhaps we'll leave most of the treasure in the cave, in case it's needed by the Friends of God.

Because I want to tell Jerome about the real treasure, which is the treasure in our hearts. I want to tell him about God's love.

I am leaping up the hillside, my body working like a spring, and there is the farm. I see it shining in the light. The Light! And there is William waving to me! And Baiona calling! Roland-Pierre! I shade my eyes with my hand, because I cannot see for the white, the brilliance of the Light!

"Let go the ropes." The Inquisitor stepped forward to the rack. The woman's form had suddenly gone slack. He disliked this work—the darkness of this underground chamber, the black heat that bellowed from the fireplace, the multiplicity of ropes and wooden pegs, the nail-studded metal coffins in which to enclose a victim, the wheel and rack and red-hot iron headbands, the spokes that gouged out eyes, the tongs that twisted limbs or pulled out fingernails. Amidst the bleeding screams, he sometimes felt he could hardly breathe; yet at the same time, he experienced an animal excitement. This work was done in the name of the most righteous service of Jesus Christ, the Lord of love, who wanted the heretics to repent, who wanted the taint removed from Mother Church.

He grimaced angrily.

"She's died."

"Fool! We're not supposed to kill them on the rack. Unstrap her quick. Revive her."

"She's only a heretic."

"She never confessed. For all we know she was a good Catholic, now dead without the sacraments."

"It's not my fault, your honor."

"You're supposed to pay attention to your work."

"I hardly twisted the ropes. She was gone before I even began."

"She never confessed. Well, give the body to the family." The Inquisitor began to strip his gloves. "Have someone notify them. It's not our business."

He wiped his hands on his clean handkerchief and turned to mount the stairs.

▣ THIRTY-THREE ▣

They found him sitting in the dark, hands dangling between his knees, and on his lap her colorless old woolen cloak.

"Why, Jerome, whatever is the matter?" Alazaïs asked, bustling into the little room. "Why are you just sitting here, the fire gone out, nothing done?"

Domergue followed slowly. He looked about him with bovine, sturdy patience while his wife twisted here, there, talking all the time.

"Why, how you've let it go!" she exclaimed. "Are you sick? Look at the dust everywhere, the animals outside untended in the yard. You haven't taken the sheep to pasture, or the pony. Here you are, sitting in the dark when it's God's good sunlight out of doors and things to be done."

She found the flint. "I'll bet you haven't eaten either. No fire to cook with. No wood to build a fire. Well, speak up, man. What's bothering you? Domergue, bring in some wood," she commanded. "The least we can do is light the fire, give the poor man some food. You'd think you were a child, sitting in the dark, alone."

Jerome cast an anguished look at her and dropped his eyes.

"Did you hear me, man?" she said. "Get up, now. Move about."

"She's dead."

"Ah, dead," repeated Domergue from the doorway. He abandoned his chore and seated himself beside Jerome, patting his knee with one hand.

Alazaïs stared at the two men, her hands on her hips. "She was a heretic." She spat out the words. "She only got what she deserved."

"I told them," said Jerome, and when he looked up they could see tears standing in his eyes. His fingers plucked the woolen cape. "I said she was a heretic."

"Well, and didn't they torture you?" asked Domergue quietly. "What do you expect? Didn't they nearly tear your shoulder out?"

He rubbed his shoulder with a puzzled expression, the mild, bewildered disbelief of a child. Two tears coursed slowly down his weathered, sun-grooved cheek.

"I can't move it anymore." He looked over at Domergue in confusion and then up at Alazaïs, standing over them. "I told them she knew the heretics. I told them she knew about the treasure."

Alazaïs and Domergue exchanged a look.

"What treasure?" asked Alazaïs.

"The Cathar treasure. The treasure of Montségur. She knew where it was hid."

"She knew where the treasure was?" Alazaïs sank down onto the other bench with a grunt.

"We were going to go get it. We talked and talked about it. She'd helped hide it. We were going to be married, and then we were going to ask you to care for our animals for a month, while we went for the treasure. We planned to tell everyone the trip was a pilgrimage. She said we would have to spend the money thriftily. She wanted to share it with you."

"With us?"

"She loved you. She said she wanted us all to share in the good fortune. She wanted to keep some of the treasure for us and give some to your family; then we'd carry the rest to Lombardy, to give to the Friends of God. It belonged to them. She said she'd take a little bit for us, for you, and take the rest to them," he repeated.

"No!" said Alazaïs, rising violently. "She was a witch. We watched how she bewitched you. She had her claws in you. You couldn't see another woman, not even my own daughter Fays, who would have made a proper wife for you soon. Then *she* came along and you took her right into your house."

She leaned down, hissing in his face. "She was a witch, with her herbs and deadly potions. She killed our Bernadette. Her, with her hands on my poor sick children's heads and murmuring her chants and spells. She borrowed my headdress, no telling what charms she was putting into that."

Jerome's jaw dropped. "It was *you* that turned her in?"

"Enchantments, that was what she did. Look at her, an old woman, and still appearing beautiful."

"Did she really know where the treasure was hidden?" asked Domergue thickly. "She would have shared with us?"

Jerome nodded.

"Well, we can still get it then," said Alazaïs. "We can do what she wanted done with it. Where's the treasure then?"

"She wouldn't tell me. She was afraid of just what happened: that I'd be arrested and say more than I meant to."

"Then she truly was a heretic," said Alazaïs. "She wouldn't have known where it was if she weren't a heretic." She looked wildly from her husband to Jerome. "And what good would it have done us, having the goods of heretics? Tainting us. What good would the treasure have done? Got us all killed, I suppose."

Domergue stood up. "Be quiet, woman."

She gasped.

"Jerome." He let one hand fall on the other man's arm.

"I miss her. I don't even have anything good that belonged to her. She didn't own a thing of any value. This cloak is all I have." He held it to his face. "It still carries her scent. Do you want to smell it?"

"I'm so sorry."

"There *was* no treasure!" Alazaïs cried passionately. "It was just another lie. She was a heretic, I tell you. She deserved to be turned in. There was no treasure, mark my words. There is no treasure. She'd not have shown you anything. Not ever."

❖ EPILOGUE ❖

Ninety years later, a violent storm uprooted the huge beech tree on the hill. Its shallow roots tore out of the soggy, stony earth, and the tree collapsed with a thunderous roar, upending the other trees and brush nearby. The drenching rain continued to fall.

In the roots a green oilskin packet could be seen. The green waterproof covering, clogged with mud, opened under the slow pressure of the rain, and if anyone had been about he could have picked up a hard brown leather case, held by a tarnished silver clasp so black it looked like iron, But no one was about anymore: the Domergue farm had been abandoned years before to briars and scrub-brush, as had Jerome's as well as the little church (its roof caved in); and no one lived any longer in so remote a spot.

The leather binding of the Holy Gospel bent and warped under the wet rain, exposing the parchment pages with their delicate black lettering, each character inked by someone's patient hand. The water splashed on the calfskin, blurring the mud-splattered pages. Each chapter opened with a capital letter painted with gold, ruby, lapis lazuli, and other precious minerals in an elaborate embroidery of fanciful animals, leaves, flowers and of tiny figures shown at play or prayer. This—the Word of God, written in the local tongue—was a treasure so valuable and so dangerous that to own it could mean death. Slowly the pages curled and tore. The book disintegrated in the sun and snow and mud.

Bibliography

Aué, Michèle. *Décourvrir: Le Pays Cathare.* Vic-en-Bigorre: MSM, 1992.

"Les Cathares: La Croisade contre le Languedoc." *Historia Special* no. 373 (1977): 1–123.

Cherry, John. *Medieval Crafts: A Book of Days.* London: Thames & Hudson, 1993.

Davis, R. H. C. *The Medieval Warhorse.* London: Thames & Hudson, 1989.

Duvernoy, Jean. *La Religion des Cathares: Le Catharisme.* Bibliotheque Historique. Toulouse: Privat, 1989.

Ennen, Edith. *The Medieval Woman.* Translated by Edmund Jephcott. Cambridge, MA: Basil Blackwell, 1989.

Fox, Sally, ed. *The Medieval Woman: An Illuminated Book of Days.* Boston: Little, Brown, 1985.

"Historia Occitanie: Le Drame Cathare." *Historama* 570 (1994): 6–39.

Le Roy Ladurie, Emmanuel. *Montaillou: The Promised Land of Error.* Translated by Barbara Bray. New York: Vintage Books, 1979.

Manchester, William. *A World Lit Only by Fire: The Medieval Mind and the Renaissance: Portrait of an Age.* Boston: Little, Brown, 1993.

Nelli, René. *La Vie Quotidienne des Cathares du Languedoc au XIIIe Siècle.* Paris: Hachette, 1969.

Oldenbourg, Zoe. *Massacre at Montségur: A History of the Albigensian Crusade.* London: Weidenfeld & Nicolson, 1961.

Roquebert, Michel. *Mourir à Montségur: L'Épopée Cathare.* Toulouse: Privat, 1989.

Rouquette, Yves. *Cathars.* Translated and adapted by Roer Depledge. Toulouse: Loubatieres, 1992.

Tannahill, Reay. *Food in History.* New York: Stein & Day, 1973.

Weis, René. *The Yellow Cross: The Story of the Last Cathars 1290–1329.* New York: Alfred A. Knopf, 2001.

The Treasure of Montségur

by Sophy Burnham

PLOT SUMMARY

The year is 1209: a baby girl, dressed in a white silk dress strewn with pearls, is found in a meadow outside the smoking city of Béziers, where 20,000 people have just been massacred. Adopted by Lady Esclarmonde, the fiery Jeanne is educated in the ways of the Cathars—the "pure ones," pacifist, vegetarian, chaste followers of Christ. But war is raging, and the Inquisition is charged with exterminating the Church of Love. It is a time of terror, with neighbor pitted against neighbor, and religious passions running high, a time of suspicion, burnings, and systematic genocide. Against this turbulent background Jeanne of Béziers finds herself embroiled in the resistance, fighting for freedom alongside William, the man whom she loves—and who is married to her best friend.

Trapped with William and more than 200 Cathars at the fortress of Montségur, Jeanne is asked to sacrifice her convictions for the security of the Cathar legacy. As the only person who can save the legendary Cathar treasure, Jeanne is propelled on a journey through the dark days of the Inquisition, eventually to a place where she discovers the true treasure of Montségur and her own destiny in keeping it alive.

This stunning novel of the Cathars, populated with real historical figures and accurate in its historical details, tells Jeanne's story of sexual passion, intrigue, mystery and the search for love and God. This extraordinary woman will linger with you long after the novel's haunting conclusion.

SOPHY BURNHAM ON WRITING
The Treasure of Montségur

I am a slow writer. It takes me years to write a book. I started researching *The Treasure of Montségur* almost ten years ago, when two different people on two different continents independently brought the story of the Cathars to me— the treasure, the doomed Good Christians trapped on the top of the mountain, the surrender, and the four Good Men who were secretly lowered on ropes down the sheer cliff face by night, to vanish into a lush landscape and keep alive the Church of Love.

What a tale! I began to ponder: What if one of those four were a woman? What if she'd lost the treasure, the three Good Men? What if she fell in love? What if she's on her own spiritual search, looking for God? That's how a story whispers itself to me, slowly, and with questioning.

What if she were a mature woman in her forties (aged by medieval standards), and I swirled that idea on my tongue like fine wine, because with our cultural idealization of youth, few books today permit a passionate love affair to an older woman. I liked that. I also liked her earlier obsessive affair; for who has not fallen in love with—had an obsession for—a man who used her callously? What if she were homeless, heretic, hunted? What if she were a Resistance Fighter?

But for me, the research into that period was made more immediate, because the war in Bosnia had just broken out, and I was reading with horror of events as appalling as those of Medieval France! Massacre, genocide, spiritual and physical passions lived out in blood and butchery, vengeance and violence, rape, mass graves, torture and atrocities; and always, as an undercurrent, the search for the God of love.

Some of my own people came originally from France, as Huguenots fleeing another religious persecution. But that's not unusual: almost any American immigrant was fleeing something—or is today. We are so blessed in our prosperity, freedom, pursuits and opportunities. Apart from acknowledging my background, I don't live in the past, or feel myself victimized for the passions of earlier generations. But I look at atrocities perpetrated in Kashmir, Croatia, Ireland, Israel, in Afghanistan, Argentina, Somalia, Sudan, in the Philippines, Timor, Sri Lanka—or on a minor scale in my own city of Washington, D. C.— is any place exempt from suffering? I look and my heart breaks. I am left shuddering and in tears.

Some people organize demonstrations, and others serve in relief camps. But all I can do is tell a story, and hope that by setting it 700 years ago those who read it will make the connection between those events and what we do to each other every day.

Are we doomed to violence evermore? And where is God in this?

The treasure has never been found. Hitler sent search parties into the Languedoc to see if they could find it. But there's another question: what *was* the treasure? Was it gold and bullion? Was it the Holy Book? Was it the Good Men and Good Women who baptized others with their light-struck spiritual hands? Or was it the simple goodness of a loving heart?

TOPICS FOR DISCUSSION:

1. One theme of the novel is the deep friendship between Baiona and Jeanne; and yet twice Baiona "takes" the man Jeanne loves. The first was not important, but all her life Jeanne loves William, and she believes that he loves her as well. Did he? Do you understand and sympathize with Jeanne's dilemma? Have you ever been in a situation of loving an unattainable person?

2. One turning point for the young girl, Jeanne, is her relationship with the boy Rogert. Why did Jeanne allow these sexual encounters with Rogert? Do you think that she was taken advantage of? Given how innocent she was and how romantic, do you think there was anything else she could have done?

3. In the end William chooses Baiona, deciding be martyred with his wife. Why? Why do you think that he chose to stay with Baiona instead of staying and marrying Jeanne? What was the result emotionally for Jeanne?

4. In the course of the novel, Jeanne drops in social position from that of a high-born lady, to bourgeois widow and resistance fighter and finally to a homeless beggar. When she meets Jerome, a free peasant farmer, she finally seems to find some happiness. Does this seem justified, or does it feel romanticized to you?

5. It is through the love of Jerome and by telling her own story that Jeanne is healed. But in telling her story she has created a conflict for the man she loves. Why can't they marry? Why can't they go get the treasure and live happily ever after?

6. What do you think was the treasure of Montségur?

7. The Lady Esclarmonde, a true historical figure, repeated a prayer whenever entering a room or eating a meal or dropping her spindle? What was so important about this prayer? Do you have a particular prayer or meditation that is especially meaningful to your spiritual life? Has it changed the way you think or relate to God?

8. The Lady Esclarmonde raises Jeanne to be a good Cathar believer and even sends her to study at Montségur under the tutelage of the great Cathar bishop Guilabert de Castres. Yet when it comes time to arrange a marriage for Jeanne, she chooses a Catholic, Gobert. Why? How have culture and faith affected your relationships?

9. Jeanne gives the *consolamentum*, a spiritual baptism, by the laying-on of hands to a dying woman. Every religion has special sacraments of baptism and initiation. What are the most important ones in your own faith tradition? Can women as well as men provide this privilege and gift?

10. When the novel opens, Jeanne is seen by many—and thinks of herself— as crazy. Yet she behaves at moments with great certainty. What do you think? Has she gone mad? Have you ever experienced or do you know anyone with post-traumatic stress syndrome?

11. Jeanne is fleeing the Inquisition. Do you know or have you heard of any people persecuted today by modern forms of Inquisition? Do you believe that use of torture is ever permissible against an enemy?

12. Holy war and the search for God are central themes of this novel. Both Catholics and Cathars believe they have found the true path, and yet both worship the same Christ, who preached only kindness and compassion. Given religious conflicts today, how far do you think we've come since the 13th century? Could another Inquisition happen?

13. According to the medieval rules of war, if a city or fortress surrendered to the attackers, all civilians and soldiers were free to leave and could not be harmed. But if the city or castle were taken by the invaders, any atrocity was allowed. At Beziers, 20,000 people were slaughtered and thousands more raped and mutilated and sent to wander in the woods. Do you know of instances today of modern atrocities committed by armies or by mobs?

Are there any rules that exist today to protect civilians in times of war? What countries have signed these rules, if there are any?

14. Jeanne becomes a Resistance Fighter, battling the French for *parage* (a way of life) and for her homeland independence. Under what circumstances would you become a freedom fighter?

15. During the course of the novel, Jeanne is betrayed again and again: she is abandoned as an orphan, betrayed by Rogert, Gobert, perhaps by her second husband as well when he commits suicide. Jeanne faced a lifetime of difficulties and obstacles; throughout, her dominant motivation is a longing for love and acceptance. What gave her courage and flexibility? Would you be able to respond with similar heroism in such trying circumstances? Did she ever truly find peace?